THE
BENCH

To Katie

Jg Carlson

2023 ALA

THE
BENCH

TY CARLSON

4 Horsemen
Publications, Inc.

The Bench
The Dadirri Saga Book 1
Copyright © 2021 Ty Carlson. All rights reserved.

4 Horsemen
Publications, Inc.

4 Horsemen Publications, Inc.
1497 Main St. Suite 169
Dunedin, FL 34698
4horsemenpublications.com

info@4horsemenpublications.com

Cover by 4 Horsemen Publications, Inc.
Typesetting by Autumn Skye
Editor Laura Mita

Library of Congress Control Number: 2021951158

Audio ISBN: 978-1-64450-415-4
Ebook ISBN: 978-1-64450-416-1
Print ISBN: 978-1-64450-417-8
Hardcover ISBN: 978-1-64450-418-5

DEDICATION:

To my wife, who wouldn't read the book until it
was done. And to my dad, I miss you.

TABLE OF CONTENTS

Acknowledgements:

First and foremost, I'd need to acknowledge what an impact my wife had on this book. Her often critical feedback was absolutely necessary in refining this story into what it is now. I can't thank her enough. Secondly, I'd like to thank my dad, who passed away in June 2020. This book deals with grief in many different ways, and my father helped me be the man I am today. He is sorely missed. I'd be a bad friend if I didn't also acknowledge the invaluable advice of Scott Sutton and Abby Baugus. You listened to my ramblings, gave me feedback, and told me what wouldn't work and why. Thank you. Also, big thanks to my editor, Laura. We started this journey at the same time and your help and feedback not only helped the story but helped me as an author. And Anthony.

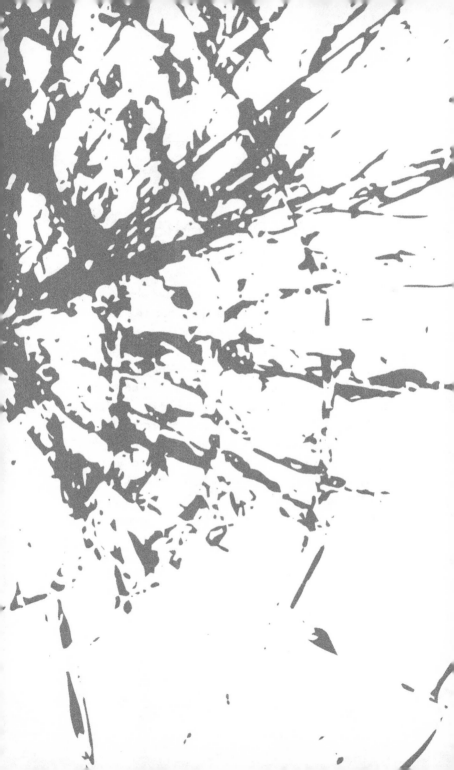

PART 1:
EVAN

CHAPTER 1

Evan Reader knew he was dreaming for two reasons. The first was an overwhelming sense that everything was fine. Not fine, in fact, but *good*, which was something he hadn't felt in some time. The second reason, and a dead giveaway, was that his wife was standing in the kitchen before him. And since she'd been dead for going on four years, the only logical explanation was that this was a dream.

Initially, he stood there, mute. Her lips were moving, but he couldn't hear her, and it was completely silent for a moment. When he tried to speak, his own voice resounded in the vast empty air that surrounded him.

"What?"

She threw her head back and laughed, rolling her eyes playfully. The brown hair he'd run his hands through countless times spilled down her bare shoulders in achingly familiar ways. He had a glimpse of the girl he met at a gas station decades before, the sun dancing on her olive skin.

And then her voice came through. "I asked how your appointment went." He knew he should be unsettled, knew that he shouldn't feel as good as he did about seeing her in his dream. But even with that knowledge, he couldn't help himself. Her voice held the tone of unequaled exasperation and desperate affection.

He blinked and screwed up his face in mild confusion. When she gestured at his arm, he understood, and as if in a script, the answer was there in his mind.

"Oh, right." He shrugged. "It was fine. Same ol' same ol' I guess. They drew blood, checked my Chip, you know. All's well. Didn't have to turn my head and cough this time." He laughed at his own joke, but his wife only smiled and rolled her eyes again.

"Did they mention the email? The invitation you got?"

He shook his head. "No, actually. They didn't, which I thought was weird, but the email was for a different appointment, anyway."

Dreams are funny. One minute you're standing in the kitchen talking with your dead wife about an email you received during your waking hours from a major tech corporation, and the next minute your best friend's now sitting at the table and it's all perfectly reasonable. The setting was too familiar. A memory of sorts, but like in any dream, it was smashed together with other memories. It was too haphazard to be real, but he remembered *this*.

Mason, Evan's best friend, was sitting calmly at the table and trying to convince him that it was all a conspiracy. A small part of himself thought, *Yeah, in this situation that's what's weird.*

"All I'm saying," Mason continued in his deep, rumbling voice as if they'd been steeped in this conversation for hours and sitting up closer to the table, "is that this Chip in our arm is mandatory and has been for a couple of decades, and it's recording everything we'll ever say, do, experience, feel, all of it. And then what, it's going to sit in a computer mainframe for the rest of time?"

Evan didn't remember if Mason had always been so paranoid, but he had a specific memory of Mason when they'd met. Evan had been out with friends to a local bar called Steelfire Grill. It was in Atlanta, Georgia, and he'd been there visiting some friends. These friends insisted on going to Steelfire for their beer. Evan hadn't ever been a big drinker, but he was beginning to feel that he could enjoy certain types of alcohol without making the face that screamed "this is disgusting."

When Evan and his friends arrived, there was a wait for a place at the bar. They sat outside on a raised brick wall watching cars drive down Green Park Lane. Mason stood nearby, and like most energetic people in uncomfortable circumstances, his friend had engaged the people around them in conversation. A man and woman behind them talked about their college experience at length. While Evan and his friends listened, interjecting the occasional "no way" or "that's crazy" to try and clue them in that their story was bordering on narcoleptic, the line stayed frustratingly still.

It wasn't until Mason spoke that Evan even remembered he was there, standing by him and listening. His deep voice had boomed out in a half-joking manner.

"So, are you guys still in college or just wish you still were?"

The conversation stopped abruptly and the silence that followed seemed abnormally loud as they waited to see if the comment would be taken offensively or in jest.

His smile was genuine and disarming, and the couple laughed and nodded as if to say "you got us there."

Immediately, the rest of the group laughed along. Mason, it turned out, was supposed to be meeting a date, but she'd stood him up. Evan's friend invited him to join them, and through the course of the night, Evan realized Mason was a genuinely kind guy. The type of guy you wanted in your corner.

And, as fate would have it, Mason lived just outside of Chicago. Evan and Mason would grow their friendship from a short distance until they moved to the same city as adults.

Evan smiled as he remembered the fun they'd had together, sometimes even feeling like children in their ability to disregard what normal people would call "age" in exchange for experience.

All of this stretched in his mind like a rapidly growing weed, and for a moment, he forgot he was standing in his kitchen talking nonchalantly with his dead wife and two best friends.

"Well, when you put it like that, it doesn't sound nefarious at all." The love of his life walked past Evan to sit at the table with Mason. Evan felt her smack his backside playfully as she passed, and Mason laughed, feigning propriety by hiding behind his hands. "It's not like there's some evil corporation out there, though." She continued chatting with the two men while Marcy, Mason's wife, appeared and began making coffee. "There's a single business, what was it, *something* Industries?" She turned to him, eyes closed in concentration. "Evan, it's the same people that you got that email from yesterday."

He snapped his fingers, remembering it easily. First from an ad he'd heard in this very kitchen years ago and then from well, the email. "Innervate. Innervate Industries."

"That's it." A cup of coffee appeared in front of her, and she nodded thanks to Marcy, who wrapped her arms around Mason's chest as she sat. "So, Innervate decided to use this information and provide some outlet for people who experienced loss."

What the hell was this dream? He remembered this conversation, parts of it, at least. All four of them were in the kitchen, then. But...

He looked down and nodded. *Of course*, he thought.

He knew for a fact that at the time the conversation took place in the waking world, he'd been wearing clothes. But the current state of his nakedness didn't seem to bother anyone else at the table. No one acknowledged it, and at that instant, he seemed to remember something else that had been discussed.

"Isn't the government the one that ultimately controls this stuff? Or is it Innervate who has rights to everyone's data?" Evan addressed the others sitting at the table.

"It was one of the big court decisions, remember?" His wife had done quite a bit of research on the subject, but his conscious brain couldn't dredge up the result. "The government issued the chip decades ago, just after the NP Wars. Their motivation for it was to maintain some measure of surveillance on everyone to keep something like that from happening again. Of course, that wasn't what they said. Instead, they said they needed ways to continue to ensure everyone's safety from what they called 'outside threats.' No one actually knew what that meant, and no one really cared; our privacy became currency a long time ago.

"Innervate's role in all of this was initially a government contract, which wasn't renewed after the first fifteen-year stint since there weren't any problems with it." Mason scoffed and nodded along. His narrative was a little more *paranoid* than it should have been.

Evan's wife continued, "Innervate Industries would develop the tech for the chips and in exchange, would be given almost exclusive rights to the data once a person had died, but only *after* that person's government had the opportunity to sift through it for 'threats.'"

Mason interrupted suddenly, "I never heard of a threat being found, by the way. Seems pretty suspicious to me that the government *never* found any issue. But that's just me, I guess."

Everyone waited until he was done, and Marcy continued the conversation, patting her husband's arm affectionately while her dark ringlets bounced back and forth with the turn of her head. "Regardless, that was the decision. Like we said, after the first contract expired at fifteen years, they didn't renew it because they believed that the threat had passed. Now, however, the government still gets first dibs *only* on people they believe to be threats. Of course, we never hear of *those* people."

Marcy was someone Evan hadn't really gotten to know until she and Mason had moved closer to him and Meredith. They'd been married for a year, and while Evan had met her, he hadn't actually had the time to get to know her until Mason was already head over heels for her.

Mason always said it was her hair that attracted him at first. It was shoulder length and fell in bouncy dark ringlets across her dark-skinned shoulders. She was African American and grew up in Chicago. She'd met Mason at some art gallery, and they'd hit it off.

Her love for Mason was obvious to anyone who saw them in the same room. Her eyes lit up when she saw him staring at her, and her smile was brilliantly echoed in her sparkling green eyes. Evan knew she was more playful than Mason, but he witnessed an argument between the two of them and also knew she could be more serious. In that particular instance, he realized she'd mastered the "finger shake" as she fired verbal cannons at Mason in their front yard.

Evan didn't have the ignorance to ask what it was about when they came back in, but he could see in Mason's cha-grined blush that he'd been called out on something or another. Mason and Marcy sat on Evan's couch without touching, but by the end of the night, they were smiling and holding hands again.

It seemed to him at that point, that they were the type of couple that knew their time together was limited and they didn't want to waste a second of it—even if the limit was few decades.

Evan directed his question at Marcy, uncertain why but feeling the script of his dream called for it.

"So, this company that emailed me—they have exclusive rights to every person's memories post-mortem?" He saw Mason nod and spread his hands in a see-what-I-mean kind of way.

As Marcy replied next to Mason, Evan smiled at her, grateful for the love that she lavished on his friend. Even if, at the moment, she was rolling her eyes in mock annoyance at her husband.

"Yes and no. And Mer—correct me if I'm wrong—but the people who die have to sign a waiver while they're alive to allow their data to be used, right?"

His dead wife nodded, sipping on her coffee. "Yep. Nail on the head, Marcy. They can only use the data if the deceased signed the waiver allowing their data to be used for any purpose once their country of origin was done with it, which is usually pretty quick, since we're all being monitored anyway, and they can determine if we're threats while we're still alive."

Evan remembered the conversation, now. Remembered how'd they'd all sat around this table—fully clothed—and continued chatting lightly about what felt to him a very serious topic. He chose to change it.

"So, they have your data, babe?"

Three pairs of eyes turned to him, and he suddenly felt every inch of uncovered skin. "Since you're, you know, dead."

The four of them silently exchanged looks, and then, they burst into laughter. He couldn't help himself; it was a funny thought. She wasn't dead. She was right here. Only his waking mind knew better, but he was stuck in his dream. Stuck and unable to stop laughing. The whole kitchen wouldn't—or couldn't—stop laughing either.

He knew this was part memory and part dream. They had laughed that day. They'd laughed a lot, and he remembered looking around at them and feeling deep warmth and affection for all of them. But this—this was some blasphemous parody. It was part of the reality that his imagination had spun to deal with whatever stressors he experienced the day before. It was no surprise that they were here.

But as they continued to laugh and look around at each other, Mason's face began to run like wet paint. His jovial laughter became distorted with dissonant octaves, and eventually, he appeared to Evan like a picture seen through a rainy window. His lips hung down below his chest and his eyes began to ooze onto his cheeks. Evan's own laughter continued even though a small, secret part of him was recoiling in terror.

Turning, he saw that Marcy's face had begun to melt in similar fashion, except it was like molten rock. Her eyes had turned a bright red and her nose was dripping into her mouth while she cawed laughter. He felt the heat of it and had to shield his eyes. He still couldn't stop laughing, though. It was funny somehow, wasn't it?

He turned to his wife, long dead and gone. Her laughter was a retching gurgle. Her pale face was crisscrossed with angry red scars that puckered the swollen flesh beneath. She looked at him with milky eyes that oozed yellow pus like tears.

At the sight of her, his own laughter finally began to die down, and he could feel his conscious mind try to take control but fail. He began to feel two hearts beat within his own chest. One was distant, and it dawned on him that it belonged to his sleeping body. It began to race as he tried to stumble away from the specter before him. But, of course, he was in a dream. So instead of falling away from her, he snapped closer.

She stood, and where neatly clean and pressed clothes had been seconds before, there were now decaying rags, decorated with gray-green moss. One pale breast was visible, sagging between the threads of a decomposing blouse.

He couldn't speak; his mouth was dry in stark contrast to the dripping specter before him.

She held out her arms to enfold him in an embrace. He stepped back the same instant as her hand brushed his shoulder and the cold clammy feel of her sodden flesh sent goosebumps writhing down his arms. When she spoke, her putrid breath clogged his senses with salty, black death. "Evan, are you okay?" Her hand suddenly lanced out and grasped his forearm. The wrinkled, rotting fingertips dug into his skin, and he was certain they were drawing blood. "You look like you've seen a ghost," she gurgled. Then, she leaned forward, cracked lips puckered and bleeding. A scream tore itself across his vocal cords, and he jerked his head away from hers.

He woke up when the back of his head connected with something hard and the dream—nightmare—disintegrated, scattering to ash in a blessedly black darkness of early morning. He tried to swallow, but his throat ached from a scream that still rang in his head and in the air around him. He tried to let his eyes adjust to the inky blackness that surrounded him, but even lying in bed and staring at the ceiling did nothing to help him. He lay there, breathing in the coolness of the pre-dawn hours trying to calm his heart. His forehead was damp with sweat, and his breath came out in uneven gasps for several minutes.

As his heart and mind calmed, he was able to feel less of the dream and more of his room, like scales tipping toward reality. Home. It was almost as if he could smell the starlight outside, an icy sharpness that pervaded the room. And there was something else that he couldn't quite pick out. A tingling sensation that he sensed more than felt, like the slight electric charge in the air before a summer storm.

He moved his hands slowly across the top of his bed. His left arm buzzed with pins-and-needles. The dream—as vivid as it was—had already begun to fade, but he rubbed the arm with a hazy recollection of cold, dead fingers. Flexing the fingers on that hand made the tingling dance everywhere up and down his arms, except for one place. The void in the middle of his arm where the tiny pinpricks were silent was the exact placement of his SafetyChip.

He wiggled the fingers again as his heart continued to hammer against his ribcage. Despite his efforts to calm, his breath came in long, winded beats along with it. In a last-ditch effort, he rubbed his eyes with the palms of his hands, and that seemed to banish the rest of the dream into little more than a blurry painting.

He took a final deep and steadying breath before moving the covers aside and placing his feet gingerly on the tile floor. He stretched and yawned, enjoying how the energy around him prickled his skin and worked the sleep out of his muddled mind.

Today was important. He had to start getting ready. His appointment was in a few hours, and he wanted to make sure he was prepared. Well, as prepared as he could be.

Evan stood and stretched in the darkness once more, his muscles groaning against the effort as he made his way to the shower. Before, the cool air helped him wake up, but it was the warmth of the shower that brought him to full awareness. He stood in the warm steam and stared at his feet as water pattered around his ankles and toes. Something sinister brushed the edge of his consciousness, and he closed his eyes tightly against it. Water trickled down his face in tiny rivulets. The random chaos of it all was almost like a drug, and the discomfort he'd felt at that fleeting memory suddenly grew into something much larger, something uncontrollable.

He sloshed through the hallways, avoiding bodies floating listlessly in the brackish water that now stood where only a few hours ago, children played and laughed... He moved a crate out of the way and a body suddenly surfaced... Pale, sodden eyes stared blankly at him in silent accusation... It's not her...

He clamped his hands over his ears to shut out the noise, but he couldn't. He grimaced as images began to float to the surface of his mind, like fingertips digging deeper and deeper into his eye sockets.

He stood slump-shouldered in the heavy rain ... the kind of rain that soaked into your soul and dripped through your bones... He stood in a pool of hopelessness... The sound was enormous in his ears... It made his head ache...

He shook his head in the shower, flinging water droplets into the air. "No," he whispered. Warm water ran into his mouth as he stood panting, the harshness of the memory beginning to fade, but not before another began to rise in its place.

He stepped over the body ... bent down to the next ... enough to catch a glimpse of the hair. Even with the dirt and mess of hair, he knew he would be able to tell his wife's from anyone's. It wasn't her hair... He moved to the next row, stepping gingerly over a body that was far too small to check... The bodies stretched into the dim corners of the tent, hundreds of them.

His hand fumbled around the shower knob before finally turning it enough to reduce the flow of water to little more than a few depressing drops.

"Shit," he whispered hoarsely, letting the water run off his parted lips.

He was shaking. His hands were cold despite the warm steam that swirled in unseen eddies above his skin. His knees buckled as he tried taking deep breaths to calm down, and he caught himself on the soap holder, praying it would hold his weight until the feeling passed.

Black spots at the edge of his vision turned into a shrinking tunnel until all he could see was a small circle of the shower wall. He took several shallow breaths, gaining a bit more control and trying to breath deeper each time. When the black tunnel had retreated to his peripherals, he could finally make his feet move to step out of the shower.

Those memories had retreated, thankfully, but he was scared. Scared that at any moment more would suddenly resurface and that this time he wouldn't be able to stop them.

The fear began to abate when he stared out the window of his bedroom. The shadows of night had been replaced with the grayness of dawn. Not yet light, his room was now in grayscale. A far cry better than the pitch blackness he'd woken to.

He dried his hair with hands that only trembled a little, and by the time he'd pulled his shirt over his head, they'd stopped trembling altogether. His breath had begun to come out in even, measured meter, with only a couple of slight hitches.

He laced his shoes and started down the stairs before grabbing his jacket and his flask—*Don't leave home without it!*—he heard in a 50's commercial voice.

He shrugged into it and felt in breast pocket again. The slight resistance told him it was still there. He knew it would be. He hadn't moved it in—how long, years? He sighed and felt those fingertips of memory begin to touch his mind, and he quickly grabbed his keys and stepped out into the pastel light of morning.

The sun was just coming over the horizon, and he could feel its warmth begin to wake up the world. A cooling breeze ruffled his still-drying hair and the grass in his front yard danced within it. The clouds in the distance, however, would soon put a stop to that. A great bank of dull blue-gray hovered over the treetops in the west, their outline visible only because the sun's rays highlighted them against the retreating night.

Turning his back on the view and hopping into his truck, his eyes lighted briefly on a packet of colorful papers on the passenger seat.

Nope, not yet. He didn't have to think about it. Not yet. There would be time at the clinic.

Instead, he thought about his life growing up. To be fair to himself, it hadn't come to him just now, but the way the hills in the distance rolled gently across the horizon sparked a memory. The collapsing barns and fresh-cut round bales he passed grew the spark to a flame. And the not-quite-day light fanned it into a fierce and warming memory.

In rural Arkansas, you grew up with two things: the distant sounds of baseball—no matter where you were or what time of day it was—and a lot of sitting around and talking, usually with the older generation. The evening air was constantly alive with sounds. If it wasn't baseball and war stories interspersed with the crackle of bugs dying in the blue light of the bug zapper, it was the joyous sounds of kids chasing lightning bugs—what the rest of the world call "fireflies."

Sitting on the back porch watching the wind whip through the maple and oak leaves would always be a staple of his childhood, a kind of moving picture framed above the mantle in his mind. The soundtrack of stories and the *crack!* and cheers of baseball had always been a balm to his soul, even though as an adult he hated sports. When he would feel down—which was often—those memories tended to help bring him out of it. Briefly, at least.

For the rest of the trip into town, the sun shone brighter and brighter on his passenger seat while he relived some of his childhood memories. Of course, Evan didn't want to admit that it was also to stave off any of those *other* memories from rearing their ugly heads. But it was pleasant enough that he didn't have to make the excuse out loud.

The freeway was nearly empty this early in the day. The commuters wouldn't come out of their hidey-holes for another hour at least. The only cars he saw on the road were a few farm trucks interspersed with taxis the closer he got to the city. It was almost hypnotic, and he found his mind slowly inching closer to what the day held. By the time he realized he was only thinking about the appointment, he couldn't stop himself.

It started with an email about a week ago.

> *Mr. Reader,*
>
> *Innervate Industries is pleased to announce that you have been selected as one of seven citizens to participate in our clinical trial of revolutionary technology called The Bench. Our trials start this evening, and you are now a*

valuable member of our research team! Your insight and experience with The Bench will help us better serve your community and give others the chance to experience a true miracle!

Sincerely,

Innervate Industries Bench Integration Team

The next day he'd received a thick manila envelope in the mail. He'd been hesitant to open it, but in the end, his curiosity got the better of him, and he cut the envelope open and dumped the packet unceremoniously on his small kitchen table. He didn't touch them until two nights after.

He'd read the brochures. Well, he'd looked over them. There was—in his opinion—too much information for them to be read in a single sitting. He'd gone through them once a few days ago, and again the previous night, which is probably what prompted the nightmare. After the second time, his head was sort of spinning, and he needed a stiff drink to settle it right.

They detailed a device called "The Bench," some marvel of technology that allowed its user to call up a representation of someone. Anyone, actually. That was one part that made him stop. Apparently, Innervate Industries had developed a way to create a digital manifestation of the subject based on the information stored within their SafetyChip. This information was then uploaded to the Intersphere, the immeasurably more powerful successor to the "internet" from the 21st century, and together with viable DNA (when applicable), was used to create an aggregate representation of an individual based on the information sourced.

The way Evan understood it was that there was so much information in the Intersphere, that Innervate had been able to smash it into a "person mold."

That was where he'd stopped the first night. It was too much to even comprehend, and he needed time to think. So, he sat down with a drink and folded his arms across his chest. What he did instead, however, was stare at the brochures across the room and wonder what the hell he'd gotten himself into.

His thought process short-circuited a bit as he passed a large green exit sign with the number "54" and "3 MILES AHEAD" in bright pearlescent foil. *My exit*, he thought as he merged into the adjacent lane.

The rhythmic blinking of the striped, yellow line separating the lanes was almost hypnotic, and his mind began drifting back to the brochures. Many notable people were listed in the brochure as Bench examples. Having been included in the original early tests of the SafetyChip, along with the DNA on file, the information on the Intersphere could be compiled to create a congruent "Intellectual DNA" as a companion to the physical DNA on file. A kind of pairing between the emotional and intellectual. Combining the two would create a "complete rendering" of the subject—up until their death, when the chip was removed and the information uploaded.

Registering the bright yellow "EXIT NOW" drew him back to the present.

He pulled off the freeway and drove the few short blocks to the address on the papers in the seat next to him. He'd memorized it by now. He'd gone over the message probably a hundred times.

He passed a bar before the address, and it reminded him of his own job at a local bar. It provided him enough money to pay the bills and little else. Not that he had the desire to do anything else. He felt like an automaton waking up, going to work, coming home, drinking until sleep overtook him, waking up and repeating it. The cycle of life that was only discussed in interventions and morality tales where the characters were described as exaggerated manifestations of negativity, but through the power of friendship, they evolved into caring and contributing people. A fairy tale is what that is. Nothing but a fucking fairy tale. But this Bench... maybe it wasn't a fairy tale.

It still made him queasy when he thought about it but in a good way. The same way your stomach clenches up when you know something great is going to happen, but you're not quite sure what it will look like.

After a few minutes of stop-and-go traffic, he pulled up to the address he'd been directed to and put the truck in park. He felt his stomach clench at the thought. He was finally at Innervate Industries. It was a tall building on the corner of what could be described as a bustling part of the city during work hours. And today, he'd arrived without any fanfare. His eyes made their way up the building. And then even farther up. A large blue logo that he couldn't quite make out was halfway up. As he looked around, he figured it matched the one on the front doors.

He grabbed the packet of papers on the seat next to him and got out, looking up and craning his neck, wishing he'd have grabbed the sunglasses five feet away in the seat of the truck. The building had to be several hundred feet high, and it glittered in the morning sunlight like a beacon.

He sighed again—telling himself to stop sighing so god-damn much—and stepped into the shadows cast by nearby skyscrapers toward Innervate Industries' headquarters. With his boots making a dull thud on the warm concrete beneath his feet, the doors opened automatically as he approached. They slid open with a seductive whisper, allowing the cool air inside to rush out and past him, making him feel as if a ghost had just escaped. He shuddered involuntarily and continued walking.

Inside was another pneumatic door that opened with a much less seductive whisper. This one sounded like a librarian hissing at someone to keep quiet as they spoke in the Holy Church of Words. Beyond the clear blue windows of the doors sat a simple reception area. He approached the desk and signed in, writing his name in quick, terse letters that could never be traced back to him on name alone, and then, he sat down in an orange chair against the far wall. For some reason he couldn't fathom, he chose the middle seat in a row of five. He only knew intrinsically that no one would sit in this row now since they'd have to sit with only a chair between themselves and the strange man nearby. A surefire way for him to keep his personal space without having to resort to being an asshole.

He wasn't sure how much time passed as he stared at the wall across from him, but there had definitely been sleep. His brain had now caught up with itself, and he felt less like two timelines moving parallel to one another and more like a single life being lived.

He sat still and silent for an interminable amount of time before a familiar sound so ingrained in his psyche made him wince. He hadn't realized his hands had moved until he heard that sound, the unmistakably crisp sound of familiar folding paper coming from his lap.

Evan made himself look down. When he saw what he was holding, he suppressed a shuddering gasp, exhaling the breath he'd unknowingly been holding in one gust of air from his burning lungs. His breath held so much grief it was practically dripping with it. The picture clenched in his hands could be seen only through a shaky watery lens.

What he now held between his fingers was wrinkled with ritual use, the folds—which had certainly been broken countless times, cutting thin and white through the figures beneath. It was discolored with age and exposure to the sun. This relic of a bygone era reflected the obsessive need both to see it and ignore it as often as possible, but Evan liked to think of it vaguely as reverence. It wasn't as pitiful in that light.

His hands and fingers trembled, but even through the tremor, he could clearly see the face and lips that he'd kissed a thousand times. The mouth that gave the ever-present smile that he had no choice in falling in love with. The grin that showed unquenchable joy. Vaguely, as if through a haze of radio static, her laughter began to echo in his head, and he was suddenly swept away in a surge of longing and painful remembrance.

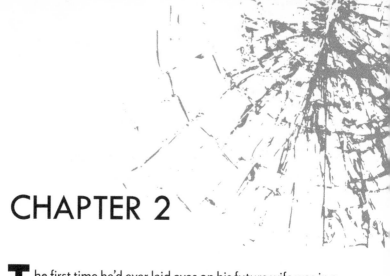

CHAPTER 2

The first time he'd ever laid eyes on his future wife was in a gas station of all places. Evan had grown up in River Fork, Arkansas. He knew the roads, the buildings, the trees, and especially the rivers. He knew that summer was changing to fall when the giant maple tree at the end of Mr. Goddard's place turned from vibrant green to searing red and then burnished copper over the course of only a few days.

The summer they met, he had nearly broken his arm by stupidly seeing if he and his friends could make the leap from the Long's Grocery roof to the Corner Station roof. The Station's roof had a concrete overhang that lessened the distance between the two buildings to around eight feet, whereas the two walls of the buildings were close to twelve feet apart. While they were only one-story buildings, since they were built back in that day, they both had attics and had to be tall enough to accommodate them.

It was the kind of stunt that millions of kids did. In a way, it was a rite of passage. Trying to prove who are the brave ones of the group and who are the cowards, easy as pie. His friend Joe had made the jump with ease. At that age, they couldn't make the argument that Joe had hit puberty the year before and, as a result, had legs that were stronger and longer, making the jump not nearly as difficult as it would be for his friends. But not to be outdone, and to the jeers of the other two, the pre-pubescent boys set themselves at the ready. Seeing how easily Joe had made it the Station's roof gave the other boys a euphoric feeling, made them energized with overconfidence.

Evan crunched his foot in the tar and gravel of the Long's Grocery roof. He took a deep breath, shook out his hands, then set off at a sprint. He raced toward the edge, feet pattering in the gravely tar for barely any time at all before lifting again. The air shimmered ahead of him in the summer heat. Joe, cheering him on from the opposite roof, was hazy through the summer film. Evan's legs pumped faster and faster, burning as he pushed them harder than he had ever pushed them before. He remembered feeling as if he were about liftoff like the planes at the airport on the outskirts of town.

Mustering all the strength and power he could, he gave one final push from the tar-stained gravel, his red cheeks puffing out with the effort. There was a final crunch as his foot left the roof of Long's Grocery. His body sailed through the air, and he felt like he was flying.

The void between the buildings that had at first seemed negligible began to yawn wider and wider beyond and below him. The roof, which had appeared to be a short distance away, sailed off into the shimmering haze of summer. The distance to the ground stretched down. Down into the deepest distance he would ever know. Down into the very depths of Hell.

He slammed his eyelids down like shutters but, in the same instant, realized he couldn't see to grab the ledge. He popped them back open just in time to watch the approaching concrete overhang fill his vision. He stretched his legs out, anticipating the collision that would jar them into a numbing but altogether self-satisfying success and prepared himself to roll across the roof of the Corner Station with the momentum. He'd jump up and give Joe a high-five, and they'd watch Dylan do the same.

But in the milliseconds between, his eyes followed the edge of the roof as it began to shift. It sailed slowly past his extended feet by mere inches. Then, his knees and crotch and stomach sank below the edge of the Station. The sudden realization that he wasn't going to make it, the elation that had lifted him from the roof of Long's Grocery, scattered from him and in its place left something terrible. A fear that gathered and whirled, as if it had been waiting for this moment, sank into his bones like frozen nails. It turned his sense of flying into the very real sensation of falling and falling fast. He flung his arms toward the edge and relief flooded through when he felt his palms connect with the hot and prickly heat of the concrete with a loud smack. That similar jarring that his feet should have felt upon landing was thrumming up his hands and to his elbows. But wait, the edge of the roof was slipping past his line of sight. That can't be. Joe's face had changed from a smile of victory into a scream of fear, his hands gripping his long hair and pulling it back from his forehead.

The feeling of elation that had gathered in his chest and sense of accomplishment evaporated as his fingertips scraped off the edge of the roof. Pain shrieked through him as the skin of his fingertips was shredded, leaving bloody lines mere feet from where Joe stood screaming and reaching for him.

The next thing he knew, he was crashing. Crashing hard on his right arm through several old boxes and onto a pile of wooden pallets stacked between the buildings. He lay there groaning and cradling his arm. He had landed at an odd angle, his body spinning through the air as momentum carried him through its strange fight with gravity. He could hear his friends rustling from the roof, clambering down the drainpipe they had used to get on the roof in the first place. They crowded around him, panting and, while none of them would admit it then, all of them on the verge of hysterical tears.

Knowing their parents would kill them if they were discovered carelessly leaping over Death's wide maw, they did what any sane adolescent would do: they avoided the adults by buying a bag of ice from the station and skirted all situations that would give up the game and show his weak right arm. They did this for a few weeks until Evan could move it easily without wincing. Though, to their pre-pubescent brains, it felt like an eternity of silence.

The new girl in town, however, had only moved to the area that same year and as luck would have it, had been present in the gas station that fateful summer day. This mystery girl watched him with curiosity and probably some concern, he told himself, as he limped down the chip aisle and leaned on Dylan, the other friend that would have jumped after Evan if things had gone differently. Blood ran freely from several scrapes and one nasty gash that arced from his injured elbow to nearly his wrist. Joe, on the other hand, was grabbing napkins from the Taste-E-Freeze station and mopping up the crimson drops as they walked, then throwing them hastily into the hole in the counter that served as a trashcan. The attendant was too busy talking up Ellie McCreery, the previous year's Miss River Fork, for him to notice a trio of boys bleeding down his chip aisle.

Once Joe was done stuffing the napkins, now pink with diluted blood, into the trash, he walked toward the cooler. Evan watched him and while he was certain Joe's demeanor was meant to convey nonchalance, it screamed "restrained hysterics" as the door to the cooler where the ice was held was yanked open. They'd actually been pretty lucky because most gas stations in River Fork—well, the other two—had their ice coolers on the outside of the building with a padlock. *People apparently steal frozen water*, Evan mused one morning while riding with his father. If they'd been at one of those stations, they'd have had to ask the attendant for the key, which would have raised questions and that was certainly something they didn't need.

Their luck was up, however, and Joe was ripping open the frozen plastic bag to grab as many ice cubes as he could and rolling them into a paper towel. Evan stood and waited. Well, he tried to stand but ended up just leaning on an end cap and grunting while trying to force his lungs to accept the air he was heaving in and out.

Unfortunately for him, the end cap had been nothing more than cheap plastic, made to hold no more weight than a dozen chocolate donut packages and a stack of candy bars. When he put his full weight on it after a rather aggressive attempt at breathing normally, he promptly crushed it along with the stacks of Twix, Snickers, and Kit Kats it had been advertising beneath signs filled with the joy of summer fun.

She had laughed at him, then. She stood at the corner of the aisle, candy bars and donut packages scattered around her yellow sneakers, and she was giggling behind her hand. Her eyes sparkled with tears, and eventually, she bent double as her body spasmed with the rhythm of downright hilarity.

He tried not to join her, but in the end, holding both his side and arm, he succumbed to nothing more than grunting chuckles and heavy wheezing while he rolled around in crushed chocolate bars. Luckily, the attendant hadn't made him pay for them. He couldn't remember the man's name. It was something that reminded him of flowers. Mr. Petal-something. He'd noticed some commotion—the piece of shit candy stand, no doubt—and came running over, his whiskered cheeks paled when he saw Evan's bleeding arm and bruising body. He'd told them to get home, or he'd tell their parents. At this, Joe and Dylan laughed a little thinking that Mr. Petal-something didn't know their parents. But then he'd looked right at Dylan and said, "I know your dad, Dylan Dickerson, so don't think I won't!" Joe and Dylan stopped laughing then and scampered out of the station, helping Evan limp out the best he could.

Her laugh, though, that's what got him, what reeled him in for good. He remembered that laugh as he lay in bed that night after dinner and tried to play off that he was just tired and wanted sleep, and that his long-sleeve tee was comfortable despite the muggy heat of the summer evening making him feel like he was suffocating. Eventually, he worked up the courage to invite her to the movie theater as part of a group date. Luckily for him, Joe came down with the flu that fall and his date, Emma, cancelled. Joe was there only because he wanted to make out in the back, but Evan wanted to watch the movie, and when he broke the news to her that the other part of their "group date" wouldn't be joining them, he was rewarded with another of those laughs. They were intoxicating.

When they met at the theatre, the Apollo, she had her hand through the sleeve of a baggy cardigan and was clenching the end of it in her fist, holding it up to her mouth to try and hide her smile. It was successfully hidden, but he could still see her eyes, and they sparkled with unbridled joy and expectation. Evan could never decide if she was actually close to crying or not, it was the kind of sparkle that was usually followed by tears, both the bitter and the sweet. Even still, he was certain if they had been tears, they would have only added to her inescapable attraction.

Contrary to what he'd originally wanted to go to the movies for, he ended up not watching much of the movie, or eating much of the six-dollar popcorn or drinking more than a sip of the four-dollar soda he'd bought for them. Instead, he watched her from the corner of his eye. The movie's light and the theatre's shadows played across her features in swirls and flashing lights. They dodged this way and that around her cute little nose and dark eyes, her perfect lips that seemed to always be on the verge of a smile, parted halfway showing the briefest glimpse of her teeth, which glimmered white in the darkness. Some part of him—at the time—kept piping up to stop being creepy, but he couldn't help it; she was a masterpiece. There wasn't another word for it, and deep down, he knew he couldn't look away even if he'd wanted to. She, however, had watched the movie and thanks to the gods of adolescent love and infatuation, hadn't seen him. But he remembered that night better than any of them. It was the night he'd always remember as the one where he'd fallen in love.

He blinked away the tears and looked around the waiting room as the memory faded back into his subconscious. Gently folding the picture in the same way he'd folded it the last time, and the time before that, and a thousand times before that, he stuffed it in his pocket, sniffed brusquely and with a sort of pained relief, sat back in his chair. The memories of her were so unwelcome, part of him mused. But the other part couldn't help but be glad that he remembered her. Even a little bit.

He picked up the packet by his side and looked at the ticket in his hand, then adjusted his hat, pulling it low over his eyes and then back up. It was an old habit he'd picked up as a kid to simultaneously keep the sweat out of his eyes and move his hair out of the way when it was too long.

Having delayed as long as he thought he could without simply walking out and coming back another day, and seeing no other way to stall the inevitable, he focused his gaze on the lightly used papers clipped together in the corner. He skipped the introduction page, having read it twice already, placing it facedown next to him. Beneath that small piece of paper were several pamphlets and the long contractual bit of paper that he was certain he would need to sign, based on the small signature boxes on the final page.

He was surprised to find that he was a little breathless. He'd printed a copy of the email, and it was clipped haphazardly into the middle of the brochures. He read through it again.

And one of seven trials? Not great odds considering the city was made up of, what, nearly 350,000 people? And many of those had lost loved ones, probably all of them, that they'd like to talk to again.

Seven. They'd been together for seven years. Well, when not counting the three months where he'd stupidly needed to "take a break and figure things out." What an idiot. Yeah, he took the time to figure out that if he didn't hurry the fuck up, she'd find someone smart enough to never let her go. So, close enough to seven years.

God, he missed her.

He shuffled through the first several pamphlets, recognizing the titles from previous perusals. He found "Coping with Loss," "What is 'The Bench' and How Does it Work?" and "Why am I Here?"

That last hit a little too close to home. When he'd read it previously, the smiling man on the front seemed to taunt him, saying "See, we'd get you in eventually. We knew that last one would get ya. Hits a little close to home, doesn't it, friend?" Evan felt another flash of inexplicable anger at the man's jaunty grin but quickly flipped to the trifold beneath. A thought began to form about what he had to do—what they'd ask him to do—and he pushed it away. He couldn't admit it. Not yet.

He looked at his watch. Still another half-hour until his appointment.

He didn't have anything else to do, so he turned his attention back to the second pamphlet, wondering if "What is 'The Bench' and How Does It Work?" could answer the question he hoped wouldn't have to be said out loud.

Inside the bright orange and green pamphlet showed the picture of a bench, dark wood with wrought-iron arms coiling toward a carpet of near-perfect blades of grass near a cliff. A man with a fedora and raincoat sat facing away from the viewer looking over a brilliantly sunlit forest. It was a beautiful picture, but it made Evan apprehensive, and he didn't know why. It had to be the height. The man looked as if he were on top of the world. What kind of head case would want to feel like they were an inch from a fall, a fall that would end with their body crunching into the ground, their insides exploding in a shower of viscera and painting the surrounding forest that had been so picturesque only a moment before, now red with gore? Not him, that's who.

He whistled a sliding note quietly to himself. Not him. He wouldn't sit on a cliff in a million years, thank you very much, you jackasses.

He browsed through the information, stumbling over words that belonged in a genetics textbook, not a layman's informational pamphlet. His disbelief began rising as he skimmed the rest of the section, stopping at the "How Does The Bench Work?" in bold lettering, realizing he could actually comprehend the words beneath it.

The disbelief ran its course with some nearly inaudible mumblings of "you've got to be kidding me" and finally culminating in a loud laugh—half bark and half disbelieving scoff.

The woman at the counter looked up abruptly at him, and he clamped his mouth shut waving once and readjusting his hat, hoping she'd believe it was a cough or that he'd sneezed in some weird way.

It seemed a bit too much like fiction but based on the state-of-the-art tech and architecture that surrounded him, Innervate appeared to be doing pretty well for itself, and Evan figured they wouldn't stay in business long if this venture was all a farce. Not to mention, they'd been in league with the government and come out on the other side—ahead, by the looks of it.

The Bench was actually—and surprisingly—an actual bench, if the one pictured in the pamphlet was to be believed. Only it was sterile white and looked like it belonged in a sci-fi movie. It was somehow simultaneously bulbous—as if it were a viscous fluid that had been suddenly frozen mid-pour—and untouchable. The kind of museum-like quality where a person watching would slap the hand of anyone who touched it.

What was interesting was that The Bench was inside a pod-like room, a sphere within which a setting could be transferred and projected onto the walls to create any desired setting, from the top of the Pyramid of Giza to the busy streets of 16th-century London. Evan was unsure why anyone would choose the latter since the next sentence explained that the room was so advanced it could generate smells as well.

No thanks.

The Bench's protocol allowed a single person to "summon" another individual, living or dead, as a compilation of every bit of verified information available, including any DNA that was on profile for this person. There didn't seem to be a time limit, that he could tell, so the conversation wouldn't be cut off like one of those old jokes his friend would tell in elementary school. Or like an old murder mystery where the detective finally tracked down a victim of the killer, but the poor sap was on his deathbed and right when they were to reveal the killer's name, the program would cut to an emergency weather announcement.

Evan's imagination was beginning to spin up, and in a kind of morbid joke, he guessed if the "subject" would know they were dead or if they'd start freaking out when they realized they weren't real.

He saw an asterisk near the paragraph he was reading, and conveniently, it stated that "For subjects that maintained their genetic profile either with DNA updates or the SafetyChip, full awareness of their lives and deaths are known, and they will not become emotionally volatile if this information is discussed or presented."

Tidy, he thought.

He looked around the room. He was still the only one there, apart from the receptionist, so he stretched out his legs and began tapping the pamphlet on the back of his hand.

No sooner had it begun when the tapping stopped. He felt the click of pieces falling into place in his mind. It suddenly made sense, all of it. Was this some kind of sick joke? Was this some pagan god's way of making him pay for his past mistakes? All his karma paid out in one swift kick to the groin?

He glanced back and forth from one pamphlet to the next, trying to convince himself that his first suspicion was wrong, but as he connected the dots, it only solidified it as the one and only end point.

He was so stupid! How could he have missed it, after all the hours spent poring through these fucking papers!

He stood up abruptly, and since he was the only other person in the room, the sudden motion caught the attention of the secretary. She looked up from her computer and smiled, eyebrows raised in the unasked question.

He approached the brilliant white desk quickly, smacking the papers down on the surface. "Hi. Yes," he began, then fumbled.

He couldn't figure out how to get it out.

It's her.

He didn't want to.

It's going to be her.

He couldn't.

It can't be her.

There wasn't a way for him to get around it.

"You can't be serious."

It was all he could think to say at the time, and he met the receptionist's stare, neither of them blinking.

He had to ask it. The question he wished he could keep inside. There was only way to get an answer, so he took a deep breath and let the words tumble from within, knowing full well it had been rolling around inside his head for days.

"You can't expect me to talk to my dead wife, can you?"

CHAPTER 3

T he young lady—probably in her 20's—gazed back at him for a moment and then blinked in surprise. "I'm sorry?"

Evan exhaled forcefully in exasperation, attempting to collect himself. When he spoke, his voice took on the intensity of a poorly concealed growl. "My wife—dead wife—is the 'subject' that you're asking me to talk to, isn't it?"

Evan's heart hammered in his chest and ears so loudly that it almost drowned out the buzzing fluorescent lights above.

In the space between his words and her answer, his blood rushed through his veins so quickly that he could feel each beat in his throbbing fingertips.

She blinked again without breaking eye contact. "Is that who you have decided to summon for the trial?"

It was Evan's turn to blink. It seemed that this was an expected response, and they'd been trained how to handle it. Had he been calmer, he would have applauded Innervate's foresight. Great job, team, we knew exactly how mourners would react and we beat them to it. Cake's in the breakroom, everyone.

But he wasn't calm. The old saying of "seeing red" rose in his mind, and he latched onto it. This must mean what it meant—this feeling, this rage that ripped through his body like an electric current. This anger was loud and bright but beneath was something else. Beneath was something he didn't like, something shaded and shy, an emotion that didn't have a place in him right now. Not yet, not here, not yet, please—

Fear.

"No, I haven't *decided* anything yet!" His neck was heating up, and he threw his hands in the air. "First off, there is no way you can 'summon' someone who is dead. It's ridiculous!" His voice rose to an emasculating squeak at the end, his tirade lost some of its edge, and he coughed.

The woman blinked again. It was starting to get on his nerves now, the way she was calm in the face of his rage at such a ridiculous idea. A timid voice broke into his head, his mental referee. *Well, that's not entirely true, you have a packet of papers that clearly explains how this could be possible. Perhaps you should—*

He silenced the voice but could hear it continuing on in a muffled, muted yawn.

She broke his gaze and looked at her computer, clicking away on the keys in quick succession with the rapid *clack clack clack* that sounded to Evan like small dice being cast across her desk.

"Well, Mr. Reader," she looked back at him, "it seems your interview will begin shortly, and I'm sure your questions will be answered by the proctor at that time." She blinked again and a smile appeared in an instant, wide and frozen in place in what he could only interpret as polite dismissal.

Turning abruptly on his heel, Evan walked briskly back to his chair, relieved that he wouldn't have to see her blink anymore but more than angry at the evasive way she'd answered his questions. Well, they weren't really questions, were they? Objections, maybe. But still, she'd avoided giving him anything at all. It was maddening. It was ludicrous. *It was on purpose,* a voice said in his head.

Exactly. That was it. She purposely hedged. She probably couldn't even answer him. *She probably isn't allowed to.* The referee voice was back with sound and thoughtful input.

He sat and tried to control his breathing. Within a few minutes, his heart stopped hammering and settled on a rhythmic pulse in his chest. He could still vaguely feel it in his fingertips, but it didn't feel like blood was going to spray from them at any moment.

His interview would start soon, anyway, and he breathed a sigh of relief. Sort of. Being called soon meant he would have to address the emotion that was stirring beneath the anger, rage, and loneliness. He'd have to begin the process of addressing his loss. He wouldn't be able to shove it under the rug or behind the curtain of booze and exhaustion. But in the words of Shakespeare, "the sooner begun, the sooner done."

He let his thoughts wander as he looked idly around the room. Eventually, his eyes settled on the brochure laying on the ghastly orange chair beside him. He stared at it unblinking and felt a familiarity rise in his subconscious. Not a familiarity, he realized as he tried to grasp it, but the thought was like steam curling between his fingers. He could feel moist warmth, but there was nothing of substance, nothing to hold onto. He focused harder, pushing all of his concentration to it. He bore into the brochure, tilting his head slightly as if listening to something in the distance. It wasn't familiarity with this, it was with something else, a close cousin to this brochure. What was it? Almost there.

Almost—

Suddenly, something clicked in his mind. Staring at the brochure, he remembered the first time this kind of technology had been publicly advertised, well at least the developing announcements, back before...

His mind trailed off as he muted it all and reached through the years toward that time. It was important, this feeling, this kindred flame of familiarity. Again, that fear seemed to bubble up. He feared some important part of him would be lost forever if he couldn't grab hold of this.

And then there it was. He seemed to snatch it out of thin air, and with a smile, his mind's eye formed the picture of a kitchen all at once. The memory came through in full. He surrendered gratefully to it.

They were standing in the kitchen with the sun—the same one in his nightmare from the previous night. But this kitchen was bright and vibrant, the sun peeking through the window and prancing around the kitchen. Their Bluetooth speakers played soft music while they made dinner. Even now, their bodies would move with practiced grace around one other to reach the knife drawer or the colander on top of the fridge. *What were we making? Summer salad with... something?* It didn't matter, he supposed.

An advert came on between songs for a new technology that promised to "shake people's understanding of life and death down to its core." It ended with "If you'd like to learn more about this incredible scientific breakthrough, you can simply respond now by saying, 'tell me more,' and you'll hear a pre-recorded explanation detailing this amazing technology now!"

Evan looked at her, then. She looked back, that same ghost of a smile playing on her lips that said *I know what you're thinking. Don't you think we should? Come on. It'll be fun.* He returned the smile in his own way, and they said at the same time, "Tell me more." Then he chuckled, and she laughed from deep in her throat, the laugh that said *I love this moment with you.*

She looked at him and winked. He hoped it was the kind of wink that meant there might be dessert *after* dessert, and he winked back at her with what he hoped was a roguish grin.

They listened raptly to the speaker for the following 20 or so minutes, their attention fixated on the little black box hung beneath their cabinet. For the first few minutes, they stood close together, his arm around her shoulders as they stood in the middle of the kitchen, both of them staring at the words that washed invisibly over them. As the message continued, however, she began to get restless. They had stopped making dinner, and he remembered that by the end of it, she was holding a kitchen cloth in one hand and running her forefinger back and forth across her bottom lip, a nervous tic she had picked up after they got married. Maybe he only noticed it after they were around each other most days. Maybe it had always been present, but the glaze of obsession and puppy love had obscured it from his perception.

The technology described was remarkable, in a word, enabling a person to speak to someone that was dead. Everyone with a SafetyChip implanted in their arm, and every child whose parents had voluntarily chipped them as well—which was even then more than half the population—had their memories or personalities called up as a digital representation. Evan was unclear exactly what part of the consciousness was being "saved." The commercial stated that there was progress being made every day on exactly how this would be initiated and maintained, but the speaker continued to reiterate how "the grave was no longer the limit."

When the commercial ended, Evan's elbows burned with the pressure he'd been putting on them as he leaned over the counter, his fingers laced together beneath his chin. The music softly began again, and he quickly tried to say, "Music, stop," but the only thing that came out was a hoarse *gurk* sound from his dry throat. He swallowed hard and cleared his throat and tried again, succeeding this time, and the music stopped, abruptly leaving the two of them in silence that was instantly too loud. It seemed as if the whole world had stopped when the music did, a yawning silence that he could feel vibrating deep in his gut.

He chanced a glance her way and saw her staring at him, still running her finger across her bottom lip. Against her pale cheeks, her lip was a bright red that bordered on vulgar. Her eyes, slightly wider than usual and glassy, were unblinking. She stared across the kitchen, stared straight through him.

"Babe?" Though it had been barely above a whisper, his voice in the silence was thunderous in his ears, and she jumped as if he had screamed it.

"What?" she answered breathlessly, and the finger on her lip stopped, curling into her fist.

Evan knew what she was thinking, though he hated it and now wished fervently that they hadn't asked for more information. The earlier hope of frisky lovemaking had just been crushed beneath the heel of unforgiving memory.

Her dad had died when she was younger. It was the reason she and her mother had moved to his town that hot summer day. But he hadn't died accidentally. He'd left and never come back. It was cliché, but he'd said he was going to the grocery store for milk. When her mother checked and said they had plenty, he'd simply smiled and said he'd be right back anyhow.

She didn't see him alive ever again.

Her mother, Sherry, received a letter in the mail one day with twenty-two dollars, a handful of coins that were effectively worthless, and a handwritten note. The handwriting was her father's familiar writing, but it was erratic, as if written while driving on a dirt road.

It hadn't said much, only that he was sorry for leaving them behind, but he wasn't cut out for being a dad. After spending his money on the unholy trinity of drugs, booze, and women, he realized he was done for and sent the rest of what he had. The letter was postmarked four weeks earlier from Las Vegas, Nevada. Sherry had then checked the obituaries and found he'd died only a day later from an overdose. They'd never know if it was accidental or not, but they settled on the fact that he had left on his own and had to have known it was the end of his run.

Whether nature or nurture, neither Sherry nor her daughter had mourned the loss for long. Sherry admitted she mourned the loss of a general partner in life instead of *her* particular partner. He hadn't ever been a great dad, they'd both all but admitted that, but he was *her* dad, and there had been *some* good times.

There was a place in every little girl's heart reserved especially for a daddy, and nothing else would ever fit there.

They had packed and moved that next week. There wasn't much to pack; they'd never been rich to the point of owning a multitude of lavish things. They lived a life of average wealth, and the job of packing was nearly done in a single weekend. All that was left after that were the things found stuffed in an unused cupboard or right out in the open like the coffeemaker on the counter.

To her credit, Sherry was nothing but respectful about her late husband, within earshot of others, at least. Evan never heard her say an unkind word about him, and he didn't think it was because she was disillusioned regarding the damage his absence had done to the both of them. Evan truly believed it was because deep down, she still loved her husband, and speaking ill of him wasn't right. She didn't glorify him by any means. In those few instances where honesty shone through the emotional walls she had to inevitably build, she was very matter of fact, and she often finished the story with: "So he left us to finish his life the way he wanted. I can't necessarily fault him for that, though it's not what I wanted for our family," accompanied by a sad smile and a shrug. She didn't want her daughter growing up on the poison she could have easily fed her about the evils of men and how they'll probably all leave. No, Sherry was a wonderful mother, and Evan could see that she made a wonderful wife, if his own was anything to go by. Evan was lucky to have met the daughter that stood across from him even though she now wore a vacant and somewhat scared expression.

She didn't talk about her father much. Even to this day, it was a subject he tried his best to avoid. Still, there were days built into the calendar that were traps, emotional whirlpools of a sort that would pull her in beneath skies of crashing thunder. Father's Day, their own wedding anniversary, and birthdays of all sorts made five days out of the year feel like inevitable typhoons, leaving plenty of emotional flotsam and his wife in foggy disarray.

And here was another, though this one an unplanned approaching storm. Would this one crack open today and pour misery and brooding into their lives? He hoped to God it wouldn't. His wife was strong, stronger than he was, but this was the secret crack to her soul. This particular subject had the ability to sneak into her heart like an oily tentacle and grasp hold, entangling itself and squeezing relentlessly.

His biggest problem was that he was never able to help her out of it. She would eventually drag herself up from the depths and start the process of healing, but until that happened, Evan was only a cheerleader on the sideline, and a muted one at that, despite how vehemently he tried. He always felt like a man offering aspirin to Christ on a cross.

"You thinking about your dad, hon?" God, how he hated to speak first on the subject, but she was already there, and maybe by showing he wasn't afraid of it, it would help her start the loathsome ritual of rebuilding her emotions.

She nodded in a slow rhythm, still not really looking at anything in particular.

"What's going on, babe? I can see the wheels turning." This was one of their scripts, used when one could tell the other's thoughts were spinning out of control and in need of a lifeline.

She blinked and her eyes returned to focus on him. Sighing, she tried to lean her back nonchalantly against the counter, but she ended up misjudging the distance and had to take a shaky step back, bumping the edge of it a little too hard and wincing. Evan didn't want to interrupt her thoughts by offering a hand since she was already walking down the stone-carved steps to that cloudy place. Her face bore the weight of each step.

His wife took another breath. "I don't know, honestly. I think I'm trying to wrap my head around the possibility of seeing him again." She looked up. "I mean, is that even a possibility? That can happen?"

She shook her head and paced around the kitchen table twice, then plopped down in a chair, her shoulders sagging, and her lower lip pooched out. "I don't even know, Evan. I mean, on the one hand, there's this possibility of seeing him again, but would it even really be him? Would I even *want* to see him?"

Evan thought about it for a minute, rubbing the stubble on his cheek, hearing the raspy whisper of it.

"Was he chipped?" The chip had become mandatory years before, and it was likely that her father had gotten himself chipped before his death. This question fell into what he called "the safe zone." Questions directly about her father were fine as long as they avoided any direct correlation with her feelings about him. Of course, there were always emotional highways that crisscrossed and had unknown exits to "danger zones," but he guessed this one with only three words was still safe.

She thought for a minute and then said, "Yeah, he was." She spoke softly, dazed, absorbed in the memory of it all. "I remember because Mom went with him, and I stayed with my friend that night. Her name was Olivia, and I was, let me think—eight. Nine, maybe."

She licked her lips, and her finger came halfway to her lip, then fell back into her lap.

She continued, "Her parents had already gotten their own chips, so Mom asked them if I could stay the night. Olivia was my best friend when I was that age, and we did everything together, so staying over wasn't anything out of the ordinary. We went to the mall that night and saw a movie. It was Dollar Theater Night, so we were able to get popcorn too." Her face lit up briefly, "God, I loved popcorn." She was silent for a moment, and then, "It was the first time her parents let us sit away from them." A smile, bittersweet, graced the corners of her lips and her eyes sparkled for only a moment. "Only two rows ahead. But still, it was a big deal to two young girls.

"When I got home the next day, I remember seeing a small bandage on Dad's forearm. He didn't try to hide it, but I remember him smacking it on the doorknob once in the afternoon when he was carrying some boxes. That's when I heard him say 'shit' for the first time." She paused, and Evan let her. "It wasn't the last time."

She blinked a few times, then said, "So that, at least, would answer that question. His memories are saved through his Chip, and I guess they could use that." She paused again. This is how it went for his bride of only a couple of years. She'd process things out loud for a few minutes or a few hours, but it was the stop-and-go traffic of a gridlocked street. Until she reached the end of the thought process, at least. "Geez this opens up all kinds of doors that make me uncomfortable." She huffed a nervous laugh.

"Like which ones?" Evan asked. His wife didn't usually show discomfort with thoughts alone. Put her in front of a room and tell her to talk, sure, but she was comfortable in her own mind. *Most of the time*, he reminded himself.

"Well first of all, for me at least, there's the moral issue of it, on a few levels. First off, these people are dead, but they don't get a say in whether they stay dead or not?"

Evan tried not to laugh because he knew she was serious. "Well, I see what you mean, but it's not really like that. It's more like a video game, I guess. They're still technically dead. I mean, not even technically, they're definitely dead, their bodies have—what's that old saying—given up the ghost, that's it. What's being created is information. Information they have given freely to whoever owns the Chip." A sudden thought occurred to him. "Unless there's some type of DNR thing where you can say 'No, don't let someone meet my digital ghost.'"

He did give a light chuckle at that and tried too late to cover his mouth. His wife was still struggling with her range of emotions, so he stopped laughing.

"I guess you're right." She huffed out another sigh and continued, "I would argue and say there's the issue of personal security or privacy, of being watched all time, but..." she lifted and showed Evan her left forearm where beneath unbroken skin lay a nearly microscopic Chip of her own, "we're already being watched all the time." She said it with a smile, but there was a hint of resignation to it too. Cynicism at the lack of privacy everyone had now. There was a time when people didn't even have computers in their homes let alone in their bodies. It seemed odd to them both, that kind of isolation. At the same time, however, how nice could it be for people to do whatever they wanted without worry that it could one day be used against them. Or even the incessant need to monitor their own newsfeeds, even knowing there wasn't anything good or new on them. The subconscious prompt to keep up to date was ingrained in them all now. What a cosmically alien thought that it hadn't always been.

She couldn't have said it any clearer. They'd both been chipped when they turned eighteen, but they knew plenty of people younger than that who were chipped as kids.

There was a huge uproar about "invasion of privacy" when the SafetyChip had been introduced all those years ago, but even during that time, people were being watched. Nearly every household had devices that let anyone ask for daily weather updates, buy concert tickets, track packages being shipped, or send a message to a contact. They were already being listened to and watched; they just didn't know it. Some conspiracy theorists spouted louder than the rest of the public, which desensitized everyone to it. "They'll listen!"

they shouted. "The government will listen and use it against you!" No one believed them. On the contrary, people believed the devices were there to *help* them.

In one instance, an intruder broke into a man's house in the middle of the day. There was a struggle, and in the end, the stranger murdered the man. There was a suspect, but there was no evidence—none whatsoever. The Supreme Court, in a landmark case, requested the recordings of the device only for that frame of time when the intruder broke into the home until he left the home, a three-hour stint. The company who owned the rights to the device at the time agreed—after some badgering by the Supreme Court and pressure from the public news media. And then, it was discovered that the devices were constantly recording without anyone's permission—anyone's *express* permission. The man was found guilty on all charges because a device that had been previously used for weather updates and ordering more batteries had recorded a murder.

The public had always suspected it, and in the end, it turned out that none of them even cared. The people spouting insane conspiracy theories were right. But because of a single event proving the usefulness of it—God forbid it have to be used that same way again—everyone was fine with Big Brother looking over their shoulder, listening to their polite dinner conversations, hearing what a husband and wife tell each other in the throes of passion. None of it mattered anymore because it was proven to be helpful *once*.

After that, it was a short step to their current status. The newsfeeds tipped it first. Rumors that everyone was going to be chipped. No longer were the conspiracy theorists shouting in the streets. A great deal of the American people began quoting Revelations in the Bible, taking a stand against "the mark of the beast." It wasn't a problem when they *might* be watched and listened to. Once it was introduced that they'd be chipped and *definitely* be watched and listened to, *then* suddenly it became a problem.

But like all things, the problem it posed wasn't a problem to anyone anymore. Evan often wondered what would be different had that company that owned the device that proved the man's guilt had denied the Supreme Court, had chosen to maintain the privacy of its customers and that of the public. Now, there were laws that protected companies in situations like that. The billions of dollars they make can't be sacrificed, but the lives of millions of people can be—they're a dime a dozen, apparently.

The laws that made it mandatory to have a SafetyChip inserted into citizens' arms also had clauses that limited the amount of data and surveilling that could take place. Those same laws had been in effect with the in-home devices too, and look at what good they did.

Now, asking people to allow the government—and now any company with access to the information—to watch and listen was apparently too much. But they got over it. Everyone always did.

Her wheels were turning again. "Do you think it's a good idea that we're still being watched and monitored?"

He shrugged. "I don't know. I think I just don't care at this point. They're going to do it anyway and already are. What's the point in fighting it? Now at least there's a good reason for it, I think."

"When I was a kid and Mom and Dad had that thing, I don't remember what it was called, but it was a girl's name. Back when they had that, people suspected someone was listening but until it became law, it wasn't a big deal." She had echoed his own thoughts almost exactly.

"Right, so now that there's a purpose to it, you think it's *more* okay?" Evan wasn't trying to "poke the bear." Now, he was genuinely curious. This was the first time they'd ever spoken about this more than just in passing.

She sat up a little straighter and spoke slowly, not as dazed as before, but as if she were thinking about each word before saying it. "I think that it is *more* okay to be watched and listened to for a purpose that can be made public, rather than a purpose that has to be kept secret." Evan nodded, momentarily fascinated and mildly—how it was possible he wasn't sure—aroused at how intelligent this woman across from him was.

"Yeah." She nodded as if she had reached a decision. "I think that's more in line with how I feel. It's like if you had a cookie and someone asked what the ingredients were and you said, 'Nothing that can kill you.' That's not going to make anyone feel good about eating that cookie despite the fact that it's true on every level, whether they followed the recipe or loaded it with horrible—but not deadly—ingredients.

"But if you list the ingredients and then say, 'Nothing that can kill you,' the phrase didn't change, but now there's ... context."

Well hot damn, Evan thought, giddy with the joy that comes from replacing old understanding with new, vibrant ideas.

"Then, there's the spiritual issue..." She let that hang in the air for a minute.

Spirituality wasn't something they had discussed much in their time together. He knew about God because he'd grown up going to church with his family, all the good it did them. He considered himself religious, but in tradition only. He didn't go to church and didn't expect his wife to, though they had great friends that were actively involved in their churches and communities.

For centuries, religion had been the driving force behind atrocities that could only be committed in the name of some god. It wasn't only Christianity like with the Spanish Inquisition and Crusades. There were atrocities committed in the name of Allah like the Twin Towers terror attacks in New York in the early 21st Century. Then, there were the Neo-Pagan wars of the recent decades. In Evan's mind, the latter weren't really "wars" in the traditional sense of the word, but they were most certainly an organized offense against anyone—people or community—who disagreed with their insane ideologies.

He didn't have a problem with religion when it served others rather than self, so this piqued his interest as it was something he enjoyed discussing with his wife.

"And...?" he prompted.

"Well, I know we haven't really talked about it much, but if these people are dead, isn't it, I don't know, almost desecrating a grave or something close to it?" She looked at him with genuine curiosity, screwing her face up into a look that would have made him laugh had it been any another instance. He didn't, this time, and gave himself a proverbial pat on the back for his discretion.

"Well, that's interesting, babe. It really is. So, you—we—believe that there's life after death, right? Everyone that's good goes to Heaven, that sort of thing?" He hated how mundane it sounded, but he went with it for the sake of simplicity.

She nodded.

"So, they're already in heaven, then. I doubt they'll be plucked from the streets of gold to come down and talk with us." He thought for a moment. "Though I do remember one story in the Bible where a guy, Saul I think, asked a witch to summon his old mentor Samuel and he did. Weird stuff."

She blew a stray lock of hair out of her face. "So, in that light, I guess it doesn't really matter. They've been judged at the pearly gates and are doing whatever they do up there, right?" He knew what they were actually discussing. Evan doubted his wife believed her father was good enough to go to Heaven, which would mean he was either nowhere or he was in Hell. He didn't want to push her to make a decision on that, not quite yet. She was wondering what the moral and spiritual repercussions to herself would be if she called the digital ghost of her father from beyond the grave. That was something she'd have to pull herself out of, as well.

He walked to the table, pulled out the chair next to her, and sat down. "I can't imagine what's going through your head, but if you need me, or anything, I'll be right here." He reached out and laid his hand on hers; she laced her fingers through his.

"I know you will, babe. And who knows? Maybe all of this is a good thing." She smiled at him, but it didn't touch her eyes.

He was always able to tell when her smile wasn't genuine, always able to tell when the smile was placating rather than participatory. This was one of those smiles. She was trying to show him that she was *fine*, she was just *fine* and would be just *fine*, and things would be normal and *fine*. And they would be. At least until they weren't, and he found her curled up under a blanket, her cheeks stained with the remains of mascara-laced tears that trickled down to also stain the couch pillows. On the floor, the aftermath of an entire tissue box scattered across the rug in a semicircle beneath his weeping and sniffling wife.

He knew that day would come; he'd get home from work and find her just like that. He hoped he wouldn't but could feel himself preparing for it, anyway. He'd need to stop by the liquor store tomorrow to get a bottle of wine and some ice cream.

Shit, he thought with half-bitter mirth. *She's doing that intermittent fasting thing and can't eat or drink after 7.* Even in the middle of a hurricane of emotion, she'd stick to that damn diet. He couldn't fault her for it. She was the most stubborn person he would ever know.

Evan sat back against the chair in the waiting room, idly tapping his fingertips on his knees while the memory faded away, the last image of his wife rubbing her lip and looking into the distance shimmered and was gone from his mind's eye.

Then the last words she spoke echoed back into his mind, as if they bounced off the thin veil of the past and into the present. *What if this is a good thing?*

His fingers stopped tapping.

The thought struck such an explosive contrast to the dour, dark clouds that had been storming through his mind, that it very realistically called a complete stop to all other mental processes.

That one phrase hung suspended in his mind as if the angel in *The Greatest Christmas Pageant Ever* had dropped from the ceiling of a theatre and hung there, swinging back and forth in the spotlight, impossible to miss or move aside, the sum of his attention focused unequivocally on that one spot. It was as if he was in the theatre, the only one in the seats staring blankly at the phrase hanging there.

What if this is a good thing?

The processes began again, cranking to life slowly and steadily catching him up to speed. *What if this was a good thing?* He'd been so depressed lately that a change may actually be good.

He could feel a small spark of hope in his chest, a chance that something could be different. It'd been the same for so long. Was it actually possible for him to change? For him to, dare he say it, live?

His name was called by Blinker, and the stage where the swinging angel named "*What if this is a good thing*" went dark. She indicated a door to the side of her desk where a handsome man stood calmly, his glasses perched at a slightly odd angle and his hands folded in front of his light blue suit, a warm smile plastered on his face.

As Evan walked by, the man said, "Good morning, sir," and nodded, the smile never changing.

Evan responded with a noncommittal grunt and brushed by him, immediately realizing he had no idea where he was going, a brief flutter of anxiety bubbling in his gut.

He was saved any embarrassment when Glasses followed him through the door and indicated a private room down the short hallway. Glasses began asking questions about his day, but Evan ignored him. Not to be dissuaded, he simply began jabbering about his own day and life. Evan still ignored him and stared around the hall as they walked.

The floor was a generic white tile, reminding Evan of his elementary school. The walls were a pristine white, and like the desk that Blinker was certainly still sitting behind, almost too bright for him to even look at directly. On the walls were several paintings, spaced every ten steps or so on both sides of the hallway. Beautiful views of the Earth from space, an aerial view of what could only be a rainforest before it and all the others were harvested into extinction, along with all the animals and plants that called them home. There was a beautiful picture beyond the room Glasses had indicated that overlooked an ocean and another on the opposite wall of a beach that now only exists in this picture, as the crystal blue waters and white sands had followed those ancient reptile kings into the history books.

He paused in front of the second picture briefly and could tell that Glasses stopped behind him. This picture wasn't a landscape. In fact, it was the first one he'd noticed that depicted people. He made a mental note to tell Glasses to put more of them up. The waiting room was too stark, and if people were actually going to be talking to their dead relatives, it would be a good reminder to have pictures of other people in their midst.

"Mr. Reader?" Glasses asked the question to prompt Evan into motion again, but Evan held up a hand to him and muttered, "Just a sec."

The picture that had captured his attention so quickly showed several children playing and laughing in the center of what he could only assume was a water park of sorts. There were two boys, both laughing merrily in mid-air, vaulting over a vertical spray of water. The other children in the picture were three girls, probably no more than 4 or 5-years-old, their long wet hair plastered to their faces where squinting eyes marked unmistakable joy. The worries of the world outside of the happiness they were experiencing was beyond their comprehension, or care. Water droplets glittered as sparkling mist in their hair and one of the girls had her hands out in front of her, trying—unsuccessfully—to stop a horizontal spray of water from hitting her square in the face. The initial white spray was hitting her palm, but because she had her fingers splayed apart, most of the splash was hitting her right in the nose. The picture was incredibly realistic, so realistic in fact, that he could nearly feel the prickling spray on his own cheeks, the tickling drips plunging from his chin while giggles and barks of laughter and jeers between friends echoed and circled in the air around him.

He began to recall something from his own life; the children he was staring at were calling it to forward, helping to push aside the ashen landscape of his life and the emotional baggage he'd buried them under. When it finally surfaced, bubbling up from the mire of memory, it was as if an old friend had stopped by for a glass of tea.

He invited it in with a silent surrendering sigh.

CHAPTER 4

Evan remembered a season when kids would normally be running around, bundled up in jackets and gloves, knitted hats failing to cover their reddening ears, but this particular day had arrived after a weekend of intense storms in the Midwest, and there wasn't anyone in their right mind wearing gloves, scarf, or jacket. Where normally the weather would be barely above freezing on a good day, the weather had warmed to late-spring and early-summer temperatures, much to the delight of children, and the relief of parents, everywhere.

In fact, most kids that Evan could currently see from the bench where he was sitting in the middle of the park were in shorts and t-shirts, many of them fitting a little tight from the previous year. He figured that there hadn't been a parent prepared for this warm day, and none had gone shopping for new summer clothes.

He sighed bitterly.

He knew nothing of those things. His intuition—or more realistically suspicions—were based solely on what he *thought* was the truth. His new reality was one where that knowledge would only be reserved for other people, people whose titles were revered and praised through the ages by some and cursed and spurned by others: *parents*.

He closed his eyes against the dull throb of his temples. As bright and warm as the sun was, he cradled his head in his hands and shielded his eyes from the light with his palms. But it persisted and shone through the trees in patches, dappling the few struggling strands of green grass around his feet and highlighting the tall stalks of weeds that decided it was their time to grow, despite the seasonal timing.

It really was a beautiful day. Evan, however, absorbed in his own thoughts, had a hard time noticing. Like the storms before the mild weather he now found himself in, his mind and marriage seemed to be in upheaval, their moods declining into cold obstinance, the joy he once felt slipping slowly away in an unidentifiable leak.

They'd been married for a short time, only a few months now, but had recently gone through all the checks that couples go through to make sure all the plumbing is in working order. He'd insisted they take the tests before they got married, but his lovely darling wife had wanted to wait. And well, Evan loved her enough to not push the point.

They'd gone to the doctor, done all the tests, including the Chip scan and the one where Evan went into the sterile room—with a TV, a chair, and access to a list of digital pornography—knowing full well that everyone else knew what was happening in there.

His wife's procedure was more invasive, and he had made sure she was still up for it. She was. Of course, she was, the agreeable little thing. The office said they'd call in a few days with the results.

With that done, they'd gone out to lunch to a little place called *Return to Sender* and had ice cream for dessert.

It had been a good day. He now wished he'd have held on to it a little longer. The storms were on the horizon. And unlike his seat on the bench—warmed by the unseasonal heat—they were bringing an icy unfamiliarity between them.

He received the call a few days later to come back to the clinic, neither of them suspecting a thing as they jumped in the car and drove merrily into town. Sure, Evan's stomach was turning, but he'd never tell her that. He didn't want to give a drop of doubt.

Besides, everything was fine.

They waited patiently for the doctor to call them to the back, his wife's dainty fingers laced through his, laughing and smiling at a few of the children tottering around the waiting room. One little boy, a fiery red-head was pretending to be a dragon and flapping his arms exaggeratedly and roaring—quietly—to the delighted squeals of who Evan could only assume was his younger sister. He could feel his wife snuggle up to him and could barely feel the corner of her mouth creased in that smile of hers as she watched with jealous expectancy. It would be the last smile he'd see for a while.

"Mr. and Mrs. Reader?" The nurse's voice cut through the playful din of the waiting room. They both stood, and he felt them take simultaneous breaths. They walked to where the nurse was waiting, graciously dodging around the playing pair of dragon and prey.

They followed the nurse through a set of double doors and back into a small office. Hand in hand they walked, confident in the outcome they both wanted.

"Please take a seat here." The nurse indicated two plush chairs facing a large and sturdy wooden desk. "The doctor will be with you in a moment." Then, she closed the door behind her.

The walls of the office were decorated with plaques and awards, but Evan noticed a weight in the pit of his stomach that hadn't been there in the waiting room. He set it aside, chalking it up to a case of the jitters.

His young wife looked at him, her eyes sparkling with expectation. "Are you nervous?" She bit her lower lip gently.

If he was honest with himself, he didn't have a good feeling about this anymore. Maybe he was being paranoid, but did the nurse give him one of those tight-lipped smiles that didn't touch her eyes when she left? The kind of smile that said, "This is all I can offer you because words won't make a difference."

"Me? Nah." Evan made a motion as if waving away a fly. "I'll say I'm excited to get this over with, but we'll be fine." He patted her knee and winked at her, something he now realized with a small bit of horror, that his father used to do.

They both stared around the room. Evan eyed the nameplate that read *Dr. Elias Gregory* and waited, both now silent. He squeezed her hand, and she squeezed back. He flashed her a "I'm not worried" smile and hoped it looked like he wasn't. Because truth was that weight in the pit of his stomach had grown. It was no longer some small thing to be ignored. It had evolved into a pot of churning and bubbling oil, and he hesitated to move lest it spill over and out his mouth.

When he heard the door click behind him, he turned to watch Dr. Elias Gregory walk around the ample desk, his white coat flaring behind him as he turned quickly and sat down. He clutched a yellow folder in one hand, and Evan's eyes followed it. Several small white edges of the papers within it stuck out.

The doctor smiled at them but glanced quickly down at his papers as he flipped the folder open. When he spoke, it was in an abruptly business-like tone, not at all what Evan expected, truth be told.

"Good morning, Mr. and Mrs. Reader. Thank you for taking the time to come in today." At this point, he folded his hands and placed them over the folder. "We have the results of your fertility tests." He sighed here, and Evan found the churning oil burst into flame in his belly, the cramp was so sudden that he nearly let out a grunt as he leaned forward to hide the sudden urge to clutch his midsection.

"There isn't an easy way to say this..."

Shit.

"...but there were some problems with the results." He turned toward Evan. "It doesn't appear, Mr. Reader, that your sperm is viable." He turned his other patient. "And Mrs. Reader, your eggs are also not viable." He turned back to face them both equally. "I wish I could say there is fertility treatment that could be done to correct this, but when talking to my patients, I'm more of a realist. I won't say there's zero chance. That's just asking to be proven wrong. But the chances of you getting pregnant without a very large amount of outside assistance is less than one percent. I am sorry. I know this news is not easy to hear or process."

The rest of what he was droning on about was lost in the high-pitched ringing that had begun in Evan's ears. The burning pot of oil now spilled over, boiling and feeling like it was cauterizing his insides. He felt his heart sinking through the chair and floor beneath it.

Evan knew that he was trying not to freeze up, and in his head, he was telling himself *speak, say thank you, move, shake his hand, look at your wife, anything*. But he couldn't. He tried to get a sense of his wife as his attention moved from his own response and focused on hers. He could feel by her crushing, white-knuckled grip that she had definitely heard dear old Dr.

Elias Gregory and was probably going through something similar to his own burning oil belly.

He finally forced his eyes to blink, but it felt as if he was fighting every force in the universe to do it. At once, it was as if a stasis field was lifted. The ringing in the room faded, and the doctor's voice began to sound more like words instead of mumbled incantations.

He turned to look at the woman who held his heart and could see a paleness in her cheeks, like the finest and most precious porcelain. Her eyes were starting to well with tears, and they glistened like crystal in the late morning light from the window.

Evan cleared his throat and adjusted his posture.

Dr. Elias Gregory continued, "There are alternatives, of course." He said this with such nonchalance that Evan blinked in surprise as if the doctor had instead said "And a hearty fuck you both."

"There is always adoption. And that will always be my first recommendation. There are plenty of children who need a loving home." He paused here as if expecting some reaction from the pair. Receiving no indication to stay on the topic of adoption, he continued. "If that doesn't feel right, there's fostering. Many families find a fulfilling life helping children in that way." Again, the two were silent, so he continued, "And finally, if you were interested, you could use a sperm donor and an egg donor to create a zygote. Mrs. Reader, your eggs may not be viable, but there was nothing we could find that suggested your uterus couldn't *carry* a baby. While adoption is my first recommendation, using donors is the *strongest* alternative at this point."

Silence hung heavily in the room. Dr. Gregory looked back and forth between the two of them. Evan swallowed and opened his mouth to speak but was cut off by the sudden emptiness where his wife's clutching grasp had been. It happened with such swiftness that for the briefest second, his brain still registered her hand in his, like the echo of it. He stared down at his empty palm in mild shock.

The smack of her palm slamming on the top of the desk sounded akin to a gunshot. Evan's attention snapped up from his empty hand.

An unironic feeling of wariness settled over him, but for the doctor's sake, not his own.

His wife, his lovely, level-headed wife was on her feet and leaning menacingly over the table at Dr. Elias Gregory. Her hair shimmered dully in the sun as it lay on her shoulders. The mouth that held that special smile was twisted into a grotesque sneer like she had just smelled the contents of the city sewer after a particularly hot day in the sun. Dr. Elias Gregory was leaning back in his chair, certainly taken aback by the abrupt change of temperature in the room and trying not to let on that he was surprised.

When she spoke, it was barely a whisper, but to his wonder—and a little to his horror—she could be heard clear as a bell. The tremble in her lower limp didn't betray her voice at all, and the unshed tears in her eyes spoke volumes to the hurt her words could not convey.

"*Strongest alternative?* That's the best you can do for us after ripping the dreams from our hearts and future, then laying them out on your desk like the remains of some gutted animal? *Strongest alternative?*" Her voice was rising in volume but not pitch. If anything, somehow getting deeper into a key that Evan couldn't remember ever hearing. "While we just found out it's not one of us broken, leaving room for at least a little hope—no, that would be too easy. Instead, *both* of us are broken, and you have the audacity, the *fucking audacity* to give us your goddamned recommendations in the same breath?" She was speaking at full volume now. Yelling actually.

The doctor adjusted his tie and rolled his shoulders—an unsuccessful attempt to appear calm, collected, and in control—and said, "Mrs. Reader, I understand you're upset. There's no reason to act in such a way that borders on hysterical. If you would please sit back d—" but he was cut off when she spoke in a calm but enormously venomous tone.

"Excuse me? Hysterical?"

The doctor, to his credit, swallowed hard. His own assumption that he was in control vanished.

"*Hysterical?*" Her nostrils flared as she took a deep, steadying breath. "This is not hysterical. If you were any type of *man* rather than an engorged tick sucking at the dollar-sized tits of couples wishing to have children, you would understand. As that's not the case, let me be clear. Hysteria is when someone loses control, and let me assure you, sir, if I had lost control, you might be little more than a pile of meaty chunks scattered around this office. Instead, I'm telling you flat out, and in an impeccably controlled voice, I might add, that your delivery of news borders on *criminal*. I don't need *you* to explain to *me* how I feel. I'm fully capable of understanding the depths of pain and grief that you've thrust so effortlessly upon me. Therefore, sir, I don't want your advice, I don't want your recommendations, and I sure as shit don't need them."

Evan found himself standing next to her. He was shocked that she was cursing so freely. Every now and then at home, one would slip out when she was tipsy or when she would stub her toe. But to be so brazen with someone she didn't even know made him more than a little wary. But also incredibly proud, he admitted to himself.

As she stood there, her body rigid like a compressed spring, he moved his hand to place it on the small of her back, to let her know that he was not only here but also that he was *here for her*. In an uncharacteristic flash of insight, however, he hesitated. He didn't want her to misconstrue the motion as placating, a non-verbal way to say, "Hey babe, settle down, will ya?" and let his hand fall back to his side. She didn't need his reassurance right now.

The doctor hesitated and when he opened his mouth to speak was abruptly cut off when Evan's wife said in a final, no-holds-barred manner, "No fucking thank you."

He saw her lower lip trembling, and while her words were still filled with a burning rage, they wavered in the air around them, and it broke his heart. She was furious, but she was also crushed. Both of them were. Her heart had been broken. A dream she'd had for decades had been splintered, shattered, and tossed aside. Oh sure, they could adopt or find donors, but she wanted her own children. Maybe it was selfish. And so what? Wasn't a person allowed to make that decision for themselves? And by extension, wasn't that person allowed to mourn when that decision was made for them by nature or God or the universe?

With her final statement made, she turned on her heel and stalked—marched—from the room, clutching her purse at her side.

Evan looked at Dr. Elias Gregory and surprised himself. Instead of shrugging an apology, which would have been his response in any normal situation, he shook his head in disbelief at the man still leaning back in his chair. Evan turned and followed his wife out. When he caught up to her in the hallway, this time he did put his hand on her back.

CHAPTER 5

Much later on, he would come to realize that the good doctor was delivering news he'd probably delivered a million times. Even still, he didn't pity the man. The doctor had incurred the wrath of a woman he'd underestimated, believing that every person would like to hear the "next steps" to take. Maybe, in that man's experience, it helped soften the blow of such heavy news. But maybe next time he'd think twice before launching into that sermon.

His wife was different. She preferred to process the issue and come to her own conclusion of what the "next steps" should be, even if they aligned perfectly with what would have been offered. If the doctor had said something along the lines of, "Would you like to hear my recommendations for next steps?" things may have turned out differently. Evan saw clearly that they would have. His wife would have politely declined, saying something about needing time to process the news first. Then, she would have thanked the good doctor, and together, they'd have left and figured out what to do. Together.

But that wasn't what happened.

After she verbally massacred the doctor, Evan had followed her out of the clinic and down the concrete steps to their car. He could tell she was miserable. Her shoulders were slumped, and she was hastily wiping her nose and eyes in that way people do when their emotions are inconveniently transparent. He opened her door, and she sat into the passenger seat. The way her shoulders began to rise and fall the second the door closed told him all he needed to know. He knew the tears hiding behind the anger upstairs in the doctor's office had muscled their way forward. The bluster and rage she'd felt had given way to the heartbreak and grief. He quickly sat in the driver's seat without looking at her and started the car.

Knowing it would make her self-conscious if he stared right at her, but also wanting to be attentive, he compromised. Out of the corner of his eye, he could see her lower lip trembling, her delicate chin creased with those dimples that come when someone is focusing all of their attention on not releasing a torrent of emotion. Despite this, tears streamed down her face in a steady flow. She tried to keep the sobs within, but they came out in light whimpers between hardy sniffs.

Evan pulled into traffic, asking tentatively if she was hungry. She shook her head without a word, continuing to wipe the tears that were spilling down her reddening cheeks. Evan reached across the space between their armrests and had felt as if he were stretching across some vast distance for her hand. He held it, but she didn't hold his.

They drove in silence from the city to their home. Evan took the time to try and come up with some way to help her. Something to say that would lighten the mood. Well, maybe not *lighten,* that would certainly be the *wrong* thing to do. No, something to help keep her head above water. There was so much to process and process it they must. But he didn't want her to go down that road of doubt, self-pity, grief, and self-deprecation that accompanied the other storms in her life.

This one involved both of them; shouldn't they face it—and rise through it—together?

When they turned into their driveway—that old familiar *crunch* of the gravel beneath the tires welcoming them home— he'd come up with nothing useful at all. On top of it, the sound of the gravel, usually a chuckling welcome, sounded today like a path laid with bones, crushed beneath the weight of the car.

He put the car in park and tried to get out quickly enough to open her door, thinking incessantly about how he could show he cared and make something—anything—easier for her, but she was already shoving it open with her foot, and before he even had time to register it, she was walking briskly up the path to the front door.

He jogged to catch up after closing her door for her, feeling helpless and stupid.

Her purse was dropped without emotion by the door. She kicked off her shoes without regard to where they landed and started up the stairs.

Evan bent to gather these items and tidy them up when her hoarse voice, thick with emotion, croaked from the stairs.

"I'm going upstairs to sleep, hopefully until tomorrow. Or forever. I don't really know. I need time. I don't care what you do."

He stood inside the front door until he heard their bedroom door close softly. This was just another storm, he told himself; it'll pass, too. He hoped desperately that it was true. The storm in him that began to rise at the news was distant; he'd pushed it away in an attempt to navigate *hers*.

The harsh "I don't care what you do" stung despite telling himself that she didn't have the emotional capacity to take his feelings into account right now. A distant part of him felt the unfairness of that lopsided thought, but it was gone before he could hone in on it.

Interpreting his wife's words had become a bit of a hobby for him. She often said things that *sounded* harsh but, in all actuality, were spoken plainly. This was often the case.

In this instance, she meant he could do what he wanted. To not worry about *her* right now. He could go see a movie or turn on the TV downstairs or take a nap with her, but whatever he chose, it wouldn't affect her. She was in survival mode. She needed time to think through what she was feeling, and for that, she needed to withdraw into herself.

Armed with this knowledge, he knew a part of him should go try to comfort her. Lying next to her and offering her nothing more than a shoulder or chest to cry on may do wonders, but he also knew that there were times when she wanted to be alone. Isolating herself usually helped her, if only in the long run, with coming out of the storm, even if it made him feel as helpless as ice in a fire.

Despite all of this, he decided to hunker down with her. Well, not *with* her, but in the same vicinity as her.

"This way," he told the empty room quietly and reassuring himself, "if she needs me..."

Fat chance.

"...I'll be here."

Over the next few days, however, he began to realize that this storm had stalled and wouldn't be moving on as quickly. Some storms would move on, where his quiet hesitation was enough of a catalyst to bring her back into the light of day.

Their interactions during this time, however, were cold. There was very little engagement—mostly from her end—and even the little that was there seemed like it was out of habit more than a conscious desire to connect and move forward together. A peck on the cheek, telling one another "I love you" before going to sleep, and a barely-uttered "thank you" when he would hand her a cup of coffee fixed just the way she liked it—touch of sugar and plenty of cream—were the only notable interactions between them.

Several times, he tried to draw her into conversation, hoping that from nothing more than rote memory she could be almost tricked into an echo of normalcy.

"Hey, Honey. Is there anything I can get you?" Evan had ordered dinner for them, and they'd eaten it on their back deck overlooking a field of tall grass that swayed lazily in the breeze.

She looked at him and smiled. "No, but thank you, Honey." The smile had not been a true smile. It was of the "I-appreciate-the-effort-but-I'm-fine" variety.

He took a deep breath and dove in. "I know there's a lot going through your head right now. I know there's a lot to process between your feelings and your grief, and well, I just want you to know that I'm here for you. I'm in this with you. I always will be."

She continued to stare out at hypnotic patterns of waving grass. After a few quiet seconds, she said, "I know you are, Evan."

He waited for more but nothing else followed. He plowed ahead and risked it all. "It doesn't really feel like it, though."

Now she turned to him, curiosity in her gaze. "What do you mean by that?" Her tone gave plenty of warning, warning that perhaps he should heed. But nothing ventured, nothing gained.

"What I mean is that it feels awfully one-sided here. I'm doing everything I can to try and make your day and time easier with all of it. And I'm happy to do it—don't get me wrong. I just feel that we should probably talk about it a little bit, you know?

Try to put words to how you—we—feel. So we can start to heal. So we can at some point move forward with our lives, I guess."

He initially took her silence as a good sign. Maybe she was thinking about what he said. Maybe she would say *You know, you're right, Evan. I'm ready to talk about it and move forward. I don't want to grieve anymore.* But she didn't.

"You want to talk about it? You want to put words to how *I* feel? Well sure, let's do that." Her tone was not a tone that was ready to heal. "Where to start. First, I feel like my own body betrayed me. You should be able to imagine how that feels, Evan, because your body betrayed you, too. Second, I can't fulfill what I've always thought I was made to do. I've dreamed about carrying a child in my body for those nine months. Yeah, sure, maybe they'd be a miserable nine months, but at least they'd be *my* nine months. Then we'd have a baby, and it would be *our* baby. It would have my nose and your eyes and my hair and as it grew up, we'd say things like, 'Wow she sure gets that from you,' or 'Doesn't he look just like you with that smile?' Instead, we have the *option* to have someone else's baby in our lives where we won't ever have those conversations. Yes, I know that sounds selfish. I know that sounds terrible. I know..." her voice cracked, and tears began to run down her cheeks, "...that it makes me a terrible person to know there are kids out there that I *could* take care of but don't want to because they didn't come from *my body*. Do you think I want to feel this way? Do you think that I feel this way because it's comfortable to me? Don't you think I'd change it if I could?"

He didn't know how to answer. His mouth worked to form an understanding and—if he was honest with himself—a response that backpedaled a little. But he couldn't manage anything more than, "Babe I'm sorry. I didn't know."

"Of course, you didn't. I barely even know. All of this is jumping around in my head, and I can't make heads or tails of it." She took a deep and steadying breath before continuing. "I only know that it takes every ounce of energy for me to get out of our bed. To sit here and not breakdown into a blubbering mess of wailing. So no, Evan, I can't talk about how I feel because *I* barely know how I feel. Yes, I appreciate all you've done these past days for me. I know it's not easy and I know how hard it is to work from home while trying to tiptoe around me. I get it, but I can't even..." She faltered a little, a sob slipping past her defenses. "I can't even think through the haze that I am feeling."

They sat out on the deck until the sun set. The chilly evening breeze brought with it the sound of oak trees whispering at the edge of the property. Birds winged through the air in the distance, and he thought he saw a bat's dark silhouette against the violet velvet of night.

Evan cleared the remains of their meal and afterward, they fell asleep on the couch together. She had hugged him, there on the couch, with his arms wrapped tightly around her. So that was something. She had cried. Hard at first, then settling into a kind of sniffling rhythm before dozing off. In a difficult way, it was nice. But the loss he felt was beginning to grow, and he didn't have time for it right now. He'd address it later when it wasn't all hands on deck.

Several days after his failed attempt at coaxing her into conversation, he tried and failed to make things semi-normal by asking enthusiastically if she wanted to see a movie. Her response was mostly the same, but she encouraged him to see it with Mason. It was then that he came to a painful realization. One that felt like a sting but grew steadily into a blossoming burn: he was trying so hard to make sure his wife didn't close the door on him, that he very nearly forgot that his grief mattered. Or would. Eventually.

The morning following this realization dawned bright and warm. It was a Saturday, and he left the house early in the morning without bothering to make a cup of coffee. If she woke up before he was back, the note on his pillow and the identical note on the table explained that he'd gone for a drive and would be back around lunchtime. He doubted she'd even notice his forethought of working to reassure her; she was too deep within her own mind to recognize the effort.

He called his best friend as he drove slowly out the driveway and turned onto Heritage Road, asking Mason to meet him at the park. The seat had been warmed in the unseasonable sun, and he took a moment to enjoy the feel of it on his skin compared to the cool days that led to this one. Mason was the only person Evan had spoken to since their interaction with Dr. Elias Gregory, and Evan desperately needed to process all of this.

"Hello?" Mason's voice was groggy, but not the groggy of having just been woken up. It was the groggy of being awake for a few minutes, at least.

Evan hesitated for a minute, but really needed his friend, so he pushed ahead. "Hey, Mason. It's Evan."

"Hey man, what's up? It's early. Everything alright?"

"Yeah. I mean it's not alright, but nothing is immediately wrong. It's the baby thing." The "baby thing" was a much easier way of naming the painful information they were processing rather than saying he was mourning or experiencing grief.

Evan could almost hear Mason's slow nod through the connection. "Oh. Yeah. I understand. What do you need?"

"Would you mind meeting me at the park this morning? I..." His throat constricted suddenly, and the corners of his eyes stung. "I think I need to talk about it all."

Mason agreed to meet at Trenthide Park as soon as he was changed and could get out the door. Now Evan sat, waiting for him and feeling the butterflies in his stomach grow and metamorphize into galloping horses as his thoughts turned more and more inward. He was beginning to look, for the first time he knew, toward the core of his emotions. And what he saw there was deep and ugly and foreign and terribly personal.

Outwardly, he imagined he looked like an everyday onlooker. His calm eyes followed several of the children playing gleefully on the monkey bars, dropping from the third or fourth rung when their little strength gave out, then laughing and running to the back of the line to try again.

There were a couple of parents grouped together near a small herd of strollers, colorful monuments to their sleepless nights and constant worry.

The sounds that washed over him through the warm waves of the day didn't register as mere noise. To him, it was music. It was the sweetest music life could produce, and to his open and inexperienced ears, it sounded like the purest and most innocent of joys.

Even in what he now knew to call grief, he could recognize how spectacular the sounds were as they made their way through the distance between them—the squeak of a shoe on the plastic slide or the rattle of the swings and their rusty cries as kids ran into them stomach-first and launching themselves into the air. Their legs and arms, freed by the squirrely momentum, reached for the clouds in front of them. The lazy arc suspended time for the briefest second at the apex, before falling back toward the ground with squeals of delight.

He felt something hit his hand and looked down. A circle of wetness was shimmering on the back of his hand, the small hairs there capturing and containing it within gossamer borders.

He wiped it away with his other hand. The wetness on his cheek was drying now, but he was surprised to feel a continued tightness in his throat. He was crying softly. His breath wasn't hitching, but his eyes had begun to leak the emotions that had been bottled up within him. The contrast surrounding him was difficult to endure. The grief had begun to worm its way out of him, all the while surrounded by the unbound vitality that could only be exhibited by children. At the same moment that this thought came, another made its way to the surface. Were the two emotions actually so different? Weren't they just two points on a circle? Without the joy and flurry of activity that children brought, could absence of such happiness bring any other response except tears of loss?

So, he didn't stop the tears, he just wiped them away when he felt their liquid weight pool beneath his eyes or slide roguishly down the side of his nose.

While watching two older kids jumping away from one another—tag, he assumed—he saw Mason. Mason was walking across the vacant space that separated the play area from the empty and out-of-season baseball fields.

Evan lifted his hand in a lazy wave, which Mason returned, flashing a small smile before closing the distance in a jog.

When he was a little closer and the sun speckled Mason's features through the leaves above, Evan stood up and stretched out his hand to shake his friend's.

Instead, Mason opened his animal arms and wrapped Evan in a bear hug. The breath was forced from him, and he grunted, but he didn't care. He found himself welcoming the pressure. He was mildly surprised at the fierce embrace, but he took a deep breath. Not knowing exactly how to react, he surrendered. He surrendered to everything he'd been hiding and ignoring, and he buried his face in Mason's shoulder.

His own shoulders shook from the sobs and moans that were finally freed from his throat in a hoarse staccato. Mason only stood there and held him. All but the words of Dr. Elias Gregory faded from around him, purged by his subconscious as he finally registered the deep ache of longing that had grown in his heart.

Less than one percent. Pretty much no chance, but he couldn't say that.

I'm never having kids, he thought, finally letting himself hear what he'd known had been waiting in the wings of his consciousness.

While his wife was still probably upstairs coping with the loss of something that hadn't even been a possibility, he was coming to grips with the fact that there would be no tiny voice to say "Daddy." No little patter of feet down the stairs asking for a drink of water after hugs and kisses had been doled out and blankets delivered. No Sunday morning snuggles, or chocolate chip pancakes, no unsightly smudges on perfect little blouses or button-ups, no snot stains on his shoulder, and no mystery smells from the backseat.

The joy of expectation had turned to the bitterness of exposure, his heart flayed open like, yes, like the animal carcass his wife had spoken of in the doctor's office. How right she had been, a keenness of mind that was appropriate on a level that she may never even realize.

Eventually, Mason patted him on the back and held him at arm's length, squeezing his shoulders. His eyes held no judgement for the tears in Evan's own, and when Mason sat on the bench, Evan sat with him, suddenly too exhausted to stand.

They were silent for a minute, the playground sounds still making their way across the open expanse to where they sat in the comfortable shade of the tree.

Mason broke the silence first. "I'd ask if you're okay, but I know that you're not. So, I'll ask a different question. What do you need?" His voice had always been deep, even in high school, but it was always his tone that surprised new people he would meet. He was the quintessential jock of every movie played or book written. With the muscled young adult body that girls fawned over, gossiping to their girlfriends about how they'd marry him some day.

Yet, despite all of that, Mason was one of the most sensitive men Evan had ever known. He had the uncanny ability to perceive a person's feelings and react appropriately to the situation. It bordered on supernatural.

And it was no different now. Evan hadn't ever wanted anyone to tell him everything would be okay, but he needed someone that could let him rage or cry if he needed. Someone who would sit and wait until he was done doing either. Mason was that person.

Evan dodged the question for the time being. He'd come back to it. "What's Marcy up to? I don't want to ruin your Saturday." A fairly weak attempt at hedging, and they both knew it.

Mason nodded after raising an eyebrow, no doubt expecting such an attempt. "Nah, Marcy is headed to your house with mimosas and cinnamon rolls for your wife. She figured if you were calling me, it was because you weren't able to talk at home. Marcy always likes to swoop in and be the hero, so I let her." He said it with good natured humor because it was true. She was the type of person that wanted to make everything better. Evan hoped desperately that she'd have some luck at his house.

"That's good. You're good together, you know." Mason chuffed a laugh and leaned back, crossing his ankles, the dirt beneath his shoes whispering agreement. "And I don't know what I need. I needed a friend, and you're here, so I can cross that off the list.

"I need to figure out where to go from here, honestly. It's like all of my plans for the next thirty years are up in smoke. Poof! just like that. With a few words—delivered in a pretty shitty way if I'm being completely honest—the entire future we'd planned together is off the rails, back to the station, square one. Whatever metaphor you wanna use would fit the bill, I'm sure.

"End result is the same, anyway. We'll never have kids, Mason. *Never.* It will always, *only,* be her and me, unless we get a dog or cat or three, and then we'll be those people that don't have kids, we have 'fur-babies,' and you know how I feel about that crap." Evan didn't have anything against pets or the people who focused their entire lives on making their pets as comfortable as possible, but to see how some people regarded their pets on the same level as children drove him crazy. He didn't want to turn into that.

Mason looked intently at Evan, listening and waiting.

"And the next issue is that no matter what happens, no matter who it is, we will always have this bitter worm in our hearts when someone tells us they're expecting." He paused and took a breath as his voice suddenly refused to continue. He tried to steady his quivering lip but continued after several unsuccessful attempts. "Mason, we'll never be able to be completely happy for anyone who is able to have what we never will. Don't get me wrong—we'll be happy for them, but in the back of our minds will always be this thought that it'll never be us." His voice cracked again. When he continued, all he could manage was a wavering whisper. "We'll never be able to have a baby shower, or one of those stupid gender reveal things you see all over the Intersphere with cake and balloons and botched unboxings. There's this gap in what we can experience and what everyone else gets to experience. It's..." He stopped himself from saying what sounded a little too petulant, even for his liking.

It's not fair.

"No, you're right. You don't need to say it. I know. It's not fair. It's also not fair that you met the love of your life at, what, eleven? Some people go through life and bounce from relationship to relationship hoping and praying that the next one is *the* one. Some people bounce between addiction and sobriety like a ping-pong ball. They're never able to experience life even when they're sober because their guard is up all the time. They aren't able to trust themselves. There are people who hate the world so much they have to cause as much division and pain in it before they leave it, and they cause pain when they leave it, too." He shrugged. "You know that better than anyone with the way your family was. No one's life is fair, even the person who has everything in the world also has some demon hiding under their bed. A demon that they can't ever shake.

"Let me reiterate this, Evan, so that it sinks in: No one's life is fair." His palm made a soft patting sound as it hit his leg on every word in metered emphasis.

"People will look at you and think you have it all together. In fact," he nodded toward the dozen or so moms and dads near the playground, "some of *them* will look at you and be jealous at the freedom you have. You're not responsible for anyone else's *soul*, Evan," Mason pointed at them dramatically, "but they are. That's a lot of responsibility, man, and I'm not sure anyone is ever ready for that."

Evan nodded and watched the playground antics for a few minutes. Mason didn't push the conversation, which is one of the things Evan appreciated about his friend.

He was right, as much as he hated to admit it. The responsibility of children went beyond just raising them right, which was a battle he knew well because of his own history. There was an adult inside each child that wouldn't show up for a good long while, and did parents have any claim on what that adult turned out to be?

And after life? Was there anything? Some people thought so, but he still wrestled with it.

Even that single question was a stressful exercise in eternal theory. Would he teach his kids there wasn't an afterlife, and when it turned out that he was wrong, the kids' souls were in jeopardy? Or would he teach them about a make-believe paradise that didn't exist just to make them feel better and less afraid of dying? He didn't know and wouldn't ever need to worry about it, in his estimation. His own parents had failed in both regards. He was already ahead of the game.

He started picking a wayward thread on the hem of his shirt and spoke again, changing the subject. "She's talking about pulling out her Chip." He didn't have to clarify who "she" was.

Mason whistled. "Whoa."

"Yeah. She said she wishes she could cut it out, so she doesn't ever have to worry about remembering this. I've told her she can request Adjustment so these memories are hazy, you know they don't ever erase them fully, but she shook her head and told me that she wants them gone. You know how she can be stubborn about stuff." He meant it as a backhanded compliment, but to his own ears, it sounded false and accusatory. *Bitter*, he thought.

Mason nodded, listening, but again, he didn't interject.

"I just, I don't know. I can't imagine that in the future this won't be an important part of our lives. Sure, it sucks, I mean it really sucks right now, but I feel like we'll overcome this at some point and look back and—hopefully—be able to say that this changed us for the better. Made us better *together*."

He sat back on the bench, brushing shoulders with Mason, and let the silence settle over them. The sun was warm, but the shadows were changing, and he knew he'd need to go soon. He wasn't sure why. There was no excitement at the thought of returning to his nearly empty home.

The slight breeze that played through the leaves was cooling but comfortable. He could hear the crunch of leaves and dirt under their shoes as they moved them in the silence.

Evan turned to Mason, blinking against a patch of sun that shone into his eyes through the wavering leaves above. "Where do we go from here?"

Mason took a deep breath, his chest rising and falling as he exhaled. "I don't know. I wish I could tell you what you need to do, but I know that there's literally nothing I could say to help this situation. All I *do* know is that things *will* get better. Probably not today, probably not tomorrow, or next week, but eventually, they will. You guys promised to stick it out, richer or poorer, better or worse. This is the 'worse' part of that vow. This is the—if you'll let me be a little abstract— the 'poorer' part, if you can think of it like that. You aren't any poorer, but it might feel like that for a while." He looked out over the playground and smiled. "You'll find ways to the 'richer' part, and while I think part of you will always mourn the fact that you'll never have kids, I also think there are freedoms allowed to kid-less adults."

The objection rose in his throat without any thought at all, based mostly in traditionalism and modern patriarchal expectations.

He was going to speak about how there's not even a comparison between the two when Mason echoed his own thoughts and held up a hand to forestall him. "I know, there's not really a comparison. I know that, okay? But even *you* can't dispute the fact that waking up at 6 or 7 a.m.—or earlier—for the rest of your life as opposed to whenever you want, isn't the part of parenting that they put on the cute little adverts. It's not attractive. Hell, Evan, it's not even enjoyable. That part, at least. And that's just based on what I've heard other people talk about.

"Also, what about the fact that you can take off work for a week and go to Rome because you both want to? You don't have to worry about finding sitters, or—" and he started to laugh a little and Evan found himself smiling a little, too "—or *paying* for a sitter. Now that," he was laughing in-between words, now, "that is *golden*!" He slapped Evan's back with each breath he took, and Evan could feel laughter rising in his own throat. He didn't tamp it down and soon found himself laughing along, even though he didn't really want to. Mason's chuckles were contagious. His didn't land as heartily as his friend's, but he gave a few, nonetheless.

After the laughter gave way to smiles, Evan turned to his friend. "Thanks for meeting me here," he said quietly with a touch of sincere modesty. "I wasn't sure what exactly was going through my mind, but you helped me process it a bit, helped me through the maze of thorns and pits. Still a ways

to go, but it's a start. A good start. So thanks." He slapped his friend's knee and stood up, leaving Mason still sitting, looking up at him with a small smile.

"Now, I think we should go back to my house and make sure that our wives aren't planning to murder us and run away to Italy to spend all our money." *Well, not your wife, but probably mine very well might fall into that category right now.*

They both smiled—Evan's a bit forced and not a tad insincere and Mason's genuine and light-hearted. After Mason stood up, Evan hugged him again. Then they walked back through the warm breeze and dry grass to where they had parked.

As they passed the playground, Evan looked over at the few kids still playing and stopped, his friend stopping next to him. When Evan spoke, it wasn't directed at Mason. It was more verbal processing than anything that required an answer or response. "It's not that I'm sad, really. I mean I *am* sad, but it's more the thought that this isn't a problem I can fix. Every other problem I can fix between us: our marriage, our fights, our disagreements, or whatever. I can fix those. This one, though..." He trailed off and looked down at his feet, pushing a small rock through the grass with his shoe. "...this one I can't fix. It's gotta play out, in all the gory detail, and I have to let it. And I think that hurts the most. I'm supposed to be the strong husband, carrying the marriage equally with my wife, and this problem is a ghost cutting us apart. I'm *so tired*." He turned and started walking toward the cars again and Mason patted his back.

"You know, Evan, Marcy and I are here for you both. Whatever you need, even if you don't think you need it, we're going to be there for you both. We love you guys."

Evan returned the sentiment with the first heart-felt smile in a couple of days at least. Then he hugged his friend and got into his car, telling Mason he'd meet him at home.

Mason followed behind in his red SUV while Evan tried to psych himself up for what he hoped wouldn't be a con-frontation. It was strange, realizing that he and his wife were at odds despite nothing really being said between them. He felt that they were on two sides of a great gorge, and he was trying to build a bridge to cross it while she tried to push the gorge farther apart.

It wasn't exactly a fair assessment, and even thinking it made his face heat in a small bit of shame. Despite his best efforts, there were times when he wasn't fair to his wife. She was a good woman, strong and resolute in most areas of her life. This one needed some time to let things slide into place. Casting her in such a light wasn't fair and it wasn't right. The shame he felt was warranted, and he let it stay for a moment before taking a deep breath and apologizing to her—or himself, he couldn't tell—in his mind.

He turned the radio on to try and drown out his ham-mering heart, but the music turned to rattling noise in his ears, and he found himself becoming more and more exasperated with it, so he snapped the knob to "off."

He tried rolling the windows down but found the wind in his face was just as irritating as the music had been. The win-dows made it halfway down before he reversed them.

Finally, he contented himself with the gentle hum of the air conditioning and the steady sound of his thumping heart as the miles clicked by on his odometer. It gave him time to think, and he was glad.

His mind began to wander down an old, disused mental path. It had been a long time since he'd thought about his childhood during the good times before it had all turned to hell. The empty fields and dilapidated farmhouses zipped by in a blur of unseen white shutters and red barns. He thought back to a time when he and his brothers hadn't hated each other, when they'd enjoyed the company of one another.

Realizing these thoughts were doing nothing for his current mood, despite the nostalgia creeping up the nape of his neck, he snipped the thread of memory as if with a pair of scissors. He came back to himself driving until he slowed and turned his blinker on, a sense of expectant dread settling over him.

As he turned into the long dirt drive to his house and he heard the familiar sound of tires on dirt, the mostly pleasant crunching brought a new level of anxiety to the surface. He wished to be anywhere but here. He thought it would be too suspicious to stop midway up the drive, so the only option was to continue on, and he did.

He felt hypersensitive to sounds, and each one became more pronounced as he slowed to a stop. The sound of his door as it creaked open was like the scream of banshee who had reached through the veil of life to lend him even more dread.

But his feet hit the ground, and it all faded.

He took a deep breath and squinted against the afternoon sun. It was warm, bordering on hot, and he'd worn jeans that morning to the park. The breeze that had pleasantly cooled the warm air was absent here. Without the shade of any trees nearby, the air was sticky, and the breath he'd taken made him cough.

Sweat immediately popped out on his forehead, and as he stepped toward the front door of his childhood home, he noticed his shirt sticking to his back. He understood he must have been sweating an awful lot on the drive here and resigned himself to the fact that he was going to be soaked by the time he faced his wife. He hung his head, briefly gathering what little strength he could and trying to still his racing heart, then he began making his way toward the front door.

Mason's crunching tires stopped with the slight squeal of breaks echoing across the yard. Evan glanced back as his friend shut the door of his car with a heavy *thunk*. It sounded like a muffled gunshot in the wide expanse around them.

Evan turned to face his home, *their* home. The large two-story house with its white siding and dark wood shutters had been here for a long time. The grass of the front yard stretched to the road that passed almost fifty yards away. It was brown this time of year, though some greenish sprigs had tried their best to shoot through last year's growth. It was usually cold, after all, and most of the grass hadn't been tricked into thinking it was springtime, not yet.

Today, however, he felt that the yard should have been glowing with verdant green grass and blooming with wild-flowers. He was unable to reconcile the weather and the physical evidence his eyes registered, but it was forgotten the moment his eyes returned to the door.

The flowers beneath the windows and those flanking the walkway to the door were dancing lazily in the mid-morning sun and seemed to mock him with their subdued cheeriness. They weren't bright by any means, not like the flowers that would seem to appear overnight when the season actually turned into spring.

Go on in, they seemed to whisper, sashaying back and forth. *This will all be over soon, and you'll be miserable. It'll be great!*

In a sudden surge of petulant immaturity that he would later remember with embarrassment, he stuck his tongue out at the light-colored petals before taking a step. Then, he took another toward the red door, painted with playful grandeur only a few months past. It seemed a lifetime ago.

Mason's footsteps brought him back as they changed from the crunch of dirt to the heavy padding of the concrete walkway. Evan silently thanked his friend for giving him some space. Still, he could almost feel the muscles in the brawny man's arms creaking with anticipation, ready as always should he turn and try to run, or something similarly unreasonable.

He pictured himself turning to run but only making it the two steps into Mason's broad chest before he was picked up and turned around, cartoon-like. It made him smile a little, and the cloud that surrounded him retreated a small distance.

He stopped feet from the front door and reached for the doorknob, but dropped his hand instead, and leaned forward until his head rested on the whimsical wooden letter "R" that hung on the door suspended from a wire. The heat from the warm day seemed to leak into him where his forehead rested, spreading comfortably down his cheeks and into his shoulders and arms. He felt himself absorbing it like a sponge, gathering it and finding strength in it. His heart began to slow, and his hands stopped their shaking almost immediately.

On the other side of the door was something he feared more than anything in the world, the misplaced anguish of someone he swore to protect from such things. Something that he could not defend against or defeat waited behind the door. It hung in the air around him, much like the letter his head now rested upon and reaching out to him through the door. It was a menacing low rhythm he felt, a constant presence. Occasionally, it reared its head and burned the day around him.

Feeling the warmth reach his fingertips, he gathered himself, much like he would before diving beneath the surface of a frigid lake. Today, he decided, today, he would fight it. He'd prepared himself for a battle, of sorts. A defensive battle, sure, but a battle nonetheless where he would need to stand firm in his conviction that life wasn't over, and his wife was still worth the world to him, and that he needed to let her know that. She was still worth the effort, even if it sucked for a while, even if— God forbid—it sucked for the rest of their life together.

Mason gently touched his shoulder. Evan felt himself nod in unspoken assent to the prompt. It was time to go in.

He reached for the knob, turned it, and felt the lazy rush of cool air from inside sweep past him, escaping into the wild of the world.

A sound reached him, riding the sweet cool air. He froze. *Oh, God, she's crying, and I've just interrupted. She's probably pouring out her heart to Marcy, and now Mason is going to see her cry, and it's going to be all my fault. Well, it was a good run.*

But then he listened and recognized that it wasn't the sound of sobbing he'd thought at first; it was the sound of laughter. *That can't be right, can it?* He hadn't heard that sound in a week or more. But it wasn't the bitter laughter that he'd heard intermittently these past several days in response to any number of suggestions, but genuine laughter. *Was that a—yes— that was a giggle.*

Evan turned back to Mason, a flush of astounded disbelief rising in his cheeks, his expression soundlessly asking Mason if he'd heard the same thing. Mason shrugged, just as mystified, and gestured for him to continue into the house with a jerk of his head.

Stepping gingerly in, as if a sign had been posted outside saying "DANGER: LAND MINES AHEAD. PREPARE TO DIE," he entered his home. He could hear Marcy talking in her musical voice. And then another voice joined in. A voice that he would recognize anywhere on Earth until the very end of his days. And his heart began to soar. The tone she spoke in wasn't angry or bitter or regretful or mournful. It was gentle. Could she be back?

He turned from the front hallway and walked slowly through the living room, taking extreme care to avoid catching his toe on something, alerting the two women in the kitchen to his and Mason's presence by hurting himself and yelling curses undiplomatically.

Their home was laid out in a way that allowed a person to enter the home through the front door and take either a right or a left around the stairwell in the middle. The left would lead through the living room where their couches and television sat, where they'd made love any number of times in the early twilight of the evening or in the sweet afternoon sunlight. This room led to the kitchen table, as they called it. If a person took the right hallway, they would have the option of entering the guest bedroom on the right and or the downstairs bathroom a bit farther on. Beneath the stairs was a small coat closet that housed their vacuum and a few odds and ends that didn't fit anywhere else. At the end of the hallway was an open door-frame that exited into the actual kitchen. Evan had grown up calling that entire back half of the house "the kitchen" because it's what his parents called it. Most people when looking at this exact layout, and eventually when this house would go on the market in several years, would separate the two areas in description as "kitchen" which is where the food was prepared and "dining room" which is where the living room connected to the back area of the house. The "dining room" is where the kitchen table now sat, where two women now sat speaking animatedly to one another.

When he could finally get a clear view of the women at the table, his eyes immediately searched his wife's face. She was facing him, and he hoped desperately to get a better grasp on the situation that he had walked into. She was smiling and the hand that picked up a fluted glass full of what he could only guess was a mimosa wasn't shaking or trembling. It was sure and steady. Marcy's back was to him, and she partially obscured his wife's features, but not all. Marcy was bent over the table, and it sounded as if she were telling some deep secret, now, but the tone was that of jaunty mirth, and he could tell that she was smiling while she spoke. *A good sign,* he desperately hoped.

Her eyes suddenly caught movement and locked onto his over Marcy's shoulder. Her other hand, the one not holding the golden drink, reached across the short distance to squeeze Marcy's. Marcy turned, following the direction of her stare. When she saw Evan, and he was certain Mason behind him, her eyes lit up, and she stood, clapping abruptly.

"Oh, you're here!" she walked toward the stunned men and opened her arms to them both, gathering Mason as she reached Evan and patting them both on the back, though she reserved a kiss for Mason after letting go of Evan. He stood to the side as she beamed up at her husband.

Evan didn't want to keep staring, but he couldn't take his eyes from the woman in the kitchen. She lifted her hand in a brief wave and mouthed "hi" to him, a shy smile tugging at the corner of her mouth. Her special smile. He walked to her and could feel Marcy and Mason's eyes on them both, but only distantly; his attention was hyper-focused on his wife.

"Hey there," he said, almost sheepishly. He wasn't sure what the proper greeting was in this situation and settled on something that he could say to both stranger and lover.

He sat in the chair across from her, and he could see a sparkle in the corners of her eyes. "Don't cry, please," he said. He'd seen enough of that and was afraid what it could mean.

She shook her head and dabbed her forefinger beneath her lids while looking up. She took a deep breath and met his gaze. "Evan, I'm sorry." Her face began to redden, and he feared it could be blossoming anger or frustration she was apologizing for.

He was momentarily taken aback. He wasn't sure what to expect, but an apology from her was something he didn't entertain in even the most unlikely of circumstances.

"I'm sorry that I started to shut you out and that I didn't even give *you* time to grieve." The tears began to spill from her eyes, and she didn't stop them, this time. Her voice became thick with emotion, and he was momentarily stunned by her candor. "I was, in no uncertain terms, a bitch. I am so sorry. You have been nothing but sweet and gentle these last few days, and I couldn't get past the fact that *my* dreams were destroyed, forgetting that they were actually *our* dreams, and that wasn't fair to you at all. Marcy," she gestured with the glass still in her other hand, "helped me see that there was something missing from my grief." She met his eyes with such intensity that Evan swallowed hard beneath the gaze. "It was you, Evan. You were missing and that's what made it so hard. I didn't have my partner. I didn't have my better half to help pull me out of the shadows and back into the light." She rested her hand on his and as she spoke, squeezed it gently. "I need you, now more than ever, and I want you to know that. You are so important to me, and I really need you to know that I know it will get better. Thank you for being my rock, Evan."

He could tell by the lump in his throat that if he started talking, he wouldn't get far. He glanced down at his hands to try and stave off the tears gathering in his own eyes, and then his eyes met hers again. "I know it's hard, but I am always here. I'm sorry that I'm not better at dealing with this. I know how to deal with the stuff like your dad and a lot of the things we've spoken about, but this, it was—" He took a shuddering breath. "It was really hard." The tears started to come, then, and try as he might, they wouldn't stop. The lump in his throat hardened, threatening to choke him, and he finally released it, allowing it to jump up and out as a great racking sob.

She got up quickly and walked around the table in a few short steps, sitting lightly on his lap and pulling his head to her breast. She began to cry, too, rocking back and forth and resting her tear-stained cheeks on the top of his head, kissing it gently.

Evan barely noticed Mason and Marcy slip out the front door gazing at each other with tears in their own eyes and hands clasped tightly around one another's shoulders. Mason gave his wife a victorious smile and a wink and shut the door behind them.

CHAPTER 6

He could feel the grin on his face widen with the memory the peals of laughter from children he'd never have. But it began to fade slowly as he felt the single cool tear sliding gingerly down his cheek. He blinked and turned from the picture, briefly heartened by the spark of joy he'd felt accompany the memory, letting the sadness gather around him like a cloud hovering above his head. No, that wasn't quite right. It was more like it settled over him. Like an old moth-eaten blanket, something familiar and comforting, but altogether, unwelcome.

Glasses was standing by a door, his hand palm-up inviting him in. Before stepping through, Evan saw blue arrows spaced periodically along the walls, pointing farther down the corridor. Inside the arrows, centered and standing out in crisp white lettering were the words *Bench Pods*.

The arrows were obscured by the doorframe as he stepped into the room, and he didn't give them a second thought.

The room was clean and bare. Two uncomfortable looking white chairs pushed against the walls, which were a stark singular white except for where the Innervate Industries' logo was painted in bright blue—an eye with two capital letter I's cordoning off the iris.

Evan sighed and sat down as Glasses closed the door behind them both and sat in the chair across from Evan. He moved methodically, almost robotic, as he took a clipboard from under his arm and looked at Evan with expectation. He cleared his throat and flipped his tie, smoothing it flat on his chest.

"Mr. Reader, how are you today? I hope the wait wasn't too long." A ballpoint pen clicked in the quiet. It had suddenly appeared in his clenched hand as if by magic.

Evan sat back, trying to do something to make himself more comfortable but settling as best he could in the cushion-less seat. "Well, it was, um, a little long. Honestly, I'm kind of just ready to get this done. Though, I do have a few questions."

"I'm sure you're ready. Absolutely. That's good to hear." His exuberant tone was over-the-top and was immediately grating to Evan's already frayed nerves. Even though they'd been in each other's company for only a couple of minutes, he had to take a deep breath to avoid rolling his eyes. "Let's get started then, and if you still have questions when we're done, we'll get to them. I'm sure June told you about the interview?"

His disappointment had to be held back. That she had a real name other than the one he'd given her was a shame. He felt that his own "Blinker" seemed to fit so much better. That and she didn't look like a "June" to him.

"Uh, she told me that I would have one, but not much more than that. Well, that and I'd get my questions answered."

Glasses nodded. "Sure, of course they will. Of course they will. My name is Jensen," Evan didn't like Jensen, "and I'm going to ask you a few questions about your past, and then afterward, we'll be sure to get to any remaining questions you have. Sound good?"

Evan nodded despite his mental response being *That doesn't sound good at all.*

"Okay, great. First off, I need you to sign these forms that protect you and protect Innervate Industries in the event that you want to sue for emotional damages or anything along those lines." He affected a nonchalant pose with a matching facial expression that he was sure meant "this isn't a big deal" and continued, "If you'd like to read everything this covers, it's detailed in the fine print at the bottom, and I'd be happy to sit here while you do that, but it could take some time and I know, as you said a moment ago, that you're anxious to get this done."

Glasses then handed Evan the forms. What he'd originally thought was a clipboard turned out to be an electronic tablet. The pen that was clipped on a small plastic holder at the top was the same pen Glasses had clicked a few minutes before. Evan made a good show of reading it carefully, but he didn't care any more about the fine print than he did about anyone's real name. He scribbled on the line indicated, signing it without another thought, then handed the device back.

Glasses—Jensen—checked his signature and nodded.

"Okay, great. Next on the docket, can you please confirm your last genetic profile update or chip verification checkpoint?"

Evan stared at Glasses dumbly as the wheels in his head began to turn. "My last update and—right." Evan ran through the last thing she could remember, his thoughts seeming to float in cold syrup as he worked to drudge them up.

When was his profile last updated? And verification checkpoint? He couldn't remember anything about those. They weren't required to be any more frequent than once a year, and he wasn't the type of person to overachieve and attend

one of those stupid things more than the minimum requirement. Even then, it was only a small fine if one was missed.

"Honestly, I can't remember. It had to have been fairly
recent, but I haven't really thought about it."

Glasses tapped on his tablet and did that stupid thing
with his head that people do when their glasses are in the way:
tilted his head down, then up and then back down again. *Just
pick one,* Evan thought brusquely.

"Hm," he continued staring at the tablet with a look of
concentration creasing his features. "Well, we can look at that
later. It's not terribly important right n-n-now."

He looked up at Evan with a smile and a nod. Evan stared
back blankly. He didn't know if it was rude to bring up the
fact that he'd stuttered or if he should ignore it, but he hadn't
noticed a single stutter up to that point, had he?

He settled the matter by nodding back at him, choosing to
ignore it as it was probably a sensitive subject for him.

Evan felt a memory tug at his attention lightly, and while
Jensen began speaking about something—not something
important, probably—he focused instead on what it was.

Evan had gone to school with a boy who stuttered. It was
always difficult to have a conversation with him because it took
twice as long for him to finish a single thought, sometimes
getting stuck on a single word, wrestling it in his mouth until
he could wrench it free and say it clearly while those listening
waited patiently. Most of the time, at least.

He remembered one time when the kid—Danny McBride—
was trying to tell a group of them about something he'd seen
on the vids that previous night. Evan and his friend Joe waiting,
while another friend stood listening nearby. Alex was that kid's
name. They stood there waiting while Danny worked to spit it
out, trying their best to be patient.

"The p-p-police were h-h-hitting this k-kid, that was pr-pr-pr-probably only twelve or-or-or thirteen bec-c-cause he flipped them the b-b-b-b-b-b-ird." The last word had been excruciating to listen to, and Evan had nearly finished his sentence for him by blurting it out, all of them knowing what he was trying to say.

Alex piped in and said he'd watched the same thing, so did Joe.

Danny nodded, grinning and continued, "D-d-id you g-g-uys see the p-p-p-art where s-s-ome older k-k-kids jumped the c-c-c-c-cops and ran a-aw-awa-away with the f-first kid? It was aw-aw-aw-" Danny's face began to redden as he struggled with this last word. He took a deep breath and ran his hand through his shaggy hair, looking sheepishly at each of them, an apology in his eyes.

Joe put his hand on his shoulder and smiled at him. "Don't worry about it, Dan. You want to finish?"

It was in this moment that Evan saw a glimpse, perhaps the first in his life, of one person acknowledging the difficulty of someone else without a hint of shame, discouragement, or inconvenience. They all knew that it was *easier* if Danny let them continue talking. Afterall, they all knew he was going to say "awesome," or at least eventually. But what was important, Evan now realized thanks to Joe, was that Danny knew they knew, and he needed to know that they were good enough friends that his success in being able to explain a story in its entirety was important to them all. His disability, if it could ever be called such, didn't need to be emphasized by his audience *understanding* the words in his story. It was that he needed to be *heard*. It wasn't terribly often when Danny couldn't get anything out, but there were times when he became more self-conscious of his stuttering, and it only made it more difficult to continue talking. This was one of those times where a random word seemed to knot his tongue and refuse to release it.

Danny began to shake his head and then looked at Evan and Alex separately, but Evan broke in, "Aw come on, Danny, I want to hear the end!"

Alex said, "Yeah man, the ending is the best part, obviously."

Seeing something in them that boosted his confidence, he nodded slowly and took a deep breath. "I-I-I was j-j-just gonna s-s-s-say that it w-w-was," he licked his lips and started the word slowly, "a-a-" He squinted his eyes closed, concentrating. "It was a-a-aw-awesome." He finished quietly and looked at his peers. All three were facing him, wide grins splitting their faces.

Joe clapped him on the shoulder and said, "It was awesome."

They kept talking about it, moving the conversation into other things they saw, giving Danny his chance to speak despite the extended turn he needed to take.

While they talked and listened, Evan remembered how he had first met Danny. Evan had been walking around the mall and watched as a group of older kids, probably high schoolers, took a kid's blue backpack and emptied it on the tile floor, a classic bully move with little imagination. Onlookers walked around the group of teasing boys and the only intervention they gave was a disapproving glare at the older boys.

When the bullies walked away pointing and laughing, Danny bent to clean up the mess, Evan walked over to him and bent down to help, smiling apologetically.

"Sorry," was all he felt he could mutter. Anything else like, "Sorry about those guys" or "Those guys are jerks" felt too much like it came straight out of a movie, and as a first impression, he didn't want this kid to think he was trying too hard.

The kid looked at him as if he were about to speak and then his mouth clamped shut. He nodded and looked back down, gathering the folders and papers, stuffing them into his backpack haphazardly and without any semblance of order.

Evan wanted to make some kind of conversation and tried a different tactic.

"I think I've seen you around school. My name is Evan Reader." He stretched out his hand after shifting a folder to the other hand and waited.

The kid looked at him, looking like he was trying to make a decision. Then, he nodded and reached out, taking Evan's hand and pumping it once.

"D-D-Danny M-m-m-m-m," he heaved a great sigh and licked his lips, "m-m-McBride!" His shoulders sagged in relief as his last name came out in a whispered shout.

"Hi Danny. Nice to meet you." Evan looked around. "I was just fixing to leave; my older brother is going to pick me up. I'm sure he could give you a ride home if you want."

Danny swallowed hard and shook his head, still looking down. "N-no thanks, m-m-m-man. My m-m-m-mom is coming to g-g-g-get m-m-m-m-" He sighed again in frustration, and Evan nodded, hoping he wasn't making a mistake in letting Danny know he didn't *have* to finish on his account.

"Well, no problem. Maybe we'll see each other at school tomorrow?"

"S-s-s-sure."

They had been friends for several years. Never very close— certainly not as close as he and Joe had been—but friends that were close enough to see movies together. The occasional sleepover occurred until it reached the level of taboo in the higher grade when boys dreaded any kind of assumption to be made about them because of how they spent their free time, especially having another boy spend the night. As an adult, Evan wished that wouldn't happen but knew it was an inevitable part of growing up.

Evan, sitting in the uncomfortable chair across from Jensen, smiled at the brief recollection. He had been a good kid and had good friends. He idly wondered where they were—Danny, Joe, and Alex—before Jensen interrupted his thoughts with a bark of laughter that echoed in the small room like glass needles in his ears.

"Now, let's get into why you're here." Evan sat up a little straighter, having no idea what caused the laughter and hoping Jensen didn't notice the blank look on his face. "I believe you know that you've been chosen for an event. A trial, of course. And one that has to do with people, a person, in your past.

"Now, it is our understanding that you lost someone," he swiped several times on his tablet, "four years ago in India? Is that correct?" Evan could feel his face flush and his throat tighten. He didn't trust his voice, so he nodded once. "Can you tell me about that? I know it may be difficult, but I assure you, it will help with your session today."

Evan sat up and cleared his throat, swallowing hard, already feeling the knot of emotion gathering above his collar line. "Yes, um, we were in Sri Lanka for a vacation, sort of a getaway from everything. She always wanted to go there." He chuckled, surprising himself at the abrupt sound after standing on the edge of an emotional precipice.

"She was always into nature and all of that stuff and this one topped her list for the old temples there. So, I decided to take her and she loved it. I mean, she couldn't believe that I had planned it since I'm not much of a planner." Evan laughed lightly again.

Jensen bobbed his head. "There was a tsunami while you were there, correct? Can you tell me about that?"

Evan's smile faltered and he looked at his hands, the knot of emotion tightening in an instant. When he spoke, his voice was wavery, but he trudged on. "We were staying on the southern coast—Matara, actually. We woke up and had this excellent breakfast. It was just a bunch of fruit—bananas, dragon fruit, you know. The sun was shining. The birds were yelling at each other." The muscles at the corners of his mouth tried to smile, but he couldn't carry it and let it die.

"Anyway, I wanted to go to a city that was a few miles north of where we were—Deiyandara. She wanted to stay at the hotel and plan the rest of the day since I'd only be gone a couple of hours at most."

He could feel his voice strengthening, growing less uneven and more substantial the more the spoke.

"I was in Deiyandara, browsing for something that she would like—something local like a hat or something. The market there was overwhelming, to say the least. It was the sounds and the crowds, all of it amplified by the narrow streets and alleys that were packed beyond capacity. I mean, people were yelling in half a dozen different languages, and there wasn't room to even turn around without bumping into the person next to you. The road was either packed dirt or flat stones. Half the time I was tripping over some of them so often that I eventually resorted to looking down instead of ahead. I was running into people every other step, but they didn't care. It was normal for that to happen, I guess." He gave a half-hearted chuckle and rubbed his cheek, the coarse scruff of his beard making the sound of sandpaper. "In fact, that's why they tell you to keep your wallet in your front pocket—which I did, of course.

"Anyway, I remember I was looking at this huge scarf thing, maroon and green, all the colors swirling around each other and almost—yeah—almost flowing into this brilliant flower in the middle, I think it's called something like a Mandela. No, that's close but not right. That's the famous guy from the 2000's, Nelson. It was a Mandala, maybe?

"I remember looking at that particular design the longest because it was mesmerizing. I had to have been there, starting at it for three or four minutes when all of a sudden, I felt the ground tremble a little. Not anything terrifying, but a rumble that caught my attention and the attention of everyone else around me. Enough to make the wall of scarves shake all at the same time with the same rhythmic dancing, as if a breeze was blowing them from top to bottom. It made me wonder what was going on, and everyone else just ... stopped. I kept staring at the scarf for a few more seconds until the stillness caught my attention, and I looked around. The whole place was silent. Silent as a graveyard. And perfectly still. Honestly, for a second, I had this weird experience that I was staring at a picture of the street instead of the actual street I was standing on." Evan stared at the floor between his feet, and for a few seconds, the memory was so vivid—sun, breeze, smells—that he felt as if he'd returned there.

"Not even the street dogs that constantly bark and growl at each other fighting for scraps made any noise. After a few more seconds of that, maybe twenty, noise crept back in, almost like it knew it shouldn't be there. Like it was intruding into the perfect silence. Then things were normal again, like nothing had happened." He paused for a second, remembering it all. "Well, almost."

Evan looked at Glasses, then back at his own hands. Jensen had been silent the entire time he was telling his story, still as a statue, not even making notes on his table, which should have struck him as odd, but he couldn't find the part of him that cared.

In the brief pause, Jensen picked up his pen and began making notes on the tablet.

He's a good listener, at least, Evan thought shrewdly and then continued his tale.

"I got this feeling, as everyone began moving again that something was wrong, or that for some reason, I wouldn't be able get back to her. I'll never know if it was only a feeling or if it was the universe or providence or some instinct that decided to manifest at that very moment, but I have no doubts that *something* told me to get moving.

"I don't remember what I was holding, but I let go and started running back toward the bus stop. I waited for what felt like forever, but I'm certain it was only a few seconds. Time felt fluid, like it was simultaneously slipping by slowly and rushing past faster than I could register.

"When the bus didn't show up, I started running in the direction of the hotel, on the same road that brought me there. I ran pretty well for myself. Running marathons and half marathons back in the states when I was in high-school and college kept my body in close-to-peak physical condition, so I was used to running, and it was only about 18 miles, a few of which I managed to hitch a ride in the back of an old truck."

Evan felt silly retelling his glory days to Jensen and wasn't sure what prompted it other than that it felt right; it felt relevant.

Evan paused briefly, listening to those distant sounds and seeing the buildings blur past as he ran as fast as his body could take him. The smells that came to mind felt like creeping vines that grew suddenly in his mind, releasing their noxious, cloying fragrance that was reminiscent of the land between Deiyandara and their hotel in Matara.

He felt his stomach turning. It was the mix of his senses falling back into that pit of memory, but most of all it was the smell. Cities that big never had great drainage, and they constantly reeked of human waste, sweat, and rot. Combined with the deep scent of the wet jungle, which on its own was pungent enough fill both nostrils like scented plugs, it was no surprise that it made his stomach turn.

He reached for the cup of water next to him and took a shaky sip, hoping to clear his mind of the nauseating memory that swirled unchecked in his mind. It helped enough that he was able to carry on.

"There was an air of expectation in the people. There weren't many buses or cars driving toward the coast, but I didn't understand why. Yet. There was something that the locals knew intrinsically that was hidden from me. I'd find out soon enough, though.

"I kept running after getting off the truck, but the closer I got, the denser the oncoming surge of people; there were very few going *toward* the coast alongside me.

"They were crying, and some were telling us something, but I couldn't understand what they were saying. Once I made it to the hotel, I understood what they were trying to communicate with their rudimentary signs that anyone with half a brain and a quarter of focus could have understood. I didn't, though. I wasn't even there. The only in thing in my head was 'get back there.' I repeated it over and over in my mind. Actually, by the sidelong glances people gave as I passed them, I'm certain it wasn't confined to my mental voice, I had to have said it out loud, too.

"What really cemented it into my mind, though, was when I crested this little hill about a mile from the coast, only a short jog to our hotel. In fact, I could see it a few blocks away. What I saw turned everything I knew to be true upside down." Evan's voice cracked, and he could feel a stinging wetness under his eyes and a tightness in his throat. He coughed and tried to clear it.

"I always have a hard time thinking about this part." He paused. "It's nearly impossible to describe to someone who hasn't seen it before. It's something that defies logic and reason, and while it's a natural occurrence, it defies everyday *nature*.

"There was ocean where there shouldn't be. There was trash, and there were cars, and trees and buildings and people." Tears began to slip down his cheeks. "The water was dark and muddy and strange and ... wrong. I started running and people kept grabbing my clothes, and this young guy tried to stop me and wouldn't let go until I yelled into his face and pushed him down. He fell, but that's all the attention I had for him.

"I started running toward the hotel where we were staying, and I couldn't stop. I was screaming her name, and I was frantic. I remember realizing that the water was getting closer, and it spurred me on, you know, thinking that I was getting much closer to the coast. But I wasn't. The coast was getting closer to me."

CHAPTER 7

Evan coughed and asked for another drink. He didn't speak again until he had emptied the plastic white cup of the clear and cool water. Jensen waited patiently while he did this, making a note here and there.

"Thanks. That's better."

Evan stared into the empty cup. It seemed to Evan that the cup was holding his gaze. All the memories he'd tried to forget or drown in alcohol were surfacing, swirling and rising like ghost ships churned up with hurricane winds. The white of the cup had begun to darken and there was no longer a bottom to it. The empty cup was turning into an endless pit, a well filled not with water but darkness, despair.

The voice was coming from far away, but the deepness before him retreated a bit.

Evan blinked again and the cup in his hand was just a cup, white and empty save for a small pearl of clear liquid gathered at the bottom.

He heard Jensen repeat himself, adding "Evan?"

"I'm sorry. What?"

"You were getting to the muddy water," Jensen prompted, looking at his tablet. Evan caught the brief glance he gave the cup in his hand, but it was so quick he wasn't sure if he'd imagined it.

"Oh, right." Evan coughed and began again. "I could smell the water before I got to it, and it was terrible, like an overflowing toilet in a sea storm: salt and shit, mixed with the smell of ruddy soil.

"I was shouting and screaming for my wife, and she wouldn't answer, and I could feel myself getting frantic, frustrated that my voice was getting lost in the din of everything else. I just kept thinking, 'answer me, answer me' but she wouldn't.

"The water began lapping at my feet, and I plunged on. I found myself waist deep in water and then it sort of stilled. I guess by the time I got there it was kind of done rushing inland; it wasn't moving around me in any direction and I was looking around and there were—" Evan stopped as his voice refused to continue and interlocked his fingers beneath his trembling lip, "—there were people floating in the water, facedown, and I couldn't see my wife. I couldn't see her. I kept walking, though. I kept looking and walking and wading and swimming at one point, slowly making my way toward our building. I had to move so much stuff out of the way. There was so much crap everywhere; coolers, cars, boards, tree limbs, anything you can think of had washed out there. I tried to go around the bodies as much as I could. There weren't a lot that I could see, but there were some.

"There was this film on the top of the water that shone iridescent in the sunlight—oil or gas, I'm sure. But it mixed with the dirty yellow bubbles that floated on the surface that obscured a lot of the floating debris. It was like Hell's chocolate milk. There were plants and reeds floating everywhere, and it coated the surface of the stinking water. It was impossible to see anything below in a lot of places.

"As I walked, I began to feel the water moving back toward the coast, kind of this slight pulling, as if I was walking down a very slight incline. It was bizarre, but I thought it was good since it helped me move faster toward our building. I sloshed through, pushing aside flotsam and climbing over cars or trees or parts of buildings." Evan stopped abruptly. "There was a dark-haired woman that I remember seeing. She was... she was trapped in a car. For the briefest, *briefest* flicker of a second, I felt my wife's name on my lips in an expulsive scream of horror, but I never said it. My mind registered that it wasn't her, and I moved on, relief and panic pushing me forward.

"There was a strange thing that I only now remember. Most of the cars had their noses down and their backends floated. The engines, I think. The front of the cars were heavier and so they sank, but at one point I remember looking over an expanse of bobbing vehicles in a turbulent wash, and it reminded me of ducks diving down. Only briefly, but it was something that gave me chills. These massive, multi-ton cars and trucks were bobbing on the surface of a raging oceanic river. It was unsettling, and I remember getting goosebumps at the sight. All kinds of horrible thoughts came with it."

He took a shuddering breath, wiping his mouth with his palm and quickly licking his lips. "I turned down a street and finally saw our building. Most of the windows on the first floor were shattered, and there was this thin line. You know, when something gets wet and the water depth decreases, it leaves this wet residue. The yellow wall of our building had a brown line about 7 feet above the street. We were on the first floor, Room 112." He paused and cocked his head. "No, that's not it. It was—" He stopped. *What room was it?* He was close, he knew. And then he remembered, feeling stupid. "It wasn't 112. It was 113. One fucking thirteen."

He stopped for a few seconds and put his hand to his head, trying not to go back to that place, back to the fear and panic, the desperation and paralyzing terror. He began talking again to avoid the all-encompassing dread approaching him like a beast stalking him in the dark. "I started to run—well, as much as I could—toward the building. By now, I had to contend with mostly water. You know, we were by the coast, so a lot of debris was behind me. I noticed, however, that there was more coming toward me from behind. And that still freaks me out." His eyes lost focus again, only for a moment, and then, he continued.

"As I got closer to the hotel, my legs started burning. I knew I'd been running for a long time. I couldn't tell if it was for hours or only seconds, but I knew I was running out of energy. The only thing that kept me going was that need to find her. I was on empty, but I pulled energy from that. I had to find her. I remember—I remember seeing the body of this little boy, maybe six or seven, stuck in a floating tree that I jumped over. The kid's arm was broken, had to be, at the angle it was bent. That didn't matter anymore, though, because there was a metal pole through the kid's chest."

Evan met his interviewer's eyes. "I don't think I can ever get that out of my head." He leaned forward and looked down at his hands, wringing them.

"I kept going, though, running toward our building. But my throat hurt so bad. I had been yelling constantly for an hour at least. In all reality, I'm not sure if it was from yelling or swallowing that retched water or what. Either way, I was... I was terrified. Afterward, the thoughts of what I should have done bombarded me, but at the time, all I could think of was getting to our room and finding her.

"I jumped over a car that had been wrapped around a tree that was in the courtyard of our hotel and finally made it to the front doors of the hotel—the glass had busted out, so I maneuvered myself into the building. There was no way I would have been able to open the doors, there was still a few feet of water around them.

"When I made it through, I was hit with the smell of moldy carpet. It was... it was terrible. Things and people had washed into the lobby and hallways, stairwells, too. There was no way out. The force of the entire ocean pushing against me made it impossible to escape.

"The first floor was still flooded, plenty of water everywhere. Sand and mud covered so much of everything. I could hear water dripping and running everywhere, echoing through the halls. It was so incredibly loud that even yelling for her I knew she wouldn't be able to hear me, or me hear her if she responded. The thundering rush of falling water made its way into every corner of the place.

"It was eerie, and looking back, it reminded me all too much of somewhere haunted. There were people that had been floating but now were laying haphazardly all over the floor and counters and chairs."

Evan swallowed hard, his eyes staring into the distance. "I'm sure that place is haunted, now."

He blinked hard and covered his eyes with his palms. The encroaching but all-too-familiar panic and blame was close, just beneath the surface, but he had to keep it in check.

After several minutes, Glasses raised a hand gently toward Evan. "Mr. Reader, I understand how difficult it must be for you. I can't imagine losing someone in this manner, but I assure you, talking about all of this will help us get a much firmer grasp on your emotional state prior to the interaction in The Bench. You are a remarkable man, and your situation is exactly why we spend millions of dollars and millions of hours developing the technology you're going to use today.

"When you're ready, please continue." He sat back and waited patiently until Evan coughed to fill the silence and continued.

Evan wasn't the type of person to trust someone simply because they appeared trustworthy. Jensen wasn't an exception to this rule. He was a stranger and was part of an organization that he knew little to nothing about. Sure, he had been understanding and accommodating, but Evan was sure there was some agenda behind the one he'd been told; he just wasn't sure what it could be. He was reluctant to continue. Not only because telling his story to a stranger didn't feel natural, but also because he could feel the overwhelming grief beneath every word he spoke. The razor-sharp sting when he remembered her face or when he thought of the hell he'd gone through to find her. It was hot as glowing wire and it hurt the same.

But his story was almost done. He was ready to continue. He had to. Who knows, maybe there would be something to this thing, and somehow, he'd find closure. He doubted it but left it open as a possibility remembering that little phrase he'd discovered in the waiting room: *What if this is a good thing?*

Gathering his courage, he continued. "I started trudging through, stepping over a body bobbing in the water and into the hallway to our room. Luckily there were no more doors except the one to our room, so it was as clear a shot as I could ask for.

"The hardest part, I think, is that I had to look at the people. I had to make sure it wasn't her. I was so afraid that one of the bodies would look familiar—well, that's not the right word because I remember seeing the guy that helped us with our luggage and a few of the kids that were playing soccer in the courtyard. Seeing them there, splayed out in unnatural positions like they'd been rolled around in a tin can and cast like dice, but—it was bizarre. I can barely describe it." Glasses only nodded.

"I was so afraid that I'd see her, or her familiar outline, face-down in the water, or—God forbid—part of her, but I had to look. The fear and need to know kept me going, so I looked all around in the lobby before going down the hall—there were more bodies there, too. The water hadn't drained out of the building yet, and it was probably at least three feet deep. I remember hitting the water in fits of anger as many times as I did in relief; none of the bodies were hers. However, I also had a feeling, a kind of backward disappointment that none of the bodies were hers." Evan felt so bitter in his heart, there wasn't a sound to utter that would adequately convey it, so he shrugged in helpless frustration. "None of those corpses were the one I was looking for. So, I made my way down to our room—113, like I said.

"I didn't want to open it, but I had to find her. I was still yelling, by the way, not sure why. At this point my voice was little more than a hoarse, gravely rasp. I think I kept yelling because it was the only thing I had control over. I shoved the door open, fighting the resistance of the water by pushing and pulling back and forth. The sodden frame was cracked, and eventually, I got it open enough to stumble into the room. I remember falling to my knees and drenching myself in the water, exhausted and relieved that I finally made it. Some of

the water got into my mouth, and it was more than the salti-
ness that made me immediately throw up. It tasted like death,
too, and I couldn't keep it in.

"After spitting into the water until my mouth felt cleaner, I
immediately noticed the window and one of the sliding glass
doors that led to a balcony. They were such a point of excitement for her after I booked the place. But they were both
busted out. There was some glass on the floor. I could see
some of it here and there and felt it crunch beneath my feet
when I waded through the room. Some of it glittered on the
bed. The covers were dark and stained with whatever mess
had washed over them. They were sodden and ruined. About
2 feet of water was still in the room, but it had begun draining
out the shattered balcony door.

"I saw our suitcase, amazingly, sitting open on the dresser."
Evan put his thumb and forefinger on the corners of his mouth
as he suddenly remembered another detail. The suitcase was
open, some of the folded neatly at the bottom but several
shirts tossed carelessly on top of them. His wife had always
felt strange about putting their clothes in the drawers of wherever they were, regardless of how long they were staying. She
liked to live out of their suitcase, and when he asked her why,
she responded with a tone that said she was glad he was cute,
"It helps remind me that we aren't moving in. And when it's
time to pack up, it's not as disappointing."

It was the cute little shrug at the end of the sentence, her
chin resting on her own shoulder, that made Evan run to her
and scoop her up in his arms. He had kissed her passionately
and laid her gently on the bed, him tugging his shirt off over
his head and her unbuttoning her jeans and sliding them down
her thighs.

He didn't relay the last thoughts to Jensen but continued on. "There wasn't any sign of my wife, though. She wasn't in the room. Like I've said before, that was a relief, but it was also terrifying.

"Our suitcase was open on the dresser, and we were told not to bring valuables with us out into the market and such, so we had left our wedding rings in a plastic bag hidden in an inside zipper pocket of the suitcase at the hotel room. I found them in the same pocket. The bag was wet, had that haze of condensation on the inside of it. I grabbed them and put them in my pocket and made my way around the rest of the room.

"I noticed the junk floating through the street out the busted balcony window at the back of the room. Standing there felt like I was on a riverbank, and everything was flowing by in the street below. I was struck so hard with a thought that I stumbled and sat, the bed made a sickening squelching noise and my pants immediately soaked up all they could despite already being wet.

"At that very minute, though, a thought hit me like a truck: What if her body was sucked back into the ocean?

"Before this vacation, I read some tsunami reports out of curiosity. I knew there had been a terrible one years ago around this same place. You know, most bodies aren't ever recovered because they end up back into the sea, along with all of the trash that gets washed back out after the initial push inland.

"It was terrifying, and I screamed her name, crying almost hysterically, at least as much as I can remember of that time. I was out on the deck, now, standing in some of the water as it flowed by and that's when I saw a flash of blue bobbing in the water. It was her favorite hat. Her brother Dennis had given it to her before he went halfway across the world to one of the Neo-Pagan uprisings when she was little. It was her brother's favorite team, the Chicago Cubs, and it was slipping uncere-moniously past me. I hated and loved it at that instant. It was picking up speed as it bounced along the balcony in the murky water. The Cubs logo both taunting and crying for help. So, I dove for it. I landed hard on my elbow and banged my knee on the railing, but I grabbed it right as it was about to get sucked between the rails and into the black current below."

Evan paused and rubbed his hands together. "I'm not sure why I did it. Maybe she might want it. If I found her."

He sniffed hard and sat quietly, staring at his hands. He didn't want to look up. Didn't want to keep going. The edges of his vision began to swim with a dark blue haze.

He tapped his fingers together, avoiding Jensen's eyes. *That fucking Cubs hat.* Despite his best efforts, the years of training himself to ignore the pull and repress the desire, a memory slammed into him with a force that made him inhale sharply and squeeze his eyes closed. It was as if the doors he had locked these past years had been weakened by the constant barrage of memories, their attempts to break through and be released into his conscious mind. The doors had no choice but to give way. Tears pooled at the corners of his eyes and began to run freely down his cheeks. He glanced at the man across from him, uncertain. Jensen sat watching calmly while Evan wept in the release.

He was picking himself up after diving for the blue Cubs hat, reaching in a last desperate attempt through the iron railing and grabbing it by the sodden bill. Water rushed past his outstretched arm and off the hat like a steady rain, but the sound was lost amidst the screams and increasing roar of raging water that filled his ears.

His elbow was bleeding where he had smacked it on the concrete balcony. His teeth had reacted by nearly biting through his tongue. He felt the click of his molars connecting distantly as his fingers held on to the hat and noticed the wound only after he flicked off the excess water. Blood splattered the wall next to him and he had followed the trajectory to its source. The gaudy crimson made his stomach clench, and as he watched, more dripped steadily into the dirty water from his cocked elbow. It swirled in the murky current like food coloring, then disappeared.

He tore his gaze from the water and blood mixing at his knees and looked out across the wreckage of what had only hours ago been a pristine tourist destination. He could feel the terror threatening to overwhelm him even as he worked to silence it.

The water was receding—slowly at first—back into the ocean and taking anything with it. The streets, still flooded, were filled with rushing water and debris, some of it getting caught on the buildings or heavier objects submerged in the water, but most of it rushing past him as if some old god were sucking it up through a cosmic straw.

As he watched, a small yellow car lurched and skittered along the street. Then, it turned and began sliding toward the sea, as if the driver was out for a nice afternoon adventure. It must have hit something underneath because it came to a sudden shuddering halt. The dirty water frothed violently behind hit. The force of all that water overcame the unseen barrier and the car tumbled over it and only becoming visible again bobbing to the surface several yards farther.

He screamed her name again, adding his noise to the tumult, no longer a verbal rush headlong into unknown territory but a desperate grasp at arms that would never enfold him. The thundering roar of the water was constant. A part of him was certain that he was not actually overcoming the din surrounding him, but he couldn't stop. His voice took on a new tone as he shouted the name. It was a fearful plea for the loss of soft morning kisses and intimate touches. The certainty and drive he'd felt fighting his way here were scattering. Fear took their place and began strangling his heart. Deep despair, loneliness, and loss slithered their way in and began to take root.

He shuddered as he saw in his mind's eye, vaulting over the balcony railing like a track star jumping hurdles into the serpentine waters beneath, desperation pushing him to find her in the waves.

He forced himself to grasp the railing to prevent that. He knew he'd never find her if he leapt into the frothy black water barely feet from where he was now standing. But he couldn't help staring into it. He pictured her perfect skin bruised and battered at the bottom of the torrent, her arm stuck at an impossible angle beneath a car or tree or building, face frozen in the serenity of death, showing no sign of the screams that preceded the terror of drowning in this watery waste. Evan wondered if, as her lungs filled with water, she realized she was dying and lost hope. Or if she had faith that he would save her somehow, in the final fleeting seconds of her life. If she died with hope ringing in her mind or despair dragging her remorselessly into the next life.

He screamed her name again. Or he thought he did, but no name came out,

only an anguished wail. He hit the railing hard with his fist and it replied with a dead metallic *clunk*. His hand stung from his pinky finger to his wrist where he had hit it. The pain was a salve, and it woke him weakly from his prison.

Evan turned on his heel and splashed through his hotel room, ignoring what little life was left within the four sodden walls.

"Sorry," said Evan as he reached for Jensen's proffered tissue. He wiped his nose and blew it, using another that was offered to him.

"Thanks" was all he said and put the tissues in a small white bin near his feet. Evan could tell his eyes were swollen and pictured what he looked like. His face was probably puffy, and his bloodshot eyes were throbbing. He needed something to drink, something that dimmed the mind a little more than water. "Do you have anything to drink other than water?"

Jensen shook his head apologetically. "I'm sorry. Water is all we have for our guests. I'll write that it might be beneficial to add more options, though."

The robotic man made a scribbling motion on his tablet before looking at Evan and gesturing for him to continue. "So, at this point, you realize that your wife is missing." Evan nodded. "What happened next? You don't need to give me a day by day, but for the next while, until you determined she was gone, should be enough information."

Evan swallowed hard.

Until you determined she was gone.

Despite the cold-hearted boldness of that statement, it was true. He had stopped looking for her eventually, and that was the root of his fear, the pinnacle of his dread: the moment when he knew she was, finally and irrevocably, gone.

"I... I started looking around and was able to move a little freer as the water level began to lower. But even at the end of the day, there was still water standing in most of the city and debris blocked every road, every sidewalk, all of it.

"I had a time walking around the city. There were people that needed help and every now and then I did what I could, but there was so much stuff everywhere that eventually it became overwhelming, and I focused on what I needed to do. I had to. I had to pass people up because I was afraid that helping one person would make me miss my chance to save ... her." He couldn't say her name yet. He wanted to. Wanted to so badly. But he couldn't form the sounds that said the word to his lips. To utter her name now, after all this time, was unthinkable. Her name had taken on the same characteristics as a deity. It was a holy word that should never be spoken in vain. Not after she'd become a martyr by that cruel goddess Mother Nature.

"There were other people meandering through the city, too, I wasn't the only one. Everyone needed help. But at times, especially once the sun sank behind the mountains, it was as silent and as abandoned as a century-old graveyard. You know the usual sounds that indicate a city is alive? The sounds of car horns, a low din of people talking, birds, animals? All of that was gone. Silence. Quiet as the grave. There were sounds of people yelling names or cries echoing here and there, but it was a primal, almost an *obscene* silence. Impossibly empty. Even the several people I saw looking around didn't say much. They kept on looking, shining flashlights or lanterns wherever they were looking. When I looked out across the city, I could see these little bubbles and beams of light, flashing like fireflies in the humid heat of the night. But through it all was the sound of running water. Not the relaxing ebb and flow of the ocean waves walking up and down the shore. It was running water rushing through the city, dripping down the sides of buildings, trickling between the overturned cars and joining another branching unnatural stream as all of it sought its home, wanting to go back to the sea.

"I hate that sound, that... that dimly familiar washing machine sound."

He paused for a moment to gather himself and then continued without the fierceness that had begun to slide effortlessly into his voice. Now it took on a resigned tone, like a horse that was finally broken and ready for the saddle.

"There was some distant crying, but even then, it was so lonely there in the darkness of this city of death. Without electricity, it was truly terrifying at times." A word blinked into existence before him. "It was hollow. Deiyandara had become a hollow shell filled with bodies.

"I was yelling her name, still. I guess I hoped that she had gone up to a roof or something." Evan stopped and began tapping the tips of his forefingers together and sat up. "Honestly..." He wiped at his dry cheeks. "Honestly, she was probably at the beach, but every time I thought that, I screamed for it to shut up and go away, you know. I couldn't even entertain that thought. Something that was supposed to be so perfect betrayed her, swallowed her up, and made her part of its meal.

"For the next several days, I searched within the city proper. I helped when I could but couldn't commit to much more than a minute here and there, if that. Like I said, I had to find her, and all of my energy had to go to it.

"Then, I turned my efforts to the outskirts of the city. The first night I did it, though, was the hardest. They had set up mobile hospitals a few miles away from where we stayed, and there were thousands of people crowding them, doing exactly what I was doing. It was no use; no one could help me. And even the ones that said they'd look never got back to me. I waited for an hour for one of the nurses to get back to me, and when she never did, I started walking through the hospital. There was blood everywhere. Normally, I'd be disgusted and more the type to run out, but the one thought of finding my wife drove me on. It's like it didn't even register as blood." He ran his hand down his cheek again in embarrassment. "I don't know. It's hard to explain."

Jensen nodded. "No, Mr. Reader, I actually do understand. Our minds tend to classify what we see based upon what our focus is. It's the same reason that people who work in hospitals can block that part of it out, but when they get home and cut their own finger, they may get faint or dizzy. Or how some parents can become uneasy at the thought of birth, but in that moment, are able to watch awestruck, the entire birth of their own child. Our brains are incredibly powerful and yours took the opportunity to prioritize its goals alongside your emotions. Your priority was finding M—"

"Don't!" Evan had reacted so quickly and in such an explosive manner that Jensen sat back with a jerk. "Sorry," Evan said, lowering his hand and swallowing hard. "Sorry. Don't say it. Don't say her name. Please. I can't—I can't stand for anyone to say it. Not yet."

Jensen nodded apprehensively before continuing. His voice gained strength as he spoke. "No need to apologize. I understand. There's a bit of mysticism in her name. I can understand that. Again, not altogether uncommon for our brains to attribute a higher status to certain names, images, and people based on our situations.

"I was going to say that your priority was finding *her*, so your brain filtered out everything that was irrelevant, and that includes your normally queasy stomach at the sight of blood. Please, continue."

Evan nodded and smiled in thin apology. "I checked all of the hospitals, none of them knew anything or helped. I checked the morgues, too, at three different hospitals. It took multiple visits and many days of continually checking them and lifting the sheets or having someone do it."

Evan hesitated and asked, "You know you mentioned that trick our brain uses to filter out unnecessary stuff?"

Jensen nodded.

"At some point, that stops. The third day, I saw a truck being loaded with bodies. They'd made these mass graves, and I'd seen these trucks before, but not being loaded. It was being loaded with bodies so that they could make room for more even more bodies. I had already looked at the ones they were loading, but it made me wonder if maybe I missed another truck at another hospital, the one she was on."

Evan paused. "I felt so helpless the entire time I was there. As if nothing I did, no effort I put forth, made any difference. I mean, in the end," he shrugged, "it didn't, did it."

The quiet that followed hung in the air for a moment. Neither of them spoke. Evan looked down at his hands and messed with the memory of a wedding ring on his finger, idly twisting what hadn't been there for countless months.

Once again, a memory floated to the surface. It followed his tale, continuing internally where he'd left off with Jensen. As it blossomed, his head began to throb with a great pumping *thump thump thump*. Some great demon had sawed open his skull with a rusty knife and was shoving the memory directly into his consciousness.

CHAPTER 8

Evan stood slump-shouldered in the rain. It was a heavy rain. Not the kind of rain that brought to light playful memories as a child. It didn't bring back the feel of summer showers and muddy boots by the backdoor. It was the kind of rain that soaked into your soul and dripped through your bones, carrying the weight of the heavens and puddling them at your feet. He stood in a pool of hopelessness as the rain pounded the dirt into sticky muck around him. The sound was enormous in his ears, as if his head were in a bucket and someone was hammering on the sides; it made his head ache. But it wasn't the only thing making his head ache, only one of *the* things.

He stared into the entrance of the brown canvas tent several yards ahead. He could make out several people milling around inside, stepping over cloth-covered bundles on the floor and making their way through the aisles of plastic tables.

He needed to step through that open tent flap. That portal into a world even darker and more grim than the rain washing over him and coating him in its slick chill.

He took a stuttering step forward. His boot drug through the mud and water, leaving a short trail that cut through water-filled tire tracks from earlier in the day. They filled again quickly from the downpour. The water swirled in small dark eddies, unseen by the figures nearly hidden through the curtain of unending rain.

He took another step and then another. His body was moving as if something was pulling him inexorably toward the door, and he was powerless to stop it. At the same time, there was a force in his head screaming for him to stop, that he didn't have to take that step, or that one. That all he had to do was stop.

And just like that he was at the tent flap. He reached a dripping hand to the vertical pole that held the entrance open. He was shaking, but even the rain felt warm. The canvas that covered the metal beneath was surprisingly smooth, a small detail that he seized hold of in his mind with the desperation of someone finding and holding to a sapling as they fell down a rocky cliff face. He rubbed his hand up and down the canvas-covered pole, stalling in a desperate attempt to avoid what he knew he must. But in spite of his efforts, his eyes roamed slowly toward that darkened entrance.

One step.

A second step.

A third step, and he was inside. Immediately, the loud hammering of the rain was replaced with the subtle sounds of mourning beneath a constant hum of it drumming on the canvas. His failing grip on that sapling that was the pole lessened. As he dropped his hand from it and completely immersed himself in the atmosphere before him, he felt his heart flutter as if he were plunging down that cliff face.

He looked around, letting his eyes adjust to the darkness within the tent. There were kerosene lanterns hung at odd intervals from the roof of the massive canvas, casting their steady golden glow in small circles that seemed to hold the dimness at bay, but only just.

The ground before him was a large rectangle, the only other light was spilling around him from the open tent flap.

Here and there, small groups—families, he assumed—huddled. Some stood resolutely, some lay across the bundles on the floor and wept, and some lifted eyes and hands toward the heavens. There were songs in Sinhala—a language he didn't speak at all—as well as mumbled prayers and comments from some of the others walking around.

He moved as if in a dream. He turned slowly toward someone in green scrubs sitting behind a makeshift table of crates with a wooden door acting as the tabletop. His eyes noticed the hole where a doorknob once sat was now covered in gray duct tape, the edges frayed like tiny white worms.

He could feel his mouth move, and knew what words he was saying, but couldn't hear anything, his ears were ringing without actually ringing, everything else was a numb mumble. It was nearly silent. For one precious heartbeat, it was blessedly silent.

The person behind the makeshift desk—a woman with dark skin and darker circles beneath exhausted green eyes—made a practiced back and forth motion with her hands while she spoke. She gestured midway up her own arm where most SafetyChips were seated. This wasn't the first time she'd given these instructions and knew it wouldn't be the last. He didn't need to hear her to understand what she was saying to him. *Just make your way back and forth checking as you go.*

I don't think I can, he thought. But he felt himself nod and turn—grudgingly—back toward the expanse of the room, moving with slow, deliberate steps.

One step.

Another.

Stop.

He looked down at the long bundle on the ground. If he squinted, it didn't look like a body wrapped in a sheet at all, only a pile of dirty laundry that someone left here.

Slowly bending down, he reached for the loose flap near what he hoped was the head.

A voice broke into his consciousness, familiar and welcome. *Stop! You don't have to do this! You can turn around and walk out that door and leave. You can LEAVE.*

It didn't stop the motion he'd already begun, and he hesitantly placed his thumb and forefinger on the sheet corner. Bracing himself, he pulled it back far enough to reveal dark hair caked with mud and sticks and leaves. It was enough to confirm this wasn't her, so he dropped the sheet and stood up. Instinctively, he knew that there would be enough horror in the coming days and weeks that he would need to spare himself as much of it as he could.

The rows of bodies continued to the back of the tent, all of them in nearly endless parallel lines from front to back. There were so many. Too many.

Then leave, the voice whispered. He had to admit to himself that it was an attractive option. He took a step over the body he'd checked and bent down to the next, gently grabbing the corner of the stained sheet and pulling back enough to catch a glimpse of the hair. Even with the dirt and mess, he knew he would be able to tell his wife's from anyone's. It wasn't *her* hair, so he replaced it and moved to the next row, stepping gingerly over a body that was far too small to check. He stifled a sob as it rose through his clenched throat. It hurt as he did so, and he could feel his neck flexing, preparing for the cries that would inevitably come, clenched throat or no. Once that stone cracked, there would be no stopping them.

Then, keep that stone in place, the voice warned.

Back in the interview room with Jensen, that stone that had been held in place for years suddenly burst. Sobs clawed their way out of his throat and into the tiny room around him, and he could do nothing but let them go.

Speaking through the racking sobs, he said, "I mean, what difference did I make? I stayed in that fucking country for weeks looking, researching, moving around to the surrounding cities. I used all of our savings, all of everything. I lost my job, I lost—"

He continued to sob until he felt the grief's grip on his voice lessen. He finished with a final, desperate whispered plea, "I lost everything."

Jensen looked at Evan with an empathetic expression. "Evan, I'm so sorry for your loss. I cannot imagine what you're feeling." He paused for several seconds while Evan collected himself, then continued on. "Evan, what happened next? Obviously, you made it home, but what—"

Evan cut him off with a mirthless laugh. "Nothing. Absolutely nothing. I gave up. In a way, I just stopped living."

Jensen was quiet for a moment, looking at him intently as if searching for more. Then, he smiled, and his voice became a little brighter, too sudden for him to have felt any whiff of what Evan himself was feeling at that moment.

"Well Evan, there is a little hope. With Innervate Industries' technology, you can finally find some peace and move on. You can get some affirmation for your efforts."

Evan met the man's smiling gaze, unabashed disbelief etched across his features. His sobs subsided as Glasses continued. "You asked if it made a difference in the end? Of course, it did. You lost everything *for her*, and I'm sure you've told yourself that at some point. Now, you can tell her that yourself. In a few minutes, you'll be able to see your wife for the first time in four years, and you'll be able to ask her anything you'd like."

Evan's heart began to calm its rapid pace and despite his initial opposition, he was actually warming up to the idea of "The Bench."

At first, it had seemed an abomination, a fantasy that could only have been thought up by some mad scientist with too much time on his hands. Now, however, after talking with this guy, Jensen, it seemed like a good thing, something that might help him sleep at night, or at the very least, get some small periods of rest while the sun gathered its energy for another day above the horizon.

"Before we start, however, I need finish getting your session ready. I've been told that your Bench Pod is ready, but there are a few superficial setting questions I need to ask before we move on." Evan nodded and blew his nose a couple more times and wiped his now-drying cheeks. The frustrated disbelief at Jensen's casual attitude regarding his loss was fading, but enough remained for him to dislike the man.

"Okay." Jensen sat up with renewed vigor, appearing energized by the nearness of the session's main purpose. "First on the list is where the session will take place." Jensen looked up at Evan with an expression that spoke volumes about his pride in this particular aspect of the process.

"We can create a realistic setting based on almost anything you can imagine, anywhere from the ocean floor all the way to the farthest planet in deep space or even one you make up. We'd need a little more time to create that from scratch based on your preferences and descriptions, but..." now he spread his hands wide in a what-else-can-I-say gesture, "we can do anything."

Evan shook his head, "No, nothing that crazy. She always loved the sea, but I doubt she'd appreciate being at the bottom of one because of, well..." He gestured around the room and Jensen nodded and winked in understanding.

Evan thought for a moment. He thought hard. The possibilities, even when endless, did little to help him decide. He didn't dare to create a setting as ostentatious as some planet or the moon. Hell, even a palace somewhere would be a missed opportunity because, when she was alive, they constantly made fun of the ridiculous lifestyle in which the privileged lived. While everyday men and women were forced to eke out their meager living under the constant threat of some warring remnant, the rich could happily avoid it all. They never had to worry about a roving band of thugs happening upon their home and stealing what little they had—or worse. It was uncommon in the States, but the rest of the world was little more than kill or be killed.

No, it had to be something that she would like—love, really.

And then it came to him as if it were whispered into his mind. Perhaps it had always been there and just needed the right outlet.

"What about the Cliffs of Moher in Ireland? Maybe Galway Bay. Can you do that?"

Jensen started typing on the tablet then paused, "Are you sure, Mr. Reader? Earlier, you said you hated the sound of water. The Cliffs of Moher are very near the—"

Evan nodded with the wisp of a smile that felt more like a grimace, and he cut Jensen off.

"I'm sure. I've hated the sound of water because it reminded me of when I lost her. If I'm going to see her again. I want water to remind me of that, too."

Jensen *tap-tap-tapped* on his tablet.

"Okay, that's doable. We can make a realistic sea breeze, smells, sounds, the works. How is that?" Evan nodded. "Second, you need to make sure that you don't touch the wall in The Bench Pod. The wall has hundreds of thousands of nano-receivers that help create the realistic view, temperature, wind, all of it. If you touch them, there's a chance that it will disengage the program that runs the ambience, and by extension, the session itself could be impacted negatively in a way that could result in the session being cut short. Do you understand?"

Evan nodded again.

"Great. That's excellent, Mr. Reader."

That tapping came from his tablet again like a miniature horse on miniature cobblestones. Then, he clasped his hands together above his lap and looked excitedly at Evan.

"That's it! Now if you'll wait here for a few minutes. You'll be escorted to your session by a Bench Agent. It shouldn't be any more than a couple of minutes."

Jensen stood up and held out his hand. "It's been a pleasure, and I hope you find the closure you so desperately seek, Mr. Reader." They shook hands and Jensen left the room.

Evan could feel his body react immediately in anxiety. His palms were already sweating, and he was fairly certain he had sweat through his shirt. The feeling the stickiness running between his shoulder blades all but confirmed it. He patted his sides and under his arms and they came back damp. Scoffing in mild frustration, which he had difficulty placing, he glanced at the tile. He could feel the sweat running down his ribs as

he stared at the tiled floor, transfixed. The cool lines of moisture that formed beneath his arms down each side were dis-
tracting, but something else had caught his attention. He had
to calm himself down, and he'd been reminded of a calming
strategy he'd been taught in grade school. If he could focus
on a single characteristic of something—anything—his mind
would short-cut the anxiety, essentially tricking himself into
believing he wasn't anxious.

He took a breath and concentrated. He tried to ignore the
way his hands shook or the pounding in his ears.

There was a pattern to the floor. Each tile was a copy of the
tile next to it. Same marbled design, same orientation, same
caramel swirl. That bothered him. The repetition looking at
the whole floor was constant. There wasn't any variability to it
at all. And yet, at the same time, it was reassuring. Something
about it was familiar, and despite his initial reaction of distaste,
it eased the tension he felt bearing down on his psyche.

When he looked at the floor from a wider perspective,
his eyes could easily pick out the swirling patterns that were
repeated over and over, ending only when a tile met the wall.
Each corner had a swirl that moved toward the center from the
bottom. His eyes moved slowly, almost lethargically across the
floor, moving in a kind of hypnotic rhythm from one curling
tendril on one tile to the reaching arm of the next tile, up
the curling tendril of that tile to the reaching arm of the next.
The tiles *did* remind him of something, something from long
ago, something familiar but hazy and distant. As his mind
began to reach and form into a coherent thought, familiarity
easing itself into his mind, a knock at the door made him
jump, and he blurted out rather abruptly in either frustration
or fright, he couldn't tell which, "What?"

The door opened and a young woman dressed in gray pants and matching jacket smiled at him, stepping demurely into the room. She greeted him softly and gestured down the hallway. "Mr. Reader, your Pod is ready."

Evan stood up and moved out of the room. Both his anxiety and his fear forgotten as he walked numbly down the hallway in the direction she had indicated. "Right this way, Mr. Reader. You'll be in Bench Pod One." His pulsed raced through his body, a deep electrical thrum that he was helpless to stop.

He followed her down the same whitewashed, fluorescently lit hallway, passing the blue arrows that stood out earlier without a second glance. Her long black hair flicked hypnotically like a cat's tail back and forth until she stopped in front of a large blue door with a giant number "1" painted down the front.

The door itself looked as if it belonged in a submarine. Metal rivets ran the perimeter of the door in perfect meter with a large metal wheel in the center of it.

Pictures flanked both sides of the metal door, and he gave the pictures little more than a cursory glance. Then Evan realized the woman was speaking, and he focused his attention back to her. "Mr. Reader, your summon is ready and present the second you open the door. Please remember, there is nothing we can do to keep the composite tethered to The Bench Pod, at least not until we upgrade our already advanced programming. With that in mind, if you wish to end your session early, for any reason, push the small red button on the other side of this door—" She indicated the one in front of them. "When that button is pushed, the program is terminated immediately, and Jensen will retrieve you for your exit interview and debriefing, which will take less time than your entrance interview. Do you understand these considerations?"

He dimly understood that she was waiting for his response and tried to nod. His eyes, however, had strayed back to one of the pictures on the wall and were captivated by it. He stared dumbly, absorbed by what he saw. The picture appeared at first glance to be nothing more than a stock photo, but now that he gave it his full attention, his understanding dawned like a cloudless sunrise.

The view that had become so captivating was almost an exact replica of his home, but under a menacing, lightning-laced sky. The shadows thrown by the bolts arcing through the blackness above the house seemed to be screaming phantoms, those dark parts of life reaching—certainly not for him, but that's how it felt—from the picture, stretching their melting mouths and grotesque visages to pull him under and shred his sanity. The rain partially obscured the home and was somehow oily. A dirty, greasy slick that coated the house in some incorporeal manifestation of approaching disaster. It appeared to Evan's wide and staring eyes that the rain and phantasms within it were sliding and shifting through the picture in ways that paint or color couldn't.

A hand touched his arm, and he very nearly screamed in terror. The cry died in his throat as his eyes, wide with fright, found the hand attached to the arm and shoulder of the woman. She was smiling at him in a kind and understanding manner, eyebrows raised questioningly. He gave himself a shake and blinked, thinking rapidly. He risked a glance back at the picture and was relieved to see it was only a picture of a rain-soaked plantation home beneath a summer storm.

He released a heavy breath and tried to reassert control over his hammering heart.

He looked back at the woman and answered the question that he only guessed she'd asked.

"Yes, sorry. I'm ready."

He nodded for what seemed the hundredth time that day. The woman smiled in response and cocked her head. "Excellent, Mr. Reader. I truly hope you find the closure you so desperately seek." The line was the same as Jensen had spoken. He'd said it with more conviction than this woman, though. "When you're ready, simply open the door and close it behind you." With that, she turned and walked back the way they'd come, her hair doing the same back-and-forth flicking as before. She disappeared through a doorway far down the hallway, leaving Evan to face a strange metal door. He flexed his hands in time with his anxious heartbeat.

He reached a tentative hand out before him but dropped it to his side and leaned forward. He rested his head against the door and let the coolness of the metal seep into his skin. He let it cool his anxious thoughts. It felt like his whole body was on fire, not with heat but with anticipation and something that bordered on panic. This was something he had wanted for so long, and now that it had come, he wasn't certain he could even go through with it.

Would it be everything he wanted it to be?

His foot shuffled a step closer to the door, and he placed both palms on the cool surface, his sweaty palms immediately feeling the ridges and valleys of the door's surface.

He drew in a deep breath, held it, and placed his hands on the wheel. He let out the breath and raised his head from the door. The wheel turned easily, with barely any effort or sound, then the loud click of the latch as the door swung inward.

He expected the *hiss* reminiscent of a sci-fi spaceship's pressure lock, but instead, he was met with an incredibly pleasant warm breeze and the lively tang of the salty ocean. His eyes followed a deep blue line that stretched across the horizon.

The submarine hatch he'd used to enter this paradoxical world had disappeared and he found himself standing on a dirt path. Flanking the rich darkness of the earth was grass so vibrant that he very nearly could *taste* the life with each breath in a summery green kind of flavor.

He looked up the path, trying to drink it all in. The path ended in a circle of the same naked earth, and there in the middle sat a bench. He gazed at The Bench.

Is that a...a cloud on it? He thought to himself with a small smile.

His eyes, still adjusting to the bright spring sunlight, were still squinting, making everything he saw a bit hazy. It was a figure, he saw, as he took a step closer. It was almost as if The Bench was shrouded in the deepest fog that the strongest lighthouse beam couldn't penetrate.

Evan took another step along the path and was amazed at the realism that surrounded him; it took his breath away. He had expected some of this as it was played up in both the brochure he read earlier and through the conversation with Glasses, but he could actually *feel* the wind and *taste* the salt in the air. The cries of gulls both far below the cliff and nearby above him sang in his ears, a kind of clashing music that spoke of the complexity and simplicity of the joy of the living. The shine of the sun reflecting off the ocean far below momentarily blinded him as he looked beyond the cliff. He winced and covered his brow to shade his eyes. All of it was surreal, but what amazed him the most was that he could *feel* the heat of the sun. It wasn't the dry heat of a vent blowing hot air to increase the temperature of a stale room in the winter; it was that the air *itself* was warmed in the sunlight, like late summer nights and the first days of spring dancing around him.

He turned on the spot, trying to see everything at the same time and feeling the grief and despair that had become old friends depart. And he let them go, not giving the emotions a second thought as he lifted his hands and took his first free breath in years.

The door that was forgotten behind him gently closed with a soft and forgotten *click*.

Turning back toward The Bench, his breath caught in his throat. There was no longer a haze hovering above The Bench. Sitting there now was a beautiful middle-aged woman. Dark brown hair waved lazily in a warm wind. As he stared, she reached to gather a wayward curl behind an ear as it whipped lightly around green eyes that regarded him warmly. The eyes glowed above a smile that sparked midsummer fires in his heart and chased the frigid winds completely from his mind.

He put a hand to his mouth and coughed out a single sob, the sob that unlocked that cloister of his wife's life, that holy of holies where her name had been locked behind fear, shame, and grief. Tears burst unbidden from his eyes and coursed freely down his cheeks, but he stood and stared at her, unable to move.

He stood for what seemed like forever, but he wasn't sure his feet would respond if he tried to move them; he'd lost all feeling below his chin. A distant worry tried to disrupt his attention, that those watching and monitoring might send someone soon to see if something was the matter, but he dismissed it easily. His breathing was quick and shallow, and it reminded him of his wedding day. What a strange thing to remember, but it was exactly the same.

He felt as if he was going to faint, once again as on his wedding day. The view was perfect, and he saw that day in his mind as he stood on that dirt path beneath a stretch of the clearest sky.

CHAPTER 9

The church the two finally settled on as the location of their wedding was an old Methodist church not far from River Fork, Arkansas. It had been built in the late 1800s by a very well-to-do family, the Corks. The Cork family had settled in Arkansas around the same time that several families from Italy did the same, most notably the Maestri and Bandini families. Finding some solace in their own countrymen, both families chose that particular part of Arkansas because the land was cheap and the climate was pleasant. There were another forty or so families that would find their way to that area from Italy, but those two families became famous in the immediate area and surrounding states for their fruit harvest. That is to say, wine. Eventually, it became such an attraction that in 1899, the first annual Fruit Festival took place. With a plethora of games, wine, and delicious home-cooked food, it would only grow from there. Each subsequent year was bigger and more celebrated than the last.

During the rise of the Italian families, another family began gaining notoriety in the same geographical area. Where the Maestri and Bandini families all but cornered the market on fruit and wine, the Cork family did something similar with industry. Personal vehicles had begun to replace the horse-drawn buggy and seeing a golden opportunity to make both a name for themselves and money to boot, they invested all of their family's remaining wealth and reputation into trucking. The Cork family started a delivery company, CJ Trucking, that would grow from a single wagon delivering only a single town nearby, to a multi-billion-dollar company that stretched across the state and eventually across the country, and only starting to branch into the international shipping market when the country came face-to-face with an insurmountable cataclysm.

In what some would call the worst year of their lives, the Fruit Festival would be cancelled for the first time in over a hundred years. The Cork family would, because all cross-country and international trade was cancelled for the foreseeable future, combine their assets and cancel all international contracts. The cause of this unbelievable turn of events would be a virus that spread across the world in the span of only a couple of weeks. The world quarantined for months to help stop the rapid spread of the virus, but it didn't help much at all. Mostly, because at that time, people were too concerned with their "rights" and "freedoms" to accept their responsibility to their fellow human. The Maestri family, now the exclusive administrators of the Fruit Festival, would opt to cancel it in 1980 to do their part to stop the spread, as opposed to enabling those who thought it was nothing more than a hoax. Unfortunately, the Maestri family would never recover from the economic stress placed upon them by a single year's Festival cancellation. The Cork family would, eventually, come out of the economic recession but would never reach the same national status from before the quarantine. They would struggle until CJ Trucking was purchased by the international shipping company Xi Chi Shipping in 2017.

With the stress of the family business traded for a hefty handful of millions, the Cork patriarch, Justin Trapper Cork, began dispensing his money into the community. One such way was to build a homeless shelter in a nearby town. Another way he divested his fortune was by building several churches across the region. One such church was The Light of the Morning Church.

Built into the hills of rural Arkansas, it echoed the styles of old Victorian and as such, was home to soaring spires that flanked large wooden doors. The tips of the church roof seemed large enough to impale a god should it descend from its heavenly throne to wreak havoc on the mortals below. The doors themselves seemed to weigh several hundred pounds each, but modern technology let them swing open and closed easily on hinges and pulleys.

The sanctuary itself had an arched ceiling that felt a mile away and between the vaulting columns and crossbeams was covered in a beautifully celestial painting. Angels—both the frightening sword-bearing Seraphim as well as the child-like Cherubim—flew across the expanse above. In the center of the painting was the artist's rendition of God. He appeared as an old man with shockingly white hair and large, kind eyes that saw all that was around him as "good."

The windows, spaced only a few yards apart, covered each wall. They let in ample, natural light as churchgoers entered from the south while the preacher spoke facing the north. The windows saw the sun most of the mornings in the east and most of the afternoons from the west. The church was shaded in summer only when the days were long and hot and the sun sank beneath the Ozark Mountains in the west, long after anyone was in attendance. In winter, the days were short and cold, and the sun worked to warm the sanctuary only briefly before it sank behind those same Ozark Mountains, only several hours earlier when the evening church crowd was still present.

The way the church was built, architecture and cardinal orientation, created a beautiful and striking setting for the biggest decision of his life.

What Evan was beginning to realize, however, is that the beauty did nothing to cool him down as he stood at the front of the church sweating profusely and taking deep, steadying breaths. It was perfect, really, now that he thought about it. The ceiling depicted the heavens, and below where he stood now was a kind of Hell, stagnant and devilishly hot.

The church had temperature control, and they had turned it on that morning while finishing up the decorations and last-minute preparations for the evening's event. It had been going all day, and yet despite that, or perhaps in spite of it, he felt like he was still melting in his tux. The church lights above were pointed directly at the pulpit, serving the dual purpose of both highlighting the ceremony and helping bake them in conjunction with the setting sun's heat through the westerly windows.

He put a finger in his collar and pulled, hoping to invite whatever cool air was near to dive down his shirt and do some work. It didn't help, and he instead cleared a sheen of sweat from his forehead and temples, wiping it carelessly on his pants leg. He knew by the dampness there, it wasn't the first time he'd done it.

He glanced over at Mason, his Best Man. Although he was on a step lower than Evan, they were eye level. Mason winked, giving Evan an inconspicuous thumbs up from the hand clasped at his belt line.

Evan noticed, with some relief, that he wasn't the only one dying a slow and roasting death. Mason's short dark curls shone in the light and were plastered in places at his temples, forehead, and neckline. Sweat was dripping down the sides of his face and gathering on his chin as well. Mason was doing his best to prevent it from becoming a steady drip, but even his best wasn't good enough.

Evan glanced at the two other men down the line. Jeff, who he'd met in college and now valued as a friend. He and Evan weren't nearly as close as he and Mason, but they were good friends nonetheless. Then, his gaze landed on Andrew, a mutual friend of all three men who'd accepted the invitation to be a groomsman with child-like excitement.

The three would meet every now and then for drinks or for the occasional game of poker, maybe dinner and movie. But overall, their interactions were limited to when their significant others could all get together. It wasn't something they spoke out loud; it was understood that the time they were able to get together was limited mostly by the women's schedules, not their own. They accepted this, if not with grace, then with a kind of understanding that only grew from resignation. Or maturity, depending on how Evan looked at it.

His mind was wandering, now, but it was taking his attention from the sweltering heat so he let it wander to his fiancée, who he would be able to call "wife" in several more unbearably hot minutes.

With poor relationships to their own siblings, their wedding party was small. Neither of them minded that part of it, which was a relief to them both when it was tentatively brought up at early wedding planning sessions.

They hadn't discussed family at length. Evan knew all about his soon-to-be wife's side, and she knew only a little about his, but enough. It wasn't something he talked about but told her a very brief family history of two selfish brothers, an oxycontin-addict mother and a womanizing father. He left it at that.

The truth of it was that his family issues went much deeper, but not much more complicated, than that. Evan's mother and father were husband and wife in name alone. His dad was a compulsive cheater, a bastard who worked in—and traveled to—cities with tall buildings made of glass walls and corner offices. Evan didn't have particularly *bad* memories of his father, but there weren't many good ones. None of the normal father-son bonding that involved fishing on the weekends or camping in the forests, baseball in the backyard, or board games on the weekends. Those memories belonged with his grandparents who died shortly after he started high school.

There were a few memories where his dad would take him to a shopping center and give him and his two brothers, Owen and Alan, a $20 bill each to spend at the local arcade. After that, his dad would disappear for an hour or two, saying he had "a meeting." They were young enough that they accepted it as truth. Well, Evan was. His older brother probably hadn't bought it. The twenty dollars didn't ever last the entire time he was gone, and Evan would usually end up on hands and knees searching for wayward quarters beneath the machines. All while his elder brother showed off for the youngest of the three pretty girls and talked to friends from school about sports.

He'd get lucky sometimes and see the distant glint of someone's lost quarter that meant more time on the games for him. More times than not, though, his knees would be red, and he'd have nothing to show for it. He'd end up sitting in the food court, surrounded by normal families with a mom and dad that *wanted* to spend time together until his dad showed up. He'd walk up to his three boys showcasing a smile that probably worked in those corner office business deals, but they did nothing for Evan's own self-worth, even at a young age. He doubted it did for his brothers, either.

He never found out what his dad was doing during those arcade trips but knew it wasn't business, at least not the professional kind. He was probably just fucking some floozy, nothing more to it than that.

He and his brothers discussed it briefly a few times. He discovered that it didn't bother his brothers as much as it did him. The older brother, Owen, idolized his father, and the younger, Alan, barely knew him. Evan was in the "goldilocks zone" for emotional injury, and he carried the pain with him, always.

His mother wasn't nearly as bad as his father. And while she did sleep around a little—believing herself to be secretive but in fact making it glaringly obvious—the harm she chose to inflict on the family wasn't because of infidelity; dad had that one covered. She was an addict. She had hurt her neck in an accident when Evan was in grade school, and she developed the addiction over the next several years. It probably bloomed fully into mind-numbing compulsion when she realized her husband was sleeping with other women. Evan couldn't fault his mother, not really. If the situation had been reversed and it was he that was being repeatedly cheated on—and ignoring his own cheating inclinations—the numbing of those emotions would be incredibly attractive. If you can't fix it, not feeling it is the next best thing, right?

What this created in his parents was a mother that was in a constant state of neutrality and a father who was always absent. Something Evan would never come to understand was why his father continued to hide the fact that most, if not all, of his work trips were actually weekend getaways with the new office secretary. He assumed it was out of habit. Perhaps it was also because he hoped, in some stupid secret ignorant part of him, that no one actually knew, that he had kept it a secret all this time and to change it at this point could expose him.

But as Evan grew up, becoming more emotionally and socially aware, he realized it may have been from shame. Though, admittedly, it was incredibly unlikely. For his father to admit that he'd been living a lie for decades might have been too much, so he continued with the sketch, scene after never-ending scene.

As for his brothers, Owen was the eldest of the three. Owen saw how their father treated women and followed his example, a perfect replication. He lived as a bachelor with a long chain of one-night stands and superficial relationships, most ending badly in the same echo of the last, usually a tantrum of one or both parties that included a lot of yelling, crying, and throwing things. Owen's indifference for decorum resulted in a new "girlfriend" at every family gathering. His father, all too often, looked on approvingly, seeing in his eldest son that which he saw in himself; the world was their oyster, and it was their jobs to eat it. This began to bother their mother, who played the moral giant of the family since the position had been vacated by their father. It reached the point where he—Evan—wouldn't even care enough to remember her name after she was introduced. She was an ornament on his brother's arm for the day or the week at most. She would be gone soon enough and replaced by another.

Owen died in a car accident when Evan was in college. It killed the girl that was with him at the time—Bethany. This name he would remember. It was forever burned into his memory because of the news article that covered the crash the next day. Well, that and the fact that Owen and his beauty Bethany weren't the only fatalities in the crash. The two were speeding through a residential neighborhood. They'd gone through plenty of green lights, some yellow, and a few red. This particular light happened to be red. The "walk" indicator was lit, and big brother was too busy drinking and probably finger fucking the girl next to him to see the three-year old holding her mommy's hand and skipping across the white crosswalk lines, laughing merrily without a care in the world. Owen's car came speeding around the bend in the road—police reported the vehicle moving at least triple the speed limit, a low-end estimate of sixty miles per hour. Both mother and daughter were struck simultaneously and killed instantly. *Thank God for small mercies*, Evan remembered thinking. The pair were on their way to the ice cream store after the girl, Ruby Estrella, had accidentally lost her first tooth during a wrestling match with her five-year old brother. The mother, Rosa Estrella, had taken the day off from the hospital after working ten straight days with barely any time to sleep between shifts. The speed of their deaths was a mercy.

Owen and Bethany had no such luck. They didn't die instantly. Evan saw this as a blessing, of sorts. He always hoped that Owen got what he deserved after treating people— women and his own family, mostly—as little more than pieces on a checkers board. The girl and his brother finally realized how fleeting life was in the moments after the crash. Their last remaining minutes leaked out of them through their many wounds, staining the leather seats of daddy's luxury car and dripping red and spreading across the dark asphalt beneath their soon-to-be corpses. Their last breaths were little more than gasps in the cool night air, creating tiny white clouds that disappeared almost instantly.

They were both pronounced dead at the scene. Their bodies were transported via ambulance to the hospital. The coroner's report stated that they died of asphyxiation and blood loss, and multiple other injuries. Evan imagined in a macabre kind of way, that they died choking on the same blood that pulsed through their veins while they were screwing.

Darkly poetic, in a way.

His younger brother Alan was another story. Evan hadn't talked to him in years. He couldn't remember the last time they'd spoken after Alan had literally slammed that door, shutting the rest of them out of his life.

Alan hadn't followed in his brother's and father's footsteps of debauchery, and he had only briefly explored the grayscale world of oxy like his mother, opting for marijuana and a very brief stint in cocaine, as far as Evan could tell and solely based on the rumors of family familiars in their hometown. The latter weren't necessarily reliable, not in the traditional sense. But there was usually something to them, as "the old maids didn't have anything better to do than listen with their ear to the ground," as the old men would say.

Instead, his younger brother had, in a fit of rage, punched their father square in the nose, surprising all of them. Then, in another surprising move, walked out of their lives forever.

It started the way most awful stories start—a fight. The five family members had gathered and were arguing in the kitchen. Their mother stood near the sink between Owen—who looked like a bouncer at a strip club with his black, too-tight shirt and crossed arms—and their father who had come in from the bedroom after deciding his half-hearted "that's enough" and inconsequential "calm down" weren't enough. On the other side of the raised counter—the family had called it "the bar" since they were children and the moniker stuck—were Alan and Evan. To be clear, Alan had started this mess; Evan just happened to be on this side of the bar.

Where Owen was in a constant state of posturing, Alan was in a constant state of processing. He worked relentlessly to understand a situation before making a decision or even deciding to make a decision. It was, in all honestly, one of the reasons he didn't have many friends growing up. He was difficult to interact with, requiring patience beyond the scope of most developing children and admittedly at times, adults.

Alan had started the argument by questioning his mother on the state of their family. Alan outlined the major issues with the family, starting with Owen, who followed the destructive lifestyle of their father, even going so far as to call out his own mother's infidelity in contrast to her husband's. This did him no favors and dear old dad had suddenly left the room, face flushed red from either anger or embarrassment. Having his lies and lifestyle laid out so plain and bare was more than he could handle. The man was a coward when it boiled down to it.

When their father returned—to follow through with his earlier comments from the bedroom—and found Alan continuing to crack open the family's chest of secrets, he'd reached over the counter and grabbed the neck of Alan's shirt. The yank that followed brought Alan's belly into the bar so hard that the sound of popping seams and the grunt could be easily heard over the yelling.

Their father had reached somewhere deep within himself and found some variation of embarrassed rage and decided to unleash it upon his youngest son, who was still mistaken for a grade-school boy despite shaving nearly every day.

The verbal lashing that he delivered upon Evan's unsuspecting—and thoughtful—little brother took everyone by surprise, even more so after the fairly level-headed and presentation-like dispute he had brought to the table.

Cursing and yelling, spittle flew across the foot of air between them and landed in Alan's curly hair. Their father laid into Alan. Evan, stunned as he was, couldn't remember even a single word of the hateful tirade. It lasted only a few seconds because, when their father brought the other hand around and pointed a finger in his face like some advancing weapon of war intent on skewering him like a pig on a spit, Alan had uncharacteristically brought his fist up behind his head and quick as a snake, pistoned it into his father's face. Blood immediately doused the front of his suit jacket and poured to the floor with a wet pattering sound that still echoed in Evan's mind on the pulpit steps.

That wasn't what had prevented them from speaking all these years, however; Evan had wanted to punch his dad nearly every day for a decade but would much rather acknowledge the dysfunction in his family and merely try to carry on. Evan was a master of not rocking the boat. After all, expected discomfort is better than surprise discomfort.

The reason Evan had opted to ignore his younger brother all this time was because of what happened *after* that fateful punch. Their mother stood still, leaning only a little on the sink for balance for the briefest second—no doubt her oxy-addled mind took extra time to process what she was seeing—and then rushed to her husband's side. The blood pouring down his face and shirt speckled the kitchen floor in what reminded Evan distantly of polka dot fabric, red dots on white. Evan's father slipped, his arms windmilling to keep balance while the blood smeared like garish red paint across the linoleum.

Their mother looked in horror from her husband to Evan and then to Alan. Owen was nowhere to be seen, a surprise to no one. Her eyes settled on Alan's fists, clenched at his sides and one of them highlighted where their father's erupting nose had primed the edges a sickening red.

Their mother reacted in a way that Evan still couldn't reconcile in his mind with the slow lethargic woman he remembered growing up with. He could tell she was high, her movements were almost as if she were in jelly, her head rolling back and forth gently as she walked. But in this instant, she moved quickly and snatched at Alan's hands. She held them in one hand, gently but firmly. The slap that raced through the air and across Alan's cheek was as surprising as it was cruel.

The sound of palm-on-cheek rang in the small kitchen, and even their father, who had retreated to the bathroom to clean up, seemed to have heard it through the walls, and the muted cursing and groans, along with the sound of splashing water, stopped in that moment.

Alan slowly reached up to his face where an angry red handprint was beginning to show. He stared at his mother, and as the look of stunned surprise faded from his face, an equally horrible expression began to manifest in its place. This one of growing frenzied rage that could be suppressed no longer, as it had been suppressed for years by the demure and thoughtful boy.

Alan lashed out and grabbed his mother by the shoulders. He shook her back and forth, her head flopping like a doll's connected by only a thread as he screamed wordlessly in her face, tears coursing down his face leaving shining paths behind and gathering on his jawline. The scream was one of fury, yes, but of the deepest heartache too. The release of a crying little boy trying desperately to be heard in the depths of adult fury. Spit shone on his lips and dripped off his chin as he screamed into his mother's terrified face. Even the oxycontin couldn't numb the wrath her third son had released.

She finally decided to engage in the family, and it was to poison her third son's world.

Then, Alan shoved her to the ground. He wasn't an overly strong young adult, but his wrath combined with their mother's drugged listlessness caused more damage than he no doubt intended. She stumbled as she fell back, slipping on the blood-soaked linoleum beneath her flats and falling on her rump, cracking the back of her head against the counter edge on the way down. The sound was a deep and fleshy *clump* that could be felt through the soles of Evan's sneakers.

For a moment, no one moved an inch. It was as if everyone in the house were stupefied at the events that had played out in front of them only seconds before. By standing still, the spell of time's endless grinding momentum was, for now, held at bay.

Evan broke the spell by running to his mother's side, understanding that the boat was, despite his greatest efforts to avoid it, now rocking and threating to tip the family into some unknowable surging depths.

Alan immediately disappeared into his room and packed everything he could into a duffel bag. At the door, he turned and gave Evan, who was now kneeling beside his mother and holding an ice-packed cloth to her head, a final glance. The front door slammed in the near silence. The only other sound that reached Evan's ears were the quiet moans coming from his mother's limp mouth. He couldn't hear his father in the bathroom anymore, nor could he see him in his limited view of the kitchen and living room.

It was the last time Alan would ever see most of his family alive.

After this brief explanation of his family—he left some of the more worrisome details out of his family tree—the wedding plans continued without any more probing questions from his fiancée.

And now here he was, waiting for her, dying in the heat that baked through the glass windows that had once been so attractive.

He reached up and tried to stretch his collar again, but the damn thing was too tight and wouldn't let any air in. He wasn't sure there was any air left in the room with him, anyway. The sweat's source wasn't confined to the physical world—the heat and sun. The other source, the one that took him a moment of introspection to discover was his exultant expectation, his heart pounded in his chest and his clammy palms were a direct result of the moment for which he'd been waiting a lifetime. He couldn't stand the wait, anymore. He was so ready for this next chapter of his life.

Music, loud and poignantly solemn, suddenly filled the church, signaling the onset of the ceremony. The doors directly opposite him stood open, and Marcy came through in a brilliant peach dress. She was stunning, and Evan looked at Mason who was smiling at his wife. Mason gave her a sly wink, to which she responded with a non-descript eye-roll, walking past them to take her place on the opposite side of the stage as the Matron of Honor.

Following Marcy was Jeff's girlfriend, Alice. Evan didn't know her well, but she was part of their circle of friends and important enough to include, so here she was in the matching peach dress, though the neckline seemed to be slightly different than the one on Marcy, he noticed. He didn't give it much more thought as she walked past him, taking her place next to and slightly below Marcy.

Next was Andrew's fiancée, Doxy. She was tattooed from shoulder to wrist on both arms with flowers and a number of other shamanistic and mythological symbols, but her face was that of an innocent child, only the nose ring actually making her appear older than a renegade adolescent. Her dark hair was cut short in a pixie cut with pink highlights that clashed garishly against the gentle peach of the bridesmaid's dress. Jeff smiled dumbly at her, clearly smitten, and Doxy winked at him in much the same way Mason had to Marcy before turning to join the other women on stage.

Suddenly, the music stopped. The world seemed poised on the tip of a knife and Evan found himself holding his breath. The priest's voice broke through the hushed shuffling that echoed through the church rafters.

"Please rise," he intoned formally.

The creaking of ancient pews that were finally relieved of their burden as people stood all at once filled the church. The organist began playing "Pachelbel's Canon in D," and Evan felt his heart stop in anticipation.

He took a deep breath, knowing he would see his fiancée— well, soon-to-be wife—in mere seconds.

The doors that had been closed after Doxy came through suddenly opened at the crescendo of the organists playing. The sunlight that shone through the windows beyond the doors momentarily blinded him, but he could see the outline of an angel.

As his eyes grew accustomed to the increased brightness, he realized it wasn't an angel at all but a goddess.

Everything else in the church faded, and for a moment, he was vaguely terrified that he was starting to faint. He felt a rush of heat within him move from his toes to his head and back again. His knees tried to buckle, but he adjusted his feet with uncharacteristic nonchalance and the feeling subsided. Breathing deeply, he calmed and stared at the woman walking down the aisle. Tiny motes of dust floated through the sunbeams and appeared to coalesce into the form of his fiancée, adding their own light to her already heightened radiance.

As she continued to approach, he could feel the anxious anticipation turn to relief and a slow grin spread across his face. The time had come. He was finally going to tie the knot and to the only person he wanted to spend the rest of his life with. They had made it despite plenty that tried to get in their way. They were finally going to be married.

They went through their vows, both of them repeating what the priest asked them to. They exchanged rings and took the two candles flanking a larger one, lighting it together and marking both their individuality and their unity as a couple.

They clasped hands after this, and the priest gently cupped their own in his. His voice rose to the rafters of the church, and he said in a loud clear voice, "I now pronounce you husband and wife. You may kiss the bride."

They turned to each other grinning, and Evan planted an enthusiastic kiss on his bride, much to the enjoyment of the onlookers who whistled and applauded their enthusiastic approval. He could feel her smiling beneath his own lips, but she was still kissing him back, their lips exultantly warm with passion.

He could vaguely hear the light laughter, and one person's catcall as they continued to kiss for more than a few seconds, but once it ended, they were both smiling and laughing. Evan stared into his wife's eyes, which sparkled with contagious joy and while it looked like she might begin crying, he knew it was for the best reason he could think of, and he smiled a knowing smile back at her.

The priest's voice rose again as they turned to face the congregated group of friends, family, and some very distant relatives. With arms raised in proclamation, their priest announced to those gathered, "It is with great pride and joy that I can now introduce to you the newest couple in God's Kingdom, Mr. Evan Jacob Reader and Mrs.—"

CHAPTER 10

"Meredith Alexandra Reader," he said breathlessly, fading seamlessly from one reality into the present one, feeling for the first time since he had woken up today that he was somehow irrevocably completely whole again.

Evan blinked several times before allowing himself to believe what his eyes were telling his brain to process. He thought himself prepared for this exact moment, but nothing could have prepared him for the sudden, simultaneous mending and breaking of his heart in a cyclical whirlwind of thunderous loss and electric joy.

Before he could say anything, the very reason he breathed turned toward him. Her hair fluttered lazily in the breeze, floating in the glow of the sun. Her long eyelashes shaded eyes that took him in slowly.

"Hi, Evan," she said. Her voice was polished crystal. Beautiful, clear, pleasing to hear, and heartbreakingly familiar.

Evan looked at her face and took her features in slowly, drinking deeply and breathing deeper. Her face was exactly how he remembered it, except for nearly imperceptible laugh lines that ran along the corners of her mouth where her special smile rested.

Evan was pleased that whatever technology made this miracle a reality had nearly matched the perfect memory of her from his mind. "Meredith," he breathed again, not quite certain how to begin speaking to the divine apparition before him.

The pounding in his ears nearly drowned out the distant crashing of waves below and crying seagulls above, leaving them in a vibrating orb of silence. A gentle breeze blew past his face, wakening his senses to the salty scent of the sea alongside a subtle and nearly desperate smell of the deepness of the earth.

Evan took a step forward and felt his arm lifting up an outstretched hand. He shuffled slowly toward The Bench, leaving tiny puffs of dust in his wake, to where his dead wife waited for him in a light blue dress that fell gracefully below her knees.

He laid a steadying hand on The Bench's back, its metallic surface smooth and cool to his clammy hands, much like the metallic door that led to this place. Evan never took his eyes off of the woman sitting there as he moved dazedly to the front of The Bench and sat stiffly upon it. Or collapsed upon it when his knees stopped supporting him.

The breeze that had brought the sea to his senses casually whispered through Meredith's hair, twisting and curling it around her lips, which were slightly pursed, a precursor to a smile. *Her smile.*

"Evan," she began, "you look as if you've seen a ghost." Her smile broadened into a grin, and she began to laugh. The sound of it was angelic, a sound he never believed he would hear again. She brought her hands to cover her mouth as tears began coursing down her lovely blushing cheeks.

Evan felt a tear slide down his cheek and soak into the stubble on his chin despite the near giddiness that was pumping through his veins.

Meredith's face grew apologetic. "Oh, Evan, it was only a joke." She reached up and cupped his cheek, wiping the wetness from his scruffy cheek with her thumb. She let her hand linger there.

He felt it. He felt her hand cup his cheek, and he closed his eyes and leaned into it, relaxing his shoulders and releasing the breath he didn't know he had been holding. He felt a sob rising from his gut, and he was powerless to stop it.

"Meredith," he began. "Meredith, I'm so sorry. I..." He broke off and cupped the hand on his cheek. Meredith moved closer to him on The Bench, and he could feel her knees touch his, could hear her dress moving as she leaned into him. It couldn't be real, could it? Meredith couldn't be here, she *wasn't* here, and he knew that, but despite all of the evidence to the contrary, he *felt* her next to him, the warmth of her body slowly spread to his, the soft slick feel of her dress against his knee.

"Meredith," he began when he felt his chest release the tension held there once he could catch his breath and pulled back from her. "Meredith I'm so sorry. I tried to find you at the hotel, but I couldn't. I felt the quake in Deiyandara, but by the time I got back to it, everything was gone, flooded. Everything. I went to our room but barely found anything except your hat." He sniffed and locked eyes with her, hoping to find something there that he couldn't feel within himself.

Meredith smiled again, her head tilting to one side.

"My Cubs hat. Oh, Evan, I loved that thing. It's one of those things I miss. Other than you, of course." Evan wasn't quite ready to smile at jokes yet, but this was just like her.

He did notice, however, that the program made slight modifications to Meredith's appearance. Probably to address the 4-year span since he'd last seen her. Nothing drastic, but compared to the picture he had of her in his head—and his pocket, he noted—there were vague differences. Her cheeks were slightly thinner, and she had those smile lines that weren't there before. Small differences, but they snapped him back to the reality that she wasn't here, merely a program running for his benefit.

And yet, even armed with that knowledge, he couldn't help himself.

She *was* there, and despite his best efforts to maintain the boundary in his own mind that he wasn't actually speaking to his dead wife, he felt that boundary begin to fade and splinter. Then, as he gazed at her, allowing his eyes to take in every detail of her, it cracked and then altogether disappeared.

"I'm so glad you're here," he heard himself say.

She nodded and began to smile at him; this one was *almost* her smile.

He found himself feeling slightly embarrassed. Here he was, sitting with his wife whom he loved with a desperate, infinite devotion, and he didn't even know where to start, how to begin a conversation in a situation he never dreamed would happen.

He laughed and ran a hand through his hair, trying to think of something—anything—to say that would bridge the distance that time's wheel had peeled from their threads.

"I've missed you."

As soon as he said it, he had to suppress a wince. That was one hell of a weak way to start.

A mental picture suddenly surfaced, and he nearly laughed out loud and its simplicity and situational perfection. He imagined himself as a jar of jelly turned on its head, the jelly inside—grape in his mind—the memories and everything he wanted to talk about. Even turned upside down, though, the jelly was stuck in the same position it had been since it was made. A little bit of grape jelly juice leaked out of the top, just as his weak attempt to start the conversation had been. But the memories, all of the substantive material he wanted to discuss with his wife, was stuck inside the jar. Eventually, he was both afraid of and hoped that it would come out without the loud sucking and slurping sound and plop on the surface below. He hoped that he could avoid that kind of mess when they would begin to speak truthfully about his loss. Because it had to. He knew that at his core that for this whole trial to work, he needed to get to the core of his grief. Otherwise, it was all a waste. All for nothing. Fearing a recurrence of the same failure he felt at not being able to find her, he braced himself for the coming difficulties.

In spite of that, he laughed a little and rubbed his scruffy jaw. "Meredith, as silly as it sounds, I'm not even sure what to say. I've wanted this for so long and now that I'm here, I..." He stopped and thought, shrugging in defeat. "I don't even know where to start."

To his utter relief, she laughed, too. This time, her smile did show in full, curving the corners of her crimson lips up. A deep, throaty chuckle escaped between them as she put a hand to her breast.

"I'm so glad I'm not the only one!" she cried in relief.

Then they both laughed, and Evan felt as if the jelly was beginning to seep out of the jar slowly, the tension and fear that held the conversation back was abating. For now, at least.

When the laughter subsided and they both sat smiling at each other, Evan knew how he should move forward with the conversation. There wasn't really anything else to talk about, and the sooner he could finish, the sooner he would feel the relief of finally receiving forgiveness for losing his wife on the other side of the world.

"Meredith, I searched desperately for you for forever. At least, it felt like it was forever. It may have only been a couple of weeks, but every day I searched and couldn't ever find you. I had no idea where to look and no one would help. It was a nightmare trying to figure out where to look while wishing I could be in a hundred places at once."

He paused, trying to work through the pain that was so near the surface, threatening to break free.

Meredith paused for several minutes while he tried to gather his thoughts. It was harder than he'd hoped, and gauging her reaction, he thought she felt it, too.

Evan stared at her and, as the silence stretched, wondered distantly if there was a glitch with the program, an unforeseen short in the system that would cause the subject to pause for so long.

Just when he was starting to get worried that he'd broken it, she turned to him, a light in her eyes that at first he mistook for playfulness.

"Evan, tell me what happened, with the tsunami. I want to know what happened from your perspective."

It was a perfectly reasonable request, and he nodded. He knew that she had access to every single memory of her own and could recall it through whatever machine ran the program. It made perfect sense that she'd want to understand the other side of it. Well, that *the program* would have a limited collection of data to pull from.

So, he told her. He recounted the tale he'd told Jensen what felt like only minutes before while part of him felt an exhaustion as if it had been days.

The memory still carried with it a keen sharpness that stabbed deep into his heart. It was impossible to tell again without showing emotion, but he felt that this time, the retelling was a little smoother with fewer emotional breaks required.

Meredith listened with an intensity that he remembered and loved her all the more for it, responding in all the right places with a nod or an empathetic hum. It really was remarkable.

When he was finished, with little fanfare, he looked into Meredith's face. She sat still for a moment. The breeze, constant and cool with a salty tang tickled his nose as he waited somewhat impatiently, trying to quiet the racing thoughts that continued to guess what her reaction would be.

Thinking rapidly, he opened his mouth to repeat himself. But she blinked and looked at him in no other way that he could describe except "quizzically." This in turn made Evan turn inward with curiosity, but he tried instead to focus on her question.

"Evan, what do you remember about the tsunami? And after it, I suppose."

He thought for a moment. There was something in her gaze that made him understand the question as more than curiosity. It held a gravity, a weight behind the words that cast a dark shadow over his understanding of it.

He licked his lips. "I remember looking for you in some of the hospitals, for days, a couple of weeks, maybe. So many were set up that it was nearly impossible to search all of them in the time I had. And if you happened to be one of the people that fell sick, there'd be no way for me to know that you were sick. If you died and, like so many others, were buried in a mass grave, I would never know." He met her eyes with a look of resignation. "You'd have been considered missing and presumed dead."

The remarkable thing about some parts of the world was that despite access to incredible technology, many of them were stuck in a kind of primal traditionalism. During his time in Sri Lanka following the tsunami, he had the chance to speak with plenty of locals, some of them civilians and some part of the local military. Well, it wasn't actually an official military. It was more like a group of people who continued to fight against tyranny and human trafficking, which was very popular in the area only a decade before.

The government, especially, continued to do the same thing that prior generations had done, if only because it was what they knew. These mass graves were another continuation of those practices. There was plenty of land, there were plenty of bodies, so the easiest—and cheapest—way to dispose of them was to dig a giant hole and dump the bodies in. Oh sure, they'd end up getting in some kind of trouble from humanitarian organizations or even the successor to the World Health Organization. But in the meantime, they had thousands of bodies to dispose of and plenty of land in which to bury them. Just as they had for hundreds of years, they took that stance that they could figure the rest out later.

Evan thought deeper about the way she framed the question, measuring the answer as satisfactory or in need of further explanation. The more he thought about it, though, the more he realized it wasn't a question for her. It was the kind of question someone asks when one knows something the other doesn't. A question meant to connect the dots. A *leading* question.

It was the kind of question that changes people's lives.

He stood up slowly and plunged his hands into his pockets. He drew in a great breath and heaved a sigh. It made him feel a little better; the crisp air seemed to move through his lungs, punching and energizing his body, however feebly.

He felt a hand on his shoulder, and she was there beside him, looking at him critically except for that smile playing at the corners of her mouth.

"Evan, what do you remember about Sri Lanka? About your last few days there?"

He stared out at the horizon, the distant sounds, both below and overhead gave him the sensation of being insubstantial, a mote of dust floating on the wind, subject to its every whim with no actual will of his own.

He had felt that before, a sort of ghostly understanding of his limited existence. Ironically enough, it had been around the time after the tsunami, when he had been surrounded by so much death and despair, the hope he kept secreted away in his chest set him apart from it all. The people he spoke to or passed mourning on the streets were the ones anchored to the world, tethered in a way that made their existence something more than simply one foot following another. That was him. His understanding was a pale, gray version of the world around him. Even the sounds seemed muted at times except one. The sound he heard over and over again in his mind was the sound of the water rushing below his hotel room door as he snatched the Cubs hat from the water's rapid unforgiving grasp.

"One of the last things that I remember is visiting a hospital outside of Akuressa, closer to Matara but still farther from the coast than I thought would matter.

"I had visited as many as I could on the coast, maybe every one within several miles of our resort. But going north I saw more and figured it would be a good place to start. They set up there because if there were going to be any aftershocks, they didn't want to be close to the coast and risk another disaster.

"So, I hitched a ride with another group of survivors looking for their loved ones and we rode north.

"There was this other girl on the bus with us. She was from England, and her husband was missing. They had come to Sri Lanka for their honeymoon, of all things, hoping to get away from everything happening in the UK, and instead of wedded bliss, found themselves in the middle of a nightmare."

He turned to her, looking across his shoulder with a flat smile. "Life's pretty cruel sometimes, isn't it? But I don't have to tell you that, do I." Her sad smile was her only response.

Her gaze returned to the horizon and he continued, "When I got to Akuressa, there were several hospital tents and plenty of the Tomb Tents. That's what most of the survivors and locals called them. Well, the locals had an actual name for them, but someone said that roughly translated it meant 'Tomb Tents,' so we picked that up and carried it. Those were the tents where they put the bodies of dead people so that people could come to identify them. There were a lot of those.

"I always checked the hospitals first. Bit of the romantic in me, I guess, but I just knew you had to be alive. I felt that if you had died, I'd have known. If only." The last part was said almost too quietly for Meredith to hear, but she did hear it, along with something like regret couched between its syllables.

"I walked through that hospital, and the next, and the next, and on and on. I never found you there. I didn't find you in the Tomb Tents, either. You were reduced in the public eye to merely another one of the thousand missing and presumed dead."

He turned to face as she walked back to sit on The Bench. "Does anything stick out to you those last few days? Anything at all, Evan?"

He thought hard. There was so much that he remembered as a faded blur. But there was something, something at the very end of his trip.

He snapped his fingers in the afternoon air and she jumped. He chuckled an apology, and she laughed a little as well, but it seemed to be only so he didn't feel left out. "I do remember something, though I'm not sure how relevant it is."

"That's alright. I want to know about it. After all, I wasn't there." She said it jokingly, but there was something else underneath. Not malice or chastisement, not anything close to sarcasm. But something that bordered on a kind of hesitation, though that wasn't the right word, either.

"Most of the hospitals there didn't have electricity. It makes sense. It's a jungle-covered island off the coast of India. There's not a lot of stuff out there. Nor is there a large enough reason to get it out in the boonies like that." That word he knew was a relic from his Midwest upbringing, but he let it go. "So almost every establishment—Tomb Tent, makeshift hospital, homes and huts—used kerosene lamps or good old-fashioned torches. Their smell wasn't great, and they often had to be relit, but there wasn't anything that could be done about it."

He waved his hand dismissively. "One of those 'traditionalism' things."

He noticed her look of pained patience and shook his head to clear it. He was getting carried away with the details of the setup.

"Anyway, one of them that I visited ended up being a Tomb Tent, of course. I went there because they had..." He hesitated and felt an overwhelming tightness in his throat;

the excitement was overwhelmed by a sudden surge of grief. After swallowing thickly, he was able to continue, but his previous vigor had faded. "They had just brought another load of bodies in, and I wanted to check them.

"It was awful. By this time, it had been some time since the tsunami. Bodies that they were bringing in were decomposing, and some I'm certain couldn't be recognized at all, even by their family members. Missing limbs and the natural progression of decay in the wet heat of that place wasn't doing anyone any favors. They were bloated and grotesque, vicious caricatures of who they were when they were living."

He hesitated, hearing what he said and wincing. "I mean it wasn't funny, not at all; it was such a juxtaposition of these corpses that were nearly unrecognizable along with their family or whoever. The people that were *supposed* to know who they were. Even now it's difficult to reconcile in my mind.

"This Tomb Tent, though, had electric lights. They weren't fancy—in fact they probably weren't safe at all. But it was a single copper wire, 12-gauge, probably, that sent electricity to the naked incandescent bulbs clipped at the base to the wire.

"It was, I suppose now that I think back to it, a live wire suspended above a bunch of bodies. There wasn't a good reason to make it any safer. That much time after the accident, there were fewer and fewer people looking for their family members that died. In fact, I remember being the only one in the tent at that time.

"There were nurses that recognized me from some of my searching. It wasn't something that I actually liked, being a frequent-enough visitor that the nurses knew my name. Makes me uncomfortable knowing how they pitied me every time I pulled the tent flap back, and they saw who it was standing there in the entrance, once again."

The frustration that began to jitter into his voice didn't surprise him, but it wasn't intentional. He had never wanted to be pitied, but knew without a doubt, as if some cosmic force were confirming it in his mind, that he had in fact been pitied each and every time.

"I waited until all of the workers had unloaded the truck bed. There were maybe twenty or so bodies stacked haphazardly there, and then I was alone in the back of the tent, where the light was dim, and the darkness threatened to choke it out.

"There wasn't anyone with a list or anything like in the weeks earlier. The makeshift desk that I'd seen that first day and most of the following days was gone. This was probably the last—or one of the last—loads they'd bring before changing it up and dumping them one by one when found. At least, that's what one of the nurses I met had said. The city was trying to get back to normal, and there were now normal problems that were beginning to pile up because so many of the usual hospital staff were helping with tsunami relief."

Evan paused and sat on The Bench next to her, his boots kicking up small puffs of dust that floated away in the breeze. She sat listening to him quietly, a look of concentration the only indication that she still had her attention. But all of it hurt. The memories were painful, like trying to tease a small splinter out of a reddened, inflamed hand.

At the same time, however, it brought with it almost the same relief. That feeling that a foreign object which was previously lodged in a place where it didn't belong was suddenly withdrawn and cast aside, the flesh and nerves finally free to move back into a normal rhythm. Back where they belong.

Evan felt that he was going back to a normal rhythm.

"Finding you was my number one priority, but after gagging a few times before, I needed help if I intended to see this to the end. I eventually brought a rag soaked in lavender oil with me. The smell within this last tent was ... well it was ungodly, and the rag did little to keep it from my nose, but it helped enough. Enough to prevent me from emptying my stomach every few feet. I learned the hard way in that regard.

"Actually, there was kindness in that ugly realm of death. A kind woman gave me the tip about the rag, actually. In English, no less. She approached me after I'd thrown up not only my lunch but also the memory of my lunch. And then, eventually I was left dry heaving in a corner.

"I felt someone touch my shoulder while I was bent double catching my breath. I was surprised, and for a second, I was afraid that I'd turn around and there'd be a bloated, decaying body touching me, its pleas for help coming out in a gurgling croak. But it was a kind, grandmotherly woman. The look on her face was one of such serenity and empathy that I immediately felt relief. Her dark and wrinkled cheeks were tear-stained, and some were still falling, making their way over the hills and valleys of her ancient skin. While her body appeared old, she moved with a grace and sureness that spoke of an understanding with the ground beneath her feet, that it surpassed a simple human's.

"She asked if I was all right, her tongue poking through a couple of gaps in her teeth while she explained that her mother had taught her the trick, and she gestured to a family hovering over one of the bodies, all of them with rags pressed gently but firmly against their nose and mouth, saying that she was teaching them this trick, too. The sadness that seemed to catch in the meager light reflecting in her dark eyes was ferociously deep as if she were also lamenting how awful a thing to have to pass down.

"I thanked her as she placed the rag in my palm and she leaned up to me—she was shorter than I was by a significant margin, but bent double as I had been, we were nearly face to face—and placed her damp cheek against my own, giving my shoulders a gentle and reassuring squeeze.

"I don't think I could ever forget what she said, then, though I think some part of me had forgotten it, until this moment. She said, 'I know it's hard now, and it will continue to be hard. The hardness will begin to fade if you let it. Listen to the softness when that happens. The softness wants you to carry on and will bring honor to the memory.'

"Then she leaned away, smiled her gap-toothed smile in a sad kind of goodbye, and went back to her family."

He felt a tear scamper quickly down his cheek, but he ignored it, and Meredith shifted in her seat next to him.

Had he really forgotten what that ancient woman had said? He couldn't remember the last time he thought of it before today, but deep down he believed it had become a kind of mantra to him when things were rough. Not the whole speech, but to remember the softness.

Evan leaned back, The Bench creaking as he looked at his wife. "And it was enough to let me walk back and forth between the bodies, trying my best to find identifying marks that you have, like that little mole behind your right ear. Despite what I said earlier, I have no doubt I could have found you, if you had been one of those bodies. I spent hours each night remembering your face. I didn't want to be one of those people who begin to forget what their dead family member looks like. I dreamed about you, and every time I dreamed about you, I held your face in my mind. I could never, ever, forget you, Meredith."

She began to cry, then. Soft tears lazily making their way down her cheek and dripping off her chin to land at the top of the space between her breasts then sliding beneath the fabric, unnoticed by them both.

Evan watched the tears on her cheeks, transfixed until she spoke. "I believe that, Evan. It makes me happy to know that you were so intent on keeping my memory alive. You're the reason I'm here, of course."

He smiled and put his hand on top of her folded ones. She was the warmth he needed on a cool autumn night, and he wished he could gather her in his arms, sweep out of the room, and take her home right then. But he knew he couldn't. He knew she was stuck in this room, in all of this stuff, forever.

Now, she reached up and wiped at the wetness beneath her eye. Evan put his hand back on his lap. It just wasn't exactly the same as holding her hand when they were alive together. There was a kind of dissonance, now, but he couldn't pinpoint exactly where it came from.

Meredith continued, "So what was weird about that night? Was it that it was the last of the Tomb Tents and the old woman?"

He smiled a small smile and shook his head, knowing full well that his wife was actually trying nicely to say "get on with it."

"No, that's not what was weird. The weird thing was when these trucks back up to one of these tents, they just haul open the sides of them. They're these great big canvas-sided tents, I guess what Mason would call an 'army tent,' though I still don't know what that means. The locals would roll up the sides on hot day. It had been raining earlier that day, so most of the sides had been rolled down to keep as much of the moisture out as possible to delay further decomposition of the bodies, but it was pretty much a lost cause at this point.

"But there I was, standing in the dimness except for the red glow of the taillights and watching as the truck backed up and lowered the tailgate. A few men hopped out before it had fully stopped, and they began to unload the bodies there. It didn't take long, and they didn't give me a second glance after an initial head nod in greeting.

"The strange thing happened when they left. They put the tailgate up and ... and..."

He put his hands to his head as there was a rushing sound in his ears, like water in a distant pipe was surging toward him. He could feel Meredith's hand on his shoulder and hear her saying something to him, but he was being swept away.

The memory he began explaining started out as a dim recollection, but soon it filled his mind, and he could see it again, clear as day. It was as if an ancient mechanism in his mind had started to crank and the more he thought about that night, the faster it turned, chugging to life and bringing with it the full recollection from his mind's darkest recesses.

The men jumped back into the cab with ease, having plenty of practice at it. But as they began to leave, instead of the truck moving away from the tent, it began to slide slowly in the sodden earth, kicking up huge gouts of the black, sticky mud that hit the sides of the canvas with deep, wet plopping sounds.

The tires kept spinning until, from that end of the tent, there was a *wump* and *crack*. Evan looked up from shielding his eyes from the mud and bright red taillight to see that the back right tire, nearly half as tall as he was, had clipped the side of the tent. That end of the tent started to sag deeply, like a giant's backend had found the perfect seat. Fearing the collapse of the tent, Evan retreated a step. The tent stopped its downward descent toward the mud-spattered grass after only a second, sagging listlessly beneath the combined weight of the canvas itself and the wetness from the day's rain. But it was enough to disrupt the delicate balance of the makeshift wire clasps connected to the lightbulbs. The lights bobbed above him, causing shadows to dance on the walls like a macabre farewell dance to the living. One of bulb-laden wires suddenly dropped onto the floor at the far end of the tent, and Evan's attention was snapped back to that corner of the tent. The bulbs dropped in rapid succession, hitting the ground and shattering immediately in concussive bursts of glassy popcorn.

The sound grew in speed and volume as it raced toward Evan, the darkness growing closer each time a kernel of light burst upon the dead mud.

He had only a split second to think, only time for one snap decision but time enough to know he couldn't move fast enough to avoid the wires completely. And in his sodden state, if those wires landed on him, it would be the equivalent of sticking a fork into a socket. At the very least, it would deliver a shock to his body, one that could potentially kill him.

Without time enough to move completely out of the way, he threw up his arms in a desperate attempt to stave off the inevitable. The wire was batted away but as soon as it touched his hand, there was a brief flare of pain, almost as if he anticipated it instead of experienced it, and then the memory was gone.

He clawed at his memory for several seconds, trying to grab the trailing threads of the thing, but it was dark in his mind, now. The lights were out, and he was left alone among the bodies.

The next thing he could remember was regular old life in the States. The way he felt this morning before coming to Innervate Industries. Wake up, go to work at the bar, come home and fall asleep wishing he was dead. But that doesn't make any sense. *There has to be something missing*, he thought to himself.

Another bizarre turn of it, too, was that there was a distinct lack of dimness that normally accompanies the passage of time without consciousness. He could remember a time in his youth when he'd been out of school with a bad case of the flu. He remembered very little of his time in bed, but his mother and father told him he'd stayed there for nearly three days. The feeling that piggybacked on those memories before he was sick felt *further* than the memories after his sickness, like the one when he was finally well enough to go outside and play with a boy down the street.

His memory of the lights falling and waking up in the States held no such feeling. It was the same dimness he felt when waking up in the morning. The previous night is close, very little *gray* between the end of the day and the start of the next. That's what he felt now, thinking back to those lights popping in the rapidly dimming tent and when he woke up in the States. It was going to sleep and waking up the next day.

He heard the faint sound of Meredith's voice coming to him from very far away, and he realized she was saying his name.

"Evan. Evan? What are you thinking about?" There was a look of concern on her face, and he patted her hand gently to reassure her.

"I'm fine, sorry. What was I saying?"

"You said that they put the tailgate up, and then I lost you for a second. What happened next?" There was something bothering him, something itching at the edge of his consciousness, like a shadow that could only be seen from the corner of his eye, and the second he looked right at it, it scampered away again into his peripheral view. He felt dizzy, as if he was on a carousel trying to watch a single wood-carved pony as it passed him in a colorful blur, disappeared, and then came back again.

When he spoke, it was dull and with little inflection. "They put the tailgate up and got in the truck. But when they were leaving, the truck hit a part of the tent, and the wired lights fell."

What was it that was peeking around the corner of his subconscious?

"All I remember is not having time enough to jump out of the way, so I tried to hit the light away from me, and I think I did. It's just..." He trailed off and Meredith nodded for him to continue.

"It's just I don't really..."

Why can't I get this out? Why is this so hard to say?

"It's that I don't remember anything after that."

Instead of the look of concern deepening in his wife's eyes, there was a flash of something else. *Recognition*, he thought mildly surprised at himself. *But how can that be?*

No, it wasn't recognition after all. It was confirmation.

"Why do you look like that, like I said something that you knew all along?" He wasn't panicked, not yet at least, but there was a slimy feeling in his chest that he felt swelling and growing, putting an uncomfortable pressure on his lungs.

"Evan, do you remember how your arms protected you?" She paused. "Which one touched the wire?" Her voice was steady, but there was an excitement to it, a kind of anticipation now. He couldn't for the life of him think why it would matter, but it was making him uneasy.

"It was my left hand, I hit it with ... with my left hand, but why ... why does that..."

The words, dropping slowly into the air between them, held with them a variation of disbelief that slowly began dawning on his face. His eyes cut down to his arm and back again at Meredith, then back to his arm. "It's the arm with my Chip, but surely..."

He trailed off as the wheels that previously had chugged to life now ground to a screeching halt. His mind hit a wall, and he couldn't think beyond it, like when he was little, and his preacher described eternity. He could think of "time" and "space" but to think of "forever" was something he couldn't comprehend. His mind would hit a wall just past the point of realizing that his life was limited to the clock and calendar, and eternity was outside of the very thing by which it can exist.

Evan's mind was still stuttering between thoughts, and he couldn't think clearly; he couldn't think in a way that would start the process up again.

He cocked his head to the side, his breath coming in sharp, quick gasps. If he'd been asked to walk around The Bench once, he wouldn't have been able to do it. There wasn't enough air in the world, and he felt like his brain was short-circuiting. *Is this a heart attack?* he thought with wild disregard for himself.

And then, with a great heaving effort that stretched the limit of his mind's capacity, a thought shoved itself forward. It came into his consciousness from somewhere else, somewhere outside and was as large as life, bigger, even. With it, his mind began thinking again, though at a sluggish, listless pace.

He looked at Meredith, feeling that his face was warm, sweat beading on his forehead and under his arms. Hot and cold goosebumps chased each other up and down his arms, his spine tingled as he began to form the words to express that one, fanatic realization.

"It's the Chip. The SafetyChip in my left arm."

It couldn't be. It was impossible.

"It was damaged, wasn't it? Somehow, by the electric current in the naked wire?"

The chances were infinitely small, negligible. They were so small that they weren't even discussed as a possibility in any Chip Center anywhere.

"Is that why there's nothing else in my mind? Only a vague blankness that eventually leads back to 'normal'?"

He looked up at her, his voice trembling with a fear that was fierce and terrible. It rose in his mind like a candle casting its wan glow upon the pallid shadowed sockets of a skull.

"What else did I miss?"

Tears sprang to life and quivered in Meredith's gaze.

She shook her head gently and the tears spilled over, cascading down her cheeks in tiny shimmering waterfalls.

"Oh, Evan." Her lower lip trembled as she finished, "Everything."

PART 2:
MEREDITH

CHAPTER 11

When Meredith was a little girl, her second-grade class watched a video about wildlife around the world. While most of the rainforests had disappeared by the time she became an adult, there were some small sanctuaries still left in the world. There was a tiny tract of land in Brazil, 50 square miles of what the public called "preserved rainforest" and what environmentalists called "too little, too late." There was another plot of land, even smaller, in what was called China at the time and is now called New Vietnam. It was barely over 3,000 acres of preserved rainforest and held only twelve percent of the native species that were previously found all over that part of the world. In India, there was a rainforest that was protected by the government early during the 20th Century. It started out as a 2,500-acre plot of land but wasn't immune to the human population growth the planet experienced, and it ended up being reduced to 1,200 acres to allow space for public housing, parking, and malls. Afterall, people needed a place to live. Oxygen, in some minds, was secondary.

The last major bastion that held against deforestation was a small measure of exotic wonder on an island south of the Indian continent. She didn't remember the exact numbers, but she did know that a good deal of the world's rarest flora and fauna could be found on the island. Her fourth-grade teacher, Ms. Eggersby, told the class that despite recent scientific breakthroughs and environmental laws, it was likely that the world's rainforests would completely disappear during her students' lifetime.

Ms. Eggersby was known around the school as one of the smartest teachers in their small city. Sure, the other teachers were smart, but the students in Ms. Eggersby's classroom were taught more about the world than any other class in the same grade. While most other classes were working on projects about American history—something becoming even more and more irrelevant, even she knew it—her class was writing papers on the projected changes in the carbon levels of the planet. Or working through records of environmental efforts happening throughout the world.

Ms. Eggersby's passion for her students' well-being and intellectual growth was rivaled only by her love of the content she taught. Meredith could tell that she was telling the truth about the rainforest, and she could also tell how sad it made their favorite teacher.

Following a unit on plant growth later that year, the class was tasked with writing about something they wanted to do when they grew up. A goal of sorts, with which to measure personal success.

While some of her classmates chewed on the ends of their pencils and looked around the room for inspiration, Meredith was scribbling her answer frantically on her paper, writing so fast that the letters blended together in some spots requiring her to go back and erase them, huffing in childish exasperation as she did so.

She didn't hesitate at all when she raised her hand to tell Ms. Eggersby that she had finished. Her heart did a tiny little jig, however, when her teacher glanced up from whatever she was doing behind her desk and found Meredith's hand in the air. The questioning eyebrow she raised as an answer before walking briskly around the desk wasn't menacing but was usually enough to make a student think twice about whether their question *really* needed to be answered right then.

"Do you have a question about the assignment, Meredith?" Her voice wasn't rude, but it was certainly direct. Ms. Eggersby decided early on in her teaching career that students could be spoken to with respect but without pandering to their egos. She believed this helped encourage her students to speak clearly about their own lives, in both questions and answers.

"No, Ms. Eggersby, I'm finished," Meredith responded, sounding even to her own ears a little pretentious despite her mild lisp.

Ms. Eggersby blinked and took Meredith's proffered essay slowly, taking care to avoid smudging the graphite sentences that Meredith had written at such a fevered pace.

Meredith watched with trepidation, her teacher's eyes moving rapidly back and forth several times until she reached the bottom of the paper. They darted rapidly back to the top and Meredith watched as her teacher read it through once more.

When she was done, a warm smile spread across her face. The woman knelt down, her long dress pooling atop her low-heeled shoes and in a conspiratorial whisper said, "I think that's one of the best answers I've ever read. And do you know what else I think?" Meredith shook her head with a sheepish blushing grin. "I think you'll reach that goal one day."

Then she winked, patted Meredith's hand as she gave the essay back, and stood up. She brushed the front of her dress and looked around the room for any other students that were done. None had worked as quickly as Meredith and not seeing any other students to help, she went back to her desk after telling Meredith to read quietly.

Meredith was too flattered to register the instruction. She only looked down at her paper with glowing pride and re-read what she had written. All the while her teacher's voice echoed warmly in her mind.

MY GOAL AS A GROWNUP

What I want to do when I grow up is to go to the island of Shri Lancka. I want to go there because Ms. Eggersby said that the animals and flowers that live there will probably die by the time I'm all grown up and I want to see them before that happens. I think it would be really neat to see all of the animals and flowers because I want to be able to tell my kids about how they looked because they will not be around for them. And that makes me sad. But it makes me happy to think that I will see them someday and be able to tell other people about them when they don't believe me that they used to be there.

Ever since that day, she had been obsessed with Sri Lanka. Ms. Eggersby's passion to help her students understand how much bigger the world is had rubbed off in the best way. Meredith knew, deep in her secret heart, that she had to visit Sri Lanka before she let life get in the way.

But like most people, her life became more than her fourth-grade goals. She always remembered that little assignment, kept the memory locked up inside her mind, floating in the back amidst a great number of her thoughts. As each birthday came and went, she felt a little bit of sadness creep into and discolor the glow of that memory. It became heavier, harder to hold on to without feeling an accompanying and unwelcome guilt.

She was becoming an adult, and with it, the childish attitude that overruled logic with possibility began to fade. She began to realize how difficult and expensive a trip like that could be, costing thousands of dollars and weeks of time away from work. Then, the Neo-Pagan wars began in her early adulthood and travelling anywhere for anyone was off the docket for the foreseeable future. If you cared about safety, that is.

Falling in love and marrying Evan had revitalized that dream a little, but with both of them freshly graduated from college and working long days to make ends meet, their dreams had to wait a little longer. In those early days of marriage when each person is either thinking of the other one naked or planning when the next time they'll both be naked, Meredith forgot her dream of visiting Sri Lanka. She forgot only for a little while, but it was the forgetting that made the remembering so difficult.

It wasn't that she forgot because it wasn't worth the mental energy to remember. She forgot because the wonder of the world had become normal. And, with much of the land spoiled due to one war or another or due to poor stewardship of the world's failing resources, the possibility of visiting an unspoiled haven shrunk, one nightly newsreel by one nightly newsreel.

One day, when the clouds threatened rain with brief gusts of chilly wind and the occasional wayward pellet of rain hit the window of her car, she decided on a whim to pull into the public library. She wasn't exactly sure why. But like Evan, she had fond memories of perusing the rows and rows of books, smelling old pages and peeking through the gaps between tomes to see who was on the other side. It was a bit of the romantic in her, she supposed as she walked up the steep stone steps flanked by two granite eagles.

When she entered through the glass doors, she told the woman at the desk that she wasn't a member, not as an adult at least. The woman told her that she could come back before leaving and pick up a library card if she would fill out a small square of paper asking name, address, and phone number.

Meredith took it and slipped it into her pocket without intending to fill it out. But she gave a polite nod and smile as the woman explained how simple it would be before thanking her and moving deeper into the rows of other people's imaginations.

She made her way through the library, marveling at how much shorter the shelves of books seemed. Thinking about it only briefly, she realized that she hadn't visited the library for a decade or more and began to understand that it was mostly due to her growth. She was taller now than she was then.

She smelled the air and was slightly disappointed that the smell she expected—old paper and aging wisdom—was sitting subtly beneath the crisp scent of purified air and manufactured flowers, most likely something to mask the musty smell that so often accompanied unread and unvisited corners of places like this. If she was honest with herself, she was surprised libraries existed. Everything had become digital, and the lack of current patrons told her that there were few times when a digital book wouldn't do.

She ran her hands down the vertical spines of the books as she passed them, reveling in the feeling of rough fabric and soft lettering that grazed her fingertips, and she smiled.

She happened to pass by a truly massive globe poised precariously above several empty children's tables. The chairs were miniature versions of those found in the adult side of the library and she chuckled. They were precious.

She glanced around then and realized that the tables themselves—devoid of any smiling and laughing children—sat atop a world map, square and intrepid in a muted inlay upon the floor.

Grinning to herself with the giddy discovery of a child, she walked onto the pale blue of the Atlantic Ocean and turned in a slow circle, taking in the vastness of the planet of which she was now master.

With her back to the Western Hemisphere, her toes poked into the west coast of Africa. She stopped. Her eyes had settled on a great green misshapen oval with thick black letters labeling it as "SRI LANKA" and her heart sank. She had a dream, once. A dream that she shared often with Evan in their early dating years but, more recently, had nearly resigned herself to the fact that it would happen "someday." And, like many adults, she was beginning to realize that she might "someday" herself into an early grave. *But isn't that adulthood? Having something you want and then working until you get it at the end of your life, so you appreciate it more?*

She stared at that island in the sea for what seemed like an hour before making her way to the front of the library and waving goodbye to the same woman who had greeted her. The small application for a library card, forgotten deep in her pocket, would come out in the wash as nothing more than a white crumble of dried lint.

Meredith left the library with a glowing sense of longing that hummed deep within her chest. She decided before starting the car that she needed to talk with Evan and revive her dream.

She drove without thinking. Her mind was busy moving through time, making its way to where and when the dream originated. Her consciousness, much like H.G. Wells described, traveled slowly through the fourth dimension, past fond timestamps of adventure and heart-wrenching blots of painful memories.

Ms. Eggersby, she found out that evening, died several years ago. Meredith had reached out to some of her old classmates and received back a notice from an old school friend who kept up with most of their class via Intersphere. That note also included an invitation to the 15-year class reunion. She and Evan didn't care about the invitation; they wouldn't have attended anyway. But the news of Ms. Eggersby's death had created a bright beam of light into her mind, and it revealed, in even greater, detail the goal she had set when she was nine. It seemed to wash away the guilt and regret that had built up along its edges like verdigris, showing in full the dream's heart: a trip to Sri Lanka to discover a few remaining vestiges of childhood wonder.

Meredith cried that night. In part for the loss of a wonderful and intellectual person whose one goal in life was to show every child she met that they were important and could become anything they worked for. But also in mourning of her goal to visit Sri Lanka and how it had become a pipe dream of sorts, something that she may eventually do but that most likely would remain an unfulfilled wish. She wanted to talk with Evan about it, but it was difficult to put into words what she was wanted specifically to talk about. Ms. Eggersby's passing? Her childhood dream passing from reality? Both?

Evan, usually sensitive to her emotions, had asked if she wanted to talk about what was bothering her. She did but didn't know how to verbalize what she felt. There was a jumble of emotions all tangled up inside of her heart. Yanking thoughtlessly on one string would tighten the intricate knot that she felt in her stomach and make it even more difficult to disentangle herself. She'd have to gently test each thread and tease every emotion from the rat's nest that was her mind. It would probably take a few days.

She didn't answer Evan but shook her head in the negative, instead. They were lying in bed, her head on his chest and his arm hugging her close to himself.

She felt his tight-lipped smile of understanding, and he squeezed her shoulder gently.

It was a wonder what years together could do for a couple. He knew that she would talk if she wanted. If he pushed her to talk about it, he risked either some measure of fighting and a few days of radio silence, or the radio silence while she worked it out for herself.

Her husband was smart in that regard. *Most of the time, at least*, she thought with half-hearted amusement.

Several days later, they sat down and talked about how she felt. She related her laments about unfulfilled dreams and childhood ignorance, all the while wishing she could simply stop feeling so sad about it.

Instead, she cried again. And again. The rawness of her emotions surprised even her.

She could tell it made Evan uncomfortable, but not because he was uncomfortable around expressed emotions. On the contrary, in fact. It was because there wasn't anything he could do about these tears now rolling down her red-dened cheeks.

Bless his heart.

Evan sat Meredith down a couple days after what she would have called a talk, but what Evan would have simply called "an emotional evening." It had been nearly a week since her library visit and her heart skipped a beat, worried that maybe something was wrong. Instead, he told her that they were going to Sri Lanka.

She thought that her ears were playing a cruel trick on her, and despite hearing the words, she couldn't believe them.

"We're going where?"

Her mind was still trying to process what he'd said, and the question was habit, without any expectation or under-standing of the answer to follow.

Evan, sitting across from her now at their kitchen table, had walked in with a carefree swing of his arms, kissed her cheek, and then sat down. He smiled now, resting his hand on hers with their knees touching and speaking slowly as if to avoid hurting someone who had begun to regain their hearing. "You and I are going to Sri Lanka."

Meredith stared. She heard the words. And her mind understood the individual letters making up the words, each with their own significance. But her heart couldn't accept them yet. "We're going to..." Her mind began catching up, now, and her heart rate followed suit. "We're going to..." It was racing now, absorbing the words, processing them. Then, full under-standing bloomed on her face and recognition dawned. Her heart and mind began celebrating them. Her heart jumped triumphantly in her chest, the blood it pumped seeming to gallop through her veins like wildfire.

She stood up suddenly, the chair falling forgotten behind her with a hollow metallic clatter, and Evan began to laugh. His laugh was a deep, throaty chuckle that surpassed simple mirth. It was filled simultaneously with both awestruck joy and a variation of the galloping freedom she felt within her own body.

Meredith nearly yelled it, now, as the full force of what he said slammed home in her conscious mind like block letters finally being seated within the wooden voids they were cut from. "We're going to Sri Lanka! Are you kidding? You're kidding. Are you serious? You're not, are you?" She turned from his laughter and put her hands on her head, her eyes wide as she paced back and forth, whispering the words "Sri Lanka" over and over like a secret prayer.

After several iterations of turning toward and away from Evan, she stopped and sat at the table again. "We're seriously going to Sri Lanka?" Her husband nodded. "When?"

"Our plane leaves in the morning. We'll need to drive to Tulsa and enjoy a few layovers, but it leaves in—" he checked his watch with a bit of a performance, "less than 16 hours."

The smile that spread across her face at this was more than a grin; it was more than Evan's special smile that she knew he loved the most about her. It was a smile that split her whole face, and when it couldn't get any bigger, she burst out laughing, tears coursing down her cheeks, and she didn't do anything to wipe them away. She threw her head back and laughed, the tears changing course and running down her temples as she laughed at the ceiling above.

She felt Evan move next to her, and she rested her head on his shoulder, the last few spasms of laughter spilling out of her mouth, and small dark spots appeared where her tears dropped onto his shirt. She loved the feel of him when he was that close, even more so now that her heart was full to bursting. The deep love she felt for him was amplified in this moment. High on adrenaline and expectation, she looked into his eyes and kissed him passionately. Their mouths couldn't completely close around one another's as their smiles didn't seem to want to leave their faces, and they ended up kissing each other's teeth a few times, initiating a few more rounds of giggles.

When they separated, Evan sighed and said with phony regret, "You know, the only reason I did it was to get some lovin' from you." He smacked his lips in a kind of apologetic smirk.

But as soon as he said it, Meredith could see instant regret, as if he'd said the only thing that could ruin her good mood. His tone had been thick with obvious sarcasm, but her husband was a sensitive one, and his humor often outweighed his forethought.

Before he could open his mouth again to insert his foot, Meredith smiled coyly and said, "Well, if that's the case, we should probably start packing. There's bound to be lots of lovin' on this trip, don't you think, Mr. Reader?" She looked at him from beneath her eyelids, adopting the same tone of phony regret he had used.

Normally, what he said would've put a sour taste in her mouth. She knew he was joking, but he—actually, men in general—were so *dumb* sometimes. It wasn't their fault that their brain hung between their legs, but lord god almighty, it was as if she had to think for the both of them.

This time, however, Evan's comments made her smile. He was a sensitive guy, and knowing that, she had to occasionally tailor her response. Not all the time, but the way she saw it, love was putting others before yourself. If changing up how she responded now and then helped him feel like he was an important part of her life and worth the effort, then it was a small change with a big reward. He did the same for her, she was certain. And in this moment, what did it hurt?

He didn't usually put himself in a position where his feelings could get hurt; he was a middle child after all. And so what if he wanted sex on this trip? Hell, she wanted sex on this trip. Realistically, he wanted sex most days. But it was a vacation for him too, wasn't it?

And to be completely honest with herself, the sex they did have was very good, having nurtured her sexuality with Evan alongside her love for him. She hadn't slept around all through school and college. Evan had been her first and continued to be her one and only, which was extremely rare. That was something she held dear to her heart and looked forward to many more years of "lovin" as he called it.

She smiled, coming back to herself and looking at him. "Let's get packing, then?"

Evan responded with a relieved smile, understanding that he hadn't stepped on an unseen landmine with his rather weak and flippant attempt at flirting, and nodded. "Yes, let's get packing. That plane won't wait for us, you know."

With that, they stood up, and Meredith wrapped her arms around her husband, their faces no more than a couple of inches away from each other.

"I love you, you know. I think you also know how much this means to me, and I am a little surprised that you set all this up without me knowing, but I'm not at all surprised that you thought of it. You're a sweetheart, and I love you. I'll have to call into work." The last was a very adult thought that spoiled the mood only a little.

Evan shook his head, his face splitting into a self-satisfied grin. "No, you won't. I called your boss, explained what we were doing, and she completely understood. You had the days for it anyway, so they'll all be paid vacation."

She sighed with relief and not a small measure of disbelief as well. The weight of planning something and taking care of the details lifted, and she felt free as a bird. As she thought about it, she was surprised a little to find herself more than a little aroused as well.

"I love you to death, Evan Reader."

She gently kissed his lips, and he wrapped his arms snugly around her with comforting firmness.

Then they walked upstairs, hands swinging genially with each step they took toward the bedroom. Evan began his search for their suitcases in the closet. As he reached up to the top shelf of their closet to retrieve their suitcases, she slid her arms seductively around his waist and ventured slightly below the waistline of his jeans with her fingertips.

She hugged him tightly, rubbing his stomach and chest while her breasts pressed firmly against his back. She could feel his body immediately tense in response and then relax to a state that she recognized and welcomed. It was a state of expectation and longing, one only she could fulfill for her husband.

She spoke into his back, her voice muffled by his shirt but still caressing his stomach and beltline seductively. "I think the suitcases can wait a little bit, don't you?"

She heard him swallow, a faint *click* sounding deep in his dry throat.

"Yeah they can, I think." He responded to her by turning and wrapping his own arms around her, then kissing her gently. They moved toward the bed, a small part of her focused on the passion moving between their lips and hands and the rest focused on moving carefully to avoid tripping backward *before* they made it to the bed.

The bags were fully packed later that evening, and they went to bed early to get a pleasant start on the day. They both slept soundly and, Meredith could assume, were both content with sexual satisfaction and an air of expectation.

While they packed and for most of the evening, she had noticed a piece of paper clenched in Evan's hand. As they gathered the few remaining items for the trip—a pair of shoes, the toothbrush and toothpaste—she saw the same crumbled paper in his hand. She tried to sneak a glance at it, but Evan clutched it protectively to his chest the moment she tried to snatch it, the writing hidden behind his hand.

Eventually, after a small amount of coy petulance and teasing, she coaxed him into letting her see. And Evan, with only slight embarrassment, revealed to her the writing scrawled across the small slip of paper.

At the top, dark words written in his half-cursive and half-print writing spelled out "To Do Before We Leave for That Place." He hastily explained to her that the list was started before the big reveal, and if by some stroke of bad luck, she had found it prior to, the title kept the destination a secret.

It stunned her that he was carrying around a list at all. Not only that, but also it turned her heart to butter in the sun. Bless him, but if she told him to go get milk, eggs, and bread at the grocery store, he would call within ten minutes and ask what the third thing was. Unless, she learned, he wrote it down. Many times, he would write something down, and from that point on, he wouldn't look at the list again. She had a sneaking suspicion that had something to do with being a middle child but didn't want to push it or make him self-conscious about something that he had no control over. Conversations about family were hard enough without adding in another "this is why you're like this" conversation.

She laughed good-naturedly with him about his list, and she kissed him again. She was giddy with excitement and part of her felt like she was ten years younger. She enjoyed feeling like this, especially with Evan. Life sometimes became so hectic that at times, Meredith felt that the only side he saw of her was the stressed-out version. It wasn't always fair, and she knew that. She wasn't sure how she was supposed to fix it but made a mental note to bring it up on their vacation. What better time to discuss life with distractions than when all distractions were gone? She also wanted to address some of her husband's own difficulties. There were times when his brightness seemed to fade—not by a large degree but enough that she noticed. A time when he would normally have laughed, he only smiled weakly. Other times, he was filled with such frustration at a minor inconvenience or an item misplaced that she wondered what *truly* bothered him. But, when she'd ask, he'd assure her that he was just tired or had a long day. But to her, his dimming felt like it came from somewhere much deeper within, somewhere that no matter what she said or did, she'd never be able to approach that place.

Despite that, Meredith adored her husband. The fact that he hadn't quite lost the child-like wonder that so many adults seemed to grow out of was a constant reminder to her of what the world *could* be. Sometimes his uncanny ability to take a serious situation and turn it into something else entirely, while still protecting the heart of whatever it was they were doing, brought cheer and no small measure of adventure to their fairly normal adult lives. Whether it was some business-like meeting they would attend or a dinner with friends, his heart was always in the right place, and he worked tirelessly to spread joy to those around it. The way she saw it, he had so much joy in life that it overflowed, and there was nothing he could do but share it with those nearby.

As they made their way to the airport through the early morning gray, they continued to smile at one another and hold hands like teenagers; his right hand clutched between both of her hands while her knees were drawn up and cocked sideways toward him.

Although she was tired, her brain was electrified with the possibilities ahead. There wasn't any room to think about anything but getting to Sri Lanka and exploring every inch of it. She was already researching what to do, and while Evan was much more of the type to simply "wake up and go do things," she wanted desperately to have a plan so that they could get the most out of the trip. Afterall, it was likely to be their only trip like this, at least for a long time.

In fact, he had made her promise that there would be some breaks between activities, even if it was as simple as sitting on the beach for a few hours. And she had promised. It wasn't a difficult promise to make. *Lie on the beach and do nothing? Yes, please.*

Now, she sat on a plane that had flown from Tulsa, Oklahoma to O'Hare airport in Chicago. Then, they had a connecting flight from Chicago to Hamad International Airport in Qatar. From there, the last flight would take them the last few hours to land in Katunayake, Sri Lanka. The trip was long, over 26 hours with a 6-hour layover in Chicago and a 2-hour layover in Qatar. The few hours' sleep she'd been able to catch during layovers or flights had helped take the edge off her exhaustion, but she was close now. She was almost to the place that she'd secreted away in her heart all those years ago, and she could feel a kind of excited static coursing up and down her arms and spine. The dream of going to Sri Lanka had been overgrown with responsibility and adult commitments to work and friends. After she'd washed it off and cleared away the proverbial ivy, it shone in her mind like a beacon, placed lovingly on a pedestal by her fourth-grade self.

She kept whispering to herself that she was actually going, and sweet Evan, no matter how many times she clarified to him, continued to look at her and ask groggily, "What's that, hon?" She'd put her hand on his cheek or pat his thigh and say, "Nothing, babe. Just thinking out loud." It was sweet that he was trying his best not to ignore her when all he really wanted to do was sleep or watch the in-flight movie, but she was able to maintain at least the idea that she wasn't annoyed that he kept on.

She couldn't tear her eyes away from the dark sky out her window. Tiny lights passed below as they passed unseen above, and she marveled at the world and how, after all these years and all these wars and atrocities, there was still some magic hidden within it.

She didn't know how long she stared at the passing mountains and rivers below, but the sky had lightened considerably when she blinked away the haze of it. She turned her head to look at her husband, his face relaxed in the deepness of sleep and head lolled to one side. The pressurized cabin was quiet. Almost everyone was asleep, and those that weren't were staring out the window like she was or moving quietly in their own seats reading or watching the screens in front of them. The peaceful silence was welcome, and she wanted to wrap herself in it, in them both. The wan light from the cabin washed her lover's face in a dull orange glow. It highlighted his cheekbones and jaw in such a way that reminded her of why she had been so attracted to him in the first place. He was solid, a firmness while the world seemed to turn around him. He'd never been terribly muscular, but he was muscular enough for her. She enjoyed the emotional stability he provided for her. He was solid in his beliefs but not unquestioning. He was strong in his dedication but not blind to his own biases.

She leaned over and brushed his lips with hers before pulling her arm back through his. She reached into her carry on for her phone and pulled up the message center. She scrolled until she found the 15-year reunion invitation she'd received weeks before. She scrolled past the bulk of the message but stopped when she got to the part about Ms. Eggersby's passing. Minutes before they'd left, she had hurriedly printed out the picture of the message and put it in her carry-on while Evan did everything but tap his foot and check his watch impatiently on the porch, their luggage already loaded and the car waiting for the two of them to get in and drive. When she finally did sweep out of the door, she had a good idea of what she was going to do, and she did it smiling.

Now in the stillness that encircled her in arms of quiet, she began writing a letter to Ms. Eggersby. Her pencil made soft swishing noises while the clouds whipped silently past her window, and her husband breathed deeply beside her. It wasn't a long letter, only a single page telling her how much her teacher's tutelage—well, it was actually more of her love—meant to her. Meredith wrote a bit about how her attitude toward life would be different if it weren't for her and ended with a simple and tear-filled "thank you."

She folded it up with the picture she had printed before they left and stuck it into an envelope. She hadn't exactly settled on what she would do with it, but she believed it to be an important part of the trip. No, it was more than that. It seemed the *purpose* of the trip, in some strange way. As if this trip had been pre-destined before the dawn of time.

She smiled ruefully to herself. Maybe not since before the dawn of time but certainly since fourth grade. Ms. Eggersby was the inspiration for this trip, after all, and it felt right to have her along, even if it was only in spirit.

Feeling a sense of peace as the letter rested quietly in the bag at her feet, she slept.

Both of them woke up a little less than an hour before landing in Katunayake. They could both tell that the jet lag was getting to them. As soon as the two-hour commute from the airport to their resort was done, they both stumbled and fumbled their way to their rooms and crawled beneath the covers. Evan was asleep almost instantly; she could tell by his deep sigh that preceded his still and steady breathing. She was asleep only moments later, her hand resting gently on his, their fingers intertwined intimately.

The last day had been little more than a blurred line running along the time zones. They didn't wake up until thirteen hours later, when the sun was starting to yawn above the horizon, spreading its glorious light and warmth across the trees and distant horizon upon sea.

CHAPTER 12

While the tears began to dry on her cheeks, not a word passed between the two figures sitting feet apart. Evan and Meredith only looked at each other, the word "everything" still echoing across the unseen walls around them. The Irish breeze ruffled their hair and caressed the two of them playfully. But their eyes were locked on one another's. A tension rose in the air, and Meredith could almost feel its tensile strength press upon her chest.

Evan swallowed and broke the silence first. "I don't understand. I'm so confused right now." He ran a hand through his hair, glancing around his feet.

Meredith knew there was so much she needed to tell him, so much she *wanted* to tell him, some of it may need to be screamed at him, but for now, she recognized the need to start at the beginning.

She cleared her throat primly and swallowed hard. "Okay. Let's start in Sri Lanka with the first day, and then we'll talk about the next day, when the initial earthquake hit and tsunami that followed.

"That first day, after we woke up from a jet-lagged nap, we spent most of the time at the beach."

Evan nodded. "Yeah, I remember it. It was a gorgeous day. But didn't we do something else? Something to do with an envelope or something?"

Meredith grinned at him affectionately. "That's right. We did. I wasn't sure it would be important enough for you to remember."

He cocked his head at her in question.

She raced to assure him, "No, that's not what I meant." And she laughed lightly. "I don't mean it wasn't important to you. I know you say all the time, 'If it's important to you, it's important to me.' I mean that it was something *very* important to me, but something you weren't involved much in. I'm glad you remember.

"Anyway, we took a letter I'd written into a park—well more like a bench in a grove of trees—and together we buried it at the base of a banyan tree."

Evan snapped his fingers in recognition. "That's right! It was a letter to an old teacher, right? Ms. Yolk or something?" He laughed at this, knowing it couldn't be right, and she followed along.

"Close, honey. Ms. Eggersby."

"Ah, I knew it was something to do with eggs. I was close."

"You were," she said, smiling at how he really hadn't changed at all. "Anyway, that pretty much summed up the first day. We went to the beach afterward, and I watched you play in the water for a little while."

"You joined me. Eventually I was able to convince you to get your hair wet." He continued to smile at her, and she returned the smile.

"Yes, you did convince me. I remember." Her smile faltered a little. "That was a good day, Evan. I loved it. I loved how you showed up, just like you always do, and made that letter important to you as well. You were so understanding that day, and I don't know if I ever told you how much I appreciated and loved you even more for it."

Evan looked down, and she saw the pink begin to suffuse his cheeks in a flush. "That means a lot to me, Meredith. I'm so glad you felt that."

She rearranged her dress, and she felt the lightness of the conversation flee as she prepared to move to that next fateful day.

"When you left that next morning, I stayed at the resort. You know that already. What you don't know, what you probably would never have known, was that I actually left the resort while you were gone."

She noticed Evan sit up a little straighter, something between curiosity and suspicion passing over his face like a ghostly vapor.

"I wanted to get you something, a 'happy present' for planning this all out and keeping it a secret from me. I'm sure that was no small feat." He returned the small smile she gave, knowing that not only could he not keep a secret, but he was also the self-proclaimed World's Worst Planner.

She continued, encouraged by his small smile. "I took a bus with several other people from the resort and headed up the coast toward Colombo. Obviously, it was a longer trip, and the city there was much bigger than Deiyandara or Akuressa, where you went. On the way there, however, our bus nearly hit a deer on the road, and when the bus swerved, we blew a tire. We were stranded for an hour while they tried to fix it.

"While we were stranded, though, I had a chance to get to know some of the other people in the group. There was an old married couple who were about as cute as could be with their matching tropical shirts and straw hats. They were adorable.

Louis and Louisa, if you can believe it. They had been married fifty years, Evan. Fifty!" She held up ten fingers, knowing it didn't mean fifty but also knowing he would understand that was what she meant, and he smiled again at her, understanding the gesture, she was certain.

"There was also a guy with his girlfriend, and they were very sweet on each other. Actually, they were more involved in each other than getting to know the rest of us, which was fine. They sucked each other's faces most of the trip and snuck off during the tire change to do something dirty, I'm sure. Part of me wonders if they were close to being eaten by the wildlife at any point," she mused dreamily. "We only caught their names once during the introduction of the outing, Donny and Vera.

"They both struck me as 'fancy,' you know, the types who buy Louis Vuitton handbags and have mimosas brought to them poolside by a handsome guy named Diego."

She laughed a little, and Evan continued to smile at her. She knew he loved her smile, and her laugh, and it cheered her a little to see his own.

She continued, "The other three people on the trip were two women, a mother and her daughter, and then the daughter's husband. The mother's name was Carol, the daughter was Paula, and her husband's name was Eric. They were nice enough although I caught some eye rolls from Eric while Carol related stories of her own life every time there was a lull in the conversation during the trip. I'm fairly certain, now, that Paula had invited her mother out of sheer guilt, and it had gone directly against what Eric wanted for them."

Meredith suddenly burst out laughing, the sound of it echoing out across the grassy expanse around them. "At one point, Carol was telling us—well, talking *at* us, really—about how hard it was during Paula's life and how her 'no-good, dirty rotten alcoholic husband' had made their lives even harder. Well, Eric had enough, and he heaved an enormous sigh and said— here she affected a deep, exaggeratedly manly voice, "'Goddammit, Carol, it's probably because he could pass out from drinking and didn't have to hear you talk anymore. Jesus, Mary, and Joseph.' Carol was shocked, and Paula, too, though she did smile a tiny bit when her mother clamped her mouth shut and avoided eye contact with anyone. I felt a little sorry for her embarrassment but..." Meredith leaned in conspiratorially, "...she was *so loud.*"

She stared at him briefly before continuing. "After getting to know them a little better, things began to feel more natural. Conversation flowed, people piped into someone else's story, and jokes were tossed about here and there. It started to feel more like a group of friends than strangers. But truth be told, I missed having you with me. You would have loved the group. And you would have fit right in, I'm sure." Meredith laughed, and Evan laughed with her. She remembered some of the moments when one of the others would say something, and she'd begin to explain how Evan would have responded to the same situation. It was fun, but it wasn't complete without him there.

"During the downtime when the tire was being fixed, Donny and Vera stood in the shade of the van. Vera had some sort of paper fanning herself relentlessly while Donny took long drags on a cigarette, squinting his eyes as he did so, then pointing the smoke to the sky when he'd exhale. It was all very ostentatious.

"The mechanic who was apparently along for just such an occasion announced that they were nearly done, which was exactly when we felt the ground tremble beneath us. It wasn't what I'd consider an earthquake. It was sort of a shudder that traveled past us. Everyone felt it, but we were silent, still as statues, and despite the flocks of birds that suddenly took wing, squalling with what sounded like raucous laughter and noise, even the jungle was quiet.

"We stared at each other, part stunned disbelief and part waiting for someone to tell us that what we were thinking right then was wrong. It wasn't an earthquake at all. Perhaps it was a low-flying plane that we'd missed."

Meredith shook her head and looked down at her hands. "Obviously, that wasn't the case. Both the mechanic and driver jumped into action and double-timed it to fix the tire, cursing and barking at each other when one of them didn't move fast enough. When it was repaired and we were back on the bus, we got moving again. But instead of heading to Colombo, they turned back and began to head to the resort."

She heaved a small and heavy sigh, pulling a stray lock of hair that was fluttering in the breeze back behind her ear. In her lap, her fingers twisted idly around one another in a mesmerizing, constant fluid motion.

When she spoke, it was in a thick whisper. "I'm not sure what would be different had we continued on to Colombo, but I know things *would be* different."

She sat silently and tried to calm her hands, which had begun to hurt from moving so rapidly. She felt Evan move closer to her and enclose her hands in his. Remarkable, that she could feel him. Close, warm, and *here*. Finally here.

She smiled up at him, a smile that he returned with both soft understanding and discerning patience.

"As we were pulling into Matara, the tsunami was announced, and everyone warned that it would be making landfall shortly, within the hour. There was chatter about how large it was and how large it could be, but none of the transmissions we heard described it as terrible as it would be. Traffic was understandable awful, as I'm sure you know, and we were merely one of the hundreds of vehicles idling while the wave marched indifferently up the beach and over the city."

She looked up at Evan as a motion caught her eye. He was rubbing his mouth with his hand, something he did when he wanted to say something but knew it would either interrupt or be irrelevant. She waited for him to speak, but when he shook his head in the negative and said, "Never mind," she continued.

"Everyone in the bus was scared. I mean there were only a few of us, but even the two lovers had taken their hands off one another long enough to look out the windows toward the ocean. The water had receded quite a bit. It left behind a sodden field of sandy dunes. Here and there smaller puddles of seawater stood still, shining like aluminum pools in the mid-morning sun, but the rest of the ocean simply packed up and left town.

"The most terrible thing, I think, was not only that we weren't moving, but that people on foot were moving around us, streaming around the bus almost like water. It would shortly do that, too." She took a steadying breath. The memory that she had buried beneath pain, regret, and anger was slowly rising to the surface. And like horses carrying a cart full of baggage, they brought those unwelcome underlying emotions along with it.

When she began again, she could feel the sting of tears in her eyes and willed them away. It was getting more difficult to tell the story, and she wasn't sure she'd even be able to finish it.

"It was Eric's idea to actually get out of the van. The shouts of the crowd around us, the horns and warning sirens swallowed us; we couldn't even talk to each other. But he stood up, and above the noise said 'Alright, that's it. Let's offload this shit-heap and get somewhere safer.' His voice was commanding, and part of me wondered, even then, if he had been military at some point. The Army or something like it. I never got the chance to find out, unfortunately, but I'll get to that.

"Everyone was in agreement. We scrambled to get our belongings as quickly as we could, helping whoever needed it. Seeing as it was only supposed to be a short trip, there wasn't much to gather up." The theme from the old Gilligan's Island show popped into her head, making the corners of her mouth tug into a brief smile at "a three-hour tour," but her humor was overshadowed by the tear that began its slow glide across her cheek.

She shook her head to refocus and continued, briskly wiping the tears away. "I only had my purse, so I helped Louisa down the steps and out the bus door. By now, there were so many people that it reminded me of a mob chasing down a mega sale or something. It was insanity, anarchy, even. We were the last off, other than Louis, Louisa's husband. The driver, Rashmi, tried helping Louis. I turned around to see if they needed help, and at the same instant, Louisa was clipped by the surge of people running by. I was holding her hand, but the force that hit her ... it was too much for both of us. The crowd didn't split around her, which admittedly is what I hoped would happen. But you know what happens to a panicked mob; they're in survival mode. Instead, the people surrounding us—and where Louisa fell—seemed to briefly pulse. There was a pause in the passing crowd, but there were so many people that I couldn't make my way through them to get to her. It was an impenetrable wall of bodies." Meredith wiped her eyes as larger tears began to swell in them.

"The worst part was that even through the tumult and the shouts and cries of everything going on around us, I could faintly hear her crying and calling for help not five feet from me. But she might as well have been a mile from me." She hated how shaky her voice had become, a large lump had formed above her collarbone that she couldn't swallow or shake loose.

"Louis tried to go to her, but Rashmi held him back. The people charging past us didn't even seem to hear her. In hindsight, I guess they probably didn't. Hers was just another crying voice among the thousands of other crying voices. But surely they felt her when they stepped over her. Didn't they?"

The question was, of course, rhetorical. She knew they heard her. She knew that the people who walked over her knew what they were doing, but they didn't care. They didn't care what the consequences of their own actions were apart from getting themselves to safety. As long as they were safe, nothing else mattered. No one else mattered.

To her immense relief, Evan squeezed her hands. The pressure there was enough to help anchor her, and she licked her lips to try and continue again.

"When the rest of the group was out of the van—we all pressed ourselves against the side of it—Rashmi, Louis, and Eric tried to muscle their way through the crowd. They were big enough men that people noticed them, at least, and let them through.

"Louisa was dead by then, I think. I didn't see her, but Louis, I could see Louis' shoulders shaking up and down, sobbing, and I saw Rashmi put his hands on his head and shout what sounded like a prayer of some kind. Three of them went through the crowd, but only two came back to us. They said that Louis wanted to stay by his wife and wouldn't listen to anything about the tsunami. We had heard on the radio that it was on its way. Through the mass of dark bodies streaming past us, I caught flashes of the old couple's bright blue and pink tropical shirts. But I didn't ever get a clear view of them, which I conceded was probably for the best. Thank god for small favors, I guess. That was the last time I saw that sweet old couple.

"Knowing we couldn't do anything for them, Rashmi and Eric led the rest of us into the crowd. We all held hands, and as long as we let the crowd carry us, we didn't run into any problems. No one charged through to separate us, thankfully. We stumbled along with the rest of them, moving through the streets, but by now, the initial influx of fleeing bodies had created a bottleneck where we now stood, and we had no choice but to stop.

"I remember looking over my shoulder to try and get an idea of what was happening behind us. I could see the beach and at first, I didn't understand what I was seeing. The water—now returning—seemed to be growing, or swelling, I don't even know how to describe it. It was an odd thing, but it was as if someone had begun to pour thick viscous liquid onto a table. It didn't stream everywhere at once, it inched forward and oozed around objects in its path. That's what the water was like, and I stood there with everyone else, transfixed." Meredith shivered with sudden mnemonic chills, and Evan squeezed her hand reassuringly. It was incredible that she could actually feel him there, that this whole Bench Pod let her feel him again.

"It may have looked slow, but even as we watched, it was rising and getting closer. Other people saw it too, and then, nearly everyone began to panic. Some people began running back the way we had come. I guess to try and make their way around the group, but most people surged forward, pressing in on those around them to hurry them along. I'm certain there were some people that were killed in that single moment because of the unbelievable weight of hundreds of bodies moving in unison toward a single point, smashing those at the front if they didn't move fast enough. Which I'm sure they didn't.

"Rashmi told the rest of the group—well, he told Eric and we were close enough to hear him—that there was a road nearby that went straight north, toward the center of the island. The only problem was that it was a bit of a hill before leveling out. He figured that would be the safest place to go, and it would help avoid the bulk of city traffic.

"He led the way, cutting perpendicular through the crowds. I think all of us were still holding hands. Rashmi held Carol's hand, Carol held Eric's, and he held Paula's. I held as tight as I could onto hers, and I know Vera was crying by the sniffles and sobs coming from behind me. She was holding my hand, and Donny was in the back holding hers.

"As good an idea as it was, we never made it to the road that would lead us up the hill. There were too many cars and vans blocking too many of the paths, and we had to stop at an intersection. It looked as if someone had tossed a bucket of toy cars onto the floor and left scattered there, haphazardly in the street.

"When I looked back toward the beach again, it wasn't there anymore. Now, it was a dark, swirling mass that was creeping down the streets and between buildings, like liquid tentacles stretching toward us. People started jumping on top of cars and climbing up the sides of buildings to get to the roof. We were surrounded by innumerable people clambering across every surface to get to safety. Rashmi had the same idea, and when the first bit of water soaked the street a hundred yards away, he jumped onto the hood of a yellow car and began to help the rest of us up. I don't remember what kind of car it was. I suppose it doesn't even matter, but it was low to the ground and large enough to hold seven people on the hood and roof, which is no doubt what saved my life."

Meredith took a long pause here. Remembering this part in particular was terribly difficult, nearly impossible. This was one part she had wanted Hazed from her memory, a long and expensive process of making a set of memories blurry in order to numb the emotion associated with them. In the end, she opted for therapy. After it was all said and done, she was happy with her choice. While it ended up costing more, it also brought more closure along with it.

"The water just kept coming. If not for my terror, I think I could have seen it as impressive. Even now, a lifetime later, it's hard to step back from it, and see it as anything other than a tremendously horrible disaster.

"Where the street had been ten seconds ago was now a frothing, raging river, and it was only rising higher. Rashmi had climbed onto the hood of a larger van adjacent to us. Carol and Paula were being pulled up while Eric pushed from below. The water had risen now to his knees and was swirling around them. At one point, he lost his footing and was nearly swept under. If not for the hood ornament that he grabbed at the last second to regain his footing, he would have been lost. He jumped up onto the hood and rested on the windshield of the car, the lower half of his shirt stained dark with the filthy water that sloshed around him and continued to rise.

"The wave from the beach started to lift and rearrange the cars. They were slowly being corralled down the street and in our direction; like reincarnated bodies, they moved in jerky, unfamiliar ways. The yellow car we were standing on was shuddering, and I felt it do a sort of jitter along the sub-merged street as grimy water began splashing across the hood. With the looks that Eric and Rashmi were giving each other, I knew we only had a few seconds before the force of the water pushed it down the road with the rest of the debris."

Meredith found herself unable to continue. She could feel the lump in her throat bobbing as she tried to swallow back the emotion. She was irritated with herself, feeling the weight of her emotions always seeming to get the better of her. She wanted to tell this story; she *needed* to tell this story. But she couldn't. She could tell she'd reached the end of her mental and emotional capacity, as if she had been emptying her memories from a watering can and the bucket into which she'd been pouring was full. There was no more space.

"I'm sorry, Evan. I can't keep telling you."

She said this through a thickness in her throat and with tears quivering in her eyes, threatening to spill down her cheeks. "I'll have to show you."

She pulled her hands from beneath his and made some quick finger movements on her wrist. A screen popped into existence as she cued up the memory from her SafetyChip and let it play for Evan in a way that mere words could never convey. The memory was recorded in haunting detail.

Evan sat forward on The Bench, rapt with attention. She watched him instead of the vid. She'd seen this one before.

She watched as Evan's eyes moved rapidly, trying to merge the details of her story and the details of the memory playing before him. Her eyes moved down across his cheeks and unruly beard. She missed that scruff. She missed nuzzling it in the mornings. Though more often than not, she moved her face *away* from his because it was tickling or poking her skin. She missed his jawline, the way he clenched it when he was either trying not to laugh or trying not to cry. He was everything to her, and she missed it all.

She glanced back at the screen—it was a window hovering several feet above the ground and showed everything in flawless recollection, terrible as it was.

It was as shaky as she remembered it, too. She could hear herself breathing heavily in the vid in front of her, and it echoed in her own mind, like feedback from a speaker too close to the microphone.

Donny, in a shirt unbuttoned to his waist, was holding onto Vera, whose previously impeccable skin-tight white capris and matching white blouse were now splashed with muck and water. He was grunting with the effort and, through clenched teeth, could be heard yelling "Come on, Vera. Come on!" He pulled her toward the same van where a dark-skinned man in a red fez cap was kneeling, holding onto a woman who was a few years shy of elderly, her silver hair matted to her face and unable to hide the terror beneath. It was Rashmi, pulling Carol up to the roof of the van.

Donny tensed briefly, then deftly placed Vera onto his shoulders with little more than a puffing of his cheeks. His look of concentration, however, blazed beneath sprays of filthy water and sweat. He was shouting to be heard above the noise, and perhaps a touch of both frustration and fear. "You're going to have to jump, Vera. I'm going to help you up there, but you've got to grab the roof rack and hang on. I'll be up in after you." His voice was deep and rough, even with the sounds of the drowning city beneath him, she had to strain her ears to hear.

Vera began to protest in a hysterical wail, "Donny, no! Don't do that! I can't!"

But either he didn't hear her, or he didn't care. He bent his knees and rose again, then did it once more. She realized what he was doing too late. She also knew she couldn't do anything to stop him; he'd committed to the act. Donny, in a burst of motion that Meredith to this day couldn't understand, appeared to try and launch Vera, screaming, from his shoulders and onto the roof of the adjacent van where Rashmi was now hauling Carol to safety.

While Meredith was privy to the ending, she desperately wanted to defend her little group by telling Evan, "I'm not saying it was stupid; anything was better than nothing, and we were all getting pretty desperate at that point." She didn't say it, though. She couldn't say it. She couldn't interrupt the perverse eulogy that was playing out for the people she'd met that day. So, she settled back against The Bench to relive again what she'd relived a hundred times before.

Either Donny had miscalculated his own strength or the stability of the car beneath him, perhaps both. His foot slid sideways on the roof of the car. At the same time, his legs and torso began an odd little jig as he tried to regain his balance. His leg, continuing to slide, plunged into the gap between the two cars and splashed into the tumultuous froth below, sending his backside crashing with a *wump* on the yellow roof.

Vera hit her head on the on the sideview mirror as they both fell, a slash of bright red appeared briefly before she was flailing beneath the roiling water.

All of this happened in less than a second. Their little party stared, transfixed. Donny's cursing screams could be heard over the splashing water. He tried to get up but because of the angle he fell and the force of the water, he was trapped between the white van where Rashmi, Paula, and Carol now huddled, and the yellow car where Meredith and Eric stared dumbly, no doubt trying to piece together some plan of rescue but rooted helplessly to the spot, instead.

She looked from one person to another, chilly water splashing around her ankles, a creeping chill making its way up her calves. Vera could be seen screaming for help and splashing in the water, a pale pink rivulet of blood skittering across her face as the water tried to wash it away as she failed repeatedly to grab anything around her. Then, she looked back to Donny, splashing and gurgling the putrid water as he tried to keep his head above the spraying. She looked back to Vera, now spinning wildly through the water, bouncing violently off large pieces of debris tumbling through the water. Her repeated cries for help were swallowed by the water because she could do little but gulp it down in mouthfuls.

Donny, for the moment, was in a safer position than Vera, who was being swept nearer death's door by the second. Meredith's eyes were fixated on the woman, whose bouncy black curls had been done professionally only hours before. The white blouse with the plunging neckline was the color of death now, black streaks of sin across the previously pure white. The panic in the woman's eyes was palpable every time her body spun back to face her acquaintances, the whites showing amidst a mask of dark water that ran persistently into her screaming mouth.

Vera had gone dozens of yards in only a couple of seconds and was nearing the side of a tall white office building. The lower windows had been blown out by the force of the tsunami and chunks of the building had been washed away, revealing rebar that stuck out like tiny wire bones. Meredith watched in stunned dismay; the horror she felt bubbled up from her stomach like the roiling water bathing her feet. The fear clawed at her throat and threatened to make her retch.

Vera, now little more than a bobbing, pastel speck in the dark water, was shoved relentlessly through that force that can only be described as primal wrath. She continued to scream at Donny and the rest of them, reaching when she was above the water for a second, but her attempts were lethargic. She must have known it was all coming to an end. And then it did. Vera slammed ferociously into the corner of the building where some of the rebar stuck out of the building. Her final shriek came out as a sickening squeal as all the air was forced from her body as her dirty white shirt sprouted several metal spikes.

Meredith screamed and tried to look away. In the safety of her own mind, she tried to convince herself there was nothing she could have done. Even still, she could only stare as Vera's head bobbed on the surface. Her arms trailed through the water, following its current without any resistance. Meredith's body began to tremble, then shake. Her fingertips were numb and the sound around her began to fade into a single ringing note.

Sound returned with the sudden realization that Donny was still trapped, screams and splashing sounds hit her like a hammer, and she moved her eyes with such dizzying speed that she put a hand to her head. No doubt her body was pumping adrenaline to keep her from fainting, but she could feel a dreadful darkness beneath it all.

Donny, in the last twenty seconds of Vera's life, continued to struggle between the two cars.

"Will one of you bastards help me up?" He was yelling and desperately holding out a hand, but there wasn't much help to be offered from the group. One of his legs was cocked behind and beneath him on the hood in splashing water up to his crotch. The other was wedged tightly between the cars. Even then she wasn't sure if it was truly crushed between the two vehicles, but instinctively knew it wouldn't matter in a few seconds.

Eric, who had been helping Paula and Carol get up to Rashmi, knelt down and tried to pull Donny up from between the vehicles. Meredith wiped sopping hair out of her eyes and did the same. Eric grabbed Donny beneath the armpits and braced himself against the other car. Meredith grabbed one of his free hands and pulled with all her might.

Eric's groans began to build into screams of effort. Meredith could feel tears of effort and powerlessness spring from her eyes. Donny began to scream as well as his leg began to rise out of the water inch by inch.

Finally, it jerked free, nearly spilling Eric into the water behind them, but he was able to steady himself and quickly got to his feet. Meredith stood, her head swimming with that dimness that threatened to overtake her. She shook it away, spraying water from her hair as she did so.

Once more, Eric grabbed Meredith's arm—gently but firmly—and said, "Your turn, Meredith." He let go of her arm and laced his fingers together, making a step for her. The rest of their group reached down, shouting encouragement to her. She glanced at Donny who was staring around wildly, like a horse that was spooked and trying with all its might to retain its training. When his eyes found Vera, pinned and bobbing against that white building, he screamed and grabbed his slick black hair.

"Oh God, no. No, no, no! Vera! God dammit. Son of a bitch. No! Vera!" Donny lost all sanity then and repeating her name in a ranting jumble of sounds, leapt into the raging currents below them. Meredith and Eric both reached for him and missed, Eric managing to grab part of his shirt, but it was no use, Donny had committed himself to his Vera.

They watched him splash into the water and disappear beneath the surface. He appeared briefly once more between Vera and themselves, but they never saw him again.

Meredith could feel shock steal the feeling from her fingertips. Her hands began shaking and the sounds around her began to fade as the edges of her vision darkened. She felt her grip on reality slipping and it was quiet in the dark.

Hands gripped her arms firmly and sound began to return.

"Meredith! Hey! Meredith!" It was a man's voice, firm and fearful. Pain blossomed on her cheek, and her head rocketed backward. The hat she'd been wearing fell into the water, forgotten in the chaos. Her eyes refocused on the figure before her and feeling began to creep its way into her hands and feet.

Water, she thought groggily. Then, *water!* And she was back. The cold water had risen incrementally and was covering the car that she and Eric now stood upon. He was staring at her intently with a look of relief and, what was that, regret? She brought a hand up to her stinging face.

"I'm sorry, Meredith. I didn't know what else to do!"

She nodded and swallowed, pushing the disbelief and incredulity away. "It's okay, Eric. It's fine."

She squinted up briefly at Paula, Carol, and Rashmi. The last of that small contingent of survivors. All of them were now reaching down toward her, Rashmi's hand shaking with punctuated shouts for her to grab on. She looked one final time to Eric, who was gesturing for her to get into his hands, laced together at the splashing water near his knees.

The sounds around them had taken on the likeness of screaming souls caught in a terrible vortex, savagely funneled down to unimaginable torment for eternity. The wind whipped around the small band of survivors, fiercely grasping at wayward strands of hair and shirtsleeves that weren't already plastered to her arms.

"I'll boost you!" Eric cried loudly as she stepped into his hands, working to keep his balance amidst the crashing roars around them. She looked down to check her footing and then up, frantically grasping the hands of both Rashmi and Paula, who lay down on their stomachs to assist. She felt herself rising as Eric's strong hands boosted her toward the relative safety of the yellow van.

Her view, as she was being pulled up, was of two panicked people. One dark-skinned, eyes wide with terror. The other white-skinned, eyes squinting with effort, but also squinted against the terrible creature below that had already claimed four of their party's lives.

The sounds of screaming hadn't stopped, but Meredith didn't have time to look around. After being pulled up—barely, as Paula and Rashmi's grip suddenly slipped, and she caught herself on the same sideview mirror that had clocked Vera on her way down to that watery grave—she stared back down at Eric. He was trying unsuccessfully to pull a limp stranger to safety. Eric had grasped his hand as the man floated by. His grunts couldn't be heard above the roar of the water and shrieks of tearing metal as rubble crashed around them, but the heaving of his sodden shoulders was evidence enough.

Paula and Carol were yelling encouragement at Eric, trying to spurn him on and join them on the roof. Meredith's own voice, hoarse and high-pitched with terror, joined in saying "Eric, you can't do anything for him. Let's go!"

It didn't do any good, though. The force of the water became too much and something sunken and heavy slammed into the van where they stood watching Eric. It brought them screaming in terror and surprise down to their knees, reaching instinctively for one another, to anchor themselves and avoid plunging into the mess below.

Rashmi wasn't fast enough, however. He was kneeling reaching for Eric and when whatever it was, another car or a boat from the harbor—*or bodies* she remembered thinking—slammed into the van, it sent Rashmi spinning off the roof, his outstretched hand reaching frantically behind him. Meredith's own hand struck out, quick as a flash, grabbed onto Rashmi's fingers, and then, they were gone. His forward momentum was too great and her hold too wet and weak, betraying her in the moment that she needed it most.

Rashmi landed hard on the roof of the yellow car, next to Eric, releasing a grunt and great gasp of air. Water was now splashing steadily across the roof, soaking him entirely alongside Eric. The stranger's limp body bobbed in the shallow water, in macabre disregard next to them. The pallid face broke the surface sporadically, his face a frozen mask of languid death.

The impact of Rashmi landing did something to the stability of the yellow car, and to their dismay, it simply began floating away. Slowly, at first, jerking to a stop every few inches until it began picking up speed and bumping unhurriedly along with the raging current.

Whatever hold the street below had on its tires, it now released it.

Rashmi was lying down, being struck time and again with crashing waves of putrid water while Eric stood in surprising surety like a superhero, arms outstretched to either side for balance. His eyes stared unbelieving across the rapidly increasing distance between his family and his life raft. He and Rashmi were pushed farther away from the three women, all of whom cried in screams of protest and disbelief. Then, in an instance, his demeanor changed. In a completely unbelievable act, he locked eyes with Paula and smiled, then shrugged his shoulders in a helpless "isn't that how it goes sometimes" manner.

When he yelled, "I love you," it was barely audible above the roaring waters around them, and the sound reached them from what seemed like a hundred miles away.

Paula, who was screaming incoherently next to her for her husband to come back, was inconsolable. Meredith screamed her own objections, swallowed by the thieving ambiance around them. She reached over to hold onto the other two women while tears began to mix with the seawater staining her cheeks.

In the distance, through watery vision, she watched as Eric helped Rashmi to his feet. He waved at them and then began praying. The car—miraculously—avoided the others on what was now a furious river of bobbing flotsam. The small car bounced almost gently off a rock wall and the three women reacted, screaming in fear as the men's balance wavered and then they once again settled. The two men on the car then disappeared around the corner of the same building that had released Vera from this wretched nightmare. The last thing they ever saw of the two men was a dark-handed wave and a teary blown kiss.

During this heart-wrenching exchange, their own van was being pushed and pulled within the current. It took all of her strength to avoid plunging into the dark death that thrashed a couple of feet beneath her. It was a miracle that she was still holding on. What felt like hours from the time Rashmi plummeted off the side until their lonesome last stand right now, only moments had passed.

Whether she wanted it or not, Meredith was the only one with the emotional bandwidth to make decisions. Alongside this thought, another became clear. If they stayed on the van, they would all end up dead, either drowned or something worse like Vera. Paula was spiraling. Her cries and screams fluctuated between lethargic surrender and frantic helplessness. She was in no state to be making life or death decisions. Carol could barely keep control of her own emotions, let alone reign in her daughter's. She held Paula in a steel trap embrace and stared at the spot Eric and Rashmi had disappeared.

It appeared the survival of the three of them fell to Meredith.

CHAPTER 13

Now, the water was crushing other cars against their own. Perhaps it had been, but the circumstances had overridden their senses, and Meredith was just registering the source of the noise. Some of the cars around them were floating in an offensive impression of ducks. The hoods sank beneath the surface and their taillights bobbed up and down at unsettling angles.

She could tell that more water was on its way by the splashing black swell moving irreverently toward them from the coast.

She cut her eyes to the beach and recoiled as several cars tumbled like leaves in an autumn wind, their undercarriages visible briefly before the roof suddenly appearing where it had been submerged only seconds before.

For the first time, and despite the instability of their current ride, she felt relatively safe to look around and assess the nightmare of what was happening to her.

The sun was warm on her skin, and she felt the goosebumps rise in response to the cool water there. She gazed in uncertain skepticism at the scene that unfolded before her. She felt the same gaze directed at her she took it all in. There were other people doing the same as she, trying to make sense of the insanity before them. She watched one person, who had been climbing a distant rock wall, plummet into the water with a brief and terrified shriek before becoming just another piece of debris.

Her eyes fixated on another person she saw clinging desperately to some kind of cooler, but it was so small and the water was so rough that they, too, disappeared beneath the surface, an unwilling sacrifice to an impartial god. A second later, the cooler surfaced twenty feet away, its desperate passenger lost to the waters.

For the rest of her life, this day would make panic rise in her chest and throat. It would always threaten to short-circuit her thought processes, and each time it crept upon her, she would hear a distant voice desperately crying *Run! Run! Run!*

Meredith blinked away the tears that had settled in her eyes. She tore her gaze from the death that continued to assault her senses and yelled at the other two women. "We've got to get somewhere stable. This van is going to kill us if we stay on it. Help me find somewhere we can get off and find higher ground!"

Carol looked at her, distantly, but nodded. Paula continued to hold onto her mother with fierce desperation. Meredith's voice was hoarse from crying and screaming, but she didn't have a choice. She had to get to safety, get them all to safety.

She got Carol's attention by waving her arms raucously in front of her. When she was certain she had it, Meredith raised a hand and pointed at a grove of trees. It was probably a park before being swallowed by the onrush of water that now danced on its lower branches and trunks.

If they could grab onto a tree and hang on, they might be able to hold out long enough for the water to at least stop churning so violently beneath them.

"Carol, do you see those trees?" She waited for Carol to respond, which seemed to take forever, but she finally gave a single nod in response. "We're going to try to climb one. Do you think you can do that?" She waited for the response, but the sound of splitting wood snapped her head back to the grove. As she watched, two of the trees began to lean and with the final sound of a gunshot, shattered. White splinters scattered into the air as they both broke and fell into the water, raising great gouts of black spray into the air. The small glow of hope she'd had sank and disappeared beneath the murk of despair.

Meredith heard herself yell furiously, "No!"

Her plan shattered with the trees and became yet another casualty to be counted in the disaster around them. There were other trees, yes, but if those weren't strong enough, what's to say the ones they grabbed would work as well?

A hint of hopeless panic whistled its way out her nostrils as she felt her throat constrict with fear. She tried to shake it away and succeeded only in part.

The three women were lucky to be where they were. The van was heavy enough to stay upright in the water as deep as it was now—up to the windows—but not so heavy that the water couldn't move it along. Any other day, it might feel as if they were in a convertible driving along the old Route 1 in California near the Pacific Ocean. But instead of the ocean being a comfortable hundred yards away, it was yawning beneath them like a hungry animal, devouring everything that was careless enough to get caught in its jaws and crushing it into near nonexistence with impunity.

Their makeshift raft had moved so rapidly that she now realized they were passing the point where Eric and Rashmi waved goodbye. She stared ahead, trying to gauge where their path would lead them but understanding there was no way to know for certain. They could hit anything unseen beneath the surface and it would, at the very, least alter their course. At worst, it could launch them into the water, snuffing out any hope of rescue and killing them all.

Throwing her plan for the trees away in disgust, she searched for another opportunity. Ahead, a bridge rose over the water; an unseen road lay at the bottom of the swirling, siphoning death trap. An immense whirlpool spun violently in front of the bridge, parts of trees from the park turned in drunken, twisting patterns amidst piles of litter and building parts.

Upon seeing this, Meredith hastily backed away from the edge of the van. Despite the distance to the vortex, the sheer size of the thing was overwhelming and seemed to swallow the very air around them, replacing it with a slurping, sucking sound.

The road narrowed beneath the bridge to a dual-pass tunnel. On any normal day two cars, moving opposite directions, could fit easily side-by-side with inches to spare. Now, however, as the rock walls funneled the water toward the tunnel, the water picked up speed and the objects within it became deadly torpedoes. The cars and chunks of buildings picked up speed and as they reached the tunnel—the water had to be 10 feet deep in this place—were sucked below the surface with a gurgling crash. Meredith could hear the objects around them skating along the bottom. A deep, thick sound reverberated through the van and her body each time, like a massive clock ticking down the seconds until their demise.

Those large items that weren't sucked beneath could be heard crashing into the bridge-wall with those same deep and forbidding *thunks* that reverberated back through the air.

With dawning horror, Meredith realized that was the fate that waited for them. "We have to get off this van," she yelled at Carol and Paula, bending her mouth as close as she could to them so she could be heard. Paula and Carol with matted hair and glassy stares looked ahead. She let their matching looks of resignation spurn her on instead of chaining her in place. She dug deep into the strength that her mother passed to her, into the strength her father made her create in herself after leaving, into the deep strength that Evan reciprocated each time she was down. She built a mental wall of resolve. She would get them to safety. The only alternative was to die trying.

Meredith looked again at the rapidly approaching tunnel; it was less than 100 yards away. They had maybe thirty seconds, certainly no more before their only lifeline in this disease of a day would be crushed—and them with it—between a wall of rocks and a wall of water.

She continued to search frantically, and a plan began to form in her mind. Not a good plan, and certainly not the simplest, but the best plan she could come up with while staring death in its baleful, glistening eye.

Gnarled branches and twisted heaps of metal scraped the sides of their van, squealing the way only metal-on-metal can. A massive branch punched straight through one of the windows, its offshoots stripped of most leaves resembled a giant's skeletal hand reaching for succor from the fatal water below.

She took a risk by doing it, but she let go of the bobbing van beneath her for a brief second and pointed to a portion of the brick wall that jutted out perpendicular to the path they were currently on. She had no idea what purpose it served before this watery hell had overrun it, but at the moment it didn't matter. It was a way off this nightmare carnival ride.

Carol and then Paula nodded numbly in what she hoped was understanding and after a gesture from Meredith, began inching along the roof of the van slowly, their legs hanging off the side of the van, the cold water splashing up their legs and onto their laps. With their backs to the approaching rock wall, Meredith felt exposed, but she knew this was the best position to be in for the approaching jump.

Briefly, she yelled at them, trying to explain again a plan that may not work. "We're going to jump onto that rock wall, the one I'm pointing to. Do you see it? There's a flagpole up away from the water, we're going to be safe there. Do you understand?"

The two stunned women nodded, and Meredith thanked god for small favors. "There won't be a second chance. You *have* to jump." Again, they both nodded.

Not exactly content but satisfied with their response, she got ready. There would be no second to spare, and there could be no hesitation. Paula and Carol brought their legs up, ready to spring.

Meredith met each of their eyes in turn, and thankfully, the other two nodded in tear-stained agreement.

All three women squatted there, waiting.

The wall approached rapidly, and Meredith understood in a deep part of her that if she didn't go first, the others wouldn't follow. A larger part of her understood, too, that by going first, she was risking their lives. If they hesitated, they'd be lost. It evened out, in a way. Either Meredith made it or they all died, and she told herself determinedly that she was going to make it. Evan was waiting for her to come back.

It wasn't the first time that her husband came to mind since the sea began waging war on the city.

There was no time to think on it any more than that. The wall was close, now. Close enough to jump. It was now or never.

Meredith stood and yelled down at Carol, "Stand up and follow me! Do not wait!" The back end of the van was floating close to the wall and the rock wall jutting out was a foot or more away. Without giving herself time to process the fear that suddenly coiled around her lungs, she took a breath and stepped forward, off the van. She used only a small amount of pressure to leap to the rock wall. Even still, she left the van rocking with the small force of her departure.

The rocks were slippery, but her momentum carried her the three feet up the wall onto the sidewalk.

She stood and turned to see Carol bent over the wall, clinging to it desperately. Paula, to Meredith's great dismay, was mid-air between the van and wall. The van had floated several feet toward the maelstrom. And because of her hesitation, Paula had to jump against the current and subsequent momentum of van, as opposed to with it had she jumped in the second following Meredith and Carol.

She was too slow. The force of her jump worked against her momentum and pushed the van farther from both the wall and her salvation. To Meredith, everything suddenly slowed down. Time stood still as she watched in abject shock.

Paula's face, wrought with intrepid expectation, changed to dismal defeat as the realization that she would miss the jump sank home in the interstices between seconds. Her eyes widened with that realization. Though, they never left the target of the rock wall.

Meredith used that time to slide down the wall, caking the seat of her pants and shirt in mud, but taking the briefest second to ensure that her shoes didn't slip on the grimy rocks and betray her into the water. Paula didn't so much as land as she did crash. Her legs splashed into the water shy of the rock wall by only a few inches. In fact, the splash from her legs hitting the surface soaked Carol who was now making her way to safety, straddling the rock on which she had lain. Paula's arms, outstretched as they were like a concert fan reaching for their idol, cuffed the rock wall with a meaty slap, her hands clenching for purchase on the slippery surface.

Paula's face, however, followed in the split second after to smack into the rock wall with a squelching crunch. Blood burst from her nose and mouth, and immediately, her body went limp. She had passed out. The gluttonous current began dragging her body inexorably toward the yawning jaws of the whirlpool, but either by luck or providence, there was a tiny eddy of swirling water behind the wall and exactly where she landed. Her legs and torso, instead of being swept rapidly into the massive current leading to the tunnel of water, drifted lazily in the eddy, her arms anchoring her to the wall and keeping her bleeding face above the splashing surface for the second it took for Meredith to reach her friend.

Meredith grasped for Paula's hand and closed down hard on her wrist, praying desperately to the god she'd only worshipped on holidays that this time her grip would hold.

She felt a sudden tightness on her legs but didn't have time to spare it any attention. She grabbed frantically for Paula, knowing with her bleeding and shattered mouth that close to the water that she could drown in a matter of seconds.

Meredith wasn't sure if Paula was dead or not, but if she was only knocked out, there was still hope.

With Carol anchoring them both to the ground by grabbing onto Meredith's legs to prevent her from going in herself, Meredith dragged Paula's lifeless body on top of her own, turning her head from the mix of mud and blood that dripped onto her. With shaking arms, she pushed Paula up the bank toward Carol, letting out a cry of energy and relief in the process.

Paula lay lifeless in Carol's lap, who was sobbing over her and trying unsuccessfully to move the bloody strands of hair out of the mess that was her face. Meredith couldn't tell if she was breathing or not. She moved to check, the distant memory of college health class coming back to her in this moment.

Suddenly, a terrible sound rent the air. A crackling spiderweb boomed through the mulling sounds of cries for help and raging water. It reminded her of the whip crack of an enraged god, come to punish the tiny beings below.

The roar that followed came from behind her, and she turned from Carol's sobbing and Paula's lifeless, mangled face and saw a nearby building crumbling into the black water beneath it. The side of the building was there one second and the next it wasn't. In its place was a rising swell filled with churning detritus and headed straight toward the three exhausted and nearly spent women.

Meredith saw exactly what she had to do. She stood up to run, intending to grab Paula under one arm while Carol grabbed the other and together, they would run up the sidewalk and out of the way of the approaching surge. Finding relative safety on the higher road where they now found themselves was paramount.

Instead, her foot slipped on the wet rocks beneath her. She felt herself slip into the water despite frantically grasping at the rocks, her fingers slipping repeatedly and never finding a grip.

She cried out in desperation. "Carol!" Her toes went in first, the water colder than she thought possible and making her jerk her legs and causing her to strike her knee on the rock. Then, more rapidly, her ankles and shins followed, and the moment the water reached her knee, its pull was more than she could fight. Impossible to withstand, unquestionable strength and fury gripped her and simply climbed up her back and down her shaking, exhausted arms. The surging swell that resulted from a collapsing building reared above the rock wall, spraying foam and harsh, stinking water across her face. Then, it began to fall. The current grasped the backs of her hands and to her dizzying horror, it seemed to pry them from the rocks to which she so desperately tried to cling.

Trying one last time, she reached for Carol, tried to plead with the glance, but there wasn't time. She opened her mouth to shout for help but was violently yanked into the current as the wave covered her and pushed her down, her chin bouncing off the rock wall as a final goodbye. Time allowed for her to take a withering breath and hold it, but she soon found herself beneath the rolling surface, whipping through the water in a way that made her feel like she was falling. Her arms and legs didn't seem to work. She tried to bring them under control, to curl into a ball and protect her organs, but they weren't hers anymore, they were the water's, and they did what it wanted now.

The scream that was stuck in her throat threatened to burst forth, but she knew that if she opened, it would be filled instantly with the death water. It would work its way into her lungs, and she would choke on it until it soaked into her very soul.

She tried to make her way to the surface, but the only thing she succeeded in was touching something in the darkness around her that made her recoil instinctively. Her body whipped around in the dim and gritty water, and she was unable to orient herself.

Her lungs began to protest, threatening to betray her. The breath she was holding began creeping its way into her throat and nose, working to burst forth in a sodden scream. Things in the water began bumping into her, touching her legs and softly sliding across her torso, some surfaces soft and tender, like an embracing tentacle. Other surfaces, coarse and rigid, missing impaling her by inches.

She wanted desperately to look at the things around her, but she was terrified of opening her eyes in the murk, afraid of what would be staring back at her.

A part of her knew she was going to die. A part of her knew that her time had come and that she would never see Evan again. Part of her also knew that her body may not ever be found.

It was this thought that finally made her change her course. Instead of recoiling and shying away from the things that brushed against her, she reached out to capture whatever thing she could. Her hand closed around something rough and hard to the touch. *Not a body,* she thought with relief amidst the screaming voice that dominated her headspace to take a deep pull of the water. She struggled through the water, heaving herself in what she hoped was up, guessing in a desperate attempt to save herself.

Her head suddenly broke through the surface, and she took an enormous gasping breath, not caring that some of the water made its way in. She tried to scream for help, but it came out as a gurgling scattered noise.

Her vision spun wildly as the current gripped her body and whipped her around. She caught glimpses of the refuse around her. A car here, a shirt there, what looked like a tree there. After a moment and another breath, the current stopped yanking her haphazardly through the water, and she was able to turn her head. Her gaze fixated on the spinning black maw before her as the roar that surrounded her was traced to that very real death ahead.

It was the tunnel that they'd tried to avoid on the van and here it was. Here was the beast that devoured everything that approached it. The squelching, sucking crunch of innumerable objects being swallowed down its liquid gullet was audible above the splashing water around her.

She grasped madly for the side of the tunnel as it approached, and she was rewarded with a ripping, tearing pain in her elbow and shoulder as the first was hyperextended and the other dislocated from the collision. But still, she held, crying out in pain and resolute resistance.

Her legs were swept into the torrent, and she found herself horizontal in the water. The wet, cloying, relentless watery grips climbed over her own and down to her feet, pulling and yanking her inexorably toward their master's maw.

The water skating past her added to its pull, and she felt herself slipping, the rocks letting her go as if ashamed, releasing her in a way a friend may apologize for an unexpected and overly harsh criticism.

The scream that she'd been holding in since her plunge into the darkness leapt from her mouth. It roared with pain and enduring stubbornness, rising in a crescendo as her tears mixed with the water encircling her.

Finally, it enfolded her within its crushing embrace, and she was sucked beneath the surface. The beast of immense darkness absorbed her unceremoniously within its murky depths.

And then she was gone.

Meredith's eyes opened abruptly, coming back to herself and snapping open. She realized that she had closed her eyes against the pain of the memory, reliving it in her own mind instead of watching it on the vid screen with Evan.

But she did look at the vid screen. It was black. Dark with indeterminate sounds before it was silent.

Evan stood up and walked toward the hole in the air trying to grab the sides of it. Meredith watched him as he stared at it in angry, resignation and whispering, "No, no. No. No. No. No." Over and over, he repeated it while staring at the darkness before him.

He was crying; the tears coursed down his cheeks and melted into his beard, shining there like tiny little crystals.

"Meredith, no. This is," he hesitated, "this is wrong." The pain in his eyes was difficult to look at and his voice was thick with a desperate wish.

Within his words, she could hear the knowledge that he'd carried with him those years ago, and the spiraling depression that led them to where they were now.

She folded her hands in her lap, trying hard to figure out how to navigate the next logical step in the conversation, the one that they—whether aware of it or not—were both terrified of verbalizing.

She cleared her throat. "Evan," she began shakily. He stood up straighter but remained where he was, now standing next to nothing as the vid screen disappeared, leaving the sanguine cliff-side setting pristine once more.

Meredith shook her head, trying to organize the whirlwind of words that whipped around inside her mind. How could she continue? What was the next thing that needed to be said? How could she move forward to help him see what she so desperately wanted—no, *needed*—him to see?

Hoping against hope that her next step landed solidly on the path toward resolution, she spoke. "Evan," she began again, more forcefully, hoping to sound secure instead of scared. "I stopped the video because there isn't anything else—"

"I know," he interrupted, abruptly moving and sitting next to her, grasping her hands in his own. "I know there isn't, Meredith. I'm sorry. I'm so sorry. I had no idea. I—"

"Let me finish, Evan." She stared at him, finding strength where there was none and confidence in her own memories. The words that whirled within her began to calm, organize themselves. The step she took felt more solid, and she felt more certain of where the path led.

She continued with more certainty, pleased that she was finding the strength she so desperately needed to convey. "I was saying that there isn't anything else *for four days*. The memories naturally Hazed themselves.

"You know how you just found out that your chip was damaged, and you missed out on memories? I was unconscious, and I don't know how, but that—" she pointed to where the vid screen had been, "isn't the end." She continued to stare at him, hoping to convey the words without having to say them aloud.

He stared at her dumbly, mouth half-open in restrained protest.

She could tell that he was trying to process what she was saying, but his mind wasn't making the connection.

"I don't... I guess I don't understand." She could tell his heart was racing, his breathing was increasingly rapid, and he blinked at her several times, closing his mouth and swallowing dryly.

She glanced away and took a steadying breath, then took another step along the path.

"I didn't die there, Evan."

He blinked, eyes bulging in surprise.

Then he blinked again, a faint smile appearing and disappearing just as fast. A connection was being made, she knew, but not the right one. "You didn't..." he said, trailing off, unable to give voice to the miracle he suspected.

"I didn't die. Right," she finished for him. "I'm going to show you what happened when I woke up. I don't remember everything in the traditional sense, but the memories are there, stored in my Chip, as if some parasite was directing a play and I'm the lead character. But almost everything else I can feel with painful acuity."

Evan nodded, the wisp of a smile that was there moments before faded beneath the seriousness with which she spoke.

She still suspected that he didn't understand—fully, at least. He was probably still trying to fit the pieces together. She could at the very least identify with him in that there were missing memories. They were alike in that respect, at least.

Watching herself, as she had countless times, play out something and being unable to feel the thread of consciousness that connected her to her then-self was unsettling at the very least. It was downright terrifying in some of the situations she saw play out before her.

She cued up the time period she wanted to show Evan and flipped it to the same vid screen in the air. The soft hum of its activation was comforting, somehow, familiar. It was something that kept her tethered here, and she hoped Evan could follow that tether and find comfort, too.

What he would see from her perspective was not going to give him any.

They both faced the vid screen, Evan still holding her hands but loosely, as if she were holding his, but he was unaware she was even there.

The screen brightened from the dormant black to a hazy white, as if looking through a translucent shower curtain, then eventually a picture came into focus. *This is when I woke up,* she thought to herself for the hundredth time. And again, for the hundredth time wondered if it was the first time she had woken up.

Meredith, although able to watch the video along with Evan, closed her eyes voluntarily this time. She knew it, knew it by heart, had lived it. And while the Hazed memories were nothing more than mumbles and vague shadows, this was something she could relive word for word, glance for glance, terrible reaction by terrible reaction.

She'd let Evan watch the video. But she preferred to play along the gossamer thread that stretched from her mind to points across the world, to those places she had been and the people she had seen.

CHAPTER 14

Meredith wasn't aware of anything but a ringing in her ears. She was weightless in a sea of dim reality. At first, she felt nothing on her skin and heard nothing. Her eyes *felt* open, but she knew that to be a trick of the mind. Slowly, like a leaky pipe, feeling began to run its way back into her body. A trickle of substance at first began in her fingertips and toes. Still weightless, she felt it move up her legs and arms toward her belly and chest. Feeling something beneath her, she told her limbs to move. They responded in a kind of lethargic spasm. Her toes, she realized, were pointing up. Her palms were down, as well. The feeling continued to creep through her veins and awareness began chugging to life in her mind. The weightlessness was replaced with vertigo, as her mind told her she wasn't perpendicular to it, she was lying parallel to it. She was stricken with nausea and felt bile rise in her throat. The thought of retching against gravity's pull helped her stamp the feeling down. She couldn't do anything for the goose-bumps that raced along her arms and legs or the prickly sweat that burst from the pores on her face and forehead.

Her eyes moved beneath their lids. She tried to lift them and might as well have tried to fly. They were heavy, stuck and crusted over. She tried to move her fingertips again and felt something scratchy beneath her. That same substance that crept through her body made its way into her mind. With some confusion, she felt a lightness spread across her body. She was between two light cloths.

Again, she tried to open her eyes and succeeded in opening them enough to have the brightness around her stab her eyes. She winced and slammed them shut again.

Meredith's fingers began to shake with adrenaline and fear. She couldn't remember what was happening to her. She couldn't remember where she went to sleep last night but knew it wasn't here. There wasn't anything that led her to that conclusion other than the fact that she didn't keep her lights that bright at home.

She was in a strange place and, with a terrible realization, became aware of exactly how her body was oriented. She was lying down on a bed between sheets.

Sound had begun to work its way through the fogginess of sleep and whatever else had kept her from wakefulness, but it was unrecognizable beneath the buzzing ring that predominated it all. Risking the blinding lights, she peeked through the slit in her eyelids again. It wasn't as bright, but in order to look around the room, she had to continue squinting against the harsh fluorescent bulbs that shone mercilessly above her. Her nerves began to calm, and she systematically began to take stock of her surroundings, working to categorize everything she was seeing.

Unfamiliar sounds—beeps, yells, barks, crying, the steady whir of a fan or cooling unit—all jostled for her attention, and while she could hear them, they very nearly didn't even register beneath that incessant, keening buzz.

What her eyes gathered turned into something she understood at some deep level. Yet it failed to align with her mind's understanding, at least at this point, and she tried to shake her head as if to clear it.

Her head felt heavy. Her hair, she knew, must be arranged somehow around her head, and it felt like it was anchoring it down as she turned and tried to raise it enough to see beyond herself.

People of all shapes, sizes, and colors moved around her and the spaces beyond the foot of a bed. She understood that she was in a bed, with a soft blue blanket covering her from the torso down over her toes, which raised the blanket like two small alien hills. Her eyes followed the rise of her legs up to where her hands lay. A clear tube ran through the air beside her, from a needle buried in the soft skin of the back of her hand to an IV bag, but her eyes couldn't focus well enough to read what it said. However, as she watched the small cylindrical tube above her shoulder, a shimmering drip the size of her thumb swelled like a clear bulbous fruit on a robotic tree and fell soundlessly into a pool of the same liquid.

She continued to blink against the light and turned her head away from the IV drip. A dull throbbing ache had slid behind her eyes, and every time it pulsed, her vision blurred and then cleared. It was nauseating, even when she closed her eyes against it.

Based on what she saw between the cycle of blurring and clearing throbs, she was in some kind of hospital. If the beds and mulling people weren't clue enough, the plethora of beeping machines would have clued her in. There were people everywhere. Some doctors or nurses, she was sure, but many more who were dressed in everyday clothes. They bustled here and there, and for a time, as she felt the headache subsiding, she watched them if for no other reason than to gather information. She had no idea where she was or why. Her first order of business was to answer those two questions. They burned in her mind with a kind of cold radiance. She feared the answer, but she also feared to ask it. Now she just needed to find someone to explain what was going on.

It was true; she was in a hospital. That wasn't the "where" of the question. The problem, the glaring issue she couldn't seem to grasp, was why she was in a hospital bed and felt like she had been disassembled and then reassembled, and not at all in the same way.

Logically, it was because she was hurt or had been recently. But other than a few bruises here and a scratch or two that she could see, there wasn't anything obviously wrong with her.

A sudden fear gripped her fiercely, and she held her breath and told her mind to wiggle her toes. When she opened her eyes and saw the tiny hills wiggling beneath the blankets, she heaved a sigh of relief.

She closed her eyes against another bout of suddenly brutal throbbing behind her eyes—it had begun to move to the middle of her forehead, now—and she tried to remember where she was. She knew her name and after only the briefest hesitation, she recalled it, saying it in her mind as certainly as she could.

Meredith, she thought with some satisfaction.

However, when she tried to remember where she had been or what she had been doing, it was as if the memory retreated into the shadows of her mind, barely out of reach. It was there, she knew it was there, and if she could chase it and catch it, everything would be fine. But it was always beyond the revealing light of understanding, her fingertips reached and missed. Tantalizingly close and frustratingly familiar.

Her attention was called to a dark-skinned man in a white coat approaching from the throng of bystanders milling about in the hall. He approached her with a clipboard and a pensive expression. When his eyes met hers, it changed to a heart-warming smile and a twinkle of laughter in his dark eyes. His hair was jet black, highlighted with silver stripes and brushed in the way aging men use to cover emerging balding spots. His chin was covered in coarse black hair with the same silver high-lights. He was not imposing but held himself in a way that com-municated that he was certainly in charge of something.

The throb in her mind, while lessening now with each burst, still prevented her from seeing the name embroidered on his white coat clearly.

The man looked up at her after scribbling something on his clipboard. "Hello, Miss. You're awake. That's very good." His accent was not thick, but she had to repeat his words to dis-entangle them enough to become recognizable. She wanted to say Indian but couldn't, not with any certainty, at least.

"Do you know who you are?" He asked the question slowly, as if she would have difficulty understanding him. He stood grasping the clipboard in both hands, which rested gently below his ample belly.

She was glad he spoke slowly. With each throb, the sounds around her turned into a squeal, like a rusty faucet cranking to release a wash of ruddy mud. In this way, she was able to catch his question between the squealing sounds.

Meredith must have winced because he drew closer to her, a look of concern ghosting across his face before being replaced with a warm—if not as genuine—smile.

She blinked up at him and nodded her head with some effort. It still seemed to be filled with a cruel combination of bricks and cotton.

When she tried to open her dry and cracked lips to speak, she coughed instead. Her throat felt filled with fur, and she didn't have any spit to swallow and moisten it.

The doctor must have been prepared for this or had it nearby. He reached out, gently handing her a small cup. With a steady hand, he held a straw close to her mouth until her lips closed around the end of it. "Drink. It will help," he said in a quiet, kindly whisper.

She did and felt the water wend its way between the valleys in her mouth and down her dusty throat, clearing the distasteful dryness and bringing some relief. Her lips stuck to the straw as she tried to pull her mouth away, and the doctor deftly hooked a finger around the bend in it, keeping it from being drawn from the cup and dripping across her neck.

She motioned vaguely with her hand at her side for the cup again. She slurped down another long gulp of water, feeling the sweet cooling effect it had on her throat as the muscles loosened and the skin of her lips and mouth absorbed it like water on sand.

"Better?" he asked before taking the cup and setting it on a small table nearby.

She nodded again and licked her lips with the blessed moisture he'd provided her. "Yes, thank you." Her voice croaked like a frog's first words but was audible and relatively painless. "Yes, I do know my name. My name is Meredith." Her voice was still gravelly, the sound that came when a particularly strong wind gusted against a window, throwing the small pieces of grit and dust against it.

The doctor nodded, and she heard scribbling from his pen and clipboard amidst the continual beeps and din of the crowded hallway.

"That's great, Miss Meredith. My name is Dr. Kushni. Do you know where you are?"

She shook her head slowly. This was much more difficult than nodding, and she brought a hand slowly to her head to steady the sudden feeling that she was spinning in the bed. The needle in her hand pulled uncomfortably, and she was forced to lower her hand before the feeling worsened.

"You are in a hospital in Colombo, Miss Meredith."

She squinted up against the glare of the lights that all seemed to point directly into her ocular nerve and said in a crackling, disbelieving rasp, "Ohio?" She couldn't understand why she'd be in Ohio; maybe she was travelling back from Michigan and had a wreck or something. That would make sense. Yes, that had to be it.

The doctor's eyes squinted briefly, in confusion she thought, but it happened so quickly that it may not have happened at all.

When he spoke, his voice was hesitant. Probing, even.

"No, Miss Meredith. We are in Colombo, Sri Lanka." His pen was poised above his clipboard as if he had gotten an answer he didn't expect and was now uncertain as to what the next steps should be.

Meredith's breath hitched in her throat briefly. When she finally did swallow, an audible *click* sounded, and the dryness that had been washed away returned.

She tried to shake her head and only succeeded in moving it enough so that a lock of hair drifted lazily into her field of vision.

Sri Lanka? she thought groggily, trying in her muddled mind to pull a map into her consciousness and place a pin where that was.

After groping blindly across the mental image of a globe, as if she were spinning it in a strobe light and gaining only brief glimpses of places she knew and places she'd only heard of, her mind found the island south of India mainland labeled "Sri Lanka." It was simultaneously familiar and completely foreign.

She could feel a small amount of terror roll in her stomach as she tried to remember what she was doing here and coming up with nothing.

She had no memory.

The last thing she remembered was ... what? What was the last thing she remembered?

She lay back on the pillow. The several inches she'd raised herself in order to take a drink now felt like a mile as her neck muscles relaxed and her head sank deeper into the softness behind her.

Reaching further into her mind and trying desperately to move aside the curtains of disquiet and fear that began sliding closed around her, she searched.

She couldn't remember anything. She knew her name, something that was remarkable by itself, but she had no reason why she knew her name and little else. She remembered her mother, she remembered being a child, and even now, staring down at the gentle rise of breasts beneath her smock and the blanket on her lap that covered adult-sized legs, she could tell she was no child. But it was as if she were a blank slate, with only a single word written at the top in ghastly white letters: MEREDITH. Everything else was ... gone. Perhaps it was waiting. Maybe. But at the moment, every aspect of who she was had flown into obscurity. She had a horrid picture of the memories sitting on the guywires in the shadows above a darkened theater stage like crows, laughing at her inability to call them down, to master them.

The fear that had been creeping up her spine and through her mind suddenly lashed out, its claws shearing through her flat affect as a gulping sob leaked from deep within her throat. It seemed to land in her lap, the sound, and she stared where it lay, trying to take stock of what she did know. The void of knowledge was overwhelming and only increased the headache that began to pound like shifting bricks within her skull.

My name is Meredith ... something.

I am in Sri Lanka.

My mother is... I don't remember, but she's alive, I think.

I am alone.

Why was I here?

Was I alone?

I need to find a Chip Center and try to recover my memories.

This last gave her a flash of hope and an idea. She looked up sharply at Dr. Kushni, the quick movement making her head swim for a dizzying second, and a collection of drums began a cacophonous rhythm behind her eyes.

"Dr. Kushni," she began, steadying her head with a shaky hand and noting a dull and aching tightness between her shoulder blades that limited her range of motion, "Where is the nearest Chip Center? I—" She hesitated, not wanting to alarm the doctor, but understanding there wasn't another way to go about this. "I don't remember anything except my name. I need to get Recovered."

Dr. Kushni nodded as he looked at her, his lips pursed. The small measure of hope she felt rise victoriously only a moment before now began to shrink under that gaze.

"I'm sorry, Miss Meredith, but the nearest Chip Center was in Matara, which was recently hit with a massive tsunami. That is why you are here. You and several others were pulled from the water by a group of people who brought you here. The coast is as close to being destroyed as possible, and the hospitals that have been set up are temporary and farther from the southern coast. This hospital isn't as temporary as those, but only just. The nearest Safety Center is going to be in New Delhi on mainland India."

Her mind took this in and slowly began sorting the words. There were several different points of interest in his response, the first of which was that bit about the tsunami. Apparently, she had been in it, and by the sounds of it, she was one of the lucky ones. The second was that apparently the hospital where she now lay underneath the comfort of a blue blanket and fluorescent lights was a temporary one. Now that she looked around, really looked, she could see that walls and ceilings didn't exactly meet at straight angles. The roof sagged between walls and the walls, while they were straight lines, gave her the impression of being *limp*. She didn't know how else to describe them. The third point of interest, and arguably the most important to her, was the nearest operational Chip Center. *New Delhi.* She knew that Sri Lanka was south of India, so while New Delhi was far away, it also wasn't as far as, say, London.

"How long do I need to stay here?" she asked.

Dr. Kushni flipped a page back on his clipboard. "You've been here for nearly twelve days. Vitals are stable, and remarkably, there's no indication of infection in any of the wounds or in your blood. Your shoulder and elbow may be sore for a few days, but they will heal if you are careful with them. In my professional opinion, you should stay for a day or two if only to speed the healing a bit." He paused. "And, now that you're awake, your brain may start to recover memories on its own."

Meredith nodded and stared past him, working up the courage to digest the words on her own, to come to terms with the swirling mass of impossibility before her.

Her eyes followed an older Caucasian man walking—well, limping—down the hallway. He was holding his left arm to his chest, and even from here, she could tell he was a victim of the tsunami. His short brown hair was tangled beneath an oddly familiar blue hat, and his eyes were sunken and hollow, haunted as his roving gaze moved back and forth, as if searching for something without the expectation of finding it. He was on a task doomed to fail, and he knew it. She wondered if he simply couldn't admit it to himself yet.

His eyes met hers without recognition, and he moved on down the hall and around the corner, his lips pursed in fierce determination. His head suddenly appeared back around the corner, his body trailing only a second behind. He stopped with enough momentum that his feet stuttered beneath him, and he nearly crashed into a crowd of people standing nearby.

When his eyes met hers across the tiled room, he blinked. The look of defeated determinism had changed to something entirely different. The change was so drastic that she couldn't give a name to his look other than desperate hope.

She looked down, embarrassed, and closed the small opening at the base of her neck with fingers that trembled slightly. She was in no way prepared to talk to a stranger, let alone the fairly handsome—if somewhat skeletal—man she speculated was hidden beneath the grime and hunger.

She lifted her arm to tuck a wayward strand of hair behind her ear and looked back up, the throb in her head subsiding in lessening waves. The man was limping toward her and even the haunted look on his face had vanished. With this look of hope, he seemed to have lost decades of worry from his pale face, and she now realized that the man couldn't be older than 40. It was as if he had made some kind of divine discovery.

The feeling of self-consciousness grew, and she pulled the blanket closer to her, trying to shield herself from his penetrating gaze. The man was close now. As she listened, she was able to pick out what he was saying from the buzzing beeps around her; fear coalesced in her chest and her nostrils flared with it.

He was saying her name.

How? was her only thought before he was standing close to her, squeezing between Dr. Kushni and her bed with a healthy mix of bearing and emaciation. His hands, filthy and crusted with mud, reached for her own while his face, a grisly countenance smeared with dried blood, reminded her of risen ghost whose body reflected its manner of passing.

"Meredith?" The voice that issued from between the man's cracked lips was jagged and uneven. It was also husky with emotion, and yet underneath it all was a simple note of adoring devotion.

She was momentarily taken aback. "Um, yes?"

Fantastic response, she thought dismally to herself.

The man, whose lip had been quivering since he'd approached her, suddenly burst into tears and reached for her hand with a shaking one of his own. Relief eased his face into something less zombie-like, but she didn't know this man. She jerked her hand away, working hard to avoid letting on that pain had exploded in her shoulder and a deep fear suddenly gripped her and was slowly twisting her intestines into knots.

Dr. Kushni, finally recovering from being made irrelevant as the man swept him aside and ignored him completely, stepped in-between the two Americans and said with only a touch of obstinance, "Excuse me, sir, may I help you?"

The man didn't even seem to notice. He continued staring at her eyes and pleaded with his own. The tears had begun to make their way through the dried blood, making tiny pink rivulets as they ran. Red blotches bloomed on the blanket covering her where the tears fell.

At the same time that Meredith began to feel claustrophobic because of the two men standing so close her bed, the stranger turned from her to answer her doctor. He glared at the doctor with ferocious disdain and said, "Yes, you *can* help me. You can get the fuck out of my way so I can see my wife."

Meredith froze and could feel her eyes bulge in their sockets.

She wasn't married. She didn't even have a boyfriend. It was impossible.

Her mind reeled and tried to make sense of how she could find herself in such a position; her memories were gone and a man was claiming her, like someone laying claim to a suitcase at the baggage claim conveyor belt. Grimy hands reached for a bag that had no choice but to go.

Did she have a choice? Or was she now this man's property? What were the laws here in Sri Lanka?

Her mind seemed to click into motion and the simplest explanation—usually the right one—came to mind.

This man, whoever he was, was obviously injured and without any prompting, approached her saying her name. Perhaps, he saw it on a chart or overheard Dr. Kushni say it; that would be the easiest and most obvious solution. Then the stranger, now knowing the name of his prey, could approach without fear of reprisal and begin groping her, all while claiming they were married. It was preposterous. Impossible? No, not really. Improbable, yes.

Riding the rising wave of fear that swelled quickly within her, she looked down at her left hand.

What if this man was telling the truth? After all, she didn't have any memories, did she? Perhaps the simplest explanation would win out. She would find a gold band on her hand, shining in the harsh light but adding its truth to the man's. She would leave the hospital with him and create a life for herself because she was, despite her feelings and fears to the contrary, married.

Instead, she found no ring on her hand. In fact, there wasn't even a tan line where a ring would be. Granted, she didn't tan easily, didn't even try to, but there would have been some physical indication, she was certain.

Meredith swallowed hard, the two men still staring at each other in the aftermath of the stranger's specific "request" for his help. The vehemence with which he'd spoken to the doctor was so certain, firm. She felt a modest kind of respect for the stranger. Even if he was crazy, which was becoming more and more likely in light of the circumstances, he had laid claim to her and expected that to be that. Luckily, she felt that it was not that easy.

She moved her head slightly to get their attention, meeting the stranger's piercing eyes as she spoke to him, a brief twinge of panic welled in her stomach like a cistern gathering rainwater. "I'm sorry, sir, but I don't even know you. I don't know who you think I am, but I'm certain that I'm not your wife."

The man's eyes were cold, but not with aggressive or subversive cruelty. It was more like untamed wildness.

His eyes focused on her and then changed. It sent terror creeping down her arms and legs, but not because it was malice or anger, which she had halfway expected. It was something else entirely. It was deepest dread. *Unbridled terror,* her mind intoned soundlessly.

The thought that followed on the heels of the previous one gave her pause. This man had lost his memory, too. What a hellish coincidence that another person would suffer the same fate she now suffered. Now, he was reaching out, trying to find his own place, his own comfort in the cosmos. "No, you're wrong." His voice was even, now, as if he were explaining something to a child. "Meredith, it's Evan. We've been married four years and have known each other since we were kids. We live in America, and we were travelling here for our anniversary trip. A trip you've wanted to take since elementary school."

Likely story, she thought, trying to tamp down the familiarity in childhood memories that included an "Evan" as a lanky adolescent boy. *Something* seemed to swell in her mind briefly, a flashbulb of recollection, but when she tried to grab hold, it disappeared.

Another time, she might reflect on how handsome the man was, and yes, there was some kind of familiarity to him. She assumed that perhaps his face was of that kind that was "an everyman's face," the kind of characteristics that exuded familiarity. At the moment, however, she was terrified that the doctor would believe the man and release her to his care. Then, she was certain of this, he'd no doubt spend his time alternating between torture and rape, locking her in a room and calling her his wife.

The doctor looked at her for some kind of confirmation. She stared gape-mouthed in return before answering. "Excuse me?" The terror that had been crawling over her like a burst spider's egg sac disappeared. Anger began to replace it. And fear, but only in half-doses.

"Absolutely not. I've never seen this man in my entire life." The fear burned within her, and the fumes of its burning was rage. "If you think some random stranger can come in here and *claim* me as his own, you'll find out that a bruised arm isn't going to stop me from bringing Hell to Earth!"

In her mind, she had been self-confident and firm, but the fear had slipped through the rage, and she heard the words as pleading and sickeningly desperate, which terrified her. The anger and outright disbelief retreated incrementally, once again leaving fear to curdle in her throat.

Her mind was reeling with all of the diverging paths that lay ahead, most of them chilling in their finality.

Dr. Kushni gently asked the man to leave. But the man, Evan, refused none too politely and leaned into the doctor's gently guiding hands.

Remarkably, at least remarkable to Meredith who had been watching the two men with growing unease, two large men in combat fatigues were standing across the open hallway. She now realized they'd been there the whole time, keeping an eye on the man as he approached her bed. They watched the interaction as it grew more and more heated, and when Evan pushed against Dr. Kushni, they moved briskly away from the wall and toward her bed with purpose. Each man grabbed Evan under the arms as he began to posture aggressively toward Dr. Kushni, despite the caretaker's kind admonitions to leave peaceably.

When he was suddenly lifted off his feet—with ease, she noticed with that kind of satisfaction that comes with a healthy serving of justice—he cried out. But under the circumstances, Meredith couldn't tell if it was from physical injury or something like frustration at being handled so easily and thoroughly.

The big brutes hauled the man away while he yelled her name over his shoulder, sounding more and more desperate the farther down the hall he was led. She felt bad for him in a way; mental illness wasn't funny, and it seemed like this guy needed help.

She licked her lips and pinched the corners of her mouth between thumb and forefinger. She was shaking. She watched her fingers tremble in the air in front of her until the doctor turned to her, a blatant look of embarrassment and apology gracing his features. "I'm terribly sorry, Miss. I know that must have been extremely upsetting." His words were comforting, but they did little to ease her anxiety.

He wrote something on his chart and looked at her again. "Miss Meredith," he hesitated, and she could tell he was feeling his way through his words with great care. "In light of your current mental state, are you absolutely certain that man is a stranger? Can you say without any doubt that he is not your husband?"

She opened her mouth to protest in earnest, but he held up a hand to forestall her briefly and spoke in quiet resignation. "I only mean, is it possible that he may be a part of your life at all?"

Her jaw dropped in disbelief.

Her mind was foggy at best, but she could feel herself slipping into frustrated helplessness. Was it because she was a woman that her word was untrustworthy? Or was it because her memory was gone? Jesus, this was something that women had been dealing with since Women's Suffrage, and it still was an issue?

Dr. Kushni must have seen the shadow of curdling rage that passed across her face, and he hastened to speak before she could release her indignation upon him. "I only mean to say that with your memories gone, if he truly is someone from your past, perhaps you could speak to him. It may help you gather a bit of your memories by talking to him. Even if he isn't part of your past, it's never hurt someone to verbally process their emotions."

She was galled. What was wrong with men that they believed they knew better than everyone? Why couldn't her word be enough? "Let me clear about this, Dr. Kushni. And understand, I'm giving you the benefit of the doubt because you've been so kind to me this morning. I am *absolutely* certain that man has nothing to do with me. How did he even get in here? You let anyone in?" As soon as she said it, she felt her argument shudder, and like a large weight on small, splintering branches, it fell in a hapless heap around her. "I know how that sounded, but you know what I mean. That man could be dangerous."

Dr. Kushni nodded placatingly and said, "We will try to discover who he is and get him the help he needs. For now, I think it best if you try to get some sleep. You're still healing, and your body needs time. Perhaps, with a few days, your mind will begin to heal as well." He put his clipboard under his arm and nodded, walking away in the direction the bulky men had dragged her "husband."

She huffed in frustration and shook her head, feeling the headache return and laid back on the bed. She closed her eyes but couldn't stop the man's horrified expression appearing and disappearing in a continual cycle behind her eyelids.

Where normally things from her past or fond memories would light up the screen of her mind, now she only saw the desperate man's rolling eyes as he called to her. Despite the blanket that covered her, a ripple suddenly ran up her arms, forming goosebumps as each pore tightened in fear. The ripple, now a chill, began to creep down her spine as she drifted into an uneasy doze.

Before her mind leapt from the cliff of consciousness into that wonderful place of weightless thought, two sudden realizations snapped her to near wakefulness. The first, a desperate hope that she'd never see that man again. And the second, how comforting it was to have someone know her, even if it turned out to be nothing more than an elaborate and desperate farce.

Both thoughts existed simultaneously. Two polar opinions existing in the same mind alongside each other. It seemed impossible, but it was almost *too* real.

In fact, the more she thought about it, the more the second thought seemed to ingest the first, sapping the energy required to maintain it and absorbing it, becoming the stronger of them both, and in the end, she decided, the more valid.

She ran the events of that morning through her mind again, from the time she woke up to when she was asked if the man could be a clue to her past. There wasn't anything that stuck out in any obvious way. There was also, she had to admit, an air of the fantastic regarding her theory that the man had overheard her name and laid claim to her. After all, she hadn't seen him in the hospital at all before he saw her. Of course, being unconscious for several days gave him the time and opportunity to find out more about her. The next thought following rapidly on the heels of the first was that Dr. Kushni would have—surely—shown some kind of recognition for the man had he been slinking around the hospital.

Meredith drifted nearer to sleep that evening with not only the uneasy feeling that she wasn't done with that strange man but also a strange relief that she would see him again.

The thought that sent her into unconsciousness came with the assurance that only a last resort can bring. If all else failed—talking to "verbally process" emotions, as her doctor had said—they could scan his chip and determine exactly who he was. Of course, documents could be faked.

CHAPTER 15

The following day dawned bright and clear. The sky adopted a hue of blue that was so clean she could practically feel it cleaning her skin. It was one of the few cloudless days since the tsunami had accosted the shoreline and devoured thousands of lives, along with the bulk of her memories.

The sun shone through the few windows on the hospital floor where she sat, eating a meager breakfast of red jello and oatmeal, neither of which she enjoyed but swallowed with distaste. The rays of sun lay across the bed in rectangular patches, warming her with their slanting golden bars. Small motes of dust drifted through their light, appearing for a moment in one and then disappearing, only to reappear a moment later in the next patch of sunlight.

She tried to follow one of the motes that was slightly bigger than the others and reflected on how it represented her current situation. She felt like she was drifting through life, remembering some of it in one sunbeam and then stumbling upon missing memories as she floated between them. She tried her best to avoid feeling sorry for herself and almost succeeded.

Today, however, she was able to look around without a headache searing through her mind like a hot needle. Upon realizing this, she took full stock of her surroundings and found she wasn't a hospital after all. Well, it wasn't a hospital before the tsunami. It looked to be some kind of business building, two or three stories tall based on how far she could see out the window down the hall a short way. The walls where she lay were makeshift canvas, separating beds in what would have been spacious rooms before their conversion.

She couldn't see much of the city, only the tops of a few buildings and the sides of several others. While she ate, she saw several pigeon-like birds fly lazily through the air, riding unseen wind currents until one landed on her window and sat. It cocked its head back and forth, peering in at her before pumping its head back and forth and strutting across the sill several times.

Another joined it, and after a minute more of strutting, she could hear faint cooing sounds from them, and she smiled as they flew away to join their companions high in the sky, beyond her field of vision.

She continued eating the last of her breakfast, which had been delivered on a tan tray that had seen plenty of use. She took her spoon and began scraping the small paper bowl—which was full of oatmeal upon its arrival—clean and licking the spoon for every last speck of nourishment. Her appetite had returned in the last twelve hours, and if she was honest with herself, it felt good to be hungry again.

When she had cleaned both bowl and spoon, an orderly approached her bed and quickly notified her that Dr. Kushni was making his rounds and would be by to check in on her.

Meredith waited, impatiently tapping her fingers against her thighs and trying desperately to recall any memory from the darkness that was the past several years.

She succeeded in recalling a few, most of them of her school days and young adult life. They were scattered thoughts, as if someone had taken a folder full of her memories and threw it high in the air. The memories fell to the ground and landed, some face up and some face down, but none of them were in any recognizable pattern or order. She had to piece them together from peripheral understanding of the memory. Understanding that this gas station had been demolished at some point—she still couldn't pinpoint how she knew—so the memory had to be prior to this one, and that one had to be after because the station wasn't there anymore.

It was an exercise in mental precision, and by the time Dr. Kushni stopped by, the effort had produced a fine sheen of sweat on her forehead, which she hastily wiped away. The headache that had been plaguing her since she woke up the previous day had blessedly disappeared, leaving her the capacity to move without feeling as if her head was going to roll from her shoulders at any second.

"Good morning, Miss Meredith. How are we feeling today?" His voice was pleasant and the smile that greeted her was reassuring, a kind of anchor she could latch on to while she flailed about inside her own mind.

"I'm feeling rather well today. Actually," she hesitated only briefly, "I had a question, about the man that came to my bed yesterday?" Her voice had lost its rasp, and she spoke clearly.

Dr. Kushni folded his hands before him, both of them grasping the clipboard he had been checking. "Yes, that was an unfortunate interaction. I am terribly sorry that it upset you as much as it did, Miss." She could tell it was something of an admission, that perhaps he realized he should have done more to stop it but realized it only after the adrenaline of confrontation had worn off.

She shook her head and smiled, "No, actually, that's okay. I simply wondered if you had a chance to find out who he was? I wanted to ask him some questions." Her voice became small as she finished, understanding that she was now agreeing with his previous recommendation after she'd vehemently opposed it.

She was surprised, however, when Dr. Kushni smiled broadly at her. He nodded once with finality and said, "I think that's an excellent idea, Miss. I will have him brought up immediately."

She sat up a little straighter. "Immediately? What do you mean? He's actually here? Already?" She idly tucked a strand of hair behind her ear.

Dr. Kushni nodded again, nearly a bow this time. "Yes, Miss. He was so adamant, and there was no record of it otherwise, that we allowed him to stay in the hospital lobby last night. He was no danger to anyone and actually apologized profusely for causing any measure of discomfort to you and my staff. He was actually very kind."

Chuckling, he continued, "After speaking with him briefly, we determined it may be relevant for him to speak with you. It could perhaps help jumpstart the memory recovery for you." Turning serious, quick as a flash, he said. "However, if he scares you or threatens you in any way, you need only to press the red button next to your bed."

He indicated a small rectangle, one end raised, the other lowered. A teeter totter for ants, she mused to herself without finding much humor in it.

"I'll have the guards that were so generous at escorting him last night wait by the nursing station until you're ready for him to leave. Will that be okay?"

Meredith was surprised that he had offered it. There were so many people that needed help, and she was only one of them. Perhaps it was the oddity of her memory loss or that she was American that made her worth the extra time. She suddenly became embarrassed at the latter thought, a blush rising in her cheeks at how arrogant it was, even within the confines of her own mind.

Regardless, she was thankful for it and told him so.

He waved her thanks away good-naturedly, told her that he'd return with the man named Evan, and began walking down the hallway, not quite at a run.

She felt more than butterflies zipping this way and that within her stomach. There must be an entire forest carousing in her midsection. She took a few deep breaths to try and calm her nerves, but it only seemed to give the damn butterflies more room.

She straightened the covers and wished desperately for a brush, as she was certain there were still sticks and mud crusting most of her hair, but when she felt her head, she was surprised to find it fairly well maintained. Perhaps the nurses had cleaned and brushed out her hair while she'd been unconscious.

But before she could grab the attention of a passing nurse, the man she had been terrified of only the night before poked his head around the curtain that sat listlessly on makeshift rails above her bed.

He looked much the same as he had yesterday, she noticed, as he moved cautiously closer to her bed. His hair was a terrible mess, caked with that same combination of mud and rusty blood down the side of his face in a haphazard crescent. His face was flushed with what she could only guess was restrained excitement, but somehow, his eyes remained sunken and haunted. They floated above garish circles of hazy bleakness, and his high cheekbones highlighted the strong jawline of Germanic descent. He didn't quite look skeletal, but a few more days of not eating, and he could be mistaken for Halloween decoration.

"Can I come in?" he asked with a sort of half-smile. She could tell that his surprise at seeing her had worn off, replaced now with caution, as if she were some frightened doe he was approaching in the forest.

She nodded and tried to smile but was afraid it came off as a bit of a sneer, the way her dried lips caught on her unbrushed teeth. Her heart hammered mercilessly in her chest, and she was positive that the blanket bulged with every beat.

He walked around the curtain, and her earlier assessment of skeletal was confirmed to an even greater degree. His clothes hung off his frame as if he were nothing more than a wire hanger. One shoulder and half his chest bare, the shirt hanging lazily below his collarbone. Small dark patches of wiry hair sprouted from the crust of mud that spattered the skin on his chest. His jeans were loose and held up by a belt that she could see had been tightened past the usual notch, the leather worn and molded with use two notches down.

She must have gasped because he looked up sharply and then clipped the bed with his leg, sending him stumbling across the space between them. He grasped for the bed and succeeded in only grabbing the top blanket, which was yanked unceremoniously to the floor as he fell. She reached for him and then found herself giggling and unable to stop. When his head popped comedically above the edge of the bed, he was wearing a goofy grin that far showed too many teeth, very much like a skull. But the wry grin was comforting and not the least bit defensive.

"Sorry," he mumbled as he got to his feet and walked to the edge of her bed. She gestured for him to sit, and he eased himself onto it, laying the blue blanket in a bundle between them.

"So," she began, a note of coy harassment in her voice. "You're my husband? Evan?" She didn't even think about it before saying it and immediately regretted it. The words were supposed to come out as playfully sarcastic, but the playful part must not have come across at all. Instead, she sounded accusatory, as if she were interviewing and accusing him of theft. In a way, she thought that maybe she was.

She saw him swallow hard, his Adam's apple bobbing up and down beneath his fuzzy chin, and he smiled, almost abashed. "I am, yeah. I mean, I have been for four years, I think. I always have a hard time with dates."

He sighed and laughed, but there was no mirth in it. "You don't remember me at all?"

His eyes may have been set in sunken sockets, but as he stared at her, she could see the pleading desperation emanating from deep within them. He wanted her to know him so badly, that she found herself wanting to lie and say she did. But that would be cruel, and she didn't want to give him any kind of false hope.

She cleared her throat. It was suddenly dry as a desert. "I've been trying to remember more of my life, and I've been successful in a way. I still don't remember you as an adult, but I do remember you as a kid. We were close, as I remember it, and I'm pretty sure we liked each other a lot."

His eyes brightened, and he nodded vigorously. "Yeah, that's right. We were fond of each other. We sort of fell away when we went to college, but there was always some string that brought us back together. I always felt like I could look over my shoulder, and you'd be there. For most of our adolescent life, we grew up together."

It sounded nice, she had to admit. Something almost out of a storybook. Girl and boy meet as children, grow up together where the friendship blossoms into romance, and get married and live happily ever after.

But she didn't know this guy—at least not as an adult. Her memories of him consisted of a scrawny boy that she had a crush on when she was little more than coming into her own as a preteen. Adult relationships—especially marriage—were much more complicated than what she remembered feeling for him back then.

Of course, it made a kind of sense that this guy would be here, the only one she knew, but they had a history together. She didn't want to admit it, but the thought wouldn't leave her, like a fly that continued to buzz about her head. No matter how much waving and batting, it always came back.

She spent so much of the past few hours trying to convince herself that there was no way that she was married to him that she forgot to take the other side and argue it. Maybe she was married to this guy, Evan. Certainly it was possible, but it wasn't *probable*. Granted, she thought, it was the *most* probable thing she'd experienced these last 24 hours.

"So, what happens now, Evan? You're going to whisk me off into the sunset and everything becomes normal again? Because I'll be honest, I'm scared as hell for a couple reasons." She counted them out on her fingers as she said them, "I'm alone in my own mind hoping someone doesn't take advantage of me. I'm hoping you're not a liar because it sure sounds nice, what you're saying. And finally, I don't know if I even know who I am. Following that, I may be the person that you were married to on the outside, but what if I'm not her on the inside?" Her thoughts strayed back to those two dichotomous notions that seemed to pop back into existence.

She looked at him, hoping he'd either say something fantastic enough to believe or fantastic enough to dismiss, and she was scared of both options. He delivered on the former, something she would always remember.

He chuckled lightly at first and then exhaled, saying, "That hasn't been the plan, no. I don't think it would help you by taking you out of here, yet. Actually, I was going to see if you wanted to get some coffee or something. I can't imagine what's going through your head, but I know you well enough to know that you don't trust at the drop of a hat. You've always been like that. You need someone to earn your trust, and it's hard. But when they do, you trust them wholly. I want to earn that trust, *your* trust, and I'll wait until I do. Is that okay?"

She stared at him, trying to pick up any derision or sarcasm in his voice. She could find no bitterness or frustration secreted away between the words, so she had no choice. In this instance, she was thankful for that. She nodded her head and swallowed. "Okay," she said, "I think I'd like that."

He nodded and got up. "I'll go grab us a cup of coffee, and we'll chat, at least until the doc says you're all clear."

When he returned, he held two steaming cups of coffee. She took a tentative sip of her own and smiled warmly at him. Two creams and two sugars, just the way she liked it.

He got lucky, she thought.

She suddenly remembered how he could get his Chip scanned and verified, and it would all be proof to his claim, so she asked him about it, sipping contentedly on her coffee while he spoke.

He shook his head and sat up a little, rubbing the location of his Chip absentmindedly. "Unfortunately, I already asked that. In fact, I asked the doctor last night—he can tell you I did, I'm not lying about it—and he said the local servers are so backed up not only with the requests for verification and Hazing, but also with logging everything that had happened that they're denying requests for anything new until they can get the backup log shortened a bit. Otherwise, I'd have already done it."

"Did they give you a timeline? Maybe a few days or a week at most?"

"They told me 'until further notice.' To me, that means more than a week, maybe even more than several weeks."

Meredith nodded. She would ask Dr. Kushni, but she had to admit to herself that it made too much sense to be a lie and a rather extravagant one at that.

It was one of the few issues that the SafetyChip was known to run into since its public distribution. The backup, verification, and Hazing process, while nearly instantaneous, still required a great deal of digital resources. In times like this, where some disaster—natural or otherwise—occurred, the requirement for those resources grew exponentially with the number of requests being generated. It was like the Internet, that precursor to the current Intersphere, when multiple pages could be open simultaneously but each additional page sapped memory resources of the computer running it, resulting in sluggish processes of everything running, not only the Internet. Haz

Modern technology was great, but it always reached a wall, some limitation that rendered it nearly obsolete no matter how advanced it was.

They sat in silence, both drinking their coffee for a few minutes before she spoke to him again. She knew Dr. Kushni would be along shortly, if not to check an adjacent patient then to check on her visitor. She might as well use the time they had right now to try and regain some memories, and maybe some trust.

"Where do we live?" she asked.

Evan cocked his head, not understanding.

"I mean in the States, where do we live?"

"Oh, I see. Sorry, I—anyway. We live in the house I grew up in, actually. Arkansas. Far enough from the city to be considered 'outside,' but close enough that a short drive of an hour to be within city limits."

It didn't spark any recognition, though she had a brief and very vague picture of a house surrounded by field, and then, it was gone.

Suddenly, a great fear gripped her, and she grabbed his forearm so hard that she flinched at her white-knuckled grip. When she spoke, her voice was a harsh, desperate whisper.

"Do I have kids?"

Evan, surprised by the sudden urgency of her words, leaned away from her, shaking his head.

"No, Mer, no we don't—don't have kids. We—" he stopped abruptly and swallowed, "Why?"

She released his arm with a small apology and took a steadying breath. She wondered what he was going to say but didn't pursue it.

"Well, I was terrified that we were both over here, and they were somewhere wondering where their mom and dad were." She looked at him with mock accusation. "That is, if I believe you. But then I started to wonder what would happen if I saw them, and since I can't remember anything..." She trailed off as her throat grew tight.

In a surprising show of tenderness, he gently picked up her hand. He didn't hold it, but he placed their palms together, bringing his other hand to sandwich hers. He squeezed gently and smiled in a way that she couldn't identify at first but understood later as revisited regret.

"No, we—we don't have to worry about that at all. Everything will be okay. In fact, the only people waiting for us are Mason and Marcy."

She didn't recognize either name and shook her head. Despite not recognizing them, she felt a sense of normalcy washing away the anxiety and fear that had gripped her so completely during their previous interaction. It was suspiciously comfortable, she noted. The coffee, the conversation, the vague memory of a home.

Evan shrugged and continued with a half-grin, "That's fine. They're good friends of ours. I managed to get ahold of them last night. They've been worried sick and have been asking for updates constantly. They were over the moon that I'd found you and wanted to fly out here when they heard you were in a hospital, but I told them not to, for several reasons. The main one, though was that the local airport is currently closed to all travel.

"They promised to be available when we get home for anything you or I need. They're pretty amazing people." He grinned fondly.

"They sound amazing." She smiled, now feeling a bit of sadness in it herself. "I wish I knew them." She laughed, now, and even though it was only an ironic laugh, Evan smiled with her.

"You will. You'll either get to know them again or remember them again. But either way, you'll love them." He sounded so *certain*, but she couldn't imagine why. There was no promise that she'd ever remember anything. If she did decide to go with him—and let it be known she hadn't—she'd essentially be travelling with a complete stranger. No, that wasn't quite right. He wasn't a *complete* stranger; he was *mostly* a stranger. An old friend she'd reconnected with at best.

She was thankful that he was kind and understanding. He wasn't pressuring her to be someone she couldn't be, and that was comforting in a way she didn't know she had the capacity to feel amidst the mental upheaval that was her current reality.

It was as if he were on an island floating above raging seas, reaching down for her hand, and all she had to do was grasp it so that it would all be safe and calm.

Dr. Kushni interrupted this scene in her mind by appearing around the curtain, cautious at first but accurately reading both of their expressions that everything *felt* fine.

"Hello, Miss. I'm glad to see you talking with Mr. Evan. Do you need anything?"

"I wonder if I could actually check out? I'm not feeling the need to stay here, I'm getting a little hungry, and I'd like to talk with Evan a little more. Somewhere with less beeping and overhead announcements. Maybe something that is not a hospital."

This brought a round of small chuckles from the three of them, and Dr. Kushni nodded in understanding.

"Of course. You are free to go. And I'm very glad to see you smiling. You have a very pretty smile, Miss."

Evan grinned at her and said, "She does, doc. It's what made me fall in love with her."

CHAPTER 16

Back in The Bench, she thumbed the vid to stop. Her heart ached to keep it going, to relive it all, to see his smile again, but she couldn't let herself.

The beeping within the memory faded from mind's eye, taking with it the sickly sweet smells of death and antiseptic, those two guardians of the infirm.

She looked at Evan who was staring at the screen in the air, now black as night and void of any accompanying memory.

It was such a strange juxtaposition to see—and remember experiencing—the deep-seated fear she had felt when Evan approached her for the first time alongside her current knowledge of love and devotion to the same man. She couldn't decide if he should see their next few meetings in the same way she'd played the previous one but knew they all led up to the same thing. That one act that left them ruined. Something she couldn't quite think about. Not yet.

"Evan," she whispered. He turned to her slowly, and surprisingly, a faint smile was playing on his lips.

"I really looked like shit, didn't I?" He said it with a tone of joviality, but she now realized that his smile, while genuine, hid all of the other emotions she expected to see. Blessed Evan, ever the optimist.

She smiled in return and a small giggle scampered out, surprising them both. "You really did, babe. But there was a sense of rugged charm hiding beneath it all. I remember thinking that you were pretty cute, even as a skeleton."

Then they laughed. It was, for her own benefit, a laugh that took the fear and unease from the room. She realized she'd nearly been holding her breath. To understand that Evan had no memory of anything that happened—even after their return to the States—had done more to her emotional stability than she'd initially given credit.

"What happened after that? What did we do?" He was hungry for the knowledge, like a child that has discovered a new favorite topic or hobby.

She let the laughter fade, but the affectionate smile remained. "We actually started dating again." This made her laugh a little more, and Evan laughed all the more loudly. The deep throaty chuckles that she missed terribly.

"Really? That doesn't sound like me. I was always such an awful date."

"No, no, you were a valorous guy while I recovered. We went on several dates over the course of ten days before coming home. We went for coffee, chai, curry, all of it. I asked questions, you answered, and there were some really beautiful nights. You were nothing short of a gentleman."

She could feel tears of suppressed nostalgia begin to sting the corners of her eyes, and she hastily wiped them away before continuing.

"We ended up coming back to the States after you verified your identity with actual documents. I know I always made fun of you for it because you were such a traditionalist, but they actually came in handy this time. They were still stuffed in the suitcase, wrapped in plastic and safe from the tsunami.

We were able to go back and get them after they cleared the city a few weeks afterward.

"They were able to verify our relationship through electronic public records. It took a couple of hours, but we weren't going anywhere, really. We took it all in stride, grabbed some lunch, talked some more, and went back to the documentation office. Once that was verified, we were able to book flights home by taking a bus north and—" She stopped, the wistful joy that came with remembering their adventure began to go gray, her enthusiasm turning into wisps of smoke in her mind.

"Anyway, it was this big thing that took way too long. We came home, and I still felt like a stranger in my own place. It was odd, unsettling, walking down our hallway and seeing pictures on the walls and in the bedroom. I had to reconcile that there was this life we had together, but it was a complete blank in my mind. I felt like a ghost floating through this other Meredith's life. I walked where she walked, slept where she slept, ate where and what she ate. I was a foreign body.

"Some days, I would walk through the house, staring at pictures for hours or holding onto blankets and pillows, breathing in the smells around me trying desperately to recall something—anything—that would jumpstart the process of regaining my memories. It didn't work.

"I remembered the house, sort of, remembered that it was an important part of my life but didn't know where it fit. For all I knew, it was my childhood home, and those memories were phantoms of my life. I had no idea that the way I felt about the home originated from the fact that my best life had been lived there."

She stopped. Evan continued to stare at her, listening intently. She began recalling where their new life became more painful. And, if she was being honest with herself, a little scary.

"One morning, I remembered finding a note on the countertop from Mason, though at the time I couldn't picture his face, either. Or Marcy. They were both strangers to me and didn't pull any kind of recollection, not even the shadow of one.

"But the note said that if we needed anything—here he had underlined the word 'anything' four times, creating a large black swath beneath it—to call him, and their number was below that."

Here it was.

"I began walking through the house trying to regain my memories and spent several hours doing it. I sat on beds, laid on the couch, looked out windows and dug into the closets. I was desperate for something that would make me feel like I was where I'd always belonged.

"I knew you'd give me some space; you said so on the plane back.

"What I didn't know is that you poured yourself a drink after bringing the luggage in and sat at the kitchen table by yourself. Obviously, at that time, I had no idea you liked to drink. Like most people, we had a liquor cabinet and a wine rack that was mostly ornamental.

"It wasn't until you started crying and speaking about how much you tried—rattled on, would be a more appropriate description—I decided to give Mason a call." Her hands were shaking, now.

Meredith looked up at him, clasping her hands in her lap and leaning toward him, almost conspiratorially. "He answered on the first ring. I told him that I had gotten his note and that I thought it might be a good idea for him to come over. I tried to describe how you were acting, but he interrupted immediately and said he'd be there in 10 minutes, then hung up." She smiled in soft bitterness. "He was there in eight because I remember watching the clock. Evan, I know you probably don't remember your drunken stupor, but don't you remember anything during that time? Don't you remember anything once we got back from Sri Lanka? Anything at all?" Her eyes were desperate and pleading. She knew it, and she felt the soft shining crescent of tears welling in her eyes as she continued to stare at him.

Evan swallowed hard. "I'm trying to understand how there could be a gap in my memory. It seemed like a small thing at first. After all, people forget events in their lives all the time. But the SafetyChip was supposed to prevent that. It was supposed to increase memory recollection almost infinitely.

"Mer, I don't-don't remember anything about it. I don't even remember getting on the plane in Sri Lanka. I don't remember landing, and I don't remember anything after that. It's like, it's like everything after that just—" He shrugged, trying not to look clueless and failing miserably. "It's impossible," he finished dejectedly.

Meredith stared at him for a few minutes, searching his eyes for any hint of deception, any indication that he was hiding something.

After a moment, she gave a final sigh and continued. "When Mason arrived, the rain started. Normally, at least the way we tend to remember it, rain begins gently and grows in intensity. This rain started and all at once it was thunder and lightning and torrential downpour. It was hammering down on the ground and the roof. It covered every noise and muted our voices that we almost had to yell to be heard.

"When it fell on the walkway outside, the drops were so big and heavy that they smacked onto the concrete; it sounded like hundreds of people were applauding the lightshow overhead.

"Mason got out of his car, and I guess you had seen the headlights shine through the windows onto the walls because you got up and started walking out the front door before I could even register you'd left the kitchen. You staggered a little, but for the most part, you were steady.

"He ran up toward the house, stopping when he saw you standing beneath the front porch roof. The rain was thunderous, but I could hear what you were saying. I was standing at the window watching through the curtains. I knew I should know you better and here was that chance. The opportunity to gain more knowledge intrigued me enough to listen to every word. Part of me wishes I hadn't. But hindsight is always twenty-twenty."

At this, she stood up and glanced around, walking a few feet from him to stand in the artificial sunlight. The wind tousled her hair gently, and she let it wave about her head. The effect was mesmerizing, as if she were underwater and her hair was being moved about by the current rather than the wind. Meredith gazed out over the cliffs below her, trying to find the words to explain everything she was feeling during that time. Evan remained on The Bench, waiting for her.

There were two separate chains of thought. What she *knew* and what she knew she *should* know. It was strange, like overlapping pictures and neither one clear enough to make out.

She came to the realization that telling it would not only be emotionally impossible, but it would be unclear. She would only be able to communicate a limited number of things. It would be much easier—and simpler—to *show* Evan. She could let him see exactly what happened.

The scene appeared to pick up where Meredith had stopped. It showed the perspective of someone looking through a window at two figures silhouetted against a rain-streaked sky. Lightning flashed in the distant black sky and the thunder of heavy rain encompassed them all.

One of the figures was Mason, his shirt soaked and clinging to his muscular torso, seeming to reach the limits by which it could contain his bulk.

Meredith watched Evan for the first few minutes. When he noticed one of the figures in the vid was him, he jumped in surprise and looked at her. Meredith nodded encouragingly, and he looked back at the screen.

He stood up, taking tentative steps closer to the hole in the air now floating above the ground and squinted, trying to get a closer look, a different angle. But it was static; it was *her* view.

The figures on the screen were moving toward one another through Meredith's recorded vision. Even now, it was difficult to believe what she saw. She knew he had always been of average height and build, never very muscular but never heavy, either. As far as athleticism, he played but never committed, and his figure was always what she'd considered "fit."

But the figure that she intrinsically knew as her husband standing on the other side of the window was a reedy echo of who he once was. Enormous raindrops pelted the grass and walkway, bouncing around the feet of her husband. He was a phantasm.

That Evan was more than simply gaunt; he seemed barely able to stand on his feet. His clothes were baggy in a way that showcased exactly how thin he had actually become. He hadn't gained much weight in the interim between her departure from the hospital and their return to the States.

When the lightning lit the sky and ground below, the shadows it cast only emphasized his sunken sockets. The chill she felt sank deep into the marrow of her bones and stayed there.

He wasn't much more than a walking skeleton, with skin as thin as paper stretched across the rickety scaffolding of his body.

Meredith sat close enough to him that she could have reached out and touched his arm, but he was so absorbed in the screen that he didn't notice the tears tumbling down her cheeks.

She could feel the dismay and oppressive hurt rising from the memories she had worked so hard to minimize. Overcome with emotion, she covered her mouth and eyes with the palms of her hands, praying for a reserve of strength she didn't believe she had.

Mason's voice spoke, muffled by the rain and window that separated Meredith and the two men outside. "Evan, what's wrong? Meredith called and I came right over. Is everything okay?"

Evan replied, "Whadurr you doon here?" Even through the clapping rain and occasional rumbling thunder, she could hear how strained—and slurred—the words were.

Mason took a step closer, looking intently into Evan's eyes. "Evan, are you drunk? What—what is going on?" There wasn't much room between them now, and Mason tried to take another step and put his arm around Evan. The sign of someone seeing a good friend hurting who is unable to pull themselves out of it.

But despite his obvious drunkenness and skeletal frailty, Evan deftly ducked and turned away out of Mason's reach.

He took a step back away from Mason, and this brought him out from under the protective shielding of the porch overhang and into the pouring rain. Immediately, he was drenched, and where previously his dry clothes sagged list-lessly with the weight of the water, they now stuck to him in odd places. In other places they appeared to be dripping off of him, draining off his bones like wet paint soaking slowly into the sodden ground.

Where Evan's clothes appeared to be dripping off his body, Mason's seemed to be painted on, soaked to the bone and sticking to every curve of muscle.

When Evan spoke, it was a little harder to hear but still clear enough to understand. His Adam's apple moved beneath the steady sheen of water coursing down his strained neck muscles. "I don' need 'ur halp, Mezzen." The last word, obvi-ously meant to be his friend's name, came out in a jumble.

Mason stepped out into the rain, blinking it away and ignoring it just as much as he ignored the rest of Evan's words.

"Buddy, it is more than obvious that you do. It seems like you need me more now than you ever have."

Meredith put her hand to her chest. The love this man had for his friend was unrivaled, and she knew that Evan was one of the luckiest men in the world to have found such loyalty.

He took a step forward. "Evan, you've just gotten home, and there's already enough going on in your life. You don't need to add to it by drinking. I'm not judging, don't feel that, but if you want Mer to come back to us, she's going to have to be reminded of the man she married, of the man she fell in love with those years ago. Not this—" he gestured vaguely in Evan's direction, "whatever this is."

The storm thundered its applause in response, but Evan stood blinking in the rain. It ran freely into his eyes and dripped off his nose, chin, and earlobes. He looked like he was drowning and didn't give a damn.

"You don even know, Macenon—Mazn." Evan stumbled over the name and looked into Mason's concerned eyes. Meredith could feel the hurt thrown at him as Mason heard the words, dripping with acid, spoken by his truest friend. He listened to the words and processed them. The pain of seeing his friend hurting and lost and quite literally wasting away was reflected in the disquieting worry that dripped from the stoic mask he now wore.

"You probbly never will." Evan lowered his head and brought his hands up to cradle it, holding it dejectedly in the downpour as the rain continued to hammer the earth. The intermittent flashes of light and occasional bolt that etched itself through the sky in the distance highlighted the two figures in the yard with surreal and jarring uncertainty—one tall and proud, the other bent and broken. But both subject to the storm.

When Evan began moving, he stumbled a little past Mason, who threw up an arm to catch him, sending an arc of water through the air. Evan was slow to react and landed on the helping arm that Mason offered but pushed back and grimaced at his friend.

The sneer that contorted his face was a grisly grin of teeth that seemed to shine pale in the eroding darkness.

Evan's voice, raised in a yell through the rain, took on a haunting quality. "You will *never* know what is like b'cus you an-an-an *Marcy*—" he nearly spit the name "have a perfeck liddle life." The words were slurred but unmistakable. His drunken and misplaced disdain for his best friends was coming through loud and clear, released from logic's gates and allowed the freedom to cast blame and hurt without direction or reason.

Mason stood up straighter, his face screwed up in a look of confused disbelief. "What? Evan, what are you talking about? Our 'perfect little life?' What the hell do you even mean?"

Evan laughed bitterly and threw his arms up, flinging tiny droplets of water through the air as lightning flashed through the sky again. It looked as if he had flung two handfuls of glitter through the air and each one sparkled for the briefest moment before being consumed by the surrounding darkness.

"Oh right, right, you don't see it. 'Course you don. You got a perfeck marriage and a perfeck baby and a perfeck house to go 'long withit."

Evan sniffed and wiped his sodden arm across his nose, attempting to wipe it and succeeding in only allowing more water to wash across it. His voice became thick with repressed emotion, cracking and groaning like a wooden ship being tossed by a watery gale. "And-and your wife knows ezzackly who you are and you don' haveta try and figure out howda convincer that you still love her no-no matter what." Meredith's eyes grew cloudy, her view of the two men wavering and then stretching as tears welled in her eyes. The words, which Evan had thrown so carelessly, hit impossibly close to the very fear she was trying to work through.

She wiped the tears away, trying to see how the two men could possibly reconcile after such haphazard accusations.

The quivering lip and frown that replaced Evan's grimace showed Mason that his friend's words were only blustering pain, trying desperately to hide the immense pain and fear that was worming its way through his heart. It also did a poor job of hiding his very real tears as they mixed with the rain that coursed down his face.

Meredith took a deep breath and looked away from the vid. Having gained some control of her own emotions, she moved her head only enough to look covertly at her husband's face. To her surprise, she noticed his own tears had formed and were coursing down his cheeks. He was watching himself in some TV episode that he didn't have any recollection of participating in.

It felt as close to impossible as it could be without crossing the line into fantasy. But that's where they were now. They were approaching that line into fantasy.

She looked back at the screen, feeling some relief at seeing the sorrow that echoed within her own soul reaching out to his.

Evan, still standing resolutely in the rain, raised a shaky, dripping finger and snarled, "Fugyoo, Mayzin," and sniffed again. His red eyes were filled with a hellish agony that the alcohol didn't create, only accentuated. It tore down the temporary curtain that he'd built to protect his wife.

Mason's sodden shoulders were sagging now, and he was nodding in understanding, as if he finally understood what Evan was feeling in the deepest recesses of his secret heart. He could finally see through the mask, through the posturing, and what he saw didn't enrage him, only empowered him to be more understanding. Rain dripped steadily off his chin and off the ends of his curly hair. His arms ran with the heavy rivulets in shimmering visceral highways.

"Evan, you think our life is perfect? You think everything is great, and we never have any issues? You *know* that's not true, Evan. You *know* that! You've seen all of our ugly, the exact same way we've seen yours. My story is not your story, Evan, but it's still worth telling."

The rain continued to fall, but Mason's voice was raised and could be heard clearly. He took a step toward Evan, his foot scoffing water out of the way in a miniscule wave that was lost to the rest of the torrent, and put a hand on his friend's shoulder. He bent closer to his friend but was forced to speak above the incessant percussiveness of the rain.

"Evan, what other choice is there? To give up and leave Meredith in a world with only half of her memories and no one she knows alive anymore? What kind of life is that?"

Evan seemed to shrink with each rhetorical question Mason delivered. It seemed to encourage Mason, so he continued.

"What would you do anyway, go somewhere else and what, start over? Look at you, Evan. You're killing yourself!"

Evan recoiled as if Mason had hit him in the face and took a step back. Several looks cycled across his face in a flash, like shadows of clouds across a sun-bathed field. A look of deep hurt was replaced by a look of surprised horror, which was quickly replaced with a look of seething rage. He snarled and shook the water out of his eyes, looking very much like a drenched animal.

Then, he charged Mason, lowering his right shoulder and head like a bull, working to spear Mason in the mid-section. It may have worked on someone his own size, but Mason was, compared to this scrawny and almost translucent Evan, nearly twice his size. Evan ran with complete disregard to the size difference, and when he was within arm's reach, Mason side-stepped easily into the grass—now little more than a small pond—and Evan skidded to a stop, splashing water and almost falling. He turned with exaggerated slowness, waving his arms disjointedly to maintain his balance. It all would have been funny under different circumstances.

Meredith gasped. It was barely audible over the rain as it assaulted the men outside. She could feel her heart hammering and hands shaking with every beat. She covered her mouth and part of her wanted to look away, part of her wanted to wake up from this whole thing, but she knew she couldn't. She was transfixed, as much a player in this as Evan and Mason. It was terrible to see. Even more terrible to remember where it led.

Evan's shoulders heaved up and down in the rain. Then he charged once more at Mason, kicking up large transparent explosions of water with each splashing step, and in a gesture that she couldn't determine if purposeful or mere accident, he slipped past Mason's broad outstretched arm by half-falling and half-dipping. Evan screamed in rage. It rent the air and seemed to slip between every raindrop that could have muffled it, and it rang through the yard with merciless clarity. To Meredith, watching behind the window, it came to her with both agony and fury, everything characteristic of a final assault. Meredith watched with mounting horror and the world slowed as Evan punched Mason square on the jaw.

Water flew in an expanding arc from his hair as Mason's head snapped to the side. His expression changed from surprise and mild pain into a disbelieving grin that in the harsh light flashing through the air with water cascading across his eyebrows could easily be seen as growing frustration. To Meredith, it appeared that his patience had been exhausted.

Meredith jumped in surprise when Evan's fist connected with Mason's jaw. It was only a moment before she began moving, rushing from the window where she'd watched the whole thing to the door. She took long strides toward it and grasped the cool, slick doorknob with her own booming frustration, and heaved the door open. Her hair fluttered around her head as the air rushed past her, but she tucked it hurriedly behind her ears, watching the two men before her.

Mason's expression had changed as he looked through the rain at his friend. It had reverted, to Meredith at least, to something closer to pity. He shook his head, ran his hands through his hair and stepped back, locking eyes with Meredith standing in the doorway.

A fine mist, the tiny children of raindrops that fell and exploded on the porch roof, now fell toward her and, in the light from the door, shone in the darkness. The look that Mason gave her said, "We are still here if you need us, but tonight, he's crossed a line." And she understood. The tears that had been threatening to fall for the past several minutes made their debut.

With that, Mason stepped close Evan with a grace that surprised her. And despite his protests of frustration and increased thrashing, Mason hugged him close to his chest, ensuring that his mouth was near Evan's ear to be heard over the continual rain. Meredith was shaking with silent sobbing as she watched the man she knew she *should* love struggling helplessly against the man her husband held so dear to his own heart.

"Are you done?" Mason yelled loud enough to be heard through the thunder that cracked through the sky like a colossal whip. "Evan, you're better than this. I know you're going through a really rough patch, but I need to know that you're done. You need to go into the house, take a cold shower, and go to bed. Sleep this off. You're scaring me, and that doesn't happen easily. But more importantly, you're scaring Meredith. Is this how you're going to help her remember?"

Water flew from his lips with every puff of breath as he spoke. And Evan, weak as he was, could do little more than flail his feet in the muddy grass.

Water dripped from Mason's nose and ears down to Evan's shoulder, joining the rest of the emptying skies as they plummeted ruthlessly toward the ground. With one final, weak thrash of his feet and arms pinned at his sides, Evan started sobbing uncontrollably and nodded his head. Mason relaxed his grip a small amount, and when Evan didn't try to wriggle or run, he set his feet gently on the ground.

Evan didn't let go, though. Instead, he wrapped his thin arms around Mason's bulging torso and sobbed into his chest.

Meredith saw the corners of Mason's mouth turn down, and his chin gained the unmistakable dimples of the effort to suppress deep emotion. Despite his efforts, his shoulders began to tremble as he, too, sobbed and held his friend.

Meredith felt like an outsider, like she was somewhere she shouldn't be. Perhaps there would be a time when she would understand the intimacy her husband shared with his friend, but she also couldn't help but wonder how it existed at all. Too many men believed intimacy with another man could only fall into two camps. The first was that it was non-existent. Friendships were only surface level. Oh sure, they could dive into a tirade about work or even a relationship, but that was it. If it went any deeper than that, it fell into the other camp. What most people would consider vulnerability, men tended to believe it emasculating to share deep feelings with another man. Meredith didn't know what she would do if she didn't have friends to share her deepest emotions with, but she also knew that men were different in that way. It was incredibly rare to see a man show emotion—deep, hidden emotion—to another man.

But she couldn't look away. She was mesmerized, completely absorbed by the tenderness between the two men standing in the rain embracing each other. They loved one another, and it reminded her distantly of a story in the Bible she'd heard as a child between a crazed king's son and his friend. Intimacy didn't always mean anything sexual, and she was thankful that her husband—stranger though he may be at this point—had someone he could rely upon in this regard. He obviously couldn't rely on her, at least not yet.

With a gentle rub and pat on the back, Mason held Evan at arm's length. Both men looked at each other, wiping the rain from their faces with unsteady hands.

Mason helped Evan toward the door, and when he was close to Meredith, she heard him say, "Go inside and get some dry clothes on. You already look like you're on death's door; don't get any closer to it. Get some sleep, and I'll come by tomorrow to check on you."

Evan continued to walk ponderously through the rain and standing water toward the door. Mason's arm still held him around the shoulder, but to Meredith, it was also helping to support him.

As he approached, she couldn't help but gaze fixedly at her husband. She moved aside when he was near, letting him pass the threshold to make muddy, splashing tracks through the house to the bathroom. She wasn't even sure he'd seen her; he hadn't looked up as he passed. Part of her hoped it had been in shame that he'd avoided her eyes. The other part feared she had been forgotten in that moment.

She looked back at Mason and found him on the front porch, water and grassy mud dripping down his sodden legs and off his fingertips, a depressing puddle expanding at his feet.

He took a deep breath and said, "I'm sorry, Meredith. Thanks for calling. Marcy is at home with Maddie; otherwise, she'd be here, too. We will come by tomorrow." His face said that he was sorry to have been needed, but glad that he had come, and his small smile was tired but reassuring.

She nodded and thanked him, tucking a strand of hair behind her ear more from habit than actual need, "Yeah, thanks for coming, Mason. I'm fine. A little shaken up." She hesitated, unsure if she wanted to hear the answer to the question that was before her. "Was he always like this?"

Mason's stance lost a fraction of height as he sagged a little in what she could only assume was tired relief. "No, Meredith, he wasn't ever like this. He rarely drank, and he was always trying hard to be on the right team, *your* team." He shook his head sadly. "The tsunami and everything else, it changed him. He's lost a part of himself that he's known for nearly twenty-five years, and that's you. He's trying to figure out where to go from here."

He stared into the house, following the trail of muddy footprints. Grunts and the slopping sounds of wet clothes landing on the hardwood floors made their way out to them despite the rain that continued to fall.

"I know you need time, but so does he. It's a lot like before you went to Sri Lanka—the whole baby thing. It's going to have to be a team effort to get back into the rhythm again. I don't know everything that you're both going through, but I know that. Please remember, Meredith. He's on your team. He always has been."

He stepped closer and looked at Meredith with a heartfelt smile. "And remember, we are here for you. If you need anything, you call me or Marcy. Both of our numbers are there on the counter, and we'll be here as fast as we can. We both know that you don't remember us, but that's not going to stop us from being here for you. We've loved you for as long as we've loved Evan."

Meredith began to shake with sobs which started out slow but grew in intensity. She covered her face with her hands, and Mason stepped toward her, wrapping his muscular arms around her and pulling her to him. She was surprised that she let him. To her, he was a stranger. But after the interaction between Mason and her husband and the subsequent intimacy she'd seen between them, she understood deeply that Mason was a man of integrity and empathy. She let him hold her until the weeping subsided into hitching gasps.

"Thank you, Mason. Really," she smiled up at him and patted his chest with her palm, "now I know why Evan appreciates you so much. You're one of the good ones, and I'm sure Marcy is, too."

Mason shrugged.

"I'll make sure Evan knows you're stopping by tomorrow. He'll probably be happy to see you. Or not. I don't really know." She gave a single chuckle that held only a small measure of honest bitterness.

They said their goodbyes, and she watched as he walked through the continuing rain to his car, opened the door with a squeal of hinges and hopped in, trying to avoid letting as much rain as possible soak the interior of his car.

When his taillights turned from their driveway, Meredith waved one last time from the porch and closed the door.

CHAPTER 17

The vid playback stopped, and the black screen collapsed quickly. The view of the sea was back, clear as ever, with no sign that a temporary screen had just shown one of the last interactions they would have together.

Evan turned to Meredith who was no more than a couple of feet away. Both of their tears had stopped falling, but the shining tracks that trailed down her cheeks were still evidence enough that the tears had barely subsided.

She smiled that same sad smile and said, "I did tell you the next day, and you were embarrassed, but you were also happy. You both apologized to one another, though to be perfectly honest I can't—even now—imagine why Mason apologized. You were a real bastard that night." She didn't mean to sound cruel but suspected that it came out that way. "Even still, Mason and Marcy came by for lunch the next day. It was nice, actually. Refreshing if I'm being honest. I remember how natural it felt being with them. It was a welcome change from the bundle of fear that churned in my stomach, my constant companion in those days."

With a small sigh, she began fixing her dress.

She felt new tears slide down her cheeks, that inevitable sign of the human inheritance, as H. G. Wells put it so callously. She couldn't imagine how many more tears were left, but she knew within her primal self, that there were still more that must be cried.

"They came by with Maddie another night, too. You were embarrassed, but they're sweet people. They forgave you, of course, and told you not to bring it up again."

"Of course, they did," he said, a look of gloomy disgust darkened his features. "I wish I hadn't been like that."

"That's one thing that still gets me."

"What do you mean?"

"How you could be so sweet and comforting, but then suddenly you began to drink, even though it was actually that one time, it was as if there were no walls between what you *wanted* to be and what was behind the calm demeanor. I mean, I get it. I'm sure it was hard to be in a one-sided relationship, but the difference was..."

"Staggering," he finished for her.

"Yes. That's exactly it. 'Staggering.'"

He shrugged. "I've never handled stress well, and even more so when it had to do with you. You held the key to a secret part of my heart. Any time something happened between the two of us, it was as if I had two separate entities in my brain. One—the loving, kind, and understanding husband, doting on his wife and working to be the person she wanted him to be. Then the second—a vile, depressed, irritated, and angry version of everything I wanted to lock up in the dark recesses of my mind forever."

She nodded. "Yeah, that makes sense, Evan. It makes a lot of sense. Explains almost everything.

"You know," she began, hoping to change the subject, "Mason and Marcy weren't the only ones who visited me—us— when we got back."

Evan looked at her and Meredith saw something kindle behind his eyes. It seemed to be pressing forward, pushing the mystery and sadness to the side. She recognized hope, there. Remembering the feeling like when she began to remember herself again.

"Really? Who would visit us?" He sat silent for a second and continued. "Other than Mason and Marcy, I can't remember—limited as my memory apparently is—who else could have even been a part of our life?" His face was screwed up in the same way that a child's would be, trying desperately to verify the last time they had a piece of candy after asking for more and being turned down by a parent.

Meredith nodded, swallowing hard. "Yes, it was a surprise to me as well. In fact—" She swallowed again. There was a lump in her throat that despite her efforts seemed to be stuck there and swallowing did nothing to ease the pressure.

Evan mistook her pause for breath as hesitation. "Was it someone nice? Someone we liked?"

She shook her head in the negative and tried to continue, lump and all. The result was that her voice sounded frail and watery. "I hadn't ever met this man before, but he knew you. He knew you very well." She folder her hands in her lap while Evan made a *hmph* sound and sat back against The Bench, his chin held in the palm of his hand. It had always been his nonverbal way to communicate a period of deep thinking. Meredith smiled despite the emotion she now felt and rubbed his leg affectionately.

He shook his head after several seconds of silent introspection, then sighed in exasperation. "I don't know, Mer. There's nothing that I can remember without more hints." He was looking at her and that small spark of hope had retreated briefly, she saw.

"It was Alan, Evan," she said quietly, hoping it was without emotion.

He continued to stare dumbly at her, his nose wrinkling. "Who—" he began and then stopped, clamping his mouth shut, recognition dawning and quickly fading to distaste.

"Alan? Alan. As in Alan my brother, Alan?"

Meredith nodded and couldn't help but laugh lightly, relishing the change of pace from sadness and despair to some semblance of joviality. His disbelief was merited, at the very least.

Evan spoke very sparingly about his family. It was a subject that she never pressed. She knew a vague overview of the circumstances that brought about his—and by extension, her—current relationship status with them, but beyond that there was nothing.

On top of that, Evan didn't like *talking* about his family, which Meredith assumed meant he also didn't like his family, either. It was true, she found, when Alan showed up, and Evan nearly went ballistic.

To be fair, she thought as he sat on The Bench stewing, he hadn't been in the best place. Not only that, but it was suspicious that Alan would show up at that time, after everything that had happened to them.

Even to this day, she wasn't sure how Alan had found their address and verified that they still lived there. It was incredibly uncommon to find someone living in the same place as public records showed, which were updated only every couple of years. Following that, most people moved into the cities following the Wars. The news kept calling it "herd mentality."

Evan's bitter chuckle brought her attention back to him. He was sitting with elbows on knees, shaking his head and staring at the ground.

"Why would he show up? What did we say? I mean, that's bizarre. It's insane! I haven't seen him since we were kids, why—and how—would he show up?"

He spoke it all in a single, rushing breath, evidence that he was truly upset. Meredith made a calming gesture with her hands, one he would certainly recognize as a nonverbal cue they'd developed over the time they spent together.

"Slow down, babe. It was strange, certainly. Instead of me telling you how it went, it would probably be better for me to show you another memory vid, if that's okay with you." While she didn't enjoy the idea of showing her viewpoint again, it was much easier for the same reasons as the Mason and Evan fight. It would explain not only what she saw but also show how she felt and thought in tandem with everything being said, like a hand to mouth or silent chuckle that went unnoticed.

Easier in some ways, but she could still tell she'd relive it within the privacy of her own mind, thinking and feeling all of those things again while her husband watched it from her perspective.

The Bench was somehow making her feel things with such pinpoint acuteness that she wanted to blame it—or the creators of it. But this was all stuff she should have dealt with instead of turning away from.

"Yeah, sure," he said shrugging. Sweet Evan, ever the compliant party, even when it was blatantly obvious that he had no desire to see his brother again.

She cued up the vid and sat back, closing her eyes and breathing deep, content to drown the sound out with her own memory.

CHAPTER 18

Their unexpected visitor came well before lunch, but long enough after breakfast that the dishes were done and drying on the counter. The last dregs of their coffee had cooled at the bottom in dark half-crescents within their mug, which sat stoically on the side tables in the living room.

Evan walked out of the bathroom, drying his hands on his shirt when he heard the muted chime of their doorbell. A relic they'd both agreed to keep for nostalgia's sake.

He stopped, a dark handprint drying on his shirt as he looked at the door quizzically. Meredith, who was reading *The Great Gatsby*, what some would call "classical literature," sat quietly on the couch closer to the door, so she placed the book on the side table next to her and moved a curtain aside to peek at their visitor.

She couldn't see the face of the person standing there but could see half an elbow in a tweed jacket and one leg in dress slacks. By the stance, she could safely assume it was a man. *A salesman*, she thought wryly, *someone trying to make a buck by selling some novel new gadget or an old one that has wormed its way back into the cultural spotlight by virtue of being nothing more than what's now considered "vintage."*

As she got up from the couch, she saw Evan watching her. His shirt—an unremarkable gray—still had fading handprints where he'd dried them, but the backs of his hands still shone with wetness. His eyes were questioning, and she wasn't sure if the curiosity was still directed at her or merely at their enigmatic gentleman caller.

She still hadn't regained her memories, despite supplying the necessary documentation to receive a Recovery from a center in the States, the nearest one in St. Louis. The waiting list was a long one. It didn't make a lick of sense to her, but she guessed the process was more involved than going into a clinic and connecting her chip wirelessly to a server and having her memories re-uploaded. Despite the tech that was developed year after year, it always struck her how the body responded, so much more complicated than any chip that could be developed. The body shut the chip down; they called it "Natural Hazing," making memories show during that time nothing more than a muted fog of moving shadows and hushed murmuring. There was no explanation for it, and there was nothing that could be done except reset the chip, re-upload all information prior to the Natural Hazing, and continue on.

What amazed her most, however, was that the Natural Hazing of specific trauma remained. The memories of that time, whether someone witnessed a murder or was raped, those memories remained muted to an extent. The mental picture could be recalled, but it was fuzzy, as if seen through a window covered in parchment paper. The sounds were present, too, but only as if heard in another room through the adjacent wall. The brain naturally recognized trauma and protected its host or the individual to which it belonged. It was remarkable.

She had tried to regain memories of Evan, but all she could recall were those smoky figures to a certain point. Of course, that was more than she had when waking up in the hospital. But it was unsatisfying to say the least. It was like being thirsty and seeing a picture of water. It only drew the lack of context in darker outlines.

Aside from that, her memory had returned to a certain extent, up to the point when she was in college. From what she could tell, that was 5 or 6 years ago. She knew Evan as a childhood friend and then a boyfriend. It didn't surprise her that they married, now on this side of the veil. She had loved him for a long time, she knew that, but she didn't *feel* it. That thread that connected her childhood crush to her lover and husband had been snipped in half. She had to find the two ends and tie them together. She'd found one but was still feeling in the dark for the other.

A frequent quote from her mother floated to the surface of her mind: "Love isn't a feeling. That's called infatuation. Love is what happens after the infatuation fades, when it becomes the choice you make every morning. Will I stay committed to this person, or will I choose to do what I want based solely on what's best for me? Choosing to work with that person—whether you want to or not—that decision is what we call 'love.'"

She knew her mother was right. Her mother, by that definition, loved her father even after he left. She hoped she would be able to mirror her in that regard. Be able to love someone to which she had little—or in her case, limited—connection.

She may not *feel* love toward Evan, but she was making choices that were leading her toward that. In a way, she thought, maybe she was choosing to love him. It wasn't easy, some small suspicious part of her whispered. Probably some remnant of that hurt girl that was left fatherless all those years ago saying that she didn't have to do this. It was getting easier to turn away from that voice, though. She was choosing to make new memories with Evan instead of continuing to mourn all the ones she lost.

He was worth the effort, she was realizing. He'd given up drinking altogether after that night with Mason. He was ashamed and that shame drove him to be better. She was proud of him and felt a stirring in her chest when she thought of how his change had to be difficult. He was loyal to her beyond anything she deserved. The days she woke up in a strange home, those times before her mind had time to catch up to her before she acted, were the worst. Yelling and screaming, fearing that she had been kidnapped and was now trapped in some strange commune, she'd run through the house looking for an exit. Evan, all the while, stayed out of her way until she calmed down, usually because she would realize he wasn't chasing her or trying to convince her otherwise. She remembered some points where he had, and those days had turned out to be the worst of them.

So now he waited while she raved and cried and yelled and—ashamedly, now she remembered—threw things. There was a picture hanging in their entry hall of Evan and her, arm in arm with Marcy and Mason. The background was a merrily lit tree, so she knew it was around Christmas, but further than that, she had no recollection of that evening.

Usually when she saw that picture, whether it took ten minutes or two hours, she would pause and take a mental—and sometimes literal—seat. She would take the picture down and stare at it, marveling at *knowing* she was present, but having no connecting feelings to that point in time. The canyon was as wide as an ocean and as thin as spider's silk, and she found herself on the edge every time. The memory was there, somewhere, but it was lost, like a budding magician asking her to pick a card and place it back in the deck, then shuffling it for the rest of eternity. It was there; she knew that at an intellectual level. But what made memories *memorable* were the feelings that they pulled with them, carried along the stream of time to comfort in dark nights or provide a respite of joy in a time of crisis.

She opened the front door for the mystery salesman, turning the burnished copper doorknob and swinging it inward in a single soft motion, the muscle memory too ingrained to be lost despite having few memories of it.

Standing across from her was a man in his mid-thirties, she guessed. His hair was dark brown, parted to the side and brushed in a non-descript business-like fashion. There was something familiar about him, something she couldn't quite place, but her gaze was drawn to his mouth. She realized at once that she was staring at his lips as he spoke and could feel the heat of self-consciousness begin to warm her face in a scarlet wave.

She blinked and met his eyes. "I'm sorry. Can you repeat that, please?"

The man showed a nervous but altogether genuine smile and shifted his stance once. "Of course, I can. I'm sorry. Sometimes when I am nervous, my words tend to blend together, and I end up speaking gibberish.

"I was asking if this is the home of Evan and Meredith Reader." His hands were folded over his ample stomach, which stretched the pale yellow button-up that bulged over his belt. He wasn't fat, but she could tell he'd reached the age where a speeding metabolism from adolescence had slowed to a crawl. The poor exercise and eating habits hadn't changed, which resulted in unsurprising weight gain, what most people called "the dad bod" years ago. He struck her as a man used to eating what he wanted and sitting around because his metabolism kept the weight off but would soon realize he'd need to change his habits, or he'd become a jiggling monstrosity in no time.

She nodded despite being mildly surprised that this stranger would know her name and cautiously said, "Yes, I'm Meredith. What can I do for you?"

She was keeping one hand on the door and preparing a response to his sales pitch in her mind, something like "I'm sorry, sir, but we aren't interested," or "That does sound wonderful, but we aren't in a place to invest the time." Anything to get him off their doorstep without unnecessary conversation.

The words waited just behind her teeth, like horses stamping in their cages before the start of the race. They waited for his opening line to be released, to race through the air between them to cut the conversation off before it could become anything more than a brief embarrassment for them both.

He smiled and said, "That's great. I've been wanting to find Evan for some time. I haven't ever had the guts, I guess."

At his smile, what he said was lost to her.

Some primal thought suddenly shouldered its way from the recesses of her subconscious, something so animalistic that she couldn't even name it, but she both dreaded and welcomed it at the same time. It was as if she were dying of thirst, and someone offered her a muddy glass of water that she guzzled with both insatiable gratefulness and irrevocable disgust. She dared not verbalize it, but she knew this was no salesman. Later, she would reflect that she could have written the next words to leave the visitor's mouth as he was speaking them, and they would have matched perfectly, a kind of psychic script that crept through her subconscious.

"I'm Evan's brother, Alan."

Meredith hadn't noticed Evan standing next to her, and when she felt a presence nearby, she jumped. She merely glanced out of the corner of her eye to confirm it was him and noticed his fists clenched at his sides, white knuckles standing out in the sunlight.

Alan noticed Evan at her side now. His smile faltered, and he swallowed hard. When he spoke, it was little more than a tremulous whisper and didn't gain much enthusiasm. "Hi, Evan. It's... it's been a while."

Evan wasn't smiling. In fact, Meredith took a small step away from him as her eyes worked their way from his clenched fists to his heaving chest and up to his face. To say he was staring daggers would have been an understatement. His expression was one she couldn't remember ever seeing, and while she hated to admit it, it scared her.

His face was flushed with rage, and his lips were pressed so tightly together they were no more than thin white lines between his flaring nostrils and dimpled chin. His jaw was clenched so tightly that the muscles stood out on his neck like the netting that might be found on a clipper ship.

Rage simmered beneath the words, like rocks at the bottom of a shallow stream, making the words waver with the heat of it.

"What the fuck could you possibly want, Alan?"

It was Alan's turn to take a step back now. After seeing and hearing the fury, it was clear that, despite the years that had passed between the hurtful events of his adolescence and now, his bigger brother still wanted nothing from him. His hands, previously folded serenely in front of him now began to wring, shining in the mid-morning sunlight with a thick sheen of clammy sweat. His face turned a pallid, chalky white, and he stammered when he spoke. Meredith wasn't sure she'd react any better had that ruthlessness been directed at her.

"Evan, I was hoping we could talk."

Evan didn't respond immediately. Instead, he reached past Meredith, slowly and with exaggerated slowness, his eyes never leaving Alan's, and grasped the doorknob between two fingers.

"There's nothing to say."

With that, he slowly closed the door on his younger brother, the latch clicking softly as a puff of warm air ruffled their hair.

Evan turned from the door and walked—stalked—toward the kitchen while Meredith remained where she was, staring dumbfounded at the door. She was trying to process what was happening, but she couldn't fit the pieces together. The interaction took no more than thirty seconds, but in her mind, it was drawn out, stretched across an interminable amount of time. It almost felt manic in her mind's eye, and she had to shake her head several times to before she could decide what action to take.

She turned to Evan quickly and spoke to the tense muscles on his back and up his spine, half pleading and half command. "Evan, stop."

He did, thankfully, but kept his back to her. She could see his shoulders relax imperceptibly and took that as a sign to continue. A hopeful sign.

"Evan, you can't ignore him like that."

Now, he did turn to her. Some of the heat had left his face, but his eyes still held all of the anger he'd shown Alan.

She continued, treading lightly but praying that he'd listen. "It seems like he's come a long way, and from the little you've told me, it's been a while since you've seen each other. It might do some good to at least hear him out." She took a tentative step toward him, her fingers twining about themselves nervously. "You don't have to hold onto that anger, honey." She used the term hoping to cool his temper a little. She hadn't called him any form of endearing pet name since they'd returned, and it had the effect she hoped for. His shoulders released more of the tension holding them and he licked his lips, the tension around his eyes and in his forehead eased, and he looked away.

"Meredith, I don't *want* to talk to him. When I said 'there's nothing to say,' I meant it. I have nothing to say to him after how he acted." She wasn't sure, but she felt like he was softening to the idea. Even as he spoke, it seemed more like he was trying to convince himself that the original reason still held water. She knew it didn't, and intuitively, she knew he would realize it, too, given enough time. The only problem was that they didn't have any. She couldn't let him pass up this opportunity. Deep down—and she didn't know if it was tied to memory or intuition—she knew he'd regret it.

She stepped back to the door and opened it, expecting to see Alan walking toward his car. Or worse, his taillights retreating into the distance.

Instead, to her surprise, he was still standing in the same spot on their concrete walkway, staring forlornly at her.

He jumped a little when she spoke, and his face flushed. She could tell he was relieved to see her, no doubt fearing Evan had come back to lay into him.

"Alan," she said, leaving the front door open and walking briskly toward him, her bare feet making a soft, pleasant padding sound on the concrete. Its warmth spread up her legs, and it was not unpleasant. "Please, come inside." She reached for him, looping her arm through his elbow and gently walking with him—leading him, she thought at the time—up the step and through the front door into the cool air of their home.

Meredith affected a pleasant smile, nearly a grin, and a good-humored tone to make up for the dour mood her husband was no doubt nurturing. Perhaps they'd balance out and it would result in nothing more than a standard conversation. She hoped for more but understood that was unlikely.

"Since we haven't been properly introduced—well, actually, I don't remember if we have or not, actually—my name is Meredith. I'm the lady of the house." She said the last bit with an air of mock superiority and curtsied dramatically.

This had the desired effect on Alan. He smiled broadly and bowed his head briefly toward her and said in a nearly British voice, "Pleasure to meet you, Mrs. Meredith Reader, Lady of the House."

She had expected him to comment on the part of her not remembering but was relieved that he didn't. She giggled at him and gestured for him to sit.

She felt Evan making his way from the kitchen into the adjacent living room where they were now chuckling, and immediately, Alan's laughter cut off and he cleared his throat with embarrassment, as if he'd been caught saying something inappropriate. He was the little brother, though, and she knew that the big brother—her husband—still held a significant amount of sway over him.

Meredith's smile faded as well, but she forced out a few more chuckles to show Evan she didn't approve of the way he was treating her brother-in-law.

There was a part of her that didn't understand why he was being so awful to him, but then a part of her waking subconscious knew that her husband had his reasons, even if she wasn't privy to them. She may disagree with him, but he was his own person. She could try to weed out the anger and perhaps together—today—they could plant something better there.

She glanced at Evan and smiled at him, raising her eyebrows to communicate that he should try to brighten up. His scowl deepened in response, but she was not dissuaded, and in fact, she couldn't help but smile. He was being purposely petulant, and despite his mood, it cheered her a little. The only thing in her way was his desire to stay angry, and that was something she could work with.

Turning to Alan once more, she put a hand on his elbow and asked if he'd like something to drink. Evan continued walking into the living room, brushing past them both and sitting on the couch with a rather loud sigh of what she could only assume was exasperation. She knew most of it was for show because he wouldn't look at either of them for longer than a second. He was doing an exemplary job at communicating his displeasure with the entire situation.

Well, that was fine; he could be angry while she entertained Alan. In a way, it was exciting to finally be meeting his little brother. She'd known of his existence but only from the times Evan mentioned him in their childhood discussions and only briefly from her recent questions. But with her memories gone, she could assume a completely neutral front with him. There was no history to blacken the interaction they could have today, and Evan couldn't change that, despite—or perhaps in spite of—his efforts.

"I'd love a glass of water, actually. My throat is as dry as a desert." Alan licked his lips, and she responded with a cheery smile of her own, gesturing for him to take a seat. She wasn't so naïve and hopeful that he would sit next to Evan, so instead of gesturing to the same couch where her sullen husband now sat with his arms crossed, she gestured to the wingback chair next to the couch. Evan was having difficulty deciding what he wanted to do more—watch her with irritation or shoot baleful glares at Alan every few seconds.

Alan sat in the seat she offered, which was farthest from Evan.

Baby steps. I may not have any memories of this place, she thought wryly to herself, *but at the very least I can try to disarm this bomb before it explodes in all of our faces.*

She walked into the kitchen, leaving Evan to stew and Alan to wring his hands. Filling up a pitcher with ice and water from the tap and stirring it with a wooden spoon helped her center her thoughts and make a plan.

She set the wooden spoon down on the counter with a sharp clatter that echoed through their kitchen, and she pulled three glasses from the cupboard, smiling a little at their hollow tinkling as the edges caressed one another as they were placed gently on a tray. The pitcher of ice water followed the cups, and Meredith brought the tray into the living room, working to ensure her face didn't betray the anxiety she felt.

She wasn't normally one to play the dutiful wife, what their modern culture called "the wife from when." It was a small jab at not only how long ago the 1950's had been, but also how the wife had a role inside the house while the husband could do anything outside of the house, something she could barely even believe was a thing.

She set the tray down on the coffee table, deftly taking the empty coffee mugs from earlier and placing a glass in front of Alan and Evan and filling them both halfway. It was easier to focus on the soft clinking of the shifting ice and the splashing gurgle of the water as it fell into them rather than the itching tingle between her shoulder blades that was either Evan's stare or the tension in the room.

Aside from the subtle hum of the air conditioner, there was only silence, and she could very nearly slice the tension with a knife. Again working to avoid dwelling on that, she poured herself a cup of ice water and sat on the couch next to Evan, strategically between him and the object of his immense displeasure.

When she took a sip of water, it was cool and refreshing. She took several swallows, waiting to see what would happen next. It reminded her of the old western movies, where two men stood in a dusty road, wind blowing tumbleweeds around their dusty boots, the only sound the whistling wind and gunslingers sucking on a piece of straw. The high whistling trill of a standoff a precursor to the draw.

She wondered, much like a bystander of the Old West, who would be the first to draw and if both would be left standing when the proverbial dust settled.

So, it surprised her when Evan spoke—drew—first, his tone holding nothing back and cutting straight to the point, without the preamble of niceties. "What are you doing here, Alan?"

Alan took a deep breath and a sip from his glass, then set it carefully on the table. To his credit, it only clacked against the smooth wood of the coffee table a couple of times as his unsteady hand set it down.

"Well, Evan, it's been going on fifteen years since I saw you last. I don't think it was right that I—we—keep each other at arm's length when we could have a relationship." Alan sighed, and Evan stayed silent, avoiding his brother's eyes by glowering at the wall across from where he sat. "To be honest, Evan, I miss you. I know things weren't great when I left all those years ago, but you have to understand that I had to get out of there."

Now, Evan looked at him, the anger that had begun to abate resurfaced, rekindling within his eyes. "*You* had to get out of there? *You*?"

Meredith took a nonchalant drink from her glass, avoiding eye contact with either. *Maybe it hadn't been a good idea to sit between them*, she thought.

Evan continued, the anger changing from a simmer to a rolling boil. "Do you even remember what you did? You say you had to get out of there, but you left *me* with a mess to clean up. You didn't 'have to get out of there.'" He clawed the air with finger quotes. "You *ran away*, you bastard, leaving your bigger brother to clean up the mess you left behind. Dad, who was nothing of the sort except in name, and mom, who was little more than a zombie most of the time. Only now, she was a new-and-improved zombie, bleeding profusely from the back of her head where *you*," he jabbed a shaking finger at Alan, "shoved her against the counter, splitting the back of her head open nearly to her skull!" Meredith swallowed the sip of water she'd taken with a *gulp* that could be heard in the silence that followed Evan's rant, which ended in nearly a shout. The words poured from him in a cascade, the dam that held them back all these years finally removed.

Alan withstood his brother's accusations, even the unspoken ones, but his face flushed in the silence, growing a deeper red than she thought necessary. Meredith was uncertain if Alan had a temper like her husband or if that flush was indicative of shame. She guessed, by the brief overview that Evan had given, that it was shame. Silently, she hoped it was.

Alan stared at Evan after a brief glance in Meredith's direction, as if to gauge what she was thinking based solely on her expression. She hoped desperately that it was as impassive as she was trying to make it.

Alan's voice shook and had a high, tinny quality as if he were trying to speak through a straw. "Yes, you're right. You're absolutely right. I did run away from them. In fact, I haven't talked to them since. To be honest," he took a deep breath, "I'm not sure if they're alive anymore. For that, I might even be a little bit ashamed." His voice quivered and cracked with emotion at the end, his eyelids sparkled in the mid-morning light with unshed tears.

Internally, she nodded in approval. Perhaps his temper was as bad as Evan's could be sometimes. She'd certainly seen more of it today than she could remember, but she realized that was a poor frame of reference.

Despite the temper she knew her husband to have, she also knew he defaulted to a stance of immeasurable tenderness. She knew that not only because of how she remembered him in their younger years, but more notably in the way she'd been treated since their return from Sri Lanka. With the one night of drinking that led to Mason hauling him inside and putting him to bed, there had been little conflict and no more drinking. He gave her space without having to be asked, understood that she was very nearly a stranger in her own life's habits, and he pressured her on nothing except getting better—for her sake, not his own.

He was a very sweet man, and she realized with no small amount of wonder that there was a small fire of desire heating in her chest. Desire wasn't the best word, as it had no sexual connotation, but it was a longing, a kind of wish to be close to him and learn more about him. Perhaps, she was falling in love with him.

His tenderness began to make its debut at this point, and she was pleased to see it. His gaze, while still undoubtedly angry, had lost some of the heat to it. Were those tears in his eyes as well?

He shifted in his seat and folded his hands in front of him. "Alan." Meredith realized that her husband wasn't sure how to continue. She knew instinctually that there was a war raging within him and could see it passing across his face in waves. One side was hell-bent on maintaining the familiar anger and rage at being wronged and the other was this new, familiarity that desired nothing more than to mend the connection with his younger brother.

The anger, which was a fair and simply a response to the wrong that had been done to him and his mother, was valid, and she knew it. But the loss of a brother fifteen years ago had set the stage for sorrow and regret as well. Like the image of gunslingers earlier, they were at opposite ends of the street, tumbleweeds of thought rolling about their feet, fueling each emotion individually and vying for control over the guns.

"Alan, I have spent countless hours thinking of what I'd do if I ever saw you again. Not that I wanted to, mind you, but there's been a plan in place for over a decade. I set it in motion when I saw you standing at the door. I had no intention of ever letting you into my house, let alone back into my life. You wounded me deeper than I thought ever possible." He took a sip of his water, the first sip since she'd poured it, and the condensation on the outside ran down the glass, leaving clear trails amidst the hazy pockets that coated the lower half of the glass and dripped, once, twice, three times into the air between his lap and the table.

Then he continued gesturing to her with the chilled glass. "And then my wife here, lovely Meredith, shot that shit to pieces."

The smile that followed was something that she hadn't expected to see at all.

It wasn't bitter, like the smile he'd worn when the doctors in Sri Lanka told him that her memory may never come back. It wasn't sardonic, like when she'd recently thrown a pillow at him in frustration, and she'd screamed, "I hope that hurt!"

The smile was... what was it?

Whimsical, she thought to herself. It was whimsical. It was the sort of smile that occurs when something unexpected yet altogether welcome happens. It was the kind of smile that greedily gulped at the nonchalant joy that bubbled from the place where frustration and fear may have previously reigned. Perhaps, they *were* ready to plant something new.

Meredith risked a glance at Alan and nearly laughed aloud at the look of pleasant surprise and cautious distrust on his face. It was the same look that she imagined was on the look of the fly when the spider invited her in for tea.

Evan must have seen it as well because he suddenly burst out laughing. It surprised both Alan and Meredith. She felt her own body tense up and jump at the same time that Alan jumped nearly out of his seat and recoil as if he expected an uncontrolled, rage-induced deluge of further accusations, his face turned from the red of recovering shame to stark white in an instant.

Evan, however, had tears coursing down his cheeks as he held his stomach and tried desperately to avoid spilling the water in the half-filled glass still clutched in his hand.

He wasn't succeeding.

His entire sleeve was dark with it as even more sloshed over the side with each movement made, rocking back and forth and clapping his hand to his stomach over and over while his face turned a brilliant scarlet. Peals of laughter echoed through the house, a welcome sound that made her feel like laughing herself. She felt tingles sprint up and down her arms, and she felt a small sting of tears in the corners of her eyes. That earlier warmth that had blossomed in her chest as she stared at her husband had begun to bloom into a something that resembled an emotional attraction instead of merely a physical one. He certainly was charming.

For a moment, Meredith feared one of two things had happened to her husband. The first, he had finally cracked beneath all the pressure of the past several months. The second, he was choking and dying in front of them while they both looked on expectantly.

She and Alan exchanged a wary glance. The smile spreading across her face seemed to ease Alan's mind as he settled back down into the chair, his mouth relaxed, changing a tense frown into the hint of a smile.

"I'm not sure I understand what's going on, Evan." Alan's voice was only a little shaky but certainly shaded with reserved hope.

Evan continued to laugh and finally put the glass down; a hard *clack* echoed through the room, rebounding off the walls alongside his laughter. By now, nearly all of the water had been splashed across Evan's wrist and arm.

He held up a forestalling hand as the laughs turned to deep guffaws and then to muffled chuckles. Meredith noted absently the wetness glistening on his wrists in the golden sunlight that warmed the living room through their windows.

Evan was wiping the tears from his cheeks when he spoke in answer. "Alan, I think I've gotten tired. Exhausted. Depleted. Whatever you want to call it. I'm done holding on to the anger and animosity. I should have done it sooner, but now I've decided to let it go. And when I did, just now, it was like I ripped away a blanket that was hiding a basket of puppies. Where I thought would be nothing but more frustration and anger or rage and regret was something more pure and unexpected than I could have imagined.

"Alan, I realize what a waste these years have been. You're my brother, and I'm going to choose to love you. I'm sure there will be things we'll argue about, or there might even be things we fight about. From now on, though, I'm going to choose to have a relationship with you."

He grew serious, the small chuckles that bubbled up from him while he was soliloquizing disappeared completely. "I'm sorry that I've been a horrible big brother. I should've been better. I should've tried to reach out. There was plenty I could have done, and I'm going to work on doing that now. If you'll let me."

He'd continued speaking over Alan's objections and the weight that had disappeared from him returned, showing in his expression and a slight tensing of his shoulders. Meredith watched him, interested more in what he had to say but also now a small measure of concern began to swirl amidst her previously unfettered excitement. The expression wasn't only sorrow or even regret. It was something more. Something much deeper. It was an unfathomable remorse, and she felt again the sting of tears at the corner of her eyes that only moments ago had been from joy. The feeling made goosebumps appear on her skin, and she began to feel her heart-rate increase, anxiety replacing mild fear. Concern and worry began to crease her own features. The seriousness with which he spoke was something that struck Meredith to her core. Her heart broke for him, even though it was still not in that place where she remembered her Evan from before. He was a deep and emotionally intelligent man, and she could certainly come to love him, she now realized fully and more completely.

She moved closer to him on the couch and grasped his hand. He looked at her in surprise—briefly—and looked back at Alan but not before she tried to smile reassuringly at him.

"Can you forgive me, Alan? Can you forgive me for being a real bastard of a brother?"

Alan looked down at his shoes, and when he looked back up, she was unsurprised to see tears making transparent trails as they fell down his cheeks.

He stood up and walked the three steps toward them both.

They both stood up, and Alan wrapped his brother in a compressing hug. She heard them both begin to cry and began to step away, wishing to give them this moment of brotherly intimacy to which she had little influence.

She acknowledged the concern she'd felt only a moment ago and set it aside. Her husband—yes, that's what he was—was hurting but was working through years of anger and regret. Of course, there would be regret; of course, there would be sorrow.

Instead of being the outsider that she knew herself to be, she felt both Alan's and Evan's arms reach out and enfold her in their embrace.

She felt her eyes begin to tingle with precursory tears, and the fear she felt melted away. Instead of crying, she began to laugh. It awed her that the power of love could transcend both years and incredible pain that had been secreted away in a bunker. That no amount of reinforcing rage and emotional cement could stop from breaking through. Love worked to ease it out, one frail thread at a time.

As she began to laugh, they did as well, and for a moment, everything was right. Everything was *normal*, and she wasn't a woman with half a memory, he wasn't a man who regretted an adolescence spent nursing a hatred for his siblings, and they weren't a couple that had a hedge maze of difficulties to traverse together.

They were a husband and a wife welcoming a new member to the family.

After several moments and when the laughter had subsided, she broke away from the hug with a contented sigh and said, "Alan, would you like to stay for lunch?"

Evan took up the offer and wouldn't allow his brother any leeway.

Alan couldn't help but accept, and his pleasantly flushed face and goofy grin betrayed his excitement to accept. "That sounds wonderful. I'd love to stay."

The three ate lunch on the back deck at a table that sat four. Their conversation was spoken beneath the cool shade of a large umbrella and between bites.

Evan updated him on everything that had happened since he watched his little brother storm out, ruffling his hair affectionately at one point to drive the point home, a good-natured reminder that he'd always be the "little brother." Meredith chanced a look at her husband when Alan had the courtesy to interrupt with some story of his own. Evan's expression was fervent, attentive, and unabashedly affectionate. His eyes, however, held little of what his face was showing. There was joy, yes. There was some contentment, too. But beneath that there lay a tightness to his eyes, a kind of gray disregard that was so out of place that she had to blink and shake her head.

When she looked again, whatever it was had retreated, and his eyes were bright with delight, and he was laughing with his brother.

Evan began telling the story of Sri Lanka after Alan finished his own story. The younger brother stopped eating and listened intently. His gasps of horror and amazement at their story of separation and reunification reminded her of two little boys listening to a librarian relating a story at a library, their immature and childish eyes wide and alight with wonder. Alan's only ever left Evan's to look at her, his mouth agape or whispering, "No way" and "That's unbelievable," including her in the telling. She felt a camaraderie with him that she hadn't expected. Something that she now realized she'd been feeling with Evan for some time now, but something more intimate.

It was wonderful, she realized, to have another person in their lives. It was as if a personality map had been drawn that included only the two of them and was skewed to one side. With Alan now in their lives, the map adjusted itself, a small arm reaching out to help balance it, to make it more round instead of a jagged scrawl.

CHAPTER 19

Meredith opened her eyes and looked at Evan. He was smiling, tears drying on his cheeks as he watched the interaction between his brother and himself. It had to be such a strange out-of-body experience seeing something so intimate that he should remember but unable to recall even the ghost of an association.

At least, it had been for her.

The joy and relief that had settled on his features as he laughed with himself and his brother was something she could actually feel within The Pod. It landed on her skin much in the same way that sunlight or mist from a waterfall did. It was light, comforting, and completely natural.

She also felt a warmth coming from him that had nothing to do with the generated Irish environment around them. It was freedom from the heavy chains of emotional baggage that he'd become accustomed to, muscles that had atrophied under their weight were finally free and able to move of their own volition, gaining intellectual strength and emotional range of motion that he probably hadn't ever dreamed possible. In all probability, he didn't even realize he was missing.

She loathed what she had to do. She hesitated a few more seconds, reveling in the naked bliss Evan felt in watching their interaction. Licking her lips, she stopped the memory and closed the video.

It faded and along with it, Evan's incandescent smile.

He looked at her, understanding that it couldn't have lasted forever. Eventually, it had to end.

"He stayed a little longer. After that, I mean, but left before dinner."

She didn't feel like she *had* to tell him this, but she did feel that it was something he would want to know.

"He told us about his life. Fairly normal for a middle-aged man. After he left your house, he found an apartment with a friend, finished school, and was able to go on and get his master's degree and PhD as a biological engineer. He's doing very well for himself. He has a husband named Dalton and a dog named Molly, who is probably the most spoiled pooch on the planet. According to him, at least."

She smiled. Evan echoed the smile in response, and they both laughed a little bit. Not as much or as heartily as they had laughed when Evan realized that love was more powerful than resentment. But still, a little.

She wouldn't tell him about what happened later that night as they lay in the dark before sleep could waltz in and seize their conscious thoughts.

In the privacy of her own thoughts, however, she let it play out over the course of several silent seconds. In her mind, the memory lasted several minutes, but to Evan it was a silence in The Pod for no more than a few blinks of his eyes.

After Alan had left, and they'd cleaned up dinner together. They'd shared laughs together and sat on the patio enjoying the cool air as the sun retreated behind the distant tree line in a eulogy of vibrant colors.

Even while they sat together on the wicker furniture, she could feel his warmth against her. The earlier thoughts of desire hadn't disappeared but had only been set behind the other, more pressing emotions.

Now, as they sat comfortably against one another, she could feel what had previously been a desire borne from knowledge changing into something more primal. Something she felt stirring within her chest as his breath whispered past her ear.

He was gently rubbing her arm, the small hairs giving a pleasant tickling that she didn't mind at all. She leaned her head back against his shoulder and felt his strong arms enfold her, gently squeezing her knees in affection. His hands, usually rough on her soft skin, had a rougher texture that she could feel traveling through her nerves, all of them.

They spoke very little, opting instead to enjoy the quiet within themselves. For the first time in several weeks, Meredith felt a kind of peace descending upon her. She was coming to grips with the fact that she had lost her memory and was now enjoying the task of falling in love again. It had been hard, that was true. But it was getting easier.

The few words they did trade with each other had to do with the beauty that was laid out before them and were spoken in hushed tones as if they dared not disturb the atmosphere coalescing around them.

The sun washed the waving landscape in a rusty red. The shadows of the tall grass and distant trees stretched for what seemed like miles. The sky, a blazing brilliant and ruddy orange, faded above them into a satiny violet and, eventually, to a black that wasn't foreboding but comforting. It was the darkness that would bring with its end a new day, another chance to do something incredible. Birds sang throughout the grasses before them, their song floating on the lazy wind and coming to them in whispered, trilling songs. When the wind did kick up briefly, it brought with it the subtle whisk of grass blades dancing against one another and leaves telling their secrets to the children of the forest.

The attention and affection he was showing her—had been showing her for several weeks—was culminating in a warmth that suffused her whole body. Her toes, bare and poking out beneath a knitted blanket he'd brought from inside—weren't cold at all. She touched them to the cushion beneath and could feel the cool cloth against her toes. She could feel the warmth of the wine washing through her body, too. She knew wine had always helped her relax anyway, but tonight, it seemed to have an amplifying effect on her. She could feel the anxiety of her current state of mind sloughing away like the skin of a snake, and she didn't mind it. She let it go, breathed it out with each breath and wished it well. Was she drunk? No, not yet. Not even close, actually. But she felt better than she had in, well, as long as she could remember.

When the glorious glow of the sunset had given way to inky blackness, they went inside and got ready for bed. She chose a loose pair of cotton shorts and a ribbed tank while Evan chose the usual—shirtless with a pair of shorts.

When they climbed into bed, she drew close to him, laying on his chest, and he again wrapped his arm around her in a firm but comforting cuddle.

After several minutes of getting comfortable in the bed, she asked Evan what he was thinking in the distance between the words he'd spoken to his brother, smiling that same whimsical smile from earlier in the day.

He was quiet for a few seconds, the question hanging in the dim room where the hushed whir of the fan's small motor overhead was the only sound.

She remembered the darkness that surrounded them. She remembered her hand, placed gingerly on his chest feeling the small curls of hair there. They hadn't made love since their trip to Sri Lanka. She couldn't keep track of the days, but she knew it had been a long time. More time than was fair. It was strange knowing they'd been intimate for an extended period of time and then, suddenly, it had to stop. It wasn't guilt she felt, and she'd certainly never felt as if Evan wanted her to feel guilt, but she knew it was something she was actively avoiding, at least on some level. Whether it was because she had been merely fond of him in the beginning or because she actually wanted to embrace it but kept letting fear hold her back, she wasn't certain. What she did know was that whatever it was had begun to change.

His voice reached through the dark toward her. She could hear the smile through the calm in his voice. "I realized something that had been hiding from me—eluding my consciousness, I guess—for the better part of my life. I realized that the anger I felt toward Alan was valid, but not to the extent that I let it get. He was responsible for leaving, sure, but the deeper anger, the rage, was more accurately labeled as hurt. A seeping, oozing wound caused by my parents that I attributed to his leaving.

"It was some ungodly amalgamation of my dad's disgusting behavior, my mom's lack of any behavior or involvement at all, and—while I hate to admit it to even myself—my other brother's death." He was quiet again. His breathing changed slightly, and Meredith could sense in the air rather than feel from any physical sensation that he was getting emotional. The way he spoke was the way someone talks when they don't want to be overheard. When they're telling a secret meant only for one person's ears. The consonants pronounced in such a way that they smacked together in the stillness. The vowels exaggerated or skipped over completely. When he spoke again, the thickness in his voice confirmed it.

"I hated Owen, my older brother, you know. He was supposed to be a role model, someone that I could follow. Instead, he was someone I didn't want to copy, to be like in any way." He laughed a short, quiet bitter laugh. More of a loud sigh than a laugh. "I guess in that way he *was* a role model or some twisted version of one. He showed me exactly what I needed to avoid. And I did, I guess, as far as I can remember.

"But it was the realization that I actually missed Owen that took me by surprise. He was an idiot, the epitome of a everything I held in contempt—the stereotypical 'guy' who had sex for the hell of it and avoided any kind of connection with people so that no one could get close enough to see the weakness in him. I couldn't stand him when he was alive, but that didn't change the fact that he was my *brother*. He was my blood, Mer. I was sad when he died, but I couldn't admit that to anyone, especially myself. If I did that, then I'd question everything I felt about everyone else, and I wasn't ready for that. Deep down, I missed him. I still do. But I didn't want to feel that way with Alan, too."

With that final admission, he started to cry. It was barely noticeable at first. Soft, jumping bursts in his chest, followed quickly by his shoulders doing the same. It evolved slowly into wracking sobs that shook his whole body, making her hand jump up and down on his chest until she moved it to cup his cheek.

He began to curl away from her, bringing his knees toward his chest, but instead, she sat up on one elbow and drew him gently toward her. She laid a hand on his temple and pushed his head against her breast, making soft rocking motions and trying desperately to think of something to say—anything—that would ease the pain he felt. She was desperate to make him feel better. She couldn't think of a single thing, and as she rocked him and he calmed, she understood that it was alright. Silence was, in this instance, exactly what he needed.

When his body stopped shaking and his breathing calmed to deep, gentle breaths, she kissed his forehead. He pushed his head against her breast lightly, affirming her kiss.

She didn't realize what she was doing until their lips pressed together. She had put a finger under his chin and lifted it to her own mouth. His cheeks were wet with tears, and she was surprised to feel her own cheeks moist with fresh ones of her own.

The kiss was tender, tentative, both of them testing the waters by dipping a toe in, for which she was grateful. Their lips were soft but fit together perfectly. She knew if he had been aggressive in the least, she'd have pulled away. But he wasn't. He was tenderly approaching her in a way that said, "I've missed you and I want this but want you to be comfortable."

Again, she had that same strange sensation for a third time of gunslingers poised on opposite ends of a street, but she pushed the thought away and decided that the water felt fine. It felt great, actually.

She opened her mouth slowly and kissed him with a little more pressure. He drew back in surprise, but she chased his lips with her own. She was sure his eyes were open, but she was tired of caring. Finally, she had decided it was okay, and there wasn't room for fear, anymore. What had replaced it instead was desire. It was a desire that resonated with her feelings earlier when she recognized the tenderness in his softening eyes, the patience in his touch, and the joy in which he held her in his mind.

And she gave herself over to it completely.

She kissed him more fervently now, letting her tongue slip seductively into his mouth while she placed a hand on the back of his neck, pulling him closer and deeper into her embrace. He responded with a sensual caress of his own, his fingertips sliding seductively down her cheek to the hollow above and between her breasts. It left pleasurable shivers in its wake.

She could feel a hardness growing between his legs as he straddled her thigh, and she felt a thrilling shiver scamper up her spine. It was frighteningly glorious in its seduction and mystery.

She could feel his desire for her in the way his hands rubbed up and down her sides, fleetingly lifting her shirt for the briefest second, his fingers tickling her waist and beneath her breasts and down her back in an exquisite storm of scattering sparks that raced across her skin wherever he touched, and in some places he didn't.

She found herself pulling his shorts down, and he was doing the same to hers. Their breaths came in gasps, each one a hair's breadth away from a moan. It was that time before sex where there was only one another, every inch of their bodies alight with the ache of passionate hunger. It burned so fiercely that she could vaguely feel a shivering vibration through her veins, a note of harmony that was struck deep within the earth thousands of years ago that sang and reverberated through her bones.

After what felt like an eternity, she felt her shorts—she wasn't wearing underwear—slip off her ankles, lost in the tangled sheets near the foot of their bed. She pulled him closer. She wanted him to be closer, wanted him to be with her, wanted him to be *in* her.

And then in rapturous ecstasy, he was.

The sigh that escaped both of them was gratifyingly delicate and unabashedly primal. They moved together in the dark, her hips rising and falling while his echoed in the transverse. She basked in the delight of their bodies joining together in a way that could only ever by mimicked but never duplicated.

It was everything she had hoped it would be, everything she wanted it to be, and for a moment, she thought she could remember something. The glimpse of a shadow out of the corner of her memory, but the growing pressure within her eclipsed the thought, and she could do nothing but let herself drift within the warming waters of passionate play.

The thrum arcing within her began gathering speed, gaining in intensity. She felt herself getting closer to climax, and by the quickening thrusts of his body—the muscles on his back slick with a light sheen of sweat—he was getting closer, too.

Their lips were touching and the moans that were transferring from her mouth to his only increased the pleasure they both felt, as if the pleasure was being given, taken, and returned between them.

Within moments, she felt his body tighten, like a coil of spring. His muscles tensed, and his thrusts became measured and pleasantly pointed. He came inside her with glorious spasms, his muscles tensing and relaxing with each plunging thrust. She could feel his warmth spread into her and his body spasmed rhythmically in pleasurable relief. He grunted, sounding out the passion he felt and release she'd delivered to him. She could feel her own climax close to the surface and repositioned herself slightly to feel him more directly.

She lifted her body once, twice, and on the third, she felt sweet and divine release. The grunting moan of pleasure that escaped came from deep within her chest, a place she didn't know could produce such a sound in this situation, but there it was. She continued to move, moaning with each subsequent thrust of her own until passion gave way to satisfaction.

She felt Evan's body slowing, his fervor slackening, and after a few more thrusts, they lay chest to chest, his face buried in the hair beneath her neck, but she could feel his wide smile on her skin. It was enough to send goosebumps dancing down her arms despite his body between her legs.

She laughed with delight and his laughter was a warm breeze on her neck. She hugged him close, and when he tried to peel himself off of her, she pushed him back down.

"Stay," was all she said, looking deeply into his eyes, two shining beacons in their dark room, "for a minute more, at least."

He lay back on top of her, and she felt his weight and heat and gloried in it all. It had been too long, for both of them. She hadn't realized what she had been missing before, but it had been missing nonetheless.

After a couple of minutes, they got up and cleaned themselves off—something the movies never told you needed to happen—and got back into bed together, both of them rustling in the bed for their shorts. They lay in the quiet, his hand rubbing gently on her back while she lay again on his chest, rubbing the soft hair there.

"I love you, Meredith." His voice came to her from above her, but she could hear the deepness of it in his throat, a great vibrating rumble next to her ear.

"I love you, too, Evan." She hadn't hesitated because she knew that she did love him. She loved him more than she could have known, and not least of all, because he was worthy of love, just as she had realized the same about herself.

Sleep came to them quickly as they lay in one another's arms. When Meredith woke the next day, she was somewhat stunned at the warmth they shared between their bodies. Their silent bodies lay in the slanting sunbeams that peeked through the blinds and landed in bright effulgent rectangles upon the bedcovers. Those brilliant shapes crept slowly up the comforter toward their faces as Meredith lay in the stillness of the morning.

When Evan woke, they made love again. Meredith felt as if things were finally starting to fall in place, memory or no memory. The lovemaking was no less passionate than the night before and full of joy and pleasure and excitement.

But it was one of the last times they ever would.

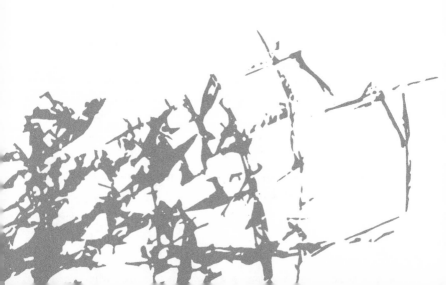

CHAPTER 20

A sudden thought struck Meredith as she sat on The Bench. Although she had lived through everything she was watching and remembered parts of it quite clearly, watching it again—perhaps now watching it with Evan made the difference—cleared the path forward. Where before there had been a multitude of trails through an ever-darkening forest of hazy decisions, now those paths remained, but she felt lights flanking one particular path.

A new perspective began winding its way through the narrative that she had been simultaneously telling and showing her husband. The time had come, she realized with both clarity and a gut-wrenching despair. Her purpose for being here had finally become clear, and it was now time to show Evan the culmination of their life together, what every word today had bought for them both.

Shakily, she stood up and walked several steps away from him. She took several steadying breaths and paced back and forth, small puffs of dust lifting and spreading into the air beneath each heel.

When she turned around, her hands writhed within one another, like octopus tentacles, and she felt a sharp pain in her lips where she was biting it. She licked her lips and tasted blood.

When she spoke, she was thankful that her voice didn't shake in rhythm with her hammering heart. "Evan, there is something else I need to show you. There's something else that you don't know—couldn't know—but you have to know it. I'm going to show you, and I want you to watch it. If I could simply tell you, I would because—" Her breath caught in her throat, and for a millisecond, she was afraid she would die from involuntary asphyxiation, betrayed by her own body much like her mind had betrayed her in Sri Lanka. She found that a part—not a small part—wished for it, wished she didn't have to continue. Wished so hard that she could feel her fists clenched at her sides, fingernails biting deep into her palms. "Because it would be simpler, and I wouldn't have to go through it again." She could feel her lower lip quivering, and she knew that even if she tried, she couldn't stop it from doing so.

Evan's posture, she noticed, was guarded. She wanted so badly to yell at him, to spoil the ending, to hell with the process her therapist said to follow.

With great tears coursing down her cheeks, she called up a final memory vid.

"This is the last memory I have of us. And for me, Evan," she hesitated, "it's not a good one."

With a note of finality in her voice that she hoped wasn't cruel, she started the video.

She felt that alongside the start to the vid, there was an inexorable march toward the end of their story, one that had been in paused, forever locked into a static mire of pain, loss, and hopelessness for far too long.

And she wept.

She wept for time lost, for unspoken words along with words that *were* said and shouldn't have been.

She wept for late-night kisses that turned passionate and wept for some that merely ended in both of them exulting in one another's natural warmth.

She wept for Evan, now. She was certain he was beginning to understand why they were here if he hadn't already.

She wept for the days she woke up, cold and alone.

She wept for Mason who lost his dearest and most intimate friend, the helplessness that they both experienced and the guilt they carried with them like a backpack stuffed with steel ingots, weighing them down and threatening to crush them every second of every day.

She wept for Marcy, who had not only taken some of that guilt and pain as more collateral damage, but who took on the mantle of supporting her own husband along with Meredith.

She wept for the memories they'd never make together. They'd never wake up together again. Never comment on the funny way the sun shone through leaves outside their kitchen window and danced on the floor. They'd never dance in the kitchen again.

They'd never take another trip together. Never kiss under the stars of a strange sky. They'd never grow old together, and they'd never sit on a front porch drinking lemonade and commenting on the weather, gray hair—if they had any—flying haphazardly around their faces.

They'd never be alive together again.

She wept because she hadn't been enough.

She had tried to convince herself that it was getting easier. That the pain, guilt, and anger were abetting incrementally, but she knew that was a lie; she was simply getting stronger. Like muscles that were worked every day, her ability to cope with the multitude of feelings that raced through her mind every second of every minute of every hour of every day of every week of every month of every year since.

Evan's voice brought her back to The Bench, although she didn't hear him at first. He was crying, now, tears streaming down his face as he continued to gaze at the vid, which had stopped the second before she'd been approved for and successfully received her Hazing.

The vid, now stopped at a single image, showed a living room—their living room—and the kitchen beyond. The same table where Marcy had helped her remember who she was despite not being able to be "mother" sat beneath the same hanging light that had borne witness to countless poker games and late-night discussions over beer and shots of whisky.

A stagnant sun could be seen hanging distantly between cracks in the curtains on the windows. It shone through them, suffusing both rooms with a warm glow that only the rising sun could create. Now however—and maybe it was because of everything this image represented—the light in the room seemed sinister and secretive, as if someone were shining a light on an idea that would harm the hearer, and gleaning enjoyment from their sudden recoil of horror.

There was an outline—a person—sitting at the table. From this perspective, a small empty glass could be seen on the table. It was dwarfed by the tall bottle of liquor, half-filled with its amber liquid of numbing poison.

The person—obviously a man—sat hunched over the table, one hand hanging limply at the side of the chair while the other lay across the table, splayed out, resembling the way a person may lay their head on their arm to nap. But this was no nap.

While Meredith had only visited this memory twice before—the first time was to verify what she asked to be Hazed and second time followed her application to Innervate

Industries, more to determine if she was prepared to face her future in The Bench—the image before her was etched so resolutely in her mind in terrible and indisputable detail that no amount of Hazing or drug could hope to scrub it free.

An object lay on the floor near the man's feet. The feet wore socks, but they were both cocked against the floor. Beneath the limp fingers of the arm, the object reflected a piece of the comatose sun. It lay as if it had been dropped there with complete disregard. It glowed delicately in the filtered light, a dark orange shape that exuded willful malice, an object whose sole purpose was to steal joy but only if it could do it absolutely. It was a pistol. Its black metal shape offensive in its used up purpose.

The wall opposite the man's hand was marred by rust-colored graffiti. Viscera spread across the previously plain robin egg blue as a monument to the pain, shame, and fear that became too overwhelming to bear. It dripped down the wall in thin rivulets. The blood had dried to a rusty burn, but the lines looked like they raced one another, where the winners pooled on the floor in crescent-shaped puddles.

Evan's response was stunned disbelief, at first. It evolved into vehement denial until it finally expanded into outraged defiance.

"Why would I do that?" The croak that came from the crying man on the floor before her tore at the protective shell she'd built around her heart. And before she could argue with herself, she was on her knees next to him, embracing him and crying into his shoulder as he held onto her like a man holding onto a buoy amidst a raging storm. She didn't want to hold onto him, but she'd waited for this moment for years, and she made herself. She knew that she would regret it if she didn't.

She tried to speak through the sobs that were raking their way out of her throat. Her breath came in ragged gasps between them, but she couldn't stop them. Her lungs cried out in pain as their normal routines were cast aside. She had to take a steadying breath before she could force her tongue and throat to form coherent words.

"I've been asking myself that for four years, Evan. After all that was going *right* in our lives, what would motivate you, make you, take that last and final step? Why would you do that one thing that you know was such a destructive part of my life when I was younger? Why would you do something so close to what my dad decided to do? Why? What help couldn't you get that would have made life livable?"

She hesitated but forced herself to say what she had really wanted answers for. The question that had burned in her with a ceaseless unforgiving heat, and on more than one occasion, had threatened to consume her sanity in a burst of wildfire. It was her true reason for coming today.

"Why wasn't I enough?"

With that, the meager wall she had built to restrain the madness of grief collapsed, and the sorrow and despair that had been pounding against the weak little dam rushed out in continual, racking sobs that were filled with grief so keen it could be felt in the air around her. She felt it on her skin, like an oily residue. She felt it settle in her hair and on her dress, and she could do nothing but grip her husband and cry for mercy to the gods of forbearance.

It was a torrent of raw emotion that clouded everything she had been through with him. Since their vacation in Sri Lanka to the dark time when she felt insubstantial and useless. Days she felt she was only a phantom floating inexplicably through the cycle of the rising and setting sun after Evan's death and the four years since.

The despair, rage and insecurity encircled her, coursing through her veins like a violent electrical wire. All of the sensations and emotions, however, paled in comparison to the great dark creature that had started as a simple question addressed to the void: *Why?*

It had grown over the years from that small question into something eldritch, careening through her mind like an uncontrollable beast that had been loosed into an otherwise quiet museum. The havoc it caused was inescapable and all-encompassing. It wrecked the few relationships she had to begin with. Some—like Marcy and Mason—would hang on until the ride was done, helping her pick up the pieces while she could feel the beast galloping onward into some other part of her life. But others—friends that couldn't withstand the onslaught of sudden episodes of hysterical crying or inexplicable rage—would recuse themselves from her life with false apologies and strangled prayers.

Her job was the next to go, which didn't take much after not having a memory, but it was yet another casualty in a long list of them. Her co-workers had always been acquaintances at best, even the ones that she spoke to on a daily basis were only what one could consider "work friends." There wasn't a relationship once they stepped outside the building. Oh, they were friendly, certainly, but when push came to shove, she was left alone to deal with it. All the while, they watched with pity and uncertainty in how to approach her, how to get on with their own jobs and pick up the slack she was leaving behind.

Her bosses claimed to be understanding, but when she would have a mental or emotional breakdown in the middle of the day, there wasn't a way around it, and eventually she had to work "off-site." Many of her daily responsibilities were handed out piecemeal to her "work friends" as her load lessened so that she could "deal with her situation" as they'd put it. That was fine until so many of her responsibilities were outsourced that they didn't have a reason to keep her around. She was let go with plenty of apology and more than a few "keep in touch" notes, but that wasn't her responsibility. She needed support, and with the exception of Mason and Marcy, she had none.

The "Beast of Why" couldn't stop there. It charged headlong into family—not much left of that anyway, but Alan had been all that remained, and the beast gobbled him up before she could gain any control of it. Their relationship, which lasted a meager three months, had been little more than a relationship-by-proxy from Evan.

When he died—*committed suicide*—she'd been quick to search out someone to lay the blame upon.

Alan, already bearing the burden of the source of a tumultuous history, was first on her list. She'd railed against him on the phone, and when he'd shown up—blessedly—to his brother's funeral, she'd railed on him in person. He and his husband had left promising that they wouldn't bother her again, but he said they'd always be willing to let her into their lives if she wanted.

The insanity of it all was that during all of these interactions, while everything she'd built crumbled around her, she was screaming in inescapable agony inside her own mind. And she was powerless to stop it. It was as if two people were controlling her. One whose single most important goal was to raze to the ground every single positive point of light and joy in her life and extinguish it. And a second, less controlling part who wanted nothing more than someone— *Evan*—to come along and hold her until the world around her stopped disintegrating.

Someone to hold her until the dust of her previous life settled and she could finally take stock of the rubble she sat upon and begin to rebuild.

Mason and Marcy had done the best they could. They were very nearly caretakers or had been for a short time, at least.

After Evan had died, she'd had no choice but to move out of his house. Not only because she couldn't afford it anymore—the payment was high on a home Outside and the cost of living in the shadow of what she would consider a fairly perfect life was taking a toll on her mental well-being—but also because the place was a vacuum.

Everywhere she looked she saw Evan. Even after Mason—probably the only other single most incredible human to have ever existed—cleaned his best friend's brains off the wall, the cost was too high. The pictures, the clothes, the smells, the echoes she heard as she walked around the house, it was all too much. Even the sound the oven made when it was opened, creaking like an ancient ironclad door, reminded her of the few times they'd used it since coming home.

It had been a terrible, disgusting irony that shortly after his death, she regained all of her memories or as near as she could tell.

She'd been sitting on the couch, the same couch where she'd witnessed the revival of her husband and brother-in-law's relationship, when she felt a sudden vertigo come over her. She didn't think much of it at first, perhaps she'd forgotten to eat the past couple of days. After all, she didn't even remember eating dinner the night before.

But when the second wave came over her and she had to put a hand out to steady herself, she knew it was no mere hunger pang.

In her mind, there was a great wave of pictures, cacophonous sounds, and raw emotions in the distance, coming toward her out of the blackness that she knew to be the section of her mind that held her lost memories. They were connected to her, though, as if someone had cast out with a giant barbed hook and snagged an incredible treasure.

With an intensity that had her reeling, the wave of memory began racing closer at an unimaginable speed, a massive rushing sound filled her ears, blocking all other sounds out. And while she couldn't be certain, she suspected that she had begun moaning and that moaning turned into screaming. Whether sound had accompanied the scream or not, she'd never know, but one thing she knew for certain was that if she couldn't withstand the onslaught, she'd be overtaken, and her mind, her sense of self, perhaps even her very soul, would be swept up and crushed beneath the enormous weight of it all.

She continued screaming as the hook pulled the memories closer, reeling them into her injured psyche with only an imagined fishing rod whizzing and whining within her.

The memories began filing rapidly into her mind one after another, a cosmic rolodex of the evidence of a life fully lived. They slotted into chronological place, each biting home with a nearly audible *snick snick snick*. The sound notecards make as they shuffled into place.

Memories of the previous four years overwhelmed her, and even amidst the terrible roaring sound of the reclaimed self, she could feel the tears coursing down her cheeks. Large and hot, they seemed to burn as they ran from her eyes and dripped from her chin; each centimeter they moved was an eternity. In the space of seconds, she bore witness to her own stars and planets coalescing, thriving, and collapsing once again into black holes of archival gravity.

When she began to hear her own hoarse voice screaming—there had been sound, after all—she noticed the deluge of memories abating. They were still filing in, but it was no longer a firehose aimed directly at her limbic system. Now, it was a faucet cranked high. But even as she took stock of her own mind and the setting around her, it diminished to a trickle.

With her eyes squeezed shut against the pain of processing that much information that quickly, she held her head in her hands, swallowing hard against the needles that felt like glass in her throat.

She felt a wetness beneath her nose and wiped it away on the back of her hand. She looked at it and saw a crimson gleam. Her nose was bleeding—there was blood on her, just like there was on the wall. She could feel herself begin to hyperventilate as she stared at the dark stripe across her skin. She wiped it on the couch, not caring that it would stain and tried again to calm her breathing.

Her shirt was wet with sweat, sticking to her back and belly in dark patches and her hair was plastered to her face where sweat seemed to pour from her temples.

She felt as if she'd plunged headfirst into a boiling lake. Sitting on the couch, she had the sudden urge to strip down to her underwear. The clothes were constricting and confining, and if she didn't get them off right now, she was going to go fucking crazy.

She jumped up, ignoring to stab of pain at the base of her skull and frantically stripped her shirt off, relishing in the cool air as it hit her damp and goosebumped flesh and ignoring the sound of fabric ripping as she pulled it over her head and tossed it aside. She had little time to enjoy it as her legs were alight with a searing, more maniacal heat. She worked at unbuttoning her pants, but her fingers were so shaky and slick with sweat that she couldn't grasp the goddamn button. With a screech of rage and frenzied fear, she yanked the jeans down without unbuttoning them, once again ignoring the feel of skin being scratched and stretched along her hips toward her ankles. Her underwear were accidentally pulled down in the process, but she didn't care.

She sat hastily and with a large measure of relief. She ignored the underwear that were pulled askew down to her thighs and reached down to her ankles to pull the pants from her clammy feet.

She was crying now. Weeping. Her fingers were going numb with pins and needles, and she couldn't tell if she was breathing or not. The air was thick, like she was working the air in and out through a coffee straw. She knew she was hyperventilating but didn't know how to stop it.

She focused on her breaths. It helped that she no longer felt the encapsulation of her clothes that they were slowly crushing her like a multitude of fiery snakes squeezing the life from her.

The lack of air moving in the living room was irritating, but even the subtle, natural movement of air currents were a welcome caress on her naked and cooling skin. Even the goosebumps felt good. They told her that she was still alive and that the memories that threatened to overwhelm her had settled into some semblance of order within her mind. She dared not look at them yet, dared not try to see if they socketed home in the correct order. Not yet.

She knew she wasn't ready to unpack them, but she knew also that there was a great deal of work to do. It would be like sifting through a box of old pictures. Only, instead of the tell-tale sign of time's unstoppable march within the sepia tone of the pictures, she would be adding color and sound and life to them all. Some, she knew, would be good. Some, however, would be bad. And she'd had enough "bad" for now.

Her breathing evened out, and she could tell that her heart, which had been racing so quickly that it had felt like one single and elongated *hum* within her chest, was slowing to not normal rhythm, but maybe less hysterical. Yes. Less hysterical at the very least.

Once more, she took stock of herself and her surroundings. She sat on the couch covered in a glassy layer of sweat with uneven, unsightly goosebumps trailing across all of her exposed skin. She was nearly naked in a white bra and disheveled gray underwear pulled nearly to her ankles. She had no issue understanding that she looked like a disaster, a victim of a terrible accident.

She reached down and pulled her underwear up to their original position. Her fingers shook, and she panted in deep and uneven gasps as she raised her hips off the couch and then settled back down, feeling a little more complete now that she wasn't sprawling on the couch in the near nude. Modesty above all, or something like that.

She decided then that she needed to call Marcy. Marcy wouldn't understand everything that she was feeling, but as a woman, she would understand the swirling mass of hysteria that was pulling her gently—but inexorably—in. It sat at the back of her mind and threatened to take control once more, but she could hold it off, at least for a few more minutes.

When she called Marcy, her voice was uneven and hoarse; she could barely form the words. All the moisture that her mouth needed in order to speak was spreading on her skin and dripping down her cheeks as both sweat and tears.

She swallowed hard and managed to rasp that she needed her to come over. Marcy hung up after quickly stating she was on her way.

She arrived a short eternity later, knocking once, calling her name, and entering with the key she and Mason had been given after Evan and Mason's thunderous battle in the front yard.

Meredith smiled in a way that said *It's great to see you, but I'm about a millisecond from shattering into a thousand pieces.*

CHAPTER 21

In the back of Meredith's mind, distantly and from a place where modesty resided, she had a sudden, stuttering hesitation as Marcy stood a few feet inside the doorway. She was lying on the couch, shivering from both the adrenaline of what had just happened to her and from the sweat that had begun cooling her burning skin, and she was nearly naked.

Her arms continued to tingle, and she felt as if she couldn't move. The distant part of her that recognized she was nearly naked was screaming for her to cover up, but she didn't have the energy to care. It was as if a clock had missed a cog on its normal rotation around the wheel, hitching for a moment, and then continuing. Another thought wormed its way into the pale spotlight that was her conscious thought. She mostly ignored—but briefly feared and then dismissed—that Marcy would see not her dear friend that had called for help, but instead, someone whose mind had cracked beneath the strain and was now wending its way to insanity. Meredith would be no more than a lunatic bound for the asylum.

"Hey Mer—" Marcy's voice faltered when she saw that tentative and exhausted smile and the glassy gaze that stared toward her but not *at* her. Meredith was certain, now, that perhaps she did look insane, but she didn't care.

"I remember," was all she managed to croak out as she moved to stand up. But before she could, Marcy rushed to her side and enfolded her in a warm and tense embrace that was not altogether uncomfortable.

Meredith started to speak again, wanting to explain—or try to—what happened and what she now knew. Instead, another round of fresh tears sprang from her eyes and fell into Marcy's hair she was rocked and held by her friend. She could feel her own knees still shaking, lightly brushing Marcy's and making a soft whispering sound that mingled with her gentle sobs.

She had made it to a half-stand, but now both of them sank slowly back onto the couch. Marcy holding her, supporting her, and keeping her tethered to sanity by nothing more than a spider's silky thread that hung inches above a tidal rush of hellish madness.

Time seemed to stand still despite the sun that stretched across the length of the living room through the still-open front door. It made shadows grow and light in the room shrink as the golden orb that willingly gave of itself sank slowly behind the horizon.

Marcy was making quiet soothing noises, gently rubbing Meredith's hair with one hand, and grasping their hands with her other. Meredith, with eyes tightly shut, could only embrace the comfort she was offered. She had no energy—or will—to disengage out of propriety.

As her breath began to ease into a more measured rhythm and feeling that she had *actually*—finally—cried all of her tears, Meredith moved slowly into a sitting position. She noticed Marcy's shirt, dark with the tears they'd shed together, and felt that she should apologize. But again, the energy to include someone else's feelings as part of her own was gone.

She met Marcy's eyes, afraid she would see accusation or doubt staring back. Afraid that she would feel shame at being found in such a state. But her friend was smiling generously with understanding and empathy sending her strength and unequivocal support within that gentle gaze.

She'd been lying on Marcy's torso beneath her breasts, and with a short gasp, she placed her hands on her friend's swollen belly. It protruded from her petite frame in such a way that they'd chuckled about it plenty, laughed that it looked like she was hiding a watermelon beneath.

"Marcy!" She could feel the sting of tears, but they blessedly stayed inside their ducts, and she held them at bay. She had to force them back and swallow the cries that were on the verge of leaping from her lips. "I'd forgotten!"

Marcy's smile timidly changed from understanding light, laughing delight. "I was afraid of how you'd react." Her own hands had moved onto Meredith's, both of them rubbing across the thin shield that protected a subsequent generation from the terrors of the outside world.

Meredith remembered now that Marcy was six months pregnant with their second child. She and Mason had already chosen a name for their little boy—Maverick. The memory that rose to her consciousness now was one filled with pain, anger, and loss. The time she and Evan had received the news that she'd never be able to have children of her own. It was sad, and there was no small measure of grief that accompanied it. But she remembered mourning that loss, and while she felt some sense that the same mourning would come again—needed to come again—she also felt excitement at the prospect of being a surrogate aunt to another child for her dearest friend.

She sobered quickly. Evan would never be an uncle. In fact, he would have been more than one of those surrogate relatives that are adopted into the family of friends like she was, those that are often dearer than family. Evan would have been more precious to that family than almost their own. Almost.

Those bittersweet memories that followed Evan's suicide were hard to remember, mostly because they followed on the heels of such a horrific event. Much to her surprise, however, they had changed a little. As if the sun were shining at a different angle of the same forest. She wasn't sure what that could mean for her, for them, but she welcomed the change.

She pulled from some secret place within herself the courage to stay in the present, to stay here with her husband for the time being. Meredith clutched onto hope, even while Evan sobbed inconsolably beside her, realizing that he'd chosen to leave the world instead of stay in it with her.

It was nearly impossible to maintain the truth that he wasn't *actually* there, only a digital composition of data, a hologram like something from a sci-fi story. It did help, though, in a strange and twisted way, for her to speak to him like this. *Tangible closure*, the letter she'd received had said. It hadn't lied. It did seem like she was approaching something like that. Not closure, not exactly, but something that resembled it as if the mirror image of it. It was a path through the ragged mountains of isolation that she'd struggled to find, and the fog of her deep despair was lifting.

She reached out her hand and placed it on his back, the tingling resistance that she hadn't noticed before tickled her palm in a way that wasn't pleasant, a feeling that cautioned of a subsequent and serious shock.

He looked at her, eyes red and swollen and cheeks wet. When he spoke, it was deep and thick with emotion, so much like her Evan that she felt an ache of longing clench her heart so fiercely that she gasped.

"Did I leave a note or anything? I can't—I can't even imagine that as a possibility, that I would leave you stranded. What kind of a selfish monster did I turn into?" His voice was an amalgamation of deep sorrow, regret, and hollow understanding. It was a Frankenstein's monster that she had felt as well.

"Yes, you did leave a note, but it didn't amount to much. It was only a few words. I don't remember exactly because I've had that part of my life Hazed. I wasn't able to function before the Hazing, and I'd say I was only marginally functional after. Your note didn't explain anything. I only remember feeling that it was something I couldn't have expected, but looking back, I should have seen the signs.

"The best that we can gather is that you were struggling at a much deeper level than any of us could pick up. I blamed myself for a long time, realizing that if I'd had my memories, I probably would have been able to pick up on certain discrepancies in your tone and affect, subtle hints that there was a war raging inside of you.

"Oh, you were happy, most of the time. But when I think back on it, the way you acted and how you treated certain parts of your life or events within it, I can see now where there may have been a darkness lurking inside."

He sniffed, and his eyes took on a curiosity. "You said 'think back.' Did you remember? Did you remember everything that you lost?"

She nodded, now embracing a mental shift where she became a source of information and nothing more.

"Yes, I remembered everything. It wasn't pleasant. It was a very sudden and exhausting event. One minute I didn't remember and the next I did. I remembered everything in that split second and it nearly drove me insane. It was only a day or two after you—died."

She continued, despite the brief pause in avoiding stating the obvious, "Even Mason didn't see it coming, though, and he blames himself as much as I blame myself or even more than I do. Even to this day. He thinks he should have seen it, not only as your best friend but also as another guy. He should have been able to see the signs of withheld anger, resentment, bitterness, sadness, whatever it was. I hold no ill will toward him whatsoever, though."

Here it comes.

"You're right, though. It was selfish, what you did."

There. She said it.

Evan nodded in understanding while she took a shuddering breath. *She actually said it. Finally.* She had come into this knowing it was what she *wanted* to say, but she knew herself well enough to know that what she *wanted* to say and what she *would* say were two separate things.

But she didn't want to dwell on that. It was a big step, one she would revel in being able to accomplish later. Even now, she could feel the demons that had held down the chains of that oppressive ignorance fleeing.

But now, however, she knew their time was coming to an end. Like the sun that sets on a field of wheat freshly harvested, so too would this day—that seemed to have lasted years, and perhaps it had—finally end.

"Speaking of Mason, he wanted to say goodbye. Obviously, he didn't get the chance to say it when you were alive, and he wasn't selected as a Bench participant, so he asked me to play this memory for you, if that's alright."

Evan wiped his eyes and smiled in gloomy resignation at her.

The same square that had taken them on a journey, through a time when their relationship was strong and where it was weakest, suddenly blinked to life. When Mason's square and bearded face floated in the air before him, a terrible sound stumbled from Evan's throat and into the room.

It broke Meredith's heart as she saw the longing and sorrow her dead husband was feeling as it came out in a type of wretched incantation, a despondent hopeless mix of formless words.

Mason's beard covered half of his face, dark and thick fur that couldn't quite cover the mouth that trembled beneath it. He was still the same muscular man from when Evan was living, but the lines in his face had become more pronounced. When he spoke, his deep and booming voice was watery with pain and grief.

"Hey, Evan. I—I wanted Meredith to show you this video because I wanted to tell you something. I needed to tell you something."

He exhaled, nervously wiping his mouth with a thick and meaty palm. His eyes cast about, as if searching for what he wanted to say. "I really thought I was ready for this."

He took a heaving breath and plowed ahead.

"I'm sorry that I wasn't there for you when—" his voice broke and he squinted hard, forcing the tears away, but his lower lip trembled as he continued in a whispering rasp, "when you needed me most. I didn't know what was going on, and if I could change one thing, it would be that I was there for you better. I love you, Evan. You were my best friend, more than a brother, and I wish you would have told me. I hope you weren't scared of what I'd think because I couldn't ever think anything but the best of you."

He was silent for several seconds. The tears he'd forced away moments ago ran freely now into the thick tangle of curly beard along his jaw.

With probably the hardest part now over, his speaking tempo quickened and took on a lighter, but no less serious, tone.

"Also, I want you to know that Meredith is gonna be fine." Sitting beside Evan and watching Mason speak, she smiled a grateful smile, still remembering when he'd asked her to record this. "Marcy and I are always with her. I mean, not always, but I'm sure there are times when she wants us to leave her alone," he chuckled, "but I'm not going to. We're not ever going to leave her alone. I promise. Sorry, Meredith." She laughed lightly, and Evan smiled wanly.

He took another deep breath and bent down. Meredith—who had only to watch him when this had been occurring—followed and another of those terrible heart-wrenching sobs escaped from Evan's gut when the screen showed a toddler, hair as red as a campfire's glow and a grin nearly as big as his daddy's.

"And finally, I wanted to introduce you to Maverick. He's almost four now, and you'd have been best friends, I have no doubt." Mason's cheeks were wet with tears that leaked steadily from his eyes, his voice shaky but persistent. "Say hi to Uncle Evan, Mav."

"Hi, Uncle Evan. I miss you." Meredith knew that Maverick had no concept of what he'd said, that he was simply repeating what Mason and Marcy had expressed countless times. But his voice, sweet and timid as a fox kit peeking through a garden of flowers, brought forth a cry of desperate gratitude from Evan. Meredith had to cover her mouth and slam her eyes closed to prevent herself from echoing it. The fact was that she was grateful. She was grateful that Mason had the idea to say hello, or goodbye, rather. She was grateful that Evan was able to see his best friend's son. She was grateful that she was here, with him, one last time.

Mason's voice vibrated through the vid screen as he suddenly spoke loudly. "Evan, you're missing a lot. I don't understand why and somewhere deep down I know that this is the closest I'll get to saying goodbye unless I'm lucky enough to be able to do what Meredith is doing, but Marcy and I—" he reached out of Meredith's field of vision and Marcy, belly growing with their third child, came and stood beside him, her own tear-stained cheeks and half-hearted smile brightening the picture exponentially. Maddie, now almost 8 stood beside her mom and dad, her own eyes swollen and red because she did know Evan. And she had loved him, too. Mason bent and picked up Maddie in the other arm. He looked very much like a pack mule with a child in each hand. "Do you want to say goodbye to Uncle Evan?" he asked her quietly. His voice was audible but soft as he spoke into his daughter's ear. She shook her head quickly, and then nodded, changing her mind as rapidly as she no doubt changed outfits.

Her bright blue eyes turned toward Evan—toward them both. She wiped away a tear and said, "Bye, Uncle Evan. I really miss you. I'm sorry you were so sad. But I love you."

Evan moaned and clutched at his shirt, looking like he would tear it from his body at any moment. His red-rimmed eyes stared longingly.

Mason put Maddie down before speaking again. But Maverick remained perched on his hand, one arm looped easily around his father's neck and the other, she now noticed, holding a toy plane. "Marcy and I love you. We have another girl on the way. We're naming her Evie because your memory is worth carrying on."

Evan was nodding, his face filled with a full range of emotions as he stared intently at the message. Sorrow, pain, heartache all present and accounted for. But hope, love, and eager enthusiasm was present as well.

"We'll see each other again, I think," Mason was saying, "and everything will be fine. Until then, you can count on us to keep your treasure safe. Meredith is closer than any of my siblings could ever dream of being, and we love her to death, all of us. You don't have to be afraid."

The image stopped with Mason's firm resolve showing through a forced smile that she was certain was meant to convey his seriousness. Evan turned to her with shaking hands and his voice choked, scratchy and spent.

"Meredith. Sorry isn't enough. I would take it back in a heartbeat if I could. I'd take it back a thousand times."

She nodded at him. She knew he would. Wouldn't anyone? Wouldn't anyone who saw the damage they left behind, the ruin left in the wake of the single-most destructive decision they could ever make in this life?

"I know. I know you would. I'm doing okay, though. I mean, I wasn't doing okay, either. There were ... dark times when I wondered if maybe I should follow you into that maw of blessed silence. They were brief, but they were there. And they helped me understand a little of why you made that decision. I think everything was too much. I think you lost perspective. That you forgot everyone around you that mattered.

"Maybe something brought you down, sucked you down into the depths of some cave stinking of death and bad decisions and you didn't know how to get out.

"Either way, I don't think it matters. I'm doing okay, better than I have been. Most days are good. Most days I'm good. I laugh, sometimes, though it sounds hollow without yours to accompany it. I miss you. Terribly. You were the single most wonderful thing that ever happened to me." She could see that he thought she was leading up to something akin to thankfulness at his untimely departure. Instead, she smiled and lifted his chin with a finger. "*I* wouldn't change that. You helped me become who I am, and I am *me* because of *you*. You've left a legacy that we may not pass to any biological children, but—" she pointed to the air where Mason's vid had been moments before, "they'll pass to that little girl, and her brother, and their sister, and their friends, and on and on.

"You are important, Evan, even now." She held his eyes with her own for a moment and brought his hand to her lips to kiss it gently.

CHAPTER 22

"It's beautiful here, Evan." She was gazing longingly out toward the sea where it met the horizon with a pale blue line. A line of fog had coalesced in a shadowed recess near the coastline and was wending its way around the rocks. A warm, salty breeze brushed her face gently, and the sun shone bright enough to make her squint against the reflecting glint on the gently yawning waves below.

She wasn't sure where to go from here. She knew their time together was coming to a close, and she felt both dread and comfort in that. She felt as if she finally had crested the hill that she'd been climbing for four years and could see that blessed city of "Moving On" in the distance.

"You know," he said from beside her in a tone of quiet calm, "I have one request, if you'll let me have one."

His voice had changed. He was no longer mournful, no longer full of despairing regret. He sounded like, well, like someone who had changed. Someone who had come to realize their role was no longer what they had understood it to be in the beginning but is now something even greater. Something with purpose.

"Sure, shoot." She wiped her nose before it could drip. She wasn't sure exactly what his request would be and wasn't even sure she could follow through on it.

"I'm not really me, right. I'm a conglomeration of all the memories that were stored in my chip. All of the memories of when things were good, mostly before I gave up, right?"

She nodded.

"So, from my perspective, if this holographic group of data can have a perspective, I'm the best version of myself that even you remember."

She nodded again, a little mystified, but smiled nonetheless.

"Here's my request: I want you to live a full life, the fullest life you could ever imagine, even fuller than the life we lived together. I want you to find someone to love and love them. If you can. I know it's not something that you'll necessarily want to entertain, but your love is the sweetest drink, and while I want so bad to keep to myself, I had my chance. I drank—drank deeply—and chose to give up on it. I want someone else to be able to experience the joy of who Meredith is, who she *really* is."

In the four years since his death, more recently probably the last two years, she'd only briefly entertained the thought of finding someone else. She had dismissed those thoughts nearly as soon as they crept up, believing that she would never be able to be a part of someone else's life the way she'd been a part of Evan's.

"Someone as beautiful, strong, smart, and brave as you shouldn't go through life alone. You deserve to be happy, and there's someone else out there who is a hopeless mess without you in their life.

"It's not like you need my permission, or even more so that you need someone to be 'complete,' but if you find someone that you enjoy being around and those feelings begin to turn into something deeper and more meaningful, it's okay to love them."

He was right. She didn't need his permission, but after all of these years, she now realized she *wanted* his permission and didn't think she'd ever get it. She wanted him to let her live, but even being the primary thinker of her body, she felt that she wouldn't ever get the chance.

She and Evan had shared such an intense and binding love that entertaining the thought of looking for—and finding—that with someone else almost felt like betrayal, an affront to his memory, like someone vandalizing his gravestone with paint—or worse.

"I love you, Evan. I've loved you for most of my life and am so thankful that you were mine, even though it seems like the shallowest of breaths shared in the river of time. Thank you for being you and letting me give you my heart."

She cupped his face and kissed his cheek, that same electrical fizz vibrating across her lips.

"You're my favorite," she whispered intimately into his ear, and his cheek touched her chin in a wide grin.

"And you're mine," he echoed.

They stared into each other's face for a time, then. Meredith worked to memorize every feature he had. She hadn't realized that in her memories, parts of him were disappearing. Perhaps not disappearing, no. But fading. Becoming pastel prints or sepia-toned.

"I think this is when we say goodbye, even though I don't want to." She could feel her eyes blinking away tears, but she didn't want to cry. She'd cried a lot in this place and for the first time—maybe the first time in four years—she didn't feel that it was out of her control. Letting go was something she'd imagined within the privacy of her own mind but never given it the chance to grow in anything more.

"I think you're right," he whispered and tucked a hair behind her ear. She leaned into his warm palm.

"I'll miss you, Evan."

"I know you will, but you know what? I think you're gonna be great. The world needs more Merediths, and I've known for a long time that you were the stronger of us."

She laughed, half in nervousness and half in relief. Evan was a good man. He'd been a good man, but he'd made a terrible mistake that cost those around him a portion of their lives that they couldn't ever get back. But he was a good man.

"Goodbye, Meredith."

Was this really the end? Was this really the last time she'd ever see him?

She could at least replace the malignant memory of his suicide as her "last memory" with this sweet moment they were sharing. And this was a good replacement.

"I love you, Evan. I'll always love you."

He nodded and leaned in to kiss her on the lips. Again, that shuffling current between their lips, but she lifted her shoulders in enjoyment and memorized every particulate of that final kiss.

She pulled away and smiled. She smiled *her* smile. The smile that he constantly told her was her best feature. The smile that she willingly and gleefully gave to him as a final parting gift.

He smiled in return, flickered for a brief second as if the connection were tapering, and then empty air replaced where the love of her life had been.

CHAPTER 23

She sat for several minutes staring into the warm space that Evan left, immediately feeling the emptiness. It was different, though. It wasn't a crushing loneliness that grew within her. Now, it was a known quantity. It was emptiness, yes, a void that was previously filled by someone she loved. But now it was *less* substantial. It was difficult for her to even understand, but she knew at the very least it was something that could be addressed and contained, if not relinquished entirely.

The room around her began changing. The sounds of gulls and the distant hum and crash of waves were fading rapidly, replaced by an electronic whine that had been cleverly covered by The Bench's technology. The steady hum of air filters and circulation were couched within the muted tones that had surrounded her. Now, they weren't being disguised and could clearly be heard.

Where previously a dazzling afternoon sunshine had suffused the room she and Evan had sat with a gloriously warm golden light, re-living their own joys and sorrows, there was now a harsh, faintly blue glare coming from the fluorescent bulbs covering the ceiling.

The walls which had been a subdued shimmering expanse around her when she entered were now dark and lifeless, the millions of receptors that covered them powered down and useless now that their transitory purpose had been fulfilled. The receptors covered the walls like a million tiny black bug eyes, glinting with a machine-like disdain for the living.

She noticed little of this, however. Only giving it enough of her attention to acknowledge it, nothing more.

She was replaying what she'd experienced with Evan. Time, that inexorable marching soldier, was far from her. She had no concept of how long she'd been with Evan, though it felt as if she'd turned a light on and the bulb had blown. A brief illumination of everything that was and could have been, plunged just as quickly back into darkness.

That wasn't entirely true, though. There wasn't complete darkness as there had been before. Evan's promise and final request still droned in her ears and from them, a radiant glow emanated, pulsing. It was weak and fragile, yes, but it was there. Something she could cultivate into maturity where it would turn into ... what?

Life.

Yes. It was the start of the next part of her life.

The first part of her life was full of joy and growth, experience and understanding.

The second was muted, the memories mulched into a dark and primordial soup of gloom.

The third was this new light. She knew it was worth the time and energy, and a small, distant part of her knew that she would share it with Mason and Marcy when she went over for dinner, a standing invitation every week since she regained her memories.

The door behind her clicked open with a stealthy *snick*, and the air pressure around her changed slightly. Turning, she saw a man in a neatly tailored suit standing there, arms clasped before him. It was the same man that brought her to The Bench after meeting her at the door to Innervate Industries.

The man, who had introduced himself as Branson Faust, spoke softly to her in a nondescript, masculine voice. "Are you ready, Ms. Reader? Are you okay?"

She nodded and stood slowly, taking a few shaky steps toward the door. The more steps she took, the steadier she became. She was fine. She was better than fine. She was, perhaps for the first time in a long time, *good*.

Branson gestured for her to precede him into the hallway, which was a stark white. Shelves with books and small plants were displayed along the walls toward the waiting room, the inception to this adventure.

"Are you okay, Ms. Reader?" he repeated the question again.

She gave him a pleasant smile, more for his sake than hers, and began walking down the hall. "Yes, I'm quite well. Thank you." And she found herself gathering that around her, that she actually was, to her infinite surprise and pleasure, quite well.

Another indicated room, this one either the same pre-session interview room or one identical to it, and she sat politely in the uncomfortable plastic white chair opposite Branson.

"Now that the session is finished, I'll ask you some questions." He spoke with the tone of a man who had this part memorized, divorced from any emotion that could be tied to the words.

"These are to gauge the effectiveness of The Bench's protocols and your experience. Your answers will help us understand successes and areas of opportunity for the program moving forward. This is not required but would be greatly appreciated."

"Of course," she stated evenly with a wan smile.

"Great." He gave a curt nod and continued. "We'll start with some simple questions about how you feel about the experience, then move on to what you thought went well and what, if anything, could be improved. Then, we'll finish with any questions *you* might have."

Meredith was still a little stunned at how quickly everything had gone. Her whole conversation with Evan seemed to have been hours ago already, though she knew it had ended only a few moments before. Now she was, what? Rating the experience like a customer survey following a Christmas shopping trip.

Her ears were ringing, and she realized that Branson had been speaking to her.

"Ms. Reader, would you like me to repeat the question?"

She scrambled back into her consciousness, retrieving the sounds she had registered but not heard.

"No, that's alright, I heard you. I'm thinking," she said hastily.

She had been thinking, that at least was true. But she wasn't thinking about how to answer the question he asked. But she remembered it now.

How would you describe your experience within The Bench?

How would she describe it? Good? No, not really. Terrifying? There were certainly parts that were terrifying, not least of all where her dead husband realized he was actually dead.

"It was interesting," she said slowly, picking each word carefully as it came in her mind. "It was not what I expected. There were issues that came up that I didn't foresee, and that made the experience ... difficult, at times."

"Are you talking about where you and the subject discovered the lack of memories?"

What else? she thought sarcastically, but then, she realized that there could be several instances that "made the experience difficult" as she'd stated.

"Yes, that's mostly what I was speaking to." A question arose inside her, and before she could stop herself, she blurted it out. "How could that have happened?" Her tone wasn't angry, but she couldn't keep all the heat from it.

Branson nodded, almost as if expecting the question. "Yes, that was a very strange occurrence. While you were with the subject, I spoke at length to several supporting techs and several experts on the SafetyChip technology, and they presented some interesting theories that may explain some of that.

"They stated that it was entirely possible that your late husband had essentially fried the chip when he tried to protect himself from the falling lights, and without subsequent warning, the chip malfunctioned, which resulted in a lapse within both the memory- and emotion-logging software.

"From that point, there seemed to be a series of unfortunate circumstances that led to the chip's malfunction never being detected, reported, and eventually, reversed."

He was animatedly relating this information to Meredith. She was curious how this could happen but was now beginning to regret asking. She didn't necessarily care *how* it happened; it was more of a question as to how they *could have let this happen.*

I should have been more precise, she thought with mild regret.

"The first point of detection that was missed would have been when requesting verification in the wake of the tsunami, but due to the colossal numbers of other people doing the same thing, his request was denied, which led to the second point of missed detection, buying tickets back to the states.

"It was stated that your Chip could have been rebooted at the nearest Chip Center in New Delhi, but due to the previously mentioned influx, the wait was undeterminable but understandably lengthy. As an alternative, I surmised that you both opted to go back to the States, where he was able to verify both of your identities with an incredibly outdated but—in this case—a very useful tool—passports, of all things. That's something we—well, Innervate Industries—would never have imagined as a way to bypass Chip functionality. In that instance, there is no law requiring a scan when passports are used to verify identification, either to buy plane tickets or, for the third missed detection point, re-entering the States. The passports were used at that time as well.

"The fourth missed detection wasn't an actual event; it was more of 'the remainder of time.' Once back in the States, there was very little reason to have a Chip scanned. He didn't need a reboot. There was no warning that showed a malfunction, and there was no rush to get yours checked.

"In fact, it's my understanding that you had requested a reboot when you returned to the States, is that correct?"

"Yes, that's right. We requested it a couple of days after our return home. We received a reply that it was 'in review,' and we would receive confirmation when it was accepted along with an appointment card and digital reminder. The only problem is that I don't think we ever received it."

Branson nodded as he wrote something down, then clicked his pen closed and looked at her, the excitement in his eyes was magnified behind the thick lens of his glasses.

"I was writing myself a note to check into peripheral indications of Chip failure. Yes, after some initial research, we were able to track down your request and the subsequent approval. Unfortunately, and this is our final failed detection because your late husband's chip was damaged—he was your emergency contact—it was never received on that end. Additionally, you'd last been pinged and registered in New Delhi, and since you'd used physical evidence of identification, there was no reason to log your registration back into the States. An oversight, to be sure, and one that I've already made sure will be addressed in some form to the committee in charge of updates and improvements.

"Therefore, the notification was sent to your previously known and scanned location, which was the Asia Zone. This wasn't detected as an error or, rather, a miscalculation. It was essentially, and to borrow a long-forgotten phrase, 'returned to sender,' where it's probably still sitting in someone's queue to review and revise."

He sat forward and looked at her sympathetically.

"Even if they did review and revise it, unless you scanned your chip in the United States, it will be returned again for review and revision. And again and again." He spread his hands in a way that said "can't do anything about it." "It's an imperfect system," he finished.

"Yeah, I'll say." Meredith could feel the bitterness creeping into her voice. She was more than irritated but was slowly realizing it would do little to no good. Even had they found a way to avoid any of those issues, the others were such that there would still have been a problem, somewhere. And who knows how long they'd have waited for some kind of reboot or Recovery.

A friend of a friend had requested recovery after her husband and child had died in a horrific car accident. It had taken nearly eight months for the process to be completed, and by that time, she had made her own progress in dealing with the trauma. And that wasn't during a crisis like a tsunami that wiped out an entire coastline.

For her own part, she'd received the tangible closure she'd been hoping for, and that was priceless in its own right.

"So other than that rather glaring issue, would you consider this experience useful for those going through the grieving process?"

This time, she actually did take a few moments to think. She turned inward and sought an answer. It was certainly something useful, something that provided relief from the constant questions plaguing those left behind by disaster. Realistically, she was actually glad that the memories had been missing from Evan's Chip. It provided the chance for her to see the Evan that she had fallen in love with.

Both times, she thought wryly.

When she spoke, she smiled a little, wanting to communicate that she wasn't bitter in this respect.

"Yes, I do. I do think that this is a useful tool for people experiencing grief."

"That's great. Thank you for that.

"The next question is what do you feel could have been better or different, speaking directly to the experience of The Bench, as we've already established the failure to indicate Chip malfunction."

"Yes, I understand." She thought back to The Bench and The Pod. The digitized walls that showed a glorious view of the ocean, the sounds of the gulls wheeling overhead, and the waves scrubbing the rocks and sand far below were all impossibly realistic. The smells of salt and wet dirt were particularly stunning. She remembered those especially. Probably because they had been ingrained in her mind from the tsunami. The warm sunlight that had lain on her exposed skin was light and comfortable, like a muslin blanket. And the breeze that tickled the fine hairs on her arm and the back of her neck, then whisked through her hair, turning it and spinning it in a way that seemed impossible in that domed room she had just left.

"It was magical," she finished. There wasn't another word for it.

Branson smiled wide and spoke with true pleasure, "Good, that's good. That's great, actually. Thank you. That's what we wanted for you. It's what we want for everyone who comes through our program. We want them to feel that magic."

He cleared his throat, and Meredith realized with only a small amount of embarrassment that he was getting a little choked up. She could understand that feeling, being so proud of something and having that pride and dedication validated by an outsider who was completely ignorant of the thousands of hours and millions of dollars invested in making it perfect.

"The final question. Is there anything else you'd like to know?" He tapped the edge of his tablet after gesturing to himself and then to her, emphasizing each pronoun.

There was something that was bothering her. Something that she was afraid to ask. No, not afraid to ask, afraid to hear the answer for. This was her chance, though, and she knew she had to take it. If not for Evan, then for her own understanding.

"What happens to Evan, or happened to Evan, after he disappeared?" She heard her own question and immediately felt self-conscious. It sounded so silly in her own ears, but Branson nodded and smiled reassuringly. She was sure he could see the scarlet flush creeping up her cheeks.

"That's okay, Ms. Reader. It's a question that we have expected. It may seem strange, but the subject—"

"Evan," she interrupted before she could stop herself. "His name is Evan, please."

"I'm sorry, yes, of course. Evan." Now, it was his turn to flush a little.

Meredith felt only a little sorry for him.

He continued, "As I was saying, it may seem strange, but Evan was only a digital representation of all the data compiled in his Chip and, if available, on the Intersphere. He wasn't alive—I'm sure you know that—not in the traditional understanding and definition accepted by those of us in this room, at least. But I understand how you may feel as if he had been alive all along in that room with you."

"Yes, but what *happens* to him, now?"

"Well, as he's simply a digitized version of data, lines of code on a hard drive. Not to be crass or insensitive, but he's a sequence of ones and zeros right now. No more real than the sounds of the seagulls and the brush of the wind against you, 'he' stops *being*." Branson used finger quotes and for some reason, it pricked at her pride. "Of course, we don't have cameras or anything like that. There's no way to monitor the data to see that it is parsed and stored in a specific place. Even if there was a way to do that, we wouldn't actually see 'Evan' as you saw him. His file is saved on our computer," he pointed vaguely, "and when we open the file, he *becomes* the Evan that you know."

He must have noticed Meredith's blank stare. He shook his hands in a reassuring, almost flippant gesture and said, "In a word, the data returns to its source, which in this case is the mainframe housed right here in this facility. Beneath our very shoes, actually."

He looked between his spread out hands and feet, indicating the area that was directly below them. Though, she was certain it would have been too coincidental to actually be directly beneath this room.

"What happens if I want to come back in 20 years and see him again? What if someone else wants to see him, like Mason or Marcy?" This question, she realized, scared her more, but she couldn't understand why.

Branson spread his hands in self-satisfaction. "That's one of the amazing things about the technology here at Innervate Industries. When someone is Summoned through The Bench, each subsequent iteration remembers the previous one, up to the very point of reintegration into the data systems. Therefore, if say, Mason comes in a year or two or five, Evan will remember the conversation you had *as well as the memories you showed him*. He'll be able to apologize to Mason for fighting if the data indicates that he would have that reaction, of course."

He paused.

"In fact, if you'll remember, you were in the room only a moment or two before the subj—I mean, Evan—came in. Evan had been going through what we call the 'Reincarnate Subroutine.' It's a program that we run the memory data through to get the person Summoned up to speed with what they experienced during their life.

"It brings them slowly into the present day by showing them events in their life leading up to the present but in the form of memories. There are certain clues we've coded into the program to begin the process. It's a fantastic formula that allows the digital code to regenerate in an almost organic manner."

He smiled almost to himself and then said quietly, "Almost like magic. Evan was going through this Subroutine in the few seconds before appearing, but to his digital mind, it lasted much longer. He arrived in the morning and went through several memories brought about by the flags and triggers placed at specific points throughout the program's environmental core. Based on his reactions to one trigger, another may show up—to him—a few minutes later as a nostalgic reminder of a childhood friend or an important event that changed the course of his life. Something along those lines."

It was incredible. It really was. The data reflected all memories up to the point when it became data in a spreadsheet somewhere, streaming about in wires and hard drives until it was opened, and he was quite literally Summoned back to the land of the living.

"Is there anything else you'd like to ask? We still have a few minutes, I believe." He glanced at his watch.

"No, I don't think so. I think that's all I wanted to know. Thank you, Branson."

He stood and gestured toward the door they'd entered from, and she walked in silence down the hallway, passing decorative bookshelves and fake plants in a kind of astounded trance.

She was more complete than she'd felt in years.

It was finished, now. She was finally done. Not done healing. No, she may never be done healing. But she could feel the cells of her sanity swelling and growing. Like a dried and crusted sponge that was suddenly fed water, she could feel herself expanding and filling up, stretching muscles that had atrophied in the dimness that was the past four years. The darkness that so frequently had threatened to overwhelm her had begun fading and was being eclipsed by something else, something she had known as a *thing* but not as a thing for *her*.

It was *hope*.

The bleak midnight that had pervaded her existence since Evan's death was turning into a gray, the gray of approaching morning, the promise of light that would make the shadows flee and give substance to things that had be secreted away.

There was hope on the horizon, and it was time to chase it down.

EPILOGUE

Evan had the briefest second to notice that he wasn't in complete darkness. He was floating, but there was no directional reference to determine whether he was an inch or a mile off the ground. And there was light coming from somewhere, but he couldn't see the source if there was one. It seemed to come from nowhere and everywhere all at once.

His mind was still reeling as he tried to gather and arrange his thoughts. He'd been sitting with Meredith on a beautifully clear day. They'd talked and cried together, and he said goodbye, something he didn't do when he was alive. But now he was, what? In a computer? Part of the computer? He understood that he was no longer alive, but beyond that, he couldn't fathom what came next.

He perceived a sensation in his hands and then understood that his fingers had begun to tingle. He glanced at them and was shocked to see an amber glow spreading from his fingertips down to his palms and nearing his wrist. It wasn't altogether painful; it was as if he were touching a wall adjacent to a room where music was playing. A deep and warm *thrum thrum* beneath his fingernails.

As he watched, his fingertips turned into almost a cartoon-version of themselves and began to separate. To drift apart, like tiny diamonds being cast lazily into the darkness around him. *Like stars,* he thought whimsically.

And then the pain began.

The tingle that was in his star-like fingertips had turned into a dull burning pain, the feeling he remembered of putting his hand too close to a heated stovetop but instead of moving it away, he moved it closer. It crept down his wrist and forearm toward his torso, and he caught a glimpse of the same light on his shoes, well, feet now. He stared in disbelief at his naked body as he began to understand what was happening.

His body was disintegrating.

Panic began to set in, but he tried to beat it down by remembering what he knew to be true.

My name is Evan Reader, I'm 37 years old, and I was married. I was married to—to—Mer-something. Who was it? Mer-e-dith!

The tingle had begun in his elbows, and the pain had reached his wrists. It was as if he had dipped his hands in molten metal and lifted them to the sky, allowing gravity to do the work for him as it drew the pain further into him.

My name is Evan reader, I'm 37 years old and I was ... married to someone. Who was it What was her name? What was her NAME?

His elbows and shins had broken into shards of glittering glass, spinning wildly away and disappearing into the dark around him. He realized with mounting terror that he was being annihilated, line of code by line of code. *Deleted.*

My name is Evan Reader, I'm 30-something, and I was doing ... something. I was somewhere. Somewhere else. Not here. I wasn't HERE!

Now his thighs and groin were beginning to burn, and he couldn't see anything past the searing stumps of his legs, drips of molten crystal moved into the distance. Parts of him as tiny reflective pixels were drifting into the nothing that was slowly swallowing him. Or rather, that he was slowly becoming.

My name is Evan Reader, I'm—I'm... What's happening to me!

His stomach had burst into starlight, and in the back of his mind, it reminded him of fireworks on the 4th of July and summer baseball.

My name is Evan. Reading—Reader.

His chest and arms were nearly gone, now, and while the pain was overwhelming, a distant image of a gaping maw closing in around him made him squeeze his eyes closed so tightly that they began to ache. He could feel tears leaking from them, but they didn't touch his cheeks. Instead, they drifted aimlessly from the corners of his eyes as if in zero gravity.

His mind was weakening. He was having trouble recalling much of anything, and his processes felt mired in thick and viscous mud.

My name is Evan. Where am I?

The panic had now taken full root. He opened his eyes, and out of their corners, he could see his shoulders skimming away like skipping crystals. The pain was unbearable, and if he could scream, he would have, but his tongue had been jettisoned into the dimness, and his mouth was tingling, certainly growing into a low burn.

My name is—is—

He couldn't remember. He couldn't remember anything.

A final fleeting thought rose to the surface of what could be called his final conscious mind.

Why am I?

It wasn't an incomplete thought. In fact, it was a burst of brilliance that the distant, final dregs of his sanity also wished someone could witness. His question encompassed not only the mystery and fear of losing what he knew to be absolute truths in his life but also what he assumed he would come to know as his life continued toward his eventual death. His mortality coming into sharp and abrupt focus.

The question addressed not only his past but also his future. And swirling through the mist of thought, it questioned what his purpose should have been.

What deed could be done by none other than him? Why was he gifted that brief time in life and then again, an even briefer breath, a truncated substance?

What import did his brief doubled existence mean to anyone?

His eyes burst into iridescent streams of memory and were rapidly consumed by the void, leaving a glowing, phosphorescence in their wake.

And then he was gone.

BOOK CLUB QUESTIONS

1. What makes a person who they are?
2. Do you believe that surveillance by any entity is wrong? What if it's used to protect you?
3. If you could capture the memories and emotions of a deceased loved one, would that make them the same person they were when alive? Why?
4. How do you see Artificial Intelligence progressing? Do you think there's a point where it can go "too far?"
5. If data could feel pain, loss, sadness, etc., would there be a moral consequence for its cause?
6. How do you think that technology like The Bench would be beneficial to grieving families? How could it be harmful?
7. How could the technology of The Bench be misused?
8. What are the religious ramifications of technology seen in this novel?
9. What ethical ramifications could there be for allowing a life to be recorded?
10. If you could sit on The Bench with a person—living or dead—who would you choose and why?

Author Bio:

Ty Carlson is a sci-fi writer who delights in the unseen strangeness and wonder of "what if". Growing up in the Ozarks of Arkansas gave him and his three siblings plenty of room to play knights and dragons or jungle explorers, igniting his imagination early on. Ty started writing at a very young age and his passion has only grown over time. He loved to read so much that he once was grounded from reading, a fact that his brothers tease him about to this day. He hopes readers discover new ways to see the world through the perspectives offered in the stories he tells.

Some of Ty's favorite reads include the classics from Fitzgerald to Tolkien to Card and has fallen in love with a multitude of worlds. When he's not writing, he's playing with his kids or enjoying some time in a video game. On the rare occasion, when his wife and him can get a few minutes to themselves, they enjoy listening to the sounds of the world waking up while enjoying a cup of coffee—with cream of course. His debut book is "The Bench" which marks his first steps as a sci-fi author like so many he's admired (and been grounded from!)!

FANTASY, SCIFI, & PARANORMAL ROMANCE

BEAU LAKE
The Beast Beside Me
The Beast Within Me
Taming the Beast: Novella
The Beast After Me
Charming the Beast: Novella
The Beast Like Me
An Eye for Emeralds
Swimming in Sapphires
Pining for Pearls

D. LAMBERT
To Walk into the Sands
Rydan
Celebrant
Northlander
Esparan
King
Traitor
His Last Name

DANIELLE ORSINO
Locked Out of Heaven
Thine Eyes of Mercy
From the Ashes
Kingdom Come

J.M. PAQUETTE
Klauden's Ring
Solyn's Body
The Inbetween
Hannah's Heart
Call Me Forth